Cedric—
This book is a.
dream, and I think Cage Jetters
is the perfect man to chase his
dream, overcoming tragedy to do so

A Splintered Dream

"Every woman's 'dream man,' baseball, fame, love
and fortune found, lost and given back a hundred fold.
In the same league as *The Natural* with Redford and
The Rookie with Quaid. Unforgettable."
— Jeanie Loiacono, literary agent

A SPLINTERED DREAM

By

Chuck Walsh

\

W& B Publishers
USA

W & B Publishers

For information:
Argus Enterprises
9001 Ridge Hill Street
Kernersville, North Carolina 27285
www.a-argusbooks.com

ISBN: 978-1-9429810-8-4
ISBN: 1-9429810-8-2

Book Cover designed by Matt Brown
Printed in the United States of America

Acknowledgments

The process of transforming **A Splintered Dream** from an "idea" into a published work was a long process--five years to be exact. There were many who played a part in the development of the characters and the storyline. Lisa Fields, Larry Webster, and Patti Scurry provided perspective with regard to finding a perfect blend between sports and a man's ability to overcome tragedy. I was extremely fortunate to tap into the invaluable knowledge of Brent Walsh and Trey Dyson with regard to not only the intricacies of baseball in the professional leagues, but the subtle strategies within the game itself. My wife, Sandy, continually emphasized the importance of keeping the storyline centered around the love between a man and his daughter, and the child's ability to stir her father's dreams from the ashes. And though I am truly thankful for their contribution to the development of the plot and the amazing characters, I would like to give a special thank you and acknowledgment to my editor, Debbie George-Jones. Her tireless efforts, insight, and relentless refusal to let me get away with clichés, helped shape and mold the story into one that I think will bring pleasure to readers everywhere. I truly appreciate her dedication in helping make this book the best it could possibly be.

-CW

Other Novels by Chuck Walsh

A Month of Tomorrows
Shadows on Iron Mountain
Backwoods Justice
A Passage Back

Dedication

To those who have chased a dream

~Prologue~

August 2009

Carnie leaned over sideways and counted the people in front of her. Thirty-six. Thirty-six people who stood a better chance than she of ending up with a front-row seat. If she hadn't missed the exit off the Dave Ryan Expressway, she'd have been first in line.

The sidewalk where they stood was a stream of constant motion, people shuffling hurriedly to begin another workday. They looked like worker ants, armed with briefcases, bringing crumbs to the mound. Carnie looked above her, the massive buildings of the Windy City making her feel claustrophobic. She looked at her watch: still an hour before the start of the show. Time flowed on a stream of molasses, and every minute seemed slower than the last. She ran her hands down the material of her brand new green dress, trying to make sure there were no wrinkles. She had second thoughts as to why she hadn't worn jeans for the comfort.

Two elderly women stood behind her, talking about the sausage casserole they'd eaten for breakfast, and they slowly appeared to be edging their way around Carnie in line.

"Excuse me," Carnie said, her hand on her hip, "but where do you ladies think you're going?"

"I beg your pardon?" asked one of the women, a frail, blue-haired, grandmotherly type. She wore blue polyester-knit pants, and a matching top of blue and white.

Standing next to the elderly woman, Carnie's smooth, chocolate complexion took on an even darker tone. "This line ain't supposed to be moving yet, but you two sure seem to be."

"I'm sorry, dearie," said the fair-skinned woman, her hazel eyes sparkling. "When Bertie and I get to running our mouths, sometimes we don't know if we're coming or going. We weren't trying to cut ahead of you."

Carnie looked into the woman's sweet eyes and wished she could take her comments back. "I'm the one who should be sorry. It's just that I've waited for years to watch the show in person, and I'm a little anxious. Patti's my favorite talk show host, and I'm not too proud to admit it."

"Honey, we love her too," said Bertie, who looked as frail and fair-skinned as her friend, and wore similar garb. "What is this, Helen, our fourth time?"

"Fourth or fifth," said Helen. "I've lost count." She looked at Carnie. "When you're our age, memory is not your friend. But I do know this—you're going to have a ball."

"I wanted a front-row seat, so I came three hours early. I had hoped to be first in line, but I made a wrong turn and got all kinda lost. Chicago is just too big for my country self."

"Did you use one of those GPS contraptions?" Helen asked. "My son Rory won't leave his driveway without his."

"I don't even know what GPS stands for, much less how to use one," Carnie replied.

"Where are you from?" Helen asked.

"South Carolina."

"So you're visiting?" Bertie asked.

"Not exactly."

The doors opened and Carnie hurried to the front row. All the chairs were taken, so she settled for a middle seat on the second. She looked around the studio, the stage, and watched the director talk with the cameramen.

"Can you believe we actually get to see Patti Richards?" she asked the portly woman sitting beside her. "Live and in person. I ain't been this excited since Meemaw told me our goat birthed an albino."

The woman simply nodded, as if unsure how to respond.

The director introduced himself as Ed, and talked with the audience for several few moments.

He explained the basic proceedings of the show. and informed them of the theme for that particular broadcast. He told them that the show would air in three weeks.

"I thought this was a live broadcast," Carnie said to no one in particular. "That's good, though. I'll get to see my own self on the Patti Richards show." She nudged the woman beside her with her elbow. "What did that man say the theme of today's show is?"

"Sacrifices we make for the ones we love," the woman said in an irritated tone.

"Sacrifices we make for the ones we love," Carnie repeated. "Does dumping Jarvis Jenkins in the dumpster for cheatin' on my cousin count?" Carnie laughed loudly and tapped the woman on the arm. "My elbows were all bloodied up that day, but it was worth it, tossin' his skinny butt in that trash can. No count is what he was."

Patti walked on stage and Carnie led a one-woman standing ovation. "Go, Patti. Go, girl."

Patti thanked the audience for attending, and promised to do her best to make it a fun time. Carnie held on to her every word. After a few minutes, Ed alerted Patti that it was time to take her seat.

The first guests were a woman and her two teenage daughters. They had traveled from Cleveland to explain the pain and agony the sisters endured when the older child donated bone marrow to save the younger one's life. Carnie shook her head and fought back tears as the youngest, age eleven, expressed great gratitude to her sister for giving her a new lease on life.

"Nothin' like family, girlfriend," Carnie said aloud as the sisters left the stage. "Um-hmm," she said through pursed lips.

Patti's next guest was a man from Austin who spoke onscreen, via satellite, about how he had scaled Mount McKinley to raise money for breast cancer, despite his fear of heights. He'd climbed the mountain to honor his mother, who had died from the disease a year prior.

"Honor thy father and thy mother," Carnie said. The woman next to Carnie gave her a curious look. "Book of Exodus," she said, ready to whip out the Good Book to provide conclusive evidence if need be.

After Patti finished interviewing the mountain climber, she took a break to talk with the audience. Ed unclipped the microphone from the lapel of her blazer, and gave her a handheld mic.

"Does anyone have a story to share that goes along with our theme today?" she asked the crowd.

Carnie jumped to her feet. "I got one," she said, frantically waving her hands above her head.

Patti saw Carnie's excited expression and walked down the steps of the stage. She motioned to Carnie, but a wobbly woman in the front row stood, holding onto a crutch for support.

"Miss Richards, can I tell you about the good Samaritan who lost his hand after pulling me out of a burning car?" the woman asked.

Patti looked as though she couldn't pass on the chance to let the woman speak. "Certainly. Tell us your story."

The woman took hold of Patti's microphone and began to talk, and Carnie slumped to her chair, dejected. As the lady explained how the man had dragged her from an overturned car that had caught on fire and burning his hand so severely that it had to be amputated, Carnie's only thought was that the woman should be telling the Cliff Notes version.

"Wrap it up, lady," she whispered, precious moments slipping by.

Finally, the woman finished her story, and then Patti thanked her. Patti looked at Ed, who pointed at his watch. She turned toward the stage when Carnie stood.

"Miss Patti, I have a story you just *have* to hear."

Patti turned and looked at her, noticing the childlike sincerity in her eyes.

"What's your name?" Patti asked.

"Carnie," she shouted, and the audience laughed. "Carnie Mack."

"Carnie, it's obvious you've got something on your mind."

"Yes'm." It was also obvious to the audience that Carnie didn't need a microphone to be heard. "It's an amazing story about the sacrifices a man made for his daughter. Tragedy and triumph. You just wouldn't believe what he's been through."

"Patti, you only have thirty seconds," Ed said loudly.

"Thanks, Ed," Patti said. "I'm sorry, Carnie. But I have to interview the next—"

"Miss Patti," Carnie interrupted, "who I'm talkin' 'bout ain't your everyday Joe. He's the shortstop for the White Sox."

The statement seemed to grab Patti's attention. "Wait a second." Patti gave Carnie an amused look.

"*Our* White Sox? Are you talking about Cape Jeffers?"

"Miss Patti, you have no idea the road that man's traveled to get where he is today." Carnie raised her hands toward the ceiling. "Praise Jesus."

The audience seemed highly amused at the spark plug from South Carolina.

"Ten seconds, Patti," Ed said.

"I'm sorry, Carnie. I wish we had time to hear the details."

Patti returned to the stage and took her seat. Ed took the hand-held microphone, and clipped the lavaliere mic back onto the lapel of Patti's blue blazer.

She covered the microphone with her hand. "Ed, grab that girl after the show. This sounds like something we should look in to. Cape Jeffers is one fine specimen, and the audience would *love* him. If there's any substance to what that girl said, let's grab hold. Our ratings have been taking a hit, and maybe this is the story to put us back on top."

If one dream should fall and break into a thousand pieces, never be afraid to pick one of those pieces up and begin again.

- Flavia Weedn

I do not think there is any other quality so essential to success of any kind as the quality of perseverance. It overcomes almost anything, even nature.

- John D. Rockefeller

Chapter One

May 1998

CAPE JEFFERS STEPPED into the batter's box and adjusted his helmet. His piercing, cobalt-blue eyes stared down the pitcher. *He's nervous*, Cape figured.

The pitcher wiped sweat from his brow and took a deep breath, and it was all he could do to keep from throwing up on the mound. He had not ever been in this situation, and he sure looked like he never wanted to be in it again. The last inning, two outs, the potential winning run standing on first base. The South Carolina state championship on the line, and staring him down at home plate, the greatest player to ever wear the black and gold of the storied Santee High Stallions.

Cape kicked the dirt and positioned his foot in the back of the box. The larger-than-life legend cast a steely stare at the boy on the mound. A damp swath of red clay covered the chest of his black jersey. A big cloud of dust hovered above the infield. The bleachers were filled, and spectators jockeyed for position along the fences. The late-afternoon sun hung above the thick row of southern pines behind the left field fence, and thin white clouds stretched across what seemed an endless summer sky. The tension in the air was so heavy it was difficult to breathe. Difficult for everyone except Cape, who had played the scene in his mind since he was old enough to hold a bat. In the dream, however, he stood at the plate in Yankee Stadium.

A starter since the eighth grade, Cape was the poster boy for all that was right about the game. With a handsome smile, strong chin, and thick brown hair that curved under his ball cap at the base of his neck, he could play himself in the movie. At six feet, two inches tall and 210 pounds, the switch-hitting shortstop oozed natural talent. His batting average was tops in the state his junior and senior years, and it didn't matter if he batted right handed or left. His athleticism showed with every ball hit his way at shortstop.

His thundering home runs were legendary, and the ball field was always packed when he came to play. He was known as much by his number as his name. "Seven's coming up to bat," and "Great play, seven," were two of the most common phrases heard when he played. Some thought he wore the number "7" because it was lucky, not knowing it was to honor Mickey Mantle, Cape's favorite Yankee of all.

If someone wanted to rob a town blind, this was the time: all of Santee was in attendance. Baseball bound the small fishing community together, providing hope to a place mired in unemployment and a depressed state of mind. In that town of lakes and slow moving streams, nothing was more important than the game of baseball. Cape was their hero, and now the fate of the state title lay on his imposing shoulders. Of all the players who had worn the black and gold of Santee High, and there were plenty who had gone on to play in college and the minor leagues, there were none the town worshipped more than Cape Jeffers.

The hostile crowd from Abington screamed and yelled. There had been numerous shouting matches throughout the game, and earlier, a fight had broken out between a pair of Abington fans and Santee's quarter-back. Abington's venom spewed toward Cape; cold, calloused obscenities that echoed across the field while they shook plastic jugs filled with pennies. Their anger made Cape grin. He was about to rip their hearts out and there was nothing they could do about it. Cape had been preparing himself for this moment for eighteen years. It was David versus Goliath, and David was out of pebbles.

Slowly, Cape rolled the handle of the bat in his hands. One practice swing, and then another. A cool stare, the bill of his helmet pulled low on his forehead. Knees slightly bent, his upper body straight and upright, Cape cleared his mind. No distractions.

The pitcher took the sign from the catcher, and glanced toward first to keep the base runner, Jevan Altekruse, close to the bag. Though Jevan represented the possible winning run, the pitcher worried about Cape.

Cape knew the pitcher wouldn't throw anything but curve balls, hoping that he'd be overanxious and swing at a bad pitch. He toyed with the idea of watching the first couple go by, just so the pitcher might think he actually had a chance to get him out. Doing so would make the fans in the stands squirm a little more in their seats, and add to the dramatics. But he decided it was time to end it.

The pitcher began his windup, his arm whipping above his head, and Cape watched the ball leave his hand. By the spin of the seams, he realized it was indeed a curve ball, a breaking ball. Cape waited until the ball pushed downward across the plate. He opened his hips, his thick forearms leading the bat in front of his body. As the ball exploded off the bat, the towering blast soared toward left field. He knew, they all knew, the instant it left the bat, it was headed for the trees beyond the outfield fence.

The Abington crowd fell into a deafening silence. One out away from clinching the state title, Cape had shown them no mercy. If misery loves company, then Abington had plenty, as Cape had caused heartache and heartbreak throughout the state for four years.

The Stallion fans were silent for a brief moment too, as the reality of winning the championship registered in their chaotic brains. And then, as if waiting for the cue to join together in a group chorus, they finally erupted.

As Cape rounded the bases, Abington's infielders turned toward the outfield, unable, or even most likely, unwilling, to watch the celebration begin. Cape ran along the base path, a stoic look hiding his excitement. He would wait until he crossed home plate before celebrating with his teammates. The best baseball player in South Carolina, Cape had the right to showboat a little. But it was not his style. Not his persona. He was there to play the game he loved, not show up the opposing team. He rounded third and looked into the eyes of his teammates standing behind home plate, and couldn't help but smile. A humble pride built within him, and he couldn't wait to celebrate with his team, his friends. He stepped on home plate, they pounced on top of him, and he became lost in a dog pile.

In the bleachers, professional scouts drooled over the possibility of signing the phenom. During his junior year, he had committed to play for the University of South Carolina, though the USC coach knew Cape would never step foot on campus. The signing bonus from the major league team lucky enough to draft him would be impossible to pass up, estimated to be ten million dollars. And since he'd laid out a fast-track plan to the majors, college would only slow that down.

***

Cape's proud parents, Randy and Pauline, were overwhelmed as the parents of other players took turns hugging them and patting them on their backs. Watching Cape play the role of hero was nothing new, though they sometimes felt the praise heaped on their son should have been equally distributed among his teammates so all the players knew they were also vital to the success of the team.

Billy, Cape's older brother, exchanged high-fives with his fraternity brothers beside the Santee dugout.

Alicia, Cape's younger sister, was more interested in finishing her cherry snow cone.

Both teams lined up at home plate and shook hands, and the pain on the faces of the Abington players was unmistakable. The three-game series between the two teams had been intense, with Abington taking the opening game 5–4, before losing the final two.

The families of the newly crowned state champs waited outside the dugout, a combustible energy within them, a certain degree of giddiness. Some of the fathers shook hands. Some even hugged. Mothers told other mothers how proud they were of their sons. A large group of girls jockeyed for position at the gate. Cape walked through and two girls hugged him while another took their picture. They tried to talk to him, but another girl stepped between them and kissed him on the cheek. He had a legion of female followers, though he committed to no one. His focus was on becoming the best baseball player the world had ever known.

***

The Stallions could finally reap the benefits of their tireless dedication, and they would admit they had felt a heavy burden as the season progressed. Everyone expected them to win, and they were reminded almost daily at school, at home, and all across town. Santee was no stranger to state championships, having won three in the last decade.

Past success, though, brought a sense of urgency to the present, and it showed in the team's preparation. Early morning workouts began in November, followed by four months of practice. Grueling work that led to a lot of sweat, aching arms, and swollen knees.

Amos Steck, the long-time coach, had a simple recipe for producing winners: hard work and incredible talent. Santee seemed to be some sort of baseball factory, churning out player after player who lived and breathed the game.

With Cape, the carefully cultivated ingredients of the Santee factory had produced the quintessential ball player. Nothing could stop the Cape Train, on its journey bound for the Hall of Fame in Cooperstown.

Chapter Two

Cape's brand-new white 4Runner pulled into the parking lot at Capital City Field. Two other vehicles sat close to the entrance gate of the small stadium, best known as the Home of the Columbia Swamp Hogs, the Rookie League team of the Atlanta Braves. The cozy ballpark had been built in the '50s for the Columbia Reds, and had received a facelift in the mid-'90s.

Cape parked at the rear of the bumpy lot, smart enough to know that errant foul balls could break the strongest of windshields. On through the gate he walked, his equipment bag on his shoulder. He had arrived an hour early, by design, what some might call a routine, or others might call an obsession. He wanted to get a feel for the place, quietly and uninterrupted. He wanted to absorb the nuance of the ball field, a blending of baseball souls.

He stood at home plate, looking out at the green expanse of outfield. He closed his eyes and imagined the roar of the crowd. He removed his high school bat from his bag, the one he had used to hit the winning home run in the state championship game. He stood in the batter's box, and stared down the vision of a pitcher. He tapped home plate with the end of his bat, and the thump echoed into the empty grandstand of blue, hard-back seats. The morning humidity hung heavy, and the sun found Cape's eyes as it rose above the wall down the third base line. He took a practice swing, and then another. He assumed his batting stance, his weight slightly on his back leg. He rolled the bat in his hands as the make-believe pitch was delivered. He ripped the ball high into the Carolina sky, and it disappeared into the trees behind center field.

"Hell of a swing," a gruff voice called from above the dugout.

Cape turned and watched a chubby man, cigar clutched tightly in his teeth, tip his brown cap toward him. He stepped out of the box, embarrassed, as the man made his way down the steps and onto the field.

"You might want to save it for the game though." Cape smiled, and tapped home plate with the bat as the man approached. "Name's Clint LeCroy." He removed his cap and gave a slight nod with his chin. "But everyone calls me Judge."

Cape extended his hand. "Nice to meet you, sir. Cape Jeffers. Why do they call you Judge?"

"Because I was one for thirty years." He shook Cape's hand. "Now I'm just an old fart tryin' to run this ball club. Maybe it's runnin' me. At least that's what my old lady would have you believe." Judge's eyes sparkled, and he grinned toward the sky as if he were privy to some well-kept secret. "Nice to meet you, son. I hear you're one fine ballplayer." Judge scratched his ear and looked out across the field. "The boys in the main office have big plans for you, so I wouldn't get too cozy in this town."

"I best not disappoint then," Cape said to Judge as he pointed the bat toward the outfield fence, as though letting it know he planned on sending many home runs over it.

***

The Braves signed Cape for the cost of $10,200,000, and they expected big results, quickly. Cape had been wise to hire agent Pete Bennett, a bulldog at the negotiations table, though it helped that Cape was the top pick in the draft. The deal contained the largest signing bonus ever, though Cape had played no part in the money negotiations. He simply wanted to play baseball.

Cape's dream was to play ball for the New York Yankees, but with the veteran Derek Stringer so firmly entrenched at shortstop, that dream looked remote at the moment. Besides, the Yankees wouldn't pay any large signing bonus for a rookie. They preferred to acquire players from other Major League teams after they had worked their way up through the minor leagues and proved themselves on the Major League stage. Cape planned on playing his tail off with the Braves in hopes that the Yankees would one day come calling. The Braves were a quality organization, and his goal was to be a major league shortstop.

If he couldn't be a Yankee, at least he could still play in Yankee Stadium, even if for the opposing team.

***

"We got time to B.S. a little," Judge said, waving his cigar like a wand in the air, "so let me show you around the place." Cape placed his bat in his equipment bag. "Son, you might want to hang that bat in your trophy case. It'll do you no good here."

Cape's days of using metal bats were long over. Professional leagues only allowed wooden bats to offset the ability and strength of Major League ballplayers. If metal bats were used, then home runs would become as common as singles and doubles, and pitchers would literally get their heads knocked off on the mound.

"I think I'll hang on to it just the same," Cape said.

They walked along the first base line and Judge pointed out the locker room. He told Cape how he had finagled a deal on a big-screen plasma television for the locker room from a local store in exchange for some free advertising. He added that it took longer to get cable hooked up than it took to secure the television, so for weeks the guys could only look at a snowy screen.

"Just to warn you, the locker room ain't exactly spacious," Judge said. "But at least it's clean."

"I don't care about all that," Cape said. "I just want to play ball."

Past the bullpen they walked, and Cape felt the soft grass under his sneakers. Dew sparkled under the morning sun, turning the green outfield into an intricately woven blanket of white. The serenity of the ball field soothed them as they walked together, both bound by the mystical power of the game.

Judge also came to the field early to enjoy the peacefulness of the stadium. It reminded him of the days when the game's focus was only on the ball field, and the possibilities of perfection that lay between the white lines, rather than today's circus atmosphere of promotions and prizes to keep the crowd entertained.

Judge held a life-long love for baseball. He'd played semi-pro for several years after high school, then coached a summer team of college players for six years, raising money, finding fields, playing games in front of crowds smaller than the ones on the field. They'd traveled to fields that weren't much more than backstops, bases, and winding chalk lines leading to cornfields and briar patches. When the Braves looked to move their Rookie team to the Midlands of South Carolina, Judge was the first to offer his time and money to run the show. Under his guidance, the club played in front of good crowds. Not always large in number, but very large in vocal support, especially on Dollar Beer Night. The area was a hotbed for baseball, and folks were passionate about the game.

The rest of the team trickled in with little fanfare or excitement. The Swamp Hogs were in second place in the Appalachian League, posting twenty-six wins against fifteen defeats. Players were firmly established in their positions, so the shortstop, Nick Simpson, wouldn't take kindly to the fact that Cape was there to take his place in the lineup.

Baseball in the minor leagues wasn't necessarily cutthroat, but each player was there for the purpose of making it to the Major League level. So the game was about individuality, about padding statistics to catch the eye of the organization. With five levels of minor league teams to climb to get to a major league team, it was a long, arduous process.

Cape and Judge made their way back to the locker room.

"Come meet the guys," Judge said, removing his cigar in order to wipe the sweat above his lip. Several players sat on stools in front of their lockers. Young men chasing their dreams, and if averages played out, one or two perhaps would step foot on a Major League field someday.

"Fellas, I want you to meet Cape Jeffers, the pride of Santee. Let's show him some hospitality and make his stay here a good one. Santee. Caught a catfish there once, the size of a Buick. Ethel, my wife, dropped it into the water when she let the friggin' net slip out of her hands. God, that woman ain't good for nothin'. But, that's a story for another day."

Nick walked past Cape, cutting his eyes over at his replacement. Cape nodded without speaking. He seemed intimidated that Cape towered over him.

"Here's your locker," Judge told him. "Go see Charley in the equipment room and he will give you a uniform and some basic equipment. Jockstraps, cups. You know, the necessities. And you can thank him for getting the jersey number you wanted. You're lucky that number 7 wasn't already taken." He slapped Cape on the back. "I'll leave you with the guys. We're expecting a good crowd today so I better get my ass in gear. Nine innings in this heat…that's a lot of beer to peddle, and a boat load of foul balls to chase." Judge was out the door.

Cape sat on his stool. He wasn't the nervous type, but he felt the stares. He had just stepped into a pressure cooker, and his every move would be closely watched. He started removing his things from his bat bag and placing them in the locker.

"Whoa, dude," a voice beside Cape said, "they loaded you up."

Cape turned. The player stooped and performed inventory in Cape's equipment bag. "Louisville Slugger bats, Rawlings Pro-line glove, Nike shoes. Your agent hooked you up, big time."

Cape shrugged. Pete Bennett *had* worked up great deals with sports equipment franchises, and Cape was set when it came to bats, gloves, and shoes. The player took hold of Cape's high school bat and took a practice swing. "Sweet bat. Reminds me of my younger days."

Cape extended his hand. "Cape Jeffers."

"Rocco Crezdon. Miami, born and raised." Rocco was short and muscular, with olive skin and short, black hair. He handed Cape the bat.

Cape leaned it against the locker. "What position do you play?"

"Centerfield. Been in Rookie ball for two seasons. Plan on moving up to Single A by August. I hear you're a beast at the plate."

"I can handle myself alright, I guess."

"Dude," he said as he moved in closer to Cape's stool, "don't take it personally how they're gonna treat you. You know what I'm sayin'? All of us are here for a reason, and that's to make it to the big leagues. If we don't look out for ourselves, who will? Guys are trying to secure their future, and when some golden boy shows up, with a gazillion dollar signing bonus, players aren't going to roll over and play dead."

"I understand. But I'm just here to play ball."
"You'll get your chance in about three hours, my man."

***

Cape stepped into the batter's box to take batting practice. Several players stood behind the screen of the rollaway cage, watching him. He didn't feel nervous. Just the opposite, as there was no place he felt more at ease. It felt great to stand at the plate again with a bat in his hands. With batting practice, he always batted right handed first. He took two warm-up swings, dug his right foot into the dirt, and readied himself. He ripped the first pitch into the gap in left center, the echo off the wooden bat making a sweet sound. He sent the next pitch into the scoreboard behind the left field fence. He felt no need to explain he'd been practicing with a wooden bat every day for the last month.

Almost game time. The crowd strolled in, most taking to the upper bleachers underneath the roof so as to escape the late-afternoon sun. The Swamp Hog fans were salt of the earth, in love with baseball and family, church, America and freedom. They could afford the ticket prices, plus it provided a cheap, built-in babysitter. Kids could roam freely between the concession stand and the playground down the left field line, while mom and dad sipped their beverage of choice.

Young boys gathered near the dugout, most of them wearing baseball gloves. They watched the Swamp Hogs swing bats and toss balls to each other, basically trying to control their pre-game jitters. In the players these boys saw heroes, young men whose shoes they hoped to fill some day. The players' girlfriends, and other girls who wanted to be, began to wander into the ballpark.

The crowd stood for the national anthem, Cape and his teammates straddling the base line between home and first, the visiting Spartanburg Nighthawks occupying the third base line.

The starting lineup was announced over the public address system, and Cape sprinted to shortstop when his name was called. The crowd roared their approval; they had anxiously awaited the arrival of the player *Baseball Weekly* anointed a "can't miss guy". Nick took a seat on the corner of the bench in the dugout, arms folded. Bo Reems, the first baseman, threw a ground ball to Cape, and he fielded it smoothly and fired back to first. He stood next to Felix Armando, the third baseman.

"You nervous, wonder boy?" the Dominican asked.

Cape shook his head. "Not a bit."

"Just to let you know, I'm taking everything that comes my way, so if I cut you off, nothing personal."

"Take whatever you can get; I've got your back if anything gets past you."

"Ain't nothin' getting past me."

Cape placed his glove against his cheek, the touch of salty leather rubbing against his skin. He looked across the infield. He inhaled the soft odor of the grass, filling his lungs as if the air he breathed would be his last. He listened to the echo of the baseball hitting the catcher's mitt as the pitcher warmed up. He looked to the western skyline as the sun slipped behind a swath of orange and iron clouds.

He stood again on the field where white chalk lines led to a world that many people entered, but only a few understood. A world where a wooden bat, glove, and ball were but mere instruments to an orchestra of honor, courage, and dedication. Where beads of sweat flowed like the blood of some sacrificial lamb in the pursuit of excellence.

The stands were a constant buzz of talk and movement as fans settled in for the first pitch. Music played over the speakers, and the hum of traffic outside the stadium wall roared like the ocean. Distractions to some, but not for Cape. He rubbed his hand inside the web of his glove and closed his eyes. The noise and the distractions outside the white lines faded like water on a hot skillet.

Time for baseball.

***

The pitcher, Kip Blalock, stepped on the mound. He was a flamethrower with raw power, but he needed to gain better control with his off-speed pitches. He had been projected to move to Double A in Macon, Georgia in August, as long as he could add the changeup to his repertoire. He struck out the first batter, and the next one popped out to first base. The next batter ripped a hard ground ball up the middle, and Cape sprinted to his left, hugging the grass line of the outfield. He dived, his body parallel to the ground, and felt for a moment like he could fly. The ball found the web of his glove; he popped to his feet and then rifled a bullet to Bo, beating the runner by a half step. Felix ran alongside Cape as they sprinted to the dugout.

"Not bad, wonder boy. Just don't try to show us up."

Cape was batting fourth as the cleanup hitter, the position designed for power hitters who could knock in base runners. He would be batting right-handed since the opposing pitcher was a lefty. Felix singled to start the game, and a ground out advanced Felix to second. Rocco popped out to left field. Cape's name was announced, and the crowd of 500 clapped loudly.

Cape wiggled his helmet, lowering the bill on his forehead. His eyes squinted slightly, eye-black liner thick below them. He took a practice swing, and then another. A deep breath. He blocked out everything around him, locked on the one-on-one battle that each at-bat presented. He loved the challenge of taking the best shot the pitcher had to offer, and sending it into the next county. Though it had only been a month since the state championship, Cape had missed the thrill of staring down a pitcher. It felt so natural, what he was born to do.

The pitcher took the sign from the catcher, and delivered a fastball high and outside. His second offering, a breaking ball, caught Cape off guard and he took it for strike one. *Bring me that one again*, he thought.

He stepped out of the batter's box, pulled the bill of his helmet closer to his eyes, and stepped back in. He searched the pitcher's eyes for fear or courage. It had to be one or the other. With this pitcher, it was fear.

The pitcher took the sign, turned his head to look at Felix to keep him close to second base, and delivered the pitch. The curve ball hugged the outside of the plate before dipping across the dish at knee level. Cape turned, his bat exploding to the ball, ripping it to left center. The crowd roared as both the center fielder and left fielder raced to the wall. They stopped at the warning track, watching the ball sail over the eight-foot fence. Cape looked at the ground below his feet as he ran the bases with a smooth, effortless trot. Music rocked and so did the crowd, but Cape showed no emotion.

A home run in the first at-bat of his professional career. *Welcome to the pros, rookie.*

The Swamp Hogs won 3–0. Cape went two-for-four for the night, hitting a single to right field in the sixth inning. A local television station interviewed him outside the dugout, trying to get his take on his first game as a professional. Several of his teammates watched, green with envy as he talked with Sandy Sullivan, the attractive sports reporter. A group of children gathered nearby, waiting to get his autograph.

Kip, who had tossed a complete game shutout, giving up only three hits, wondered for a moment if Sandy would interview him. He milled around the dugout, stalling for time but when he saw Sandy and the cameraman heading for the stands, he grumbled and headed for the locker room.

Cape stepped into the showers where Bo rinsed soap off his thick shoulders. Cape nodded and said, "Nice game."

Bo shut off the water and walked out without speaking.

Cape returned to his locker, drying his hair with a towel. On the field, his initiation into the wonderful world of professional baseball was off to a good start. Off the field, as smooth as a cat's tongue. He reached his locker, and Nick, already dressed, stepped in front of him, driving his shoulder into Cape's chest.

"Watch where you're going, numb nuts," Nick said, the impact knocking Cape over a stool and into an open locker.

He jumped to his feet and grabbed Nick by the shirt. "What's your problem?"

"They got it all laid out for you, don't they? The easy path to the top. Interviews, autographs. A one-man band. Everybody's hero."

"I can't control any of that. I'm just here to play ball, same as you."

"Same as me, huh? I can't do much ball playing from the bench. Thanks to you." He poked his finger in Cape's chest, and Cape knocked his hand away.

"Maybe if you played a little better, they wouldn't have brought me here to replace you."

Nick took a swing at Cape, but he dodged it.

Judge ran into the locker room. "What's goin' on in here?" he asked, separating the two.

"You better watch your back," Nick said, pushing Judge's hand away. He turned and headed for the door.

"Bite me."

"Shut your mouth, son," Judge said, pointing his finger at Cape.

Cape gave Judge a surprised look. "Why are you jumping on me? He started it."

"I don't give a coon's ass who started it. They'll be no division in my ranks. You're the new guy, so you need to keep your mouth shut and just play ball."

***

Evening had softened the day's heat and sunset was just minutes away. Kasey Prentiss pulled in front of the convenience store, turned off the car's engine, and rubbed her temple. Her head felt like it had been in a vice grip for a week. Babysitting her two nephews tended to do that. She longed for an aspirin, something made of chocolate, and a nap, and not necessarily in that order.

Cape didn't notice Kasey's Honda Civic when he drove into the parking lot, or anything else for that matter. He was busy looking down the street in either direction. He didn't notice her getting out of her car and walking inside either. He studied an address scribbled on a folded piece of notebook paper. Apparently he hadn't paid close enough attention to Judge's directions; he couldn't find Heyward Street for anything. Instead of standing in front of his new apartment, he found himself at the corner of "Walk" and "Don't Walk".

He stuffed the paper into his pocket and then went inside the store for a drink. He wore his black Stallion cap, striped seersucker shorts and a blue t-shirt he'd changed into after the game. He checked the cooler up and down, settling for a Gatorade. As he walked toward the register, he couldn't stop thinking about the confrontation with Nick. He turned the corner beside the chips rack and slammed into Kasey, knocking her keys, purse, and clunky Nokia cell phone to the floor. She stumbled against the chips rack and a beer display, and Cape reached out and caught her by the arm, preventing her from ending up spread eagle on the bottles of sixteen-ounce tall boys and salt-and-vinegar potato chips that had landed on the floor.

"Whoa, my bad," he said as he tried to balance them both.

"Holy crap!" she said. "Why don't you watch where you're going." Dazed, she looked for her purse, her headache approaching migraine level. "Idiot," she said to herself.

After steadying her, Cape reached under the overturned chips stand and grabbed her phone. She snatched it from him, placing it in the back pocket of her jeans, then combed her tussled auburn hair back from her face with her hand.

"Let me help you," he said.

"You've done enough already." She wanted to, but couldn't curb the biting sarcasm.

"Ease up. I didn't do it on purpose."

She took a deep breath. Her china-blue eyes tried to split him in two. "Just forget it," she said, squatting to gather the other items scattered on the floor. "This is so not what I needed today."

As if to prove he wanted to make amends, he stooped again, picking up her sunglasses and a tampon.

She took the tampon and shoved it in her purse. "If you're trying to embarrass me, you're doing a great job." She finished collecting her things, and tried not to let his rugged good looks soften her anger. She felt ticked off, and wanted to enjoy the moment.

"Listen, I'm really sorry," Cape said in an extremely apologetic tone.

"If you don't mind, I'd like to leave before you knock me into the magazine rack." His mild tone hadn't softened her demeanor.

Cape stepped aside and then waved his arm like a matador, as if to let her know he wouldn't waste any more of her time. "Have a nice day."

Kasey had no trouble picking up the sarcasm in his voice.

***

In the parking lot, Cape looked once again at the directions Judge had given him. He checked his pocket for the key, just for reassurance he had a way to get into his apartment. Assuming he ever found it.

Kasey got back in her car and then noticed him standing in the lot like a homeless puppy. She lowered her passenger window. "Don't tell me. You're lost."

"Is it that obvious?" Cape asked, stooping down to make eye contact.

"You make me want to put a collar on you and give you a bowl of water."

"I'm looking for Heyward Street. Am I close?"

"Very. Take a right out of the parking lot. It's two blocks up."

Cape tipped his hat. "Thanks. Sorry again about the collision."

"Sorry I snapped at you. It's been a rough day."

He nodded to let her know there were no hard feelings. She watched him get in his car, anger no longer clouding her mind, and she realized that she'd just bumped into the cutest guy she'd ever seen.

Chapter Three

Kevin Bondurant pulled into the semi-circular driveway, and the first thing he saw was a black Escalade, chrome wheels sparkling in the sun. In front of the rich vehicle sat a late model Mercedes E Class, also black. To Kevin, the vehicles seemed a perfect complement to the three-story, red-brick home behind them.

Two white columns stood like sentinels, making the place seem intimidating. It was the most impressive house Kevin had ever seen, and when he got out of his small, older silver Toyota truck, he felt inadequate.

A tall Jamaican with huge, tree-trunk sized biceps answered the door. He led Kevin through several spacious rooms to a large den that had a pool table and bar. A man in black slacks and a white golf shirt sat at a round table beside a window overlooking a kidney-shaped pool. The man stood and shook Kevin's hand, giving him a warm smile that didn't seem genuine.

"Hey, man," he said. "Thanks for stopping by. Have a seat." He looked toward the bar and the man standing behind it. "Cleve, I'll have another Rock and Rye, and get my friend Kevin whatever he wants."

Cleve looked at Kevin without speaking.

"Cleve's a little short on patience. Just tell him what you want to drink."

"A beer is fine."

The man at the table swirled his drink as Kevin sat, the cubes clinking together. "So, how well do you know Cape Jeffers?"

Kevin took a long sip of his cold Stella. Then he noticed two girls lying on lounge chairs next to the pool, long legs, tanned, wearing small bikinis.

"Known him all my life, basically," he replied. "We played Little League ball together. Were high school teammates, too. He played short. I played second."

"In case you don't know it, I make a very good living taking care of other people's money. Ballplayers, specifically. And so, I have a business proposition for you. I need an *in* to Cape Jeffers, and you can provide that. I need you to let him know I'm the best there is at investing, at making money. Tell him I'll do more with his signing bonus than anyone. Tell him I'm trustworthy, and I've got a long list of clients to prove it."

"Why do you need me to tell him? You're the businessman."

"Because it's all about getting your foot in the door. It's about getting to know someone to gain their trust." He tapped at his glass for a moment. "So, can I count on you?"

He shrugged his shoulders. "Yeah, I guess so."

"I can't settle for 'guess so'. Either you can, or you can't. Either you will, or you won't. If you do, I'll make it worth your while. How are things? Could you use a little extra bank?"

"Sure. Who couldn't?" He looked around the room, impressed with the leather couches and the large screen plasma television. "Well, except you, maybe."

The girls from the pool walked in and smiled at him, towels wrapped around their midsections.

"Ladies, this is a good friend of mine. Kevin, these are the ladies." Kevin nodded and struggled to look them in the eyes, their skimpy suits a major distraction. "Take him out by the pool. Work with him on his backstroke." The man looked at Kevin. "How about it, Kev? Want to take a swim with Erin and Lindsay?"

"I didn't bring anything to swim in."

"I got you covered." He looked at Cleve. "Bring my man here a pair of trunks." He placed a heavy hand on Kevin's shoulder. "Go change, take your beer and catch some sun with the girls while I finish up some work."

One of the girls took Kevin by the arm. "Come on, honey, and I'll show you where you can change."

Kevin looked at the man and smiled.

"Remember, Kev, you take care of Cape, and I'll take care of you."

***

Kasey's cell phone rang, waking her from a deep sleep. She wiped the hair from her eyes. "Hello," she mumbled, trying to focus her eyes on the clock on the nightstand. 8:43 a.m.

"Wake up, you slacker," Lauren said, much too cheerfully.

"Why are you calling so early?"

"Early? It's almost nine."

"I finally got a day off from the hospital," she said, rubbing her hand through her hair. "I need sleep."

"All you're doing is summer intern work. It's not like you're performing surgeries."

"It's still work. Plus my classes. I'm tired."

"Anyways, I'm on my way to the pool," Lauren continued, ignoring Kasey's comments. "I sweet-talked Bob into letting me work the early shift. Wanted to see if you want to go to the Swamp Hogs game tonight. Grace has tickets and we're going to check out the new team hottie, Cape Jeffers. He's my future husband, and he needs to know that as soon as possible."

"Yeah, you better alert him. The media too."

"We'll pick you up at 6:45. Try to be up by then."

Lauren, Grace, and Kasey were childhood friends, and they always made a point to spend time together in the summer.

Lauren and Grace attended Clemson University. Kasey had moved forty miles south of their small town to attend the University of South Carolina. Unlike Kasey, Grace and Lauren moved home for the summer. Living in a place where listening to the sound of chirping crickets was considered entertainment, Lauren and Grace were eager to see the bright lights of Columbia.

***

Kasey brushed her shoulder-length hair with the pink brush she'd gotten for Christmas when she was only thirteen. She sat in front of her dresser, her eyes sparkling from the sun's reflection slipping through the bedroom window and onto the mirror. She thought about calling Lauren to cancel going to the baseball game. She had a biology exam coming up in two days, and she needed to study.

***

Lauren and Grace showed up early at Kasey's door, eager to get to the ballpark. Kasey just couldn't force herself to share the same enthusiasm.

Lauren wanted to arrive ahead of the crowd to give the players an unobstructed view of them when they walked in the stadium. Lauren was an authority on the new Swamp Hogs ballplayer, mainly because her brother had played against Cape in high school.

"Okay, girls, help me find him," Lauren said once they stood behind the dugout, trying to act as nonchalant as possible. "He's number seven. I've heard he's just as good-looking as he is a stud ballplayer."

"Number seven?" Kasey asked. "Who does this guy think he is, Mickey Mantle?"

The girls, dressed in the latest style of shorts and tops, gave a glimpse of how Mother Nature had blessed them. Petite, small waists, long legs. They say that milk does a body good, and it looked as if these ladies had guzzled it their entire lives.

The opposing team, the Florence Bobcats, was taking fielding practice. Cape sat in the dugout, tightening the laces to his glove, focusing on the game ahead. Most of the Swamp Hogs stood outside the dugout talking and looking at the females in the crowd. Felix nudged the catcher, Kelly Landrum, who then smiled at Grace.

Lauren elbowed Grace. "Don't look now, but number eighteen is checking you out."

"He's cute," Grace said, trying to act disinterested.

"I hope you both meet your dream guys tonight so I don't have to come to any more of these stupid games."

"You like baseball and you know it," Grace said.

"I don't have a problem with the game. Just the boys who play it."

"Just because Cal broke your heart junior year, you still think all ballplayers are scum?" asked Lauren.

"Well, maybe not all of them, but it sure seems to be a common theme."

The girls took their seats four rows up, halfway between the backstop and the dugout. With the sun on its way down, they didn't need the shade of the overhang. Lauren looked for number seven, anxious to see if he was as advertised. Finally, the Swamp Hogs took the field.

Cape sprinted to shortstop and Lauren took hold of Kasey's arm.

"There he is," Lauren said, sighing. "Look at him. He's just plain pretty. Nice build, too."

"Nice butt," added Grace.

Kasey shook her head. "You're both savages. I'm going to turn the hose on the two of you."

She looked at Cape, but with his hat pulled low, eye-black on his face, Kasey didn't recognize him as the guy she'd waltzed with over strewn bottles of beer and bags of chips.

The teams straddled the foul line for the National Anthem, and the girls settled back in their seats.

The Bobcats struck first, scoring two runs on a double down the left field line.

When the Swamp Hogs came up to bat, the girls in the crowd sat up and took notice. A lot of young ladies dreamed of landing a ballplayer, especially one moving up to the big leagues, and they came to pro games just for the chance to meet one. It didn't seem to matter that baseball players had the reputation of being skirt chasers, of being young bucks looking to make the most of their youth. It seemed each girl figured they'd be able to corral their ballplayer and make him a true-blue mate.

When Cape stepped on-deck, Lauren hoped to draw his attention, but he ignored the crowd. He held two bats in his right hand, doing a strange version of a one-armed backstroke to loosen his shoulder.

"He is absolutely flawless," Lauren said.

"Amen to that," added Grace.

"He's alright, I guess," Kasey said, shrugging her shoulders, still clueless that she had already had actual physical contact with him.

"You're crazy," Lauren said. "He's perfect."

Kasey ignored her and watched as the mascot, Harry the Swamp Hog, placed its giant mouth on top of some unsuspecting, elderly man's head.

Cape hit the second pitch to centerfield, and rounded first base to the crowd's noisy approval. Lauren and Grace clapped enthusiastically.

"I want to bear his children," Lauren said.

Kasey looked at her friends and shook her head.

By the seventh inning, the Swamp Hogs had built a comfortable six-run lead. The fans had watched the dizzy bat race and the mascot foul pole trot. Throughout the game, Harry danced in the aisles, trying not to show his frustration when kids yanked on his swirly tail. By the ninth inning, the crowd thinned, and the soft skies and light summer breeze reminded the few hard-core fans that remained why Carolina summer nights were magical.

***

After the game, the friends stood near the dugout. The players walked past on their way to the locker room, talking to girls, signing hats, balls, or the shirts on the backs of youngsters. Lauren positioned herself close to the fence in hopes of getting Cape's attention. She'd bought a Swamp Hog hat from the concession stand for him to autograph. Even if she made no impression on the boy, she at least wanted something that might be valuable some day.

"Here he comes," she said, lifting her hair from her shoulders, adjusting the strap on her blue top. When she held out the hat to him, pen extended, he stopped and smiled.

"How are you ladies doing?"

Lauren and Grace couldn't speak. He signed it and returned it to Lauren. Kasey turned to look at the crowd exiting the game, disinterested by it all. A girl, maybe five years old, blonde hair tucked under a Swamp Hog cap, walked up with a pen and a ball, her parents behind her. She smiled when Cape knelt.

"Hey there," Cape said. "What's your name?" He began writing his name carefully on the white rawhide.

"Becca," she answered softly.

"That's a pretty name. Do you like baseball?" Becca nodded, biting her lower lip. "Hey, would you mind autographing my hat?" The little girl looked up at her mother with confusion. Cape removed his cap and handed it, and the pen, to her. "I want your autograph, because I figure you'll be Miss America in about fifteen years." After some prodding from her father, Becca scrawled her name on the inside of the cap's bill. "I'm going to get a new hat so I can put this one on my dresser." He tugged gently on the bill of her cap and smiled. "Thank you, Becca. You just made my day."

Surely Becca's heart, and most likely the heart of every girl watching, melted. Kasey, oblivious, turned to ask Lauren if she was ready to leave. When she did, she found herself looking into Cape's eyes.

"Hey, you," Cape said with surprise.

Lauren and Grace looked at Kasey in amazement.

"Oh, hey," Kasey said. She ran her hair behind her ear, completely caught off guard.

"Been knocked into a beer stand lately?" he asked with a smile.

Kasey looked down at her feet, embarrassed.

"I guess it's not everyday you get steamrolled at the convenience store. I hope I didn't shake you up too bad."

"No, not at all," Kasey said, trying to hide her feeling of awkwardness.

"Hey, let me make it up to you," he said, grabbing a pen from a young boy.

"Huh?"

"Let me take you to dinner." His eyes fixed on hers as he signed his name across the back of the boy's shirt.

Kasey needed to act indifferently to the dinner proposition, though she suddenly thought it might be a good idea. "Oh, that's not necessary."

Lauren gave Kasey an "are you crazy?" look.

"Come on. At least let me do it for steering me toward my apartment. Without you I'd have slept in my car."

"You really don't have to do that." She felt her stonewalling abilities fading.

"I just want to show you I can be a little more fun than I was the other night. Less clumsy too. Can I get your number?"

"You sure can," Grace said, nudging Kasey with her elbow.

"Other than the concession stand, I have no clue about who serves food in this town. So, it might be best if you choose the restaurant." He took the pen and held it to his wrist. "Ok, I'm ready." Kasey stammered through the number and Cape scribbled it on his skin. "That takes care of that. Call you tomorrow?"

"Okay," she said, because she couldn't think of anything else.

Grace and Lauren looked stunned, almost unable to move.

Cape turned toward the locker room, stopped, turned, and glanced back at Kasey. "Wait. I don't even know your name."

"My name?"

"Yes. You know. What your mom calls you when it's time for dinner."

"Kasey," she stammered. "Kasey Prentiss."

"Nice to see you again, Kasey Prentiss. I'm Cape Jeffers."

"Nice to see you again too."

On the ride home, Grace and Lauren considered Kasey's stroke of luck comparable to winning the lottery. Kasey didn't give it much thought.

Chapter Four

Kasey walked across the hospital parking lot. The steamy heat rose from the asphalt like a furnace, a liquid haze distorting the long line of cars like a desert mirage. Her phone rang and she fumbled through her purse.

"Kasey?" Cape asked politely.

"Yes?" She knew it was him, but didn't want to sound obvious.

"It's Cape. How are you?"

"I'm good. Just getting off of work. How are you?"

"Not bad. Getting ready to take on the Wilmington Sharks."

"Are you calling me from the on-deck circle? Shouldn't you be focusing on fast balls or something?"

Cape laughed. "The game doesn't start for another forty-five minutes. We just finished batting practice, and I came to the locker room while Wilmington takes infield. Anyways, I wanted to see if you were still up for dinner."

It was unlike Mr. Baseball, the great Cape Jeffers, to give even a passing thought to a girl before a game. Kasey didn't know that, and in fact, she assumed Cape intended for her to become another notch on his baseball bat.

"Sure," she responded, fumbling for her keys. "When?" For someone wondering if she was Cape's next intended conquest, she agreed to dinner very quickly.

"We're off Thursday. Are you free then?"

Tell him you're working. It'd be so easy to do. "Thursday sounds good." She popped her palm against her forehead. *Stupid.*

"Is 5:30 too early?"

Five-thirty? Where is he taking me, McDonald's? She had no idea he could afford to buy McDonald's. Several McDonald's. "No, that's fine," she answered.

"One of the guys told me about a place named Stellini's. That sound okay?"

Kasey gave her approval, and her address, and headed home.

***

Cape had just gotten out of the shower and was putting on a green t-shirt when his cell phone rang.

"Cape, my favorite ballplayer," Pete Bennett said. "How's life in the pros?"

"Not bad, although I could use a chef to fix my meals before games, though. Wasn't that a provision in my contract?"

His agent laughed. "No, somehow we overlooked that one. Hey, you're off to a great start, just like I knew you would. You're going to the top, dude. Is there anything I can do for you? You know, to make life more comfortable? I am a people pleaser, you know."

"Well, if you're not offering up your cooking skills, I have no use for you."

"Wish I could help you, bud. By the way, did you call Jim Cummings yet?"

"Who?"

"The investor I told you about when you signed your contract. Your first signing bonus disbursement is supposed to be distributed on August 1. Make sure you let Jim manage and invest it for you. With that kind of big money, you have to be careful, and Jim is the best."

Cape's phone beeped and he looked at the caller I.D. "Hang on, Pete. Mom's calling. I need to take this."

"No problem. Look, I'll call you right back. Let it go into voicemail and I'll leave you Jim's number. Make sure you call him. Very reputable guy."

"Thanks, Pete."

While Cape talked with his mother, Pete left Jim Cumming's phone number on Cape's voicemail.

Cape forgot to listen to the message.

***

Kasey felt nervous. Fifteen minutes before Cape was to arrive, and she had tried on six different outfits, none that thrilled her. *What's the big fuss?* she wondered. *He's just a ballplayer.* A ballplayer with food, and surely something else, on his mind. She examined herself closely in the mirror as she tried to convince herself that she wasn't fixing herself up for him. Rather, for the girls at Stellini's who would be staring at and critiquing her every move. Since the Italian restaurant was one of the more elegant eateries in the city, she settled on a sleeveless black dress that fell to mid-thigh. She chose two bangle bracelets and the pearl and diamond necklace she'd received from her parents for graduation.

Cape smiled with boyish innocence when she opened the door.

"Hey there," he said softly, handing her a yellow rose. "This is for you."

He wore dark slacks and a purple, long-sleeve shirt. She'd not seen him without a hat. and she was attracted to the thickness of his dark hair, and how the contrast made his eyes look even more stunning. He smelled lightly of cologne, and though she wasn't familiar with it, she loved the fragrance. *He's not fighting fair,* she thought. His warm smile lowered her protective shield immediately.

"Aren't you sweet?" She tried to focus on the flower and not his eyes. "Come in while I find a vase."

Cape stepped into her apartment, and he was impressed that it didn't look like the typical college student living quarters. Although he hadn't intended to snoop, he couldn't help but notice a canvas and easel in a room to the right of the hallway. He heard the kitchen faucet running, and figured while Kasey took care of the flower, he'd slip in and take a closer look.

All along the floor and leaning against the wall were acrylic paintings. The wooden easel held a partially completed painting of a stream carving its way through a plush valley. Tubes of paint and a variety of brushes were strewn on a small table next to the easel. Cape knelt and picked up one of a white, wooden house beside a rose garden. The colors were so vibrant that Cape traced his fingers along the canvas.

Kasey poked her head in the room. "There you are."

He stood and looked at her. "Did you do this?"

She nodded.

"Wow." He looked at the other paintings. "I had no idea you were an artist, but now it seems to make perfect sense."

"What do you mean?"

Cape squinted one eye as he searched his mind for an answer. "Heck, I don't know. Just sounded like a smart thing to say."

She looked unsure as what to think of his response. "Well, okay then."

"How long have you been doing this? Painting, that is."

"Since middle school. My grandfather took me to an art store on my twelfth birthday and he bought me a starter kit. I've been painting ever since." She picked up a painting of a girl wearing a pastel blue dress and white, floppy hat. She held a fishing rod, and beside her stood an elderly man pointing toward the water.

"This is my favorite."

"Let me guess. Your grandfather and you?"

She nodded. "We used to fish after church on Sunday afternoons. As soon as dinner was over, we'd head to the pond outside Papa's house. We wouldn't even change out of our Sunday clothes. Mom wasn't too thrilled about it. Anyway, these paintings are of people and times in my life that mean a lot to me."

Cape looked around the room and the array of beautiful colors. "Well, you are very good. I could lie and tell you that I can paint like this, but I can't draw a straight line with a pencil and a ruler."

"Don't underestimate yourself. Everyone can paint or draw to some degree. Your interpretation and your presentation are just going to be different than mine."

He looked at the unfinished painting on the easel. "What's the story behind this one?"

"This one is my aunt's house in Asheville. We used to spend our summers there."

Cape saw a sparkle in her eyes when she spoke, as if she were a mother talking about her children.

"How long does it take to paint something like this?"

"I've spent about six weeks on this one so far. It all depends on how much spare time I have. I never put a time limit on it. I just listen to my music, and try to create something with the brush. I can paint for hours if I have the time, and if the music's right."

"What do you listen to when you paint?"

"Depends on the mood." She pointed to the player on a desk. Beside the player sat stacks of CDs.

"Dang, girl, what a collection. You could start your own radio station." He picked up a Van Morrison CD. "Good choice."

"You like Van Morrison?" she asked, as though surprised a ballplayer would like his music.

"'Tupelo Honey' is my favorite song."

"I think 'Into The Mystic' is his best."

"You can't go wrong with that one either." Cape looked around the room. "Have you ever painted any of these with the intention of selling them?"

Kasey ran her fingers through her hair. "Are you interested? Let's start the bidding."

"I'll buy one. Don't suppose you have any of ballplayers."

"Not yet, but who knows?"

***

By the looks of the parking lot, Stellini's wasn't crowded yet. Cape went around his SUV to open Kasey's door and took her hand. "Thanks," she said, liking the firmness of his fingers. He seemed to be a true gentleman, but she'd been around ballplayers enough to know they'd go to great lengths to get what they wanted.

Cape requested a booth near the back that looked out over a flowered cobblestone wall. His teammate Felix had told him it was the best spot in the restaurant. He made sure Kasey sat before he slid into the booth opposite of her. The waitress, a pretty brunette with big brown eyes, was clearly drawn to him. She introduced herself, and when she spoke about the evening's specials, she only addressed him, as if Kasey wasn't even at the table.

She brought them glasses of tea, and then placed a basket of freshly baked bread on the table. "Again, my name's Summer, and if there's anything you need, be sure to let me know." She gently placed her hand on Cape's shoulder before turning away.

"Looks like you've got a fan," Kasey said.

"What do you mean?"

"You've already won over Summer." She cattily emphasized the word Summer with a southern belle accent for effect.

"Ah, you're crazy. They do work for tips, you know."

"If you say so."

As they nibbled on delicious ciabatta bread, Cape asked Kasey about her home and where she grew up.

"Well, where do I begin?" she asked rhetorically. "I grew up in the middle of nowhere, in a tiny place called Salem Crossroads. If it's trees you're after, it's the perfect place to live. I went to a school so small my graduating class had only twenty-nine people. How's that for cozy?"

"Twenty-nine? Did you all carpool together?"

"A mini-van could have held us. Anyways, I have three sisters, and I don't know how my father survived being the only guy. My mom is like Doctor Doolittle and spends her days searching for abandoned wildlife. You know, fawns whose mothers got run over by a car. She takes them home and nurses them until they are able to survive on their own. My two older sisters are now out of college. The older one, Morgan, has two boys, which made dad very happy. I'd just finished babysitting them the day you tossed me to the floor at the Quick Stop."

"Throwing that up in my face," he said, shaking his head in mock disgust. "I'm never gonna live that down, am I?"

"Not a chance. My youngest sister's eight, but think's she's twenty-five." Cape seemed drawn to the sparkle in her eyes, and the way she smiled softly when she talked about her family. "I'm on the three-and-a-half-year plan at Carolina, my favorite color is blue, and I don't like corn flakes for breakfast."

"Now that was in-depth."

"Yep. Now you get to do the same."

Within a few minutes, Kasey could easily tell that his two loves were his family and baseball. "My brother, Billy, attends the College of Charleston. Very smart. A bit of a preppie. My sister, Alicia, is headed for the seventh grade and would rather do most anything than play baseball. And then there's Mom and Dad. Mom never missed a game of mine. Well, not until I began playing for the Swamp Hogs. She was one of those quiet moms in the bleachers. Never screamed or yelled. I like that about her. My dad taught me how to play baseball, and we went to the ball field most every day if it wasn't raining. He has a collection of video clips of Mickey Mantle, old black-and-whites from the '50s and '60s. Mickey was Dad's favorite player, and so naturally he became mine as well, even though his career ended long before I was born. I became such a big fan of The Mick, I'd pretend I was him whenever Dad took me to the field, and I'd knock imaginary game-winning home runs against the dreaded Boston Red Sox. My dream is to play at Yankee Stadium some day."

Kasey was so hungry that she had trouble keeping her stomach from growling, and a hard time not devouring the bread Summer had left. But after listening to the childlike way Cape talked of his family, food was no longer important.

"Baseball kind of came easy to me, and I think it was more because of my love and understanding of the game than my ability. I committed to play at Carolina the first day of my junior year, though in the back of my mind I wanted to be drafted and go straight into the minor leagues, which is what happened. Now, then, as far as my favorite color," he concluded, "I have to agree with you and say blue. Oh, and I don't like corn flakes either."

A perfect match.

After they finished dinner, Summer told Cape and Kasey how much she enjoyed serving them, though she never took her eyes off Cape as she spoke. Kasey was amazed that he appeared oblivious to Summer's fawning.

Cape stood and helped Kasey from her seat. When they walked outside, the early evening sun hung softly in the western sky, sending shadows long and linear across the car-filled parking lot.

"You want to make a road trip and show me where you grew up?" Cape asked as he opened the car door for her.

"Maybe some other time. We'll go when you're in the mood to see a deer or a turkey. Are you a hunter?"

"Nope. Fisherman. Where I come from, it's baseball and bass boats."

***

Kasey led him around the university campus. They drove past the nursing school where most of her classes took place. From there she showed him a new chic condo and restaurant development on the Congaree River. They crossed over the Gervais Street Bridge, and when Kasey pointed to a parking lot where he could turn around, he spotted Freddie's Fun Park in the distance.

"What's that place?" he asked.

"Freddie's? Games and more games. Mom used to pack us in the van and take us there the first week of summer vacation. We'd stay all day long, dropping tokens in the machines like trained monkeys."

It didn't take much prodding to convince Kasey to let him pull in the parking lot. Inside, they heard a chaotic blend of engines racing, bells ringing, and music playing.

Cape suggested they play a game where they raced motorbikes on a simulated racetrack. Kasey's eye caught a hunting game, where points were awarded for slaying anything from moose to gophers.

"Come on, let's try this one," she said.

She figured it a good idea to show she didn't subscribe to the theory that girls should bow down to their dates during competition in order to feed their egos.

He changed several dollars for tokens, and after he inserted four into the box, she handed him a rifle. "Okay, baseball boy, let's see how you handle a weapon."

The animals flashed across the large screen, and shots rang out, though they were drowned out by the beat of the dance game beside them. Cape shot left-handed, Kasey right. Points were tallied as the pair popped anything that qualified as wildlife. For several minutes they blasted away, both concentrating on the prey zipping across the display. When the game ended, they looked at the scores. Cape realized Kasey had nearly doubled him in points. He shook his head and smiled.

"Guess I shouldn't have taken on a cowgirl, huh?"

"You got that right. You may have been born with a bat in your hand, but I was born with a Remington automatic in mine."

"That's why we're heading to that racetrack out back. Come on, Annie Oakley."

Kasey hopped in a pink and white car. Cape was left to ride in a purple one that looked like a giant Easter egg. They waited side-by-side for the hired help to raise the checkered flag. Off they went with a dozen small-engine go-carts shaped like racecars. Richard Petty would have been proud as Kasey cut Cape off in the second turn, and though his pedal was to the metal, his engine could not roar. Soon he was in dead last. By the time he had completed his third circuit, he'd been lapped by the entire field. Kasey battled some pre-teens for first place, giving no more than a passing glance to Cape as she flew by.

She was sitting on the railing by the time Cape crossed the finish line.

He looked at the skinny teenager who waited to park his vehicle for the next group of racers.

"Hey, dude, you might want to overhaul the engine on this one."

The boy disregarded Cape's suggestion and drove the car to the back of the line. Cape approached Kasey and smiled, raising his hands as if he had no explanation, and her heart fluttered at the boyish charm in his face.

"Was that a racecar or grocery cart?" she teased.

"That does it. Let's find the batting cages."

"Uh-oh."

"Uh-oh is right. Come on."

The bat Cape chose was dented and dimpled, a pale gray, but it looked to be the best available. He took two practice swings, and then settled into the right-handed batter's box. The balls rocketed off the old bat and loud pings carried across the cage. Onlookers watching their family or friends began to notice Cape's monster swings and congregated at the fence behind him. He mashed line drive after line drive, and after he slipped another token in the machine, he moved into the left-handed batter's box. The fence behind the pitching machine rattled with each rocket he launched.

When he was done, the ball bin empty, the crowd began to clap.

"Showoff," Kasey said, looking at the adoring crowd.

"My manhood was at stake. I had no choice." He handed her the bat. "Now it's your turn."

"No way I'm following that. I concede and declare you the winner."

***

Cape hooked his pinky finger around Kasey's as they strolled through the dim parking lot outside of her apartment. His elbow touched hers. There was a quiet calmness about them as though they were content to not talk. The stars above them sparkled faintly, dimmed by the lights of the city.

They arrived at Kasey's door, the aroma of mint chocolate chip ice cream on their breath, and the normally confident Cape seemed a little nervous. Kasey, who had planned on a one-and-done date, was eager for Cape to ask her out again.

"I had a great time," she volunteered, leaning her back against the door. "Especially kicking your butt on the race track. You drive like a toddler."

"I knew if I didn't let you win, you'd whine like a baby. So the way I see it, you're the toddler."

"Yeah, right."

She tugged at his shirt. Their eyes softened, and their smiles disappeared. She pulled him closer, tugging tighter on his shirt, and he tilted his head slightly as his lips met hers. Softly they kissed, eyes closed. She sighed, and her lips trembled. The anticipation and excitement of the first kiss made her heart jump.

He lightly held her elbows as if guiding her to him. Slowly, he pulled away, and when she opened her eyes, he drew his fingers gently along her cheek.

"I'm guessing my chances for a second date are looking pretty good," he said. She rubbed her hands along his sculpted shoulders, and then pressed them along his chest as though trying to remove wrinkles from his shirt.

"Don't be so sure," she said playfully.

She pulled him to her and they kissed again. She parted her lips, and he did the same. Their tongues softly touched, and he slid his hands along the small of her back, pulling her closer. She took hold of his arms, tracing his biceps. She never knew a kiss could stir her heart the way it did. She leaned away and looked at him, her eyes soft.

"Now your chances are looking really good."

Chapter Five

Kasey attended most every Swamp Hog home game. She clipped out the standings from the newspaper each week and posted them on her refrigerator with a glove-shaped magnet. She learned the name of every starter and uniform number and the position he played.

"For someone who swore off baseball, and more specifically, baseball players, you sure are knee deep in the game," Lauren teased her. "But don't forget—I saw him first!"

One Saturday evening, the Swamp Hogs played the Burlington Indians, and Kasey arrived late. She had spent the afternoon at her parents' house for her sister's ninth birthday.

"Hey, Leah," Kasey said as she joined Rocco's girlfriend in the stands.

"How was the party?"

"It was good. Jordan got a Black Lab puppy. He's the cutest little thing. How's the game?"

"Pretty uneventful."

Three young ladies took seats in front of Kasey and Leah, two of them holding a can of beer. The third had a soft drink and a pretzel. Pitcher Parker Kral warmed up on the mound for the Swamp Hogs and Bo threw ground balls to the infielders to keep their arms loose. Cape fielded the ball thrown to him and one of the girls in front of Kasey shook her head.

"I'll be glad when they ship Jeffers up to Myrtle Beach," she said. She was a stunningly pretty girl, with thick, dark hair and big brown eyes. To Kasey she looked

Italian or Greek. She wore petite khaki shorts that showed her long, tanned legs. "Nick says Jeffers gets treated like he's God. Says all the coaches kiss his ass. Says all the publicity for the team centers around him." She took a sip of beer. "I don't see what all the fuss is about. Nick's just as good as he is."

"I think his good-guy persona is just an act," said the girl to her right. Her brown hair was streaked with blonde and she wore a low-cut lavender blouse. "I wonder what he's like when he's not in the spotlight?"

Cape didn't talk much about the jealousy, nor the individualism that often took place, but Kasey noticed.

He rarely walked out of the locker room after games with another player, except for Rocco. The rest of the team usually left in pairs or in bunches.

Perhaps they knew Cape was a short-timer, and Columbia just a steppingstone. There were only so many slots available in the minor league levels above them, and to have a player like Cape come in and steal the show, so to speak, did nothing to enhance their chances of being promoted.

Kasey wouldn't deny that Cape was the center of attention, the marquee player for the Swamp Hogs. Cape realized it too, but didn't concern himself with it. The more attention he got, the faster he could move up through the minors. Kasey wasn't ignorant to the fact that Cape stood out like some kind of Hollywood hero. He looked like Adonis when he stood at home plate, in his batting stance, and she guessed her pulse wasn't the only one racing in the stands.

The Swamp Hogs wasn't a non-profit organization, obviously, and Judge needed fannies in the seats to turn a profit, or just to break even, and promoting dizzy bat races and pizza-eating contests could only do so much. When a player like Cape came along, the selling point turned to the action on the field, not the frills and the gimmicks surrounding it. The adoration from fans had Kasey, who had never been the possessive kind, almost ready to pin Cape's picture on her blouse with "HE'S MINE" emblazoned across it.

After that night, Kasey began to distance herself from the players' girlfriends, except for Leah.

***

The crowds grew as the Swamp Hogs climbed to first place in the South Atlantic Division. Cape led the league in hitting, batting .401. He hit seven home runs in his first sixteen games, four of those left-handed. Rookie League played what was dubbed a 'short season', but made up for it by scheduling games almost every night. Half of the season was spent on the road, which meant long bus rides through the night and cheap hotels in nameless towns.

Kasey found herself missing Cape terribly when the team took to the road. They made up for it when he returned, however. After home games, Cape headed straight to her apartment, splitting time between kisses and ice cream. Kasey loved to spoon-feed Cape, kissing away the ice cream she purposely placed on his lips with her spoon.

The Swamp Hogs team held a five-game lead by August. The road trips, the time spent on buses, and the down time before games did little to help Cape develop friendships with his teammates. Other than Rocco, the players kept their distance, which was so different from Cape's high school team where players were the best of friends.

Cape began to treat Nick as if he didn't even exist, figuring it would keep them from fighting. During games, Nick talked trash about Cape from the dugout. The few times Cape struck out, Nick would comment "that wonder boy Cape Jeffers isn't invincible after all." Since Nick was on the team before Cape arrived, his teammates sided with him. And it showed most on the road trips. The rest of the players ate dinner together after the games, and often times pursued the girls waiting outside the locker room. Cape never received an invite to do either. He came to understand that jealousy and seclusion was something he'd have to endure to make it to the major leagues, though at times it wasn't easy.

***

On a Friday night in sleepy town of Florence, South Carolina, most of the team took taxis to the Crazy Horse Nightclub after the game. Rocco and Cape decided to skip the wild nightlife and walk to the Waffle House next door. The pair spent many evenings together on the road, eating at late-night food joints in walking distance of their hotel.

They sat at two empty stools at the counter. There were only a handful of patrons, one waitress, and a cook who looked like his tattoos weighed more than he did. Tobacco smoke hovered above them, a hazy ceiling of gray that looked like it had been there since the Reagan Administration.

"What'll it be?" the waitress asked from behind the counter.

Rocco looked at her nametag. "Hey, Rita, what are the specials tonight?"

Rita, dressed in black slacks, black and white plaid collared shirt, and a yellow apron, placed a hand on her bony hip and scratched her chin with her pencil.

"Specials? The menu ain't changed in thirty-five years." She looked at the cook and back at Rocco. "I'm sorry, darlin', I clearly forgot Earl's offerin' up a baked quail and filet mignon combo tonight for $29.95."

Ouch.

"I guess I'll just have a waffle," Rocco said.

"Going out on a limb there, ain't you, big boy?" she asked. "What about you, sailor?" She looked at Cape and held her pencil to her pad.

"I better play it safe and go with the waffle too. Make it two. And a side order of scrambled eggs. I can use the protein."

Rita shouted the order to Earl and he mechanically poured batter into the waffle iron. Cape had second thoughts about asking for a glass of tea, thinking it might just cause Rita to jab him with her pencil.

"This ain't the way I figured the life of a pro ballplayer would be," Rocco said, stirring the ice in his dingy glass of tap water.

"It's different from what I pictured too," added Cape.

"Sometimes I think we have to be a little crazy to do this for a living. It's so friggin' hard to make it to the majors. Hell, it's almost as hard just to move up a level in the minors."

"It's supposed to be hard. Otherwise, anybody could do it."

"For guys like me, it's brutal. We aren't all made of the same stock as you. You're one of those guys that comes along every twenty or thirty years."

"I think you're stretching things a bit."

"Let me ask you something."

"What's that?"

"What drives you to play the game? Every night you look like it's your first time. Like a kid at Christmas."

Cape had never been asked that question, and he thought about it for a moment. "It's what I was born to do." Simple as that. "From the time I was a little kid, I knew it. The first time I put on a glove. The first time I swung a bat. And buddy, when I put on that uniform, the world took on new meaning. I had a purpose. My dad took me to the field most every summer day, and I'd wait impatiently at the door for him to get home from work. Can you remember the sound the first time you hit a baseball? It was the sweetest sound I'd ever heard."

"I know what you're talking about, man. Nothing like it."

"This game lights a fire inside me. And it's not just hitting and fielding. It's the dirt under your feet. It's the sweat under your cap and the sun on your shoulders. It's that one-on-one duel between you and the pitcher."

Cape didn't realize that Rita stood at the counter, listening to him talk.

"You obsess a bit much, doncha think?" she asked.

Cape and Rocco laughed.

"Yes, ma'am," Cape said.

They shared their dreams of playing in the majors, and told each other their baseball history, memories of their first games, dramatic finishes in high school, and basically anything that had to do with baseball.

Superstitions were admitted, no matter how off the wall they seemed. Beside the game itself, Rocco made the road trips bearable for Cape.

***

The Swamp Hogs tried to survive the grind of playing night after night, but the oppressive Carolina heat wore them down. They played the second of a three-game series with Florence, the last of a nine-game home stand. The humidity was thick as country butter, the air stagnant, and the mood of the teams and fans alike was listless at best. Florence had built up a seven-run lead after four innings, and the crowd seemed more interested in kicking back draft beer than watching the game.

In the seventh inning, Columbia struck for five runs. In the bottom of the eighth, with the crowd thinning, the Swamp Hogs scored again to close the deficit to one run. Bo singled, and Rocco followed with a double off the wall. Cape stood on-deck, taking practice swings, while Florence changed pitchers. "Welcome to the Jungle" blared through the speakers. The relief pitcher stepped on the mound and Cape readied himself. He watched the first pitch go by, a called strike that he thought was a just bit outside. The next two pitches were low, and he was ahead in the count. When he ripped a shot down the left field line that curved foul, a collective relief fell over the Florence dugout. Cape worked the count to three balls and two strikes, and figured the pitcher would walk him since first base was open, setting up a force play on the next batter. The pitcher delivered a pitch that was outside the strike zone, a breaking ball Cape didn't pick up on until it dipped back and caught the corner for strike three. A moan drifted across the stands, and Cape tapped the bat against his helmet in disgust.

He removed his helmet and heard Nick say from the bench, "That's the way to put that signing bonus to good use. You ain't the crowd favorite tonight."

Cape cut a stare at Nick, but grabbed his glove and hat and ran to short.

The Swamp Hogs didn't score in the ninth, and Florence escaped with a one-run victory. Cape took his time going to the locker room, running that final pitch through his mind again and again. How had he gotten fooled like that?

Fuming, he finally went to the locker room, which thankfully had cleared out. He showered, and went back to his locker to put on some shorts and a t-shirt. The top shelf was conspicuously bare: a framed photo of Kasey, sitting in front of her mother's flower garden, was now missing. He searched through his locker. No luck. He looked around the floor to see if it had fallen. Still he found nothing, so he headed to Charley's office to see if he'd found it while gathering towels.

Kasey's photo was taped above the office door; above it, a hand-written sign said 'Slut of the Month'.

Cape grabbed a nearby chair, stood on it, and snatched the photo, crumpling the sign into a ball. He ripped off the masking tape, put the frame in his locker, and ran for the parking lot.

A few players stood talking beside their cars, and Cape spotted Nick talking with Bo.

Bo noticed Cape sprinting toward them. "He looks pissed," Bo said, nodding his head as if trying to steer Nick's eyes to the quickly approaching teammate.

Cape rammed Nick into the side of a car, knocking him to the ground. He yanked Nick off the pavement by his shirt, and punched him twice in the right eye. Nick's head smashed into the car door. When Cape pulled his fist back for another blow, Bo grabbed his arm. Nick shook his head and made it to his feet. He lunged for Cape, reaching across Bo's shoulders. Parker jumped into the fray, taking hold of Nick's arm.

"I'm sick of your games, Simpson," Cape snarled. "Grow up."

"Can't take a joke, huh, Jeffers?" Nick blinked as his eye began to swell.

"The only joke around here is you. You just touch anything else of mine and I'll kick your ass."

Behind the protection of his teammates, Nick said, "Anytime you're ready, golden boy."

***

Grace and Lauren came with Kasey to watch Cape's final game of the season. Grace didn't pass up the chance to give Kasey a hard time.

"Remember how you whined about coming to see the Swamp Hogs play?" she asked.

"I didn't whine," Kasey replied.

"You moaned like a first grader sitting in time out," Lauren said. "I don't like baseball," she said in mock attempt of a spoiled child. "I don't like ballplayers. Waah, waah."

"I don't know what you two are going on about." Kasey paused and looked toward the outfield. "But I'm sure glad y'all made me come."

"Thanks to us, you hit the jackpot, and we don't get to help you spend any of the loot," said Grace.

"You got that right," Kasey said. "This loot is all mine."

***

Game time was fifteen minutes away. Most of the guys were cutting up and talking about their off-season plans, but Cape concentrated on rubbing down his bat handle with pine tar. He looked up when Judge walked to the dugout.

"Hey, Santee," he said with a grin, his cigar clenched as tightly in his teeth as a squid in a shark's mouth. "We need you to step to the plate in about five minutes. You've been named League Player of the Year, and we want to give you a little something to prove it. There's a good crowd here tonight, so be sure not to trip or pick your nose when you walk up to the plate to get the award." Judge looked over the top of the dugout and shielded his eyes from the setting sun. "Jiminy Christmas, Bubba just knocked over his beer cart." Judge hobbled toward the gate beside the dugout. "Bubba, you dumb ass," he yelled as the gate clanked shut.

"Well, the hits just keep on coming, huh, Jeffers?" Nick said from his seat on the bench. "Player of the year. Judge will probably name the stadium after you in the off season."

Cape put his bat down and walked over to Nick. "Simpson, I've had about all I can take from you."

Nick stood, an attempted show of toughness. "Is that a fact? Well, why don't you do something about it, pretty boy?"

"He can't do anything without a bat in his hand," Bo said.

Cape looked at Bo. "All y'all can kiss my ass. I'm sick of taking crap just because I play this game like it means something. Except for Crezdon, you're all a bunch of back-stabbing babies." Cape had everyone's attention, and the dugout became deathly quiet. Cape stepped back from Nick. "Maybe I'm in the spotlight more than you guys, but that's not my choice, or decision. I'm here to play baseball, not seek rock-star status. I came here to play, thinking we were all in this together. Man, how wrong I was!" He looked at his teammates, as if searching for someone who felt the same way.

"This is supposed to be a team game, but y'all make it the exact opposite. I know we're all here because we want to play in the majors. This isn't church softball. It's a job. But we're a team. Well, we are supposed to be, anyway."

"According to Judge, and the league, *you're* the team," Nick said. "The sooner you're moved up, the sooner we'll be a team again."

"Well, I guess that can take place about five minutes after this game's over."

"Are you that certain they'll move you up next season?" Nick asked. "Geez, you're cocky."

"I'll give them part of my signing bonus if that's what it takes to not come back and listen to you bitch and moan. You can *have* your position back. That's what you want, right?"

***

When Cape accepted the plaque at home plate from Judge, he had mixed emotions. He felt honored to be voted the top player in the league. That's what he strove to be: the best. But he didn't want to be singled out, to make it look that he was all about awards, feeding off the attention and the limelight. He wanted to keep the focus on the game.

The Swamp Hogs beat Burlington that night, making them the official league champions. Cape appeared at the top of most statistical categories. He was batting .349 with seventeen home runs in just forty-two games. He led the team in runs-batted-in with sixty-eight. And his fielding percentage at shortstop was as close to perfect as possible. He refused to let his supposed "teammates" lessen his love for the game. It was a job now, but he still loved what the game represented. He loved the feel of the bat in his hands. He loved the smoothness of rawhide when he held a ball. He loved the competition.

***

Cape and Kasey ate lunch at an outdoor café in town before making the two-hour ride to Santee. They took back roads that cut across cornfields and deep rows of longleaf pine trees. The highways were asphalt ribbons, straight and flat. They passed through small towns with quiet streets and little movement, no look of hurry to the day. It was old country, rural South Carolina. On through the town of Lone Star and the land of dark water. Past swamps and slow moving rivers hidden by giant oaks and cypress trees. Kasey had never been to that part of the state, and she liked the look of the land.

Cape took her hand as she looked out the window. "You're not nervous, are you?"

"What do you think? Your mom will put me under the microscope. After all, I *am* dating her precious son. And no telling about your dad."

"You got nothin' to worry about. Mom's going to love you. They all will." Cape hesitated. "There is one thing I haven't told you about my mom, though."

"What is it?" She turned and looked at Cape as he drove.

"She was diagnosed with Parkinson's this past Christmas."

"Parkinson's?" she repeated. Somehow that was the only thing she could think of to say.

"Yep. As you can guess, it was a blow. Mom's always been so independent. Very athletic. She played tennis; she ran in 10K races. Apparently she had warning signs, but she tried to hide it. From herself, and from us. I don't know how, but she's kept a great attitude. At least around us. No telling how she deals with it when no one is around."

"With medication they can slow the progression, right? Maybe with her it will go slowly, or possibly they can keep it stable."

"Hers seems to be developing slowly, but I don't know enough about it to know if that's normal or not. Dad says her hands are starting to shake more and more. She tends to drop things, and he's having to help her with stuff around the house."

Kasey reached up and rubbed her hand through his thick hair. "I'm sorry, Cape. But it sounds like she has great family support."

"She's always been there for us, and now it's our turn. It's tough seeing her lose her balance, or feeling her hands shake when she hugs me." Tears rose in the corners of his eyes.

"She's lucky to have you for a son."

"Dad, Alicia; they've been great. I wish I could be there more to help."

"I sure do love your tender heart." She took his hand. "And I sure do love you, Cape."

He slowed the car and pulled onto the shoulder of the lonely road. He felt she was opening the door to her heart with those magical words. "You love me?"

"Of course." She looked at him as if she thought he was deranged.

"Of course, what?"

"Of course I love you."

Done. She said it. He took her by the chin and led her lips to his. After a long, soft kiss, he looked at her as though she were a new creation, one that God had kept secret for all time until that moment.

"And I am so in love with you."

***

Cape's parents opened the front door the minute Cape pulled into the semi-circle driveway. Alicia, age thirteen, sat in a swing under a massive pecan tree, busily reading the latest Harry Potter book. She hopped off and came running. She had Cape's blue eyes and warm smile, long, brown hair, and was on her way to being a heart stopper. She hugged Cape as soon as he got out of the car.

"Hey, kiddo." He squeezed her and she hung on to him. He walked around the SUV and opened Kasey's door. "Say hello to Kasey."

Alicia slid one of her arms from around Cape's neck and held it out toward Kasey. "Hi," she said.

Kasey stepped out of the car, took the girl's hand and shook it. "Hi, Alicia."

Alicia released her grip on Cape's neck and he set her feet on the ground. Cape's mother ran up and hugged him from behind.

"Welcome home," she said, trying to squeeze him, though her arms struggled with the embrace. Pauline then took Kasey's hand. "Hi, Kasey." There was only slight movement in her fingers, a shaking sensation.

Kasey tried to act like she didn't notice. "Hello, Mrs. Jeffers. It's so nice to meet you."

Randy placed his arm around Cape's shoulder.

"Good to see you, son." He extended his hand to Kasey. "I'm Randy Jeffers. It's a pleasure to meet you."

They moved inside. Pauline led Kasey to the guest bedroom and Cape followed with her suitcase. After the nickel tour, Kasey stopped to look at family pictures in the hallway. It was hard to find a picture of Cape where he wasn't wearing a baseball uniform, and even harder to find one where he wasn't wearing his ball cap.

Cape walked by and found her looking intently at a family photo. "You were *too* cute," she said as she pointed to a four-by-six picture in a silver frame. "How old were you in this picture? And what is that you're holding in your arms?"

"That's Buddy, my baseball genie."

"Call it a genie if you want, but where I come from, that's called a doll."

"He wasn't a doll. He was just a fluffy, little baseball genie."

"The great Cape Jeffers played with dolls."

"It's not a doll." He tugged her hair and faked a mean look.

"I had dolls, and my sisters had dolls, so I know what I'm talking about."

"Well, doll or not, Buddy was the key to my t-ball success. In fact, I got him sittin' on the shelf in my bedroom."

Cape and his dad grilled the steaks, and Kasey and Alicia helped Pauline prepare a potato casserole and sourdough bread. Cape tended to ears of corn on the grill. Randy poked at the steaks with tongs. When dinner was ready, they ate on the patio, the sun hiding softly behind powdery red clouds above tall pines in the distance. The land was flat around them. Soybean fields spread in all directions. Row after row of greenery. The winds were calm, and the air draped them in delicate solitude.

"Kasey, Cape tells me you're an artist," Pauline said, refilling Kasey's glass with tea.

"I paint, but I don't know if I qualify as an artist. I just do it for the fun of it."

"What kind of painting?" asked Alicia.

"Acrylics."

"Have you ever painted something like out of a Harry Potter scene?" she asked. "Or Lord of the Rings?"

Kasey laughed. "No, mine aren't that creative. I do mundane stuff: people, places, peaceful settings."

After dinner, the girls took care of the dishes and Cape helped his dad clean the grill. Randy was armed with steel wool, a bucket, and some liquid dish soap. Cape held the grill panel upright while Randy scraped and scrubbed.

"I spoke with Arthur Baker at the bank just last Tuesday," his dad said. "He mentioned he hadn't heard from you, and wanted to know what you planned to do with your bonus."

Cape's signing bonus was a two-installment deal; he'd received the first in mid-August. The second would come in January for tax purposes. After taxes, his first installment check was $2.2 million. His first order of business had been to pay Pete Bennett $310,000, so his bank account held roughly $1.9 million. Randy wanted Cape to invest his signing bonus and had opened a regular checking account for him the day before he'd moved to Columbia. Since Cape made only $750 a month for the Swamp Hogs, Randy wanted him to use the $15,000 in that account, originally created as a college fund, for living expenses.

"Arthur said he has a friend who works for a top-notch investment firm," Randy continued, "but I told him your agent had already set you up with an investor. What's the status?"

The adjustment to living on his own, playing baseball six days a week, and spending time with Kasey had erased Jim Cummings completely from Cape's mind. Randy was a stickler with his money, and Cape knew he was serious about being financially sound.

"Actually, I'm supposed to talk with Cummings on Monday," Cape said, in an attempt to calm his father's worries.

"Well, your money's been in the bank for over a month, and you don't want it to sit idle, not when you've got someone waiting to make it grow. That kind of money can take care of you for a lifetime if you invest it well."

"Yes, sir. I'll be sure to take care of it as soon as I get back home."

Randy pointed at his head with a pair of tongs. "It pays to be smart with your money."

***

The next day, Cape drove Kasey around Santee and showed her where he'd gone to school. They held hands and walked onto the tiny Little League ball field bordered by tobacco fields and encased by endless rows of tall pines. A shrine carved from the swamplands. He pinpointed with amazing recall the spot where his first home run had landed; he was only eight at the time. He shared favorite moments of his Little League days. He talked of the excitement he felt each time he'd stepped foot on the field.

They walked to home plate, and she placed her hands against his face and pulled his lips to hers. As their lips touched, she stared into his eyes in such a manner that he moaned slightly.

"How does that compare to your first home run?" she asked, rubbing her fingers along his strong chin.

"I'm thinking your lips felt a little warmer than that aluminum bat," he said. "To warn you though, I slept with that bat the night I hit the home run."

"Well, I got a feeling Mama Jeffers will make sure that doesn't happen with me tonight."

He held his hands out, palms upward. "It was worth a shot."

"Someday." She squeezed his hand, grinning. "Someday."

He led her onto the outfield grass and they sat in centerfield. The grass was soft and warm, and Kasey laid her head in Cape's lap. Her eyes sparkled in the sunlight. She rubbed her fingers along his forearm.

"Baby, I'm so glad you brought me here," she said. "You have no idea what it means to me. Just me knowing that you wanted me to meet your family, to see where you grew up, and where you played baseball. All the things that made you who you are."

Cape took her hand and held it to his face. "I've wanted to do this for some time. It's like showing you a home movie of my childhood, except you're in the movie with me."

"I love you," she said, placing her hand behind his neck and pulling him to her. She kissed him, and in that moment she felt everything within her pour through her lips, aimed for his heart.

"I love you too." He ran the back of his fingers along her cheek. "Now you have to promise to show me where you grew up."

"You got it. I'll parade you up and down Main Street and show the town that my love slave is the great Cape Jeffers."

"Only if you promise not to mention my baseball genie."

"I'm not sure if I can make that promise."

He started tickling her. "I can torture-tickle you until you give in to my demand."

She cackled, slapping at his hands until he stopped. "You stand a better chance of keeping me quiet if you kiss me."

He gently lifted her head from his lap, and guided her so she sat facing him. He took her by the hips and lifted her off the grass so that she straddled him. He looked into her eyes as though he were looking at the most rare jewel in the world, and caressed her face with the back of his hand. His lips met hers, and she sighed so sweetly and placed her hands around his neck. A tear fell from her eye.

"I love, love, love you, Cape Jeffers."

Chapter Six

Les Jamison tapped his pen against the wooden table and looked out the window toward the parking lot. He saw Cape pull up, so he adjusted his tie, rubbed his finger along the band of his Submariner Rolex, then straightened his leather notepad. He prepped the waitress to make sure Cape's every need was tended to, and with the utmost courtesy. Her ability to do so would result in a tip so large she'd be tempted to take the rest of the day off and go shopping.

Cape arrived promptly at 5:30, wearing black dress slacks and a white Polo shirt. He slipped his feet under the white linen tablecloth to hide the fact that he didn't have on socks with his black Bass shoes. Les had removed his charcoal-gray Dolce & Gabbana blazer and placed it over the back of an empty chair. He wore a crisp blue dress shirt, red-striped tie, and black Edward Green shoes. He was strong and confident, and he didn't plan to leave until he had Cape's signature.

Les ordered calamari and spring roll appetizers and told Cape to order whatever he wanted. Cape was overwhelmed by the menu, unaware that fish could be cooked in such a variety of ways, or what a medallion of veal might look like. He would have been just as happy to talk business over a burger and fries.

As Cape sat quietly, searching the menu for something not cooked in saffron or goat cheese, Les did a little name-dropping of other athletes who'd entrusted him with their money. He pulled paperwork out of his leather notepad. Cape drank water from a stem glass that the waitress had brought him when he arrived.

"See here?" he told Cape while they waited for the appetizers. "With me, you can turn that signing bonus into enough capital to make you sleep like a baby for the rest of your life. No worries; full retirement when you hang up your baseball cleats."

He had a diversified portfolio with guaranteed rates of return. He was a financial genius ready to make Cape look like one too.

"So, how long have you known Kevin?" Cape asked, trying to stall.

Les stopped for a second to recall the name. And then calmly, assuredly, said, "Kev and I go way back. Great guy. He told me you are life-long friends."

"We've known each other since grade school. He's a good dude. When he called and told me about you, I was a little skeptical. In fact, I have a guy my agent wants me to call, but I just haven't gotten around to it. I figured since you are close to home, I'd talk with you first."

"I really appreciate that, Cape. I'll do my best to show you why I'm the one you should go with."

"Kevin told me you've done a great job investing for other ballplayers."

"I hate to talk about myself, you know? But, yes, I've made my clients a ton of money. You're familiar with some, I'm sure. Rob Bannister is a client." Rob was a baseball player from nearby Summerville who had just made it to the Major League club for the Milwaukee Brewers. "Antwan Haynes, NBA player, is another. The list is long, and getting longer. No matter how long the list gets, though, it's all about individual attention. For me, this job isn't about personal gain or glory. Sure, I love the finer things in life, and this job provides that. But what makes me tick is finding great athletes, young guys like you, and helping secure their future. That's what gets me out of bed in the morning. It's what gives me a rush.

Your love is hitting balls out of the park. I love making money for my clients. You know, Kevin spoke so highly of you that I wanted to bring you on board. I've found a goldmine in land development, and it's foolproof. We're buying and selling up and down the entire North and South Carolina coastlines. Those Yankees are so anxious to move where they don't have to freeze their asses off any longer, they will plop down big bucks to do it. I'm telling you, we can't find enough wheelbarrows to haul in the cash. Not only that, I've got a proven method with other investments, and the stock market." Les removed a stack of papers from his briefcase. "Here, check this out. You'll see an ROI that will blow your mind, and you won't have to do a thing except play ball and watch your bank account grow to obscene heights."

"ROI?"

"Return on investment. I apologize. I get so jacked up talking about money that I get carried away. You don't have to worry about the boring details. You'll just have to figure out what you want to do with all that money. You do like money, don't you, Cape?"

"Well, it's not something that keeps me up nights. But I do want to make sure my future is secure." Cape looked around the restaurant, nicer than any place he'd ever eaten. He looked at Les, and couldn't help but notice the Rolex, the suit and tie, and the way he carried himself with a look of success. He fought against the guilt of not contacting Jim Cummings, since he was the man Pete had recommended.

After Cape had finished his pasta primavera, Les was ready to finish the deal.

"So, Cape," he said, removing a gold-plated pen from a slot on his leather pad, "if you're comfortable with what I have to offer, I would like to start working for you today. I'll hit the pavement running, and you can be sure I will do my absolute best to secure your future."

Cape looked over the facts and figures, and it looked good as far as he could tell. Finance was not his strong suit, and for a moment he wished his father was there.

Cape took the pen, clicking it over and over as he looked at the projected income based on the level of money invested.

"How much were you planning on investing?" Les asked, trying to look like Cape's future concerned him the most. "They are breaking up the bonus in two checks, right? One now, one after the new year?"

"That's correct. I got the first one last month, and after taxes and my agent's cut, I have roughly two million left. I'll get the same in January."

"So, four mil. As you know, the more you invest, the better it pays off in the end. You want to make sure you'll never have to work again when your playing days are done."

Cape looked at Les, trying to gauge the sincerity in his eyes. "Let's put in one-point-five million now. And you say these are all safe investments?"

"Rock solid. Foolproof. So good it really should be illegal." Cape frowned. "I'm kidding, of course. Don't worry. You take care of climbing the baseball ladder, and I'll take care of the rest."

"I have a surprise planned for my parents that will cost me about 500K. So let's go with another one-point-seven-five in January."

Cape signed the papers and Les had a large piece of strawberry amaretto cake brought to the table, a small way of saying thanks for the right to control $3,250,000.

***

Spring training started two days later though the mid-February cold made it feel like spring was nowhere in the near future. Cape would be gone six weeks, and then would find out whether he was returning to Columbia or moving to Myrtle Beach. He hoped he didn't have to go back to the Swamp Hogs, to the backstabbing and bitterness that plagued him there. With his departure, and the uncertainty of where he would be assigned, Kasey couldn't help but feel uptight and uneasy.

For their last night together, Cape took Kasey to Stellini's, site of their first date. They sat at the same booth, and a dozen yellow roses awaited Kasey in a cut-glass vase. They'd dated for almost nine months, and had become such a huge part of each other's daily life, the thought of separation was hard to take. Kasey ordered a chef salad, but could only pick over it, while Cape ate salmon and garlic mashed potatoes. They didn't talk much. He hated the look of sadness in her eyes, and tried to make her smile, but it did no good.

They finished dinner and walked somberly to the car. On the way home, the 4Runner deathly quiet, Cape's phone rang.

"This is Cape. Hey, Buster. What's up, dude?" A moment of silence. "You need what?" Cape switched hands with the phone. After a brief pause, "Yeah, I can do that. It will take me about fifteen minutes to get there. Sure, no problem." He placed his phone on the dash.

"Who's Buster?" asked Kasey.

"The groundskeeper. Thinks he left the sprinklers on at the field. He's home and doesn't want to have to drive back across town, so he wondered if I could swing by and turn them off. Do you mind?"

"No, I don't mind a bit."

***

They pulled into the parking lot, a single streetlight next to the ticket booth providing the only light. Cape parked next to the booth.

"Want me to wait in the car?" Kasey asked.

"I might get scared in the dark. Come with me."

"Tough guy."

"Watch it, woman," he said with a laugh.

Cape took her hand and they walked through the gate that led past the locker room, the streetlight carving a path into the ballpark. There was an eerie silence in the dark, empty stadium. The chill of the night air clung closely to the ground.

"Looks like someone's already turned them off," she said. "Let's get out of here. This is spooky."

Cape ignored her and kept walking. As they rounded the corner of the dugout, strings of white Christmas lights formed walkway to home plate, illuminating a small table and two chairs. Cape led her down the path and her eyes filled with confusion.

"What is this?" she asked.

He pulled out a chair and said, "Sit."

"Cape…"

He placed his index finger to her mouth, and smiled. "Shhhh."

Several round, lit candles sat on small mirrors on a white linen tablecloth; the table also held photos of her and Cape. Two yellow roses lay on the table, pointing to the middle, where a baseball and paintbrush lay side by side. At the head of the table were two goblets and a bottle of champagne. He smiled at her, turned and walked to the pitcher's mound. Once there he reached down and grabbed the small package. Walking back toward her he noticed Kasey looking at the candles, the sting of Christmas lights and the framed photos. She looked like a child who had been taken to some fantasy world. Her eyes sparkled in the candlelight and her face glowed, shadows moving across it from a gentle breeze that made the candle flames dance. He knelt beside her and tears filled his eyes.

"Ever since our first date," he began, "I knew there was something incredibly amazing about you. I saw it in your eyes. I heard it in your voice. I felt it in your touch. Before I met you, my life centered around baseball. It defined me as a man. It's still important to me, but only if you are part of it too."

Kasey's eyes welled and her hands trembled like a timid dove seeking shelter.

"I want to know the desires of your heart, to know your dreams, to know everything there is to know about you. The things in life that make you smile, that make you truly happy. We've only known each other a short time, but I've come to realize that my day isn't complete unless you're in it. My mama told me that when I met the girl of my dreams, I'd know it without any doubt."

He placed a burgundy box in her hand and fought to keep his composure. "Kasey, will you marry me?"

Kasey began to cry, unable to speak. She rubbed her finger along the edge of the box, as though it held the key to all her happiness. She opened it and looked at the engagement ring, diamonds capturing the flames of the candlelight. She slid off her chair and hugged him close, wrapping her arms tightly around his neck.

"Is that a yes?"

Crying, she nodded. "Yes." She kissed him and he tasted the tears rolling down her cheeks. "Oh, God, yes!"

They stood, and the lights of the stadium came on. Cape's family ran out from the third base dugout. Pauline was the first to reach Kasey, fighting hard to keep her balance. Kasey tried to speak but couldn't, so they simply hugged and cried. Randy placed his arm around his son's shoulder. Then Alicia waved toward the other dugout, and Kasey's family emerged with cheers and tears of their own. Her father, Doug, watched as Kasey hugged her mother and sisters. He just couldn't fight the emotions of realizing his little girl was all grown up. He hugged her, too sad to speak.

On the way to the car, Cape told Kasey how he'd slipped up to Salem's Crossroads to get permission from her father to marry her.

***

Cape closed the back of his SUV. It was time to begin the seven-hour ride to Orlando for spring training.

Kasey stood at the door of the vehicle, the buzz of getting engaged still fresh in her mind. She cried as he pulled out of the parking lot.

Suddenly she felt alone.

Chapter Seven

Kasey missed Cape immensely, although school kept her busy. She tried reminding herself that she'd see him soon, but she had a difficult time convincing herself, especially at night.

She and Cape set their wedding date for the first Saturday in October. Her older sisters, along with Lauren, Grace, and Cape's sister Alicia, would be her bridesmaids, and Jordan would be the flower girl.

Kasey's favorite part of the planning was trying on wedding dresses. She wanted her bridesmaids all to wear yellow since Cape always brought her yellow roses, but they refused.

"No one, and I mean *no one,* looks that good in yellow," Lauren told her. "You can use yellow roses for your flowers, but I will not wear it as my dress!"

They finally agreed on simple chocolate brown, tea-length dresses.

Together, Cape and Kasey's families planned to invite hundreds to the wedding, and even Kasey had to agree that chocolate ink on the invitations looked far nicer than yellow ever would.

The wedding, an afternoon affair, would take place at Kasey's home church, St. James Baptist. Then the reception would be held at Mandolin Hall, a refurbished mansion on a private lake. Honeymoon plans were in the works. Through it all, the unanimous conclusion was that there would never be a more beautiful bride and a more handsome groom.

***

Cape stayed busy on the ball field, and it felt good to swing a bat and field ground balls. The smell of freshly cut grass, the echo of the ball zipping across the stadium, made Cape feel like a kid again. As with Kasey, nighttime was hard on him. For most players, spring training meant enjoying the nightlife of Orlando, but now Cape had no interest. Even if he weren't engaged to Kasey, or dating anyone for that matter, he wasn't one for the bar-hopping scene.

Cape received word during the final week of spring training that he would be heading to Myrtle Beach to play for the Pelicans in the Carolina League. Single A ball, and his first jump in the minors. If all went according to plan, he would be on a Major League roster by the time he was twenty-one.

Kasey had mixed emotions. They would have to be separated for five months, though she would visit as often as her internship and summer courses would allow. Myrtle Beach was only a three-hour drive, and she couldn't think of any other place she'd rather hang out. She figured she could work on her tan and spend time at the ballpark.

Myrtle Beach was a great location as far as Cape was concerned; merely two hours from his parents' home, it was where his family had spent most summer vacations since he was old enough to walk. He also thought it would be a good time to take up surfing.

***

After spring training, Cape drove to Columbia to spend a few precious hours with Kasey. From there, he would head for Santee and an overnight stay with his family before reporting the next day at Myrtle Beach.

They met at Mindy's Diner and sat on the patio deck. They shared kisses, hugging each other like two grizzlies trying to keep warm.

Cape couldn't let go of her hand long enough to eat. He loved the look of the engagement ring on her slender finger.

A bittersweet aura surrounded them. They knew they had only a brief amount of time together. The season before, seeing each other almost daily, had spoiled them.

The time spent apart served to remind Cape just how much he loved and needed Kasey. He missed little things about her, quirky habits that made her so adorable. He loved her Argyle socks, with individual slots for each toe, that made it look like she wore gloves on her feet; her pink, round hair brush that looked like something that came with a Barbie set, and the way she brushed her hair for what seemed like hours a day; her Snoopy toothbrush; the oversized Piggly-Wiggly t-shirt she wore when she painted. To Cape, those eccentricities kept her a child at heart. Though she was twenty, excelled at school, and took her job at the hospital seriously, she maintained a playful, junior high air about her.

Kasey hand fed Cape chicken strips and French fries and they talked about the wedding.

"I've worked it out so I can come to Myrtle Beach next month for the weekend series against Kinston," she told him.

"Really? That's great. Wish you could work it out to come to every weekend series."

"Tell me about it. I can't wait until we're together for good." She bit into a fry, and placed the remainder in Cape's mouth. "This long distance stuff bites."

"We only have to put up with it for about five more months."

"That's true, to a point, but road trips will always be a part of your life. Our lives. It's hard giving you up so much of the time. I don't know if I'm that unselfish a person."

Cape touched her face and stared into her eyes, and she fought back tears. "Just think of all the time we'll have together. In the offseason, five months, every day, every night. Think about it. By the time spring training rolls around each February, you'll be ready for me to get out from under your feet."

She pressed his hand against her cheek. "I'll be holding on to your suitcase, trying my best to keep you from leaving."

Kasey felt uneasy, and not just because of the distance between them. The move to Myrtle Beach could pose major distractions with the hordes of coeds working there each summer. Kasey's sister Maddie had lived there two summers prior, and she and her friends had attended several Pelican games just to meet ballplayers. Girls have flocked to baseball players since Abner Doubleday stitched the first ball, but the atmosphere for player-fan interaction was especially explosive at the beach, like stringing up a gutted calf in front of hungry lions.

Cape stood at his car in front of the restaurant, tracing Kasey's face with the back of his fingers, as if committing her high cheekbones, dimples, and the shape of her lips to memory. As if someday he might be old and blind, touch his only way to identify her. She cried as she watched him drive away.

***

The drive to Santee seemed longer than normal. Cape wanted to turn around and drive back to Kasey. He missed her so. When he pulled into the driveway of his childhood home in Santee, his spirits lifted. He knew he'd soon get a good dose of mom's cooking and catch up on his family's life.

He didn't know that Parkinson's had taken a toll on his mother, limiting her ability to be self-sufficient. Her hands shook more and more. She struggled to sleep at night, and the weariness showed in her eyes. Her hands vibrated against his back when she hugged him, and his heart sank. She kissed him on the cheek, her smile thinly veiling her frustrations.

With Alicia's help, she had prepared strawberry shortcake, and he saw it under the glass bell of the cake dish when he walked in the kitchen. Over cake and sweet tea, he talked with the family about spring training and the brutal daily regimen of workouts.

He lay in his own bed that night, looking at the baseball shrine that was his room. A poster of Mickey Mantle, taking a hellacious cut, hung on the wall. On the opposite side of the room, a poster of Ruth and Gehrig striking a pose, side by side. Felt pennants for New York and Cleveland adorned the wall next to the mirror. Buddy, the baseball genie, sat on the shelf as if watching over Cape. The warmth of childhood returned, and with it, images of Mom reading in the den, Dad watching the evening news, Billy and Alicia somewhere close by.

***

The sun finally climbed above the endless row of long leaf pines to the east and the bright sky was a vaulted ceiling of Carolina blue. Cape put his bag in the back of his car, and looked at his cell phone to check the time. He was to report in Myrtle Beach by four that afternoon. But he had unfinished business to tend to first. He escorted his parents to the car and tried to act nonchalant.

"Where's the fire?" his dad asked, opening the back door for Pauline.

"Where are you taking us?" she asked, as Cape fastened her seat belt.

"To the taking place."

He drove southeast, the highway splitting the lakes of Marion and Moultrie. He tried to engage his parents in small talk so they wouldn't ask about their destination, and got them chatting about Alicia's upcoming recital. His sister played the clarinet in the orchestra at Santee Middle School, the only one in the family who had any musical ability. By the time they moved on to Billy's new obsession with sailing, they had traveled fifty miles through black-water swamps and small tributaries. Thick, moss-covered cypress trees towered above the murky dark waters like the markers of watery graves. Cape turned onto Leaphart Road and could no longer keep their destination a secret.

"Cape, are you taking us to Live Oak?" Pauline asked.

"Yes, ma'am."

"I haven't been down this road in fifteen years," she said. "It's just too sad, seeing the old home wasting away, weeds up to the windows. We should have found a way to keep the farm in the family."

Cape grinned.

He turned east onto a dusty side road with no street sign, the ridges and crevices in the dirt faint reminders of past travelers. A road forgotten, except in the recesses of his mother's mind. It cut through waist-high weeds in abandoned fields. A mile down, the road curved sharply to the right, slipping between a thin belt of pines and oaks that had once served as a border to crop fields. Cape drove through the trees and into an open field, revealing a landscape reminiscent of days long ago. Tulips and rose bushes surrounded a small pond to the east. The grounds were neatly trimmed around the water, and a small bridge led across the pond to a tiny island with a gazebo. Above the pond, on a slight rise, an old house looked alive again, aglow in fresh paint, a stately white standing sharp against the dark backdrop of woods.

Pauline put her hands together, and her trembling fingers touched her lips. "What in the world?" was all she could manage.

"Good Lord, someone's fixed up the place," Randy said. "Looks like they finally sold it to somebody who appreciates what they've got here. I haven't ever understood how the people who bought it let it fall apart like they did."

"It's just beautiful," Pauline said. "Just beautiful."

"Cape, how did you know about this? Do you know the owner?"

"I sure do."

"Somebody we know?"

"You know them very well," Cape said.

Randy looked for a car, for movement, but there was none. "Well, who owns it?"

"You do."

"What?" he asked, looking at the grin on Cape's face.

"Cape, what are you talking about?" his mom asked.

"The house, the land, it's yours."

"What do you mean it's ours?"

"I bought it for you back in the fall, and I've had the whole place redone. The house, the yard, the pond. I wanted it to look the way it did when you were young, Mom."

Cape parked, and the trio walked toward the house. They moved slowly, Randy helping his wife keep a steady footing, and a flood of memories washed over her. She stood in front of the house, tears flowing down her face. Tears of renewal. If two people had been more tongue-tied, Cape would have liked to have seen it.

Randy walked out onto the bridge and looked at the water. Pauline circled the house with Cape holding her by the elbow. She looked up at her bedroom window at the back corner of the house, and thought of the times she'd gazed out that window in the evenings, watching for her father to come home from the fields.

"I don't know what to say, son," she said. "This beats anything I've ever seen."

"Well, let's go inside and see if it gets any better."

He handed her the keys, and she looked at them for a moment. She tried to open the door lock, but her condition, along with her excitement, made that simple task impossible, so Cape placed the key in the lock and opened the door with a flourish.

Inside, the hardwood floors were buffed and shiny. The large bay window in the den held white lace curtains, tied back to give an unobstructed view of the pond. They walked into the sunny yellow kitchen, and Pauline glided her fragile hand along the granite countertop. Cape walked to the back door and opened it. On the screened-in porch were two rockers and a ceiling fan.

"Thought you and Dad could watch the sun set back here. You have a budget to furnish the house, too, because I wasn't sure what you wanted. I did choose the rockers and the fan. And the curtains in the bay window. I think they look pretty cool, even if I did pick them out."

Pauline placed her head on her son's shoulder and began to sob. "It's the most beautiful sight. I don't know what to say."

"Say you plan on spending weekends and summer days here. Stay here every day if that's what you want."

"This is all too much, son," Randy said, standing in the doorway.

"Well, it's a gift, and you can't return it. I had the financial ability, and it's what I wanted to do for you both. And now this place can stay in the family forever. I still remember you talking about how special this place was, Mom. It can be that way again, and stay that way."

Chapter Eight

Cape drove in silence, the look in his mother's eyes still fresh in his mind. He knew he could never repay his parents for the caring way they'd raised him, and the way they'd nurtured his talent and dreams. Purchasing and restoring his mother's beloved childhood home was a small way to show how much he loved them, how much he appreciated them.

His thoughts turned to Kasey, and he smiled, knowing a lifetime with her awaited. Tempted to ask God why he'd been so blessed, he scoffed at the notion that God was required to explain His reasons.

***

Cape leased a two-bedroom duplex near the stadium but off the main thoroughfares, away from the hectic summer beach traffic. Seven of his teammates rented apartments in the same complex. Joining a new team meant a new group of players to try and build some sort of friendship with during the six-month season. He had gotten to know some of the guys in spring training, but with everyone jockeying for position on the career ladder, everyone had focused on getting in shape and playing in top form, rather than becoming buddies. He hoped his teammates were nothing like the back-stabbing players in Columbia.

In Rookie League, the crowd knew the players were mere babes, and they showed more patience. The fans didn't come seeking their money's worth in victories since ticket prices were cheap; it was just a way to watch a ball game, eat hotdogs and nachos, drink beer, and let go of the stress of the day. Not so much with Single A baseball, as the players weren't considered newbies any longer. They would be treated to all sorts of verbal abuse. At least at shortstop, he'd be far enough from the stands that he wouldn't hear individual taunts.

***

Opening Day was the time for eternal optimism. Players envisioned themselves winning Most Valuable Player awards for leading the league in home runs, runs-batted-in, and batting average. Pitchers imagined they were throwing no-hit games. One hundred games awaited them in Single A ball. At the Major League level, that number grew to 162. Plenty of chances to chase their dreams.

Cape had a nervous energy about him, like waiting for recess in elementary school. The pilot light waiting in the furnace of the child within him sparked. With seasons came rituals. He fixed a power shake with bananas and blueberries. He watched Sports Center on ESPN and ate a turkey and roast beef sandwich on wheat bread for lunch. He carried a bat around the apartment, gripping it, and swinging it as he watched himself in a mirror. Time moved like a lead balloon.

Finally, Cape gave up and went to the stadium. He placed a picture of his family, taken at Christmas, in his locker. Beside that, he placed one of Kasey sitting on a large rock beside the Saluda River. She hadn't realized he was taking her picture; he had told her he was shooting photographs of the river in the distance. Cape had been able to capture her, lost in solemn expression, a three-quarter turn of her face to the camera. Her blue eyes told of deep thought, a glimpse into the matters of her heart.

The coach, Spike Marzan, walked into the locker room. He showed up early for all home games because he enjoyed the peace and quiet before the players arrived. Spike was a short, slender abrupt man with silver hair and a handle bar mustache. He lived alone near the Boardwalk, and it was never quiet down by the Boardwalk.

"A little anxious, aren't you?" Spike asked Cape, looking at his watch. "You're an hour and a half early."

"I'm just ready to play some ball, skipper." It was common for a player to call his coach by that name, an "old school" moniker that Cape felt showed respect. He placed his hand inside his glove. "Ever notice how slow time moves before the game, but after that first pitch is thrown, everything runs in super speed? It's the waiting beforehand that gets to me."

"That's the way it's supposed to be. When I was in the minors, playing for the Pirates, I'd get so revved up I couldn't eat. All I wanted was to put on my uniform, hear the roar of the crowd, and step between those white lines."

"Nothing brings a rush like stepping between those white lines."

"Always remember that, kid. There'll be tough times. Everybody goes through them. So, don't forget what this game is all about."

"Yes, sir."

"Not many shortstops switch-hit, hit for power, and roam the bases with your kind of speed. I've seen others come in here with loads of ability, but they didn't have the drive. Those guys never made it. But you always look like a kid playing his first game, and that is the kind of excitement is generated down deep. I noticed that in spring training. You bring enthusiasm to the field, and that's the way this game is meant to be played."

Cape nodded. "It's all I ever wanted. Still can't believe I get paid to do it."

"Well, how about you earn your money today?" Spike laughed. "That way you'll help me earn mine, and I won't end up selling used tires at my cousin's store in Hoboken."

Seventy-degree temperatures and a soft, crystal clear sky made it a perfect Opening Day. The announcer introduced the starting lineups for the Pelicans and their opponent, the Salem Red Sox. Cape's name echoed over the public address system, bringing him chills; the crowd of 6,000, the largest Cape had ever played in front of, roared their approval. Although everything within the white lines pushed him to play his best, he wanted to please those who came to see him play.

Jose Vargas, a fierce competitor who tried to intimidate batters by staring them down, threw the first pitch and Cape's butterflies disappeared. The game was on. It was Jose's second year at Myrtle Beach, scratching and clawing in hopes of moving to Double A. He'd been discovered at a North Florida junior college. His speed wasn't overpowering, but he did have great command of his pitches, including a wicked breaking ball that seemed to drop under the hitter's bat. He retired the first batter by way of a soft fly to centerfield. Then, after walking the next batter, the third baseman belted a double to left center, putting runners on second and third.

Jose struck out the next batter, and Bart Adele stepped to the plate. The crowd softly murmured his praises, as if they didn't want to acknowledge that any opposing athlete could be a good ballplayer. Bart was a high school phenom like Cape, and the Red Sox expected to elevate him quickly. A power hitter, six-foot four, and forearms like bowling pins, the massive first baseman swung at the first pitch. The liner was headed to the gap between short and third. Cape ran to his right for ten feet, dropped his right knee to the dirt, and backhanded the ball. He stood, pivoted immediately with his left leg and threw a bullet to first, beating Bart to the bag by two steps. The crowd screamed, and everyone sitting behind the dugout gave him a standing ovation as he jogged off the field.

Cape batted fourth in the lineup. Since the pitcher for Salem was a right-handed thrower, Cape would bat left-handed. In baseball, statistically speaking, it's best to put right-handed hitters against left-handed pitchers, and left-handed hitters against righties, the theory being that pitches were easier to hit when they moved toward the batter.

The Pelicans struck first in the scoring column. With center fielder Daniel Wilkins on second, and two outs, Cape stepped into the batter's box. Though the fans screamed and cheered, Cape didn't hear them, his only focus the hurler on the mound. He adjusted his helmet, sent an icy stare to the pitcher. He took a practice swing, and then another. He watched the first pitch sail in a little high and tight for ball one. He fouled off the second pitch, a breaking ball, and he tried to figure out what pitch was coming next. He guessed fastball, and guessed right. The pitch came in straight, knee-high on the inside corner, and Cape stepped slightly toward the ball, extending his arms, twisting his hips sharply. The sound of the bat making contact with the ball was sweeter than a jug of honey.

The right fielder raced toward the wall. He had the path of the ball lined up perfectly, and when his cleats detected the soft dirt of the warning track, he reached for the wall as he prepared to jump. He stretched skyward, his body now suspended in air. The ball shot past his outstretched glove and hit the wall, careening off just as he slammed into the dark green wooden fence.

The crowd yelled as Cape headed for second, and when he saw the third base coach waving him on, he picked up speed, sliding headfirst into third just as the third baseman caught the ball. The crowd cheered as Cape dusted off his pants and the third base coach patted his backside.

Cape's hot start in Single A ball continued as he doubled in the seventh, knocking in what proved to be the winning run.

After the game, the players gathered their gear while a large group of fans, mostly children, flocked beside the dugout, waiting with balls, caps, game programs, and team posters.

"Nice game," Daniel said to Cape in the dugout. "We ought to win a bunch of games with you in the lineup."

"Thanks, man. I appreciate it. You too."

"Hey, Jeffers, buy you a beer later?" asked Jose.

"If I was a drinking man, sure," Cape said with a smile. "But a Gatorade would be nice."

Parents held smaller children in their arms or on their shoulders, many looking as enthusiastic as the kids. Some of the players ignored the autograph seekers and went straight to the locker room, seemingly intent to shower and soak in the nightlife of Myrtle Beach. With a season or two of Rookie Ball and Single A under their belts, the newness of autograph seekers had worn off. To them, minor league ball was a job, and hopefully, was a stepping stone.

The largest gathering was in front of Cape, who believed the game was meant to be celebrated. He spoke to each child, thanking each for the chance to sign. He looked as excited as them, amazed that anyone would want his autograph. The little girls tugged at his heart. He imagined his own daughter, wearing a ball cap twice the size of her head, throwing a ball to him.

A dozen college-age girls stood behind the smaller children, waiting their turn. Some of them just wanted Cape's autograph, some his phone number, or to offer theirs in case he wanted an escorted tour of Myrtle Beach.

He provided autographs, but politely declined requests for anything else. The girls turned away, knowing they had an entire season to make Cape take notice.

The guys showered and left. Cape took his time, sitting alone at his locker after he'd showered and changed, playing scenes from the game through his mind. He wondered what he could have done better, always hoping to play the perfect game.

In walked Spike, déjà vu all over again, as baseball legend Yogi Berra used to say. He grinned when he saw Cape.

"Son, you may as well move your gear in here if you're going to spend this much time at the stadium. Now, get the hell out of here. Get some sleep. Salem's pissed we beat them today, so tomorrow they'll be meaner than my ex-mother-in-law."

"Alright, alright. I'm leaving."

***

In his apartment, lying on his bed, Cape phoned Kasey. He held a bat in one hand and the phone in the other.

"Hello," the sweet voice said.

"Hi, my name is Harry the Swamp Hog. I have misplaced my head and wanted to know if you've seen it."

"I'm wearing it, actually. It's a good look for me, I think. Bug eyes. Large nose with ugly tusks. It makes me irresistible."

"How are you, baby?"

"Missing you, that's how I am. I think about you all day, every day. I'm pathetic."

"I know. I'm the same way."

"How did the opening game go?"

"Good. We won 4–2. I think I am going to like these guys. So different than those boys in Columbia."

"Did you play well?"

"I did alright."

She loved his modesty. "Only alright? You mean you didn't hit four home runs and catch a pop fly with your cap on top of the dugout?"

"Only three home runs," he joked. "And the catch *was* on the dugout, but I used my glove."

"I think at least once a game you should stand in the batter's box, point your bat to the outfield wall, and say, 'the home run I'm about to hit is for Kasey Prentiss, the love of my life, the reason I exist, the wind beneath my wings, and the best dang race car driver that Freddie's Fun Park has ever seen.'"

"How about I get the equipment manager to screen print your picture on the back of my jersey?"

"How big a picture are we talking? I'm thinking at least twelve by twenty. And a button on your cap that says 'Cape loves Kasey'. You do that and I think we've got a deal."

"What I wouldn't give to kiss you right now. I miss everything about you."

"I know, baby. I know. Some days when I make the mistake of calculating how many days till I see you again, I truly have trouble breathing."

"Not much longer, sweet girl, and you're going to be with me forever."

"I love you, Cape. More than you'll ever know."

***

The team's first road trip took them to Potomac, the Single A team of the Washington Nationals. Since Cape was considered one of the premier players, his every move would be scrutinized.

In the third and final game against Potomac, a trio of large, obviously non-athletic men sat three rows back. They had consumed enough beer to satisfy an entire section of fans, and taunted Cape throughout the game, especially since he'd struck out his first two at-bats. Cape stepped to the on-deck circle at the top of the seventh.

"Hey Jeffers, why don't you try using your bat this time?" one of them shouted. "You haven't touched a ball all day, limp wrist."

"Switch-hitter my ass," another said, his cap on backwards, a sleeveless t-shirt revealing way too much arm flab. "We know what kind of switch-hitter you are. It ain't skirts you're chasin'."

Cape took his practice swings, trying to keep his focus between the white lines.

"I got a bat you can swing," the third one said. "It's the bat you swing best."

Cape walked confidently to the plate. *I'll show you what I can do with a bat.* He stepped into the left-hander's box, and eyed the righty on the mound. *Two strikeouts to this guy. He's nothing but meat.* Cape took a breaking ball for a called strike.

"You suck, Jeffers," one of the trio yelled.

The second pitch came to the plate, and Cape flicked his wrists toward the ball, just enough to make contact. The ball flew into the stands, hitting the guy wearing the backwards hat on the elbow. Cape turned and grinned as the three spectators fell silent.

The next pitch was a low fastball and Cape drove it to deep centerfield. The centerfielder raced toward the wall, but could only watch as the ball caromed off the scoreboard thirty feet past the fence. Cape rounded third base and the trio booed. One threw his cup of beer on the field. Cape stepped on home plate, removed his helmet, and after trading high fives with his teammates, gave a quick wink to the loudmouths.

The Pelicans scored two more runs that inning and won 5–4 for a three-game sweep.

As much as hecklers aggravated Cape on the road, other distractions lurked, veiled in skimpy tops and shorts. Locals learned where visiting teams stayed, and young ladies occupied the lobby and hotel bar. Some of them came looking for a one-night conquest, others looking for a long-term relationship with a budding star who might soon become a multi-millionaire.

Cape was one of the few players who tended to stay in his room on the road. He usually ate with Jose or Sam Bryson, a relief pitcher. Both were married, and they didn't care for the nightclub scene. When he wasn't eating with Jose or Sam, he was in his room on the phone with Kasey or watching ESPN's Sports Center.

***

One Friday night in Winston-Salem, the game was called on account of a day-long rain. The team milled around the hotel, in their rooms or the hotel restaurant. Several of the players decided to take a shuttle downtown to Hooligan's Bar & Grille. Cape stayed in his room to watch the New York Yankees and Boston Red Sox play in Yankee Stadium. Even though he played for the Braves, he still dreamed of playing for the Yankees, decked out in those famous pinstripes.

Cape had pent-up energy, so lying on his bed made him stir crazy. Around 10 p.m., he went downstairs to the gift shop to buy a Gatorade. When he got off the elevator, he walked past a sunken atrium surrounding a waterfall nestled in a colorful arrangement of plants. The water carved out a peaceful melody in the background as a man in a tux played soft classical music on a baby grand piano off to the side. Young professionals mingled, a handsome crowd of twenty-somethings. Past the gift shop was The Flightdeck, the hotel bar. A few couples stood outside the bar, discussing whether to carry the party downtown or not.

Two girls standing near the gift shop shagged to a Drifters beach song that blared from inside the bar. Cape watched them as he approached the entrance.

With Gatorade in hand, Cape walked back to the elevator. He looked behind the piano and noticed the Yankee game playing on a flat-screen television in a small alcove. He had no desire to return to his empty room, so he took a seat at a table next to a window overlooking the pool. The steady rain kept the pool in constant movement. For the first two innings, he watched the game undisturbed.

"Cape?" a soft voice asked. "Cape Jeffers?"

A blonde-haired woman approached the table, wearing a shiny short black dress that clung tightly to her slender figure and showed off her smooth, bronze arms and legs.

"Yes?" Cape responded, looking curiously at the unfamiliar face.

"Hi. I'm Angela Dennison. My younger brother Dylan played for South Florence."

"No kidding? Dylan's sister. He was a great ballplayer." He stood and extended his hand. He immediately noticed her emerald-green eyes.

"We hated playing you guys. The school threw a party after you graduated because we would never have to face you again. Would've been nice if you had let us win once." A playful laugh.

"We did seem to have luck on our side when we played you."

"Luck didn't have anything to do with it. If you had played for us, all the *luck* would have been ours. I remember watching all those kids at the games race to the outfield fence in hopes of catching one of your home runs."

"I didn't hit that many."

"I'll allow you the courtesy of having memory loss since you are a customer."

"Customer. You work here?"

"I'm an intern for the summer. Hotel and resort management. Wake Forest University. Go Deac's."

"That's cool. How do you like it?"

"It's been fun so far. I'm hoping to find a job along the coast when I graduate. Hilton Head. Destin, Florida. Somewhere there's sun, sand, and salt water. As you can see, there's not much of that around here. So, why are you hiding in the corner?" She looked up at the television. "Oh, I should have guessed."

"We got rained out." He looked out the window; the onslaught of drops had not abated. "I guess it doesn't take a rocket scientist to figure that out. So, I've got my Gatorade and the Yankees to hold me over."

"I'll be glad when Gonzalez gets out of his slump. The Yankees seem lost if he's not hitting."

"You're a Yankees fan?"

"I sleep with Mickey Mantle every night." She saw the puzzled look on Cape's face. "I mean, I have a poster of Mickey on my bedroom wall, silly. How's that for obsession?"

"Add me to that list—I slept with Mickey too. He's on my bedroom wall in Santee."

"Listen, I've got to check on a problem in the laundry room. I wish I could stay and chat."

"I understand. Thanks. It was nice talking to you. Tell Dylan hello for me."

"I sure will." She smiled and walked away.

The piano player's mini-concerto ended, and above the noise of the television, Cape heard piped-in music emanate from the ceiling speakers. Angela startled him by placing a huge plate of nachos on his table. She wore a Yankees hat, her hair pulled underneath in a cute ponytail.

"I'm off the clock, so I thought we could watch the Yankees win. I got the boys in the kitchen to whip this up."

"Wow. Now this is a snack."

Angela reached in a small bag and removed two beers. "To wash down the jalapeños." She hadn't given thought that Cape was still a year shy of the legal drinking age.

"I'm good. Still nursing this Gatorade." Cape stood and pulled out the chair beside him so Angela could sit.

"Thanks." She opened a bottle and took a sip. "Bring me up to speed." As Cape gave her a play-by-play recap, they pecked away at the food. Angela kept close tabs on the current state of her beloved Yankees.

"Do you know how hard it is to find a Yankees fan in this state?" she asked. "It's much easier searching for leprechauns. Nothing but Panther fans, NASCAR fans, Tar Heel basketball junkies. Cameron Crazies at Duke."

"An army of one. How do you survive? And I bet you stand out in this town wearing that hat." With her pretty face, she'd stand out regardless.

She placed her finger just under her lip to nudge a chip in her mouth. After chasing it with a swig of beer, she said, "So, what's your plan for moving Stringer off shortstop so you can take his spot?"

"I haven't decided. Either I'm going to slice his Achilles tendon in his sleep, or see if I can find some hot movie starlet to take him away to some exotic island. It's my only hope."

"He is a great player, isn't he?"

"Unbelievable. Of course, you have forgotten one tiny, important aspect."

"What's that?"

"I play for the Braves."

"Oh, yeah. That could pose a problem."

"It might."

"Well, how's Whitley doing these days in Atlanta? Maybe you'll move him out of the lineup."

"Right now I had better worry about keeping my position with the Pelicans," he said, laughing. "If I keep moving up, step by step, hopefully I'll be in Atlanta soon. As long as I make it to the majors I'll be a happy pup, but between you and me, I've always wanted to play for the Yankees. My idea of heaven is to stand at home plate at Yankee Stadium, in front of a packed house, and hit a home run in the bottom of the ninth to win the pennant. I've played that scenario through my head a thousand times."

"Well, here's to hoping that dream comes true." She held her beer bottle out and Cape tapped it with his Gatorade. "Speaking of Yankee Stadium, my father went to a game when he was a boy. My grandfather took him by train from New Brunswick where he grew up. Yankee blood runs deep in my family. Anyways, he got to watch the Yankees pound the Indians 12–2. He also got Mickey Mantle's autograph after the game."

"Really?"

"Yes. A reporter got Mickey to pose with Dad for a picture, although he never saw a copy. Dad always wondered what happened to that picture."

"He didn't know who the photographer worked for?"

"No. The man took down Dad's name and address and said he'd mail him a copy. Never heard from him."

"Bummer. Your dad should contact the Yankee organization and get them to check their archives or something."

"Impossible. Dad passed away four years ago."

"I'm sorry to hear that."

"It's okay. Besides, too many years have passed. I'm sure they've chunked the picture by now."

The game ended and Angela removed her cap. "Well, the night is still young. Want to step out and see what's going on downtown? I'm parked in the garage."

"That'd be fun, but I best not. I'm engaged."

Angela blushed. "Well, do I feel foolish."

"It's okay. But if I wasn't, I would have jumped at the chance."

"Well, I guess I'll head on home then." She stood and ran her fingers through her hair. "Thanks. It was great spending time with you."

"You too."

A bit embarrassed, she feigned a smile. "Maybe I'll see you around the hotel again this weekend."

***

Sunday morning, Cape walked through the lobby on the way to board the team bus back to the stadium. Angela stood behind the counter at the front desk. "Good luck today."

Cape turned and smiled. "Thanks. Hey, I enjoyed watching the game with you the other night. Don't take any grief off these people when you wear that Yankees hat."

"I won't. Maybe I'll see you in August when you come back. It'll be my last weekend before I return to school."

"Will free nachos be on the menu? You've spoiled me."

"I'll serve it to you on a silver platter. Will you be bringing the Gatorade?"

"Absolutely."

They exchanged smiles, and she watched him walk away.

He occupied her thoughts the rest of the day.

Chapter Nine

Cape's stats at midseason break were good—he'd batted .311 with sixteen home runs. Sixty-seven games took a toll on the players, physically and mentally, and Cape felt like the three-day break arrived at the perfect time.

He'd been selected to play in the July 4th All-Star game, which, much to Cape's liking, took place at the Pelican's stadium in Myrtle Beach. His family drove over for the weekend, staying at a hotel in walking distance of the stadium. Kasey, Grace, and Lauren bunked at Grace's beach house in North Myrtle Beach.

Cape was one of two Pelican players on the All-Star team, and the locals roared their prideful respect for the home-team boys. Cape won the Home Run Derby contest before the game, which had built the fans into a frenzy. A local girl who'd signed a music contract in Nashville sang the national anthem while red, white, and blue balloons raced to the sky's ceiling. America and baseball.

Cape went two-for-four in the game, belting a three-run double in the fifth to earn MVP honors. After the game, Cape took his family and Kasey to a late-night dinner at a local pancake house. The restaurant was crowded, and several people took notice when they walked to a booth near the kitchen. Several of the patrons recognized Cape and asked for an autograph. An elderly man who sat alone in a booth next to them chatted with his waitress while she refilled his coffee mug.

"Hey, Maggie, you see that guy over there?" the old man asked, pointing his bony finger toward Cape. "He's a great ballplayer."

Maggie turned and looked at Cape with a wary eye. "Is that right, Mr. Charley?"

"Yes, that's right. He plays for the Pelicans. Saw him hit a home run tonight that must have gone five-hundred feet. Ain't that right, Cape?"

Cape shrugged his shoulders. "Oh, come on now. I think you're exaggerating just a bit."

"I know what I'm talking about. Five-hundred feet. How can you hit a ball that far?"

"I use a corked bat."

Charley laughed, a phlegm-filled chuckle that turned into a hacking cough. He waved away Cape's comment. "Well, you must have one hell of a cork inside it."

They stayed well past the midnight hour, eating and drinking coffee, laughing and talking about nothing. About everything. Cape couldn't have asked for a more perfect evening, and he'd spent it with the people he cared most about.

***

A four-game series at Lynchburg and a three-game battle at Kinston followed the All-Star break. Cape began to realize how tough the game could be on the body, and on the heart. His knees began to ache, forcing him to sleep with them elevated. The elbow on his right arm – his throwing arm – throbbed and sometimes felt like it was being probed by a carpenter's drill bit. Gauze and antiseptic salve were a nightly ritual to clean bloody kneecaps.

Seeing his family, seeing Kasey, did recharge him, but it also reminded him how much he missed them. He told himself it was a necessary sacrifice to chase his dream.

His dad often told him that God had blessed him with special abilities, and he should make the most of those talents. "The Lord has filled your belt with tools," he told Cape, "so go out and build Him a mansion for all the world to see."

Randy had taught Cape he wasn't just playing the game for himself, but for heroes of the past. "Never forget Mickey Mantle, Gehrig, or the Babe," his dad would say. "It's what they did that laid the groundwork for what you are going to do."

The season went into August, and Cape continued to punish opposing pitchers. He batted .379 and riled the opposing fans. They yelled and screamed during the games to distract him, though if pressed, would surely admit to be in awe of his ability.

***

The next stop was Salem, Virginia, a rematch from the season opener. Cape had circled the weekend series against the Red Sox on his mental calendar because his parents, sister, and Kasey were going to be there. Randy's brother, Carl, lived in Salem, and the game was a perfect reason for the family to visit relatives and watch Cape play baseball.

Randy and Pauline checked in at the Marriott and took the luggage to their rooms. Alicia and Kasey waited by the lobby door, wearing excited expressions, looking like two kids waiting for a pop star. The bus pulled up and Cape stepped off.

Alicia slipped in ahead of Kasey, stealing a bear hug from her brother. Kasey waited at the curb, letting her eyes show that the one who owned her heart stood before her.

"Hey, girl," he said before kissing her, wrapping his arms tightly around her back. "Man, is it great to see you."

"My knees almost buckled when I saw you get off that bus." She took his face with both hands and kissed him again. "I've missed those beautiful, blue eyes."

Cape's teammates stopped walking into the hotel and watched the lovebirds' display of affection.

"Oh, Sam, how I've missed those baby blues," left fielder Caleb Andrews said, placing his head on Sam's shoulder.

"I've missed you too, precious." Sam pressed his hand behind Caleb's head, pulling him closer.

"Ease up, fellas," Cape laughed. "It's been a long time."

***

The evening was muggy, and humidity hung thick in the air. With no breeze, the game felt as though it was being played in a tobacco warehouse.

Cape got Kasey and his family tickets three rows behind the Pelican's dugout. They stocked up on soft drinks, peanuts, and sunflower seeds, the necessities for watching baseball.

"There are some cute guys on this team," Alicia said, filling her hand with sunflower seeds.

"Let's pick one out for you," Kasey said.

"Let's do."

"What are you going to do once we pick him out?"

Alicia scrunched her nose. "Not exactly sure. He'll probably run and hide."

"You better get ready, because in a few years the boys are going to come running, and you'll certainly need a personal assistant just to keep them all straight."

While the girls were chatting, Pauline looked both nervous and excited; the game didn't have the laid-back atmosphere of the All-Star game, or the fun of high school. She and Randy knew that Cape's performance directly affected his ability to climb the baseball ladder. Winning the game wasn't the ultimate goal, and they had trouble adjusting to that fact.

One hundred games into the season made it tough to maintain enthusiasm, even for someone like Cape who loved the game so much, but having Kasey and his family in attendance rejuvenated him. He liked seeing the faces of the people he loved most in the world in the stands. Rumors that Cape would be promoted to Double A in the spring only added to his enthusiasm.

He stepped on the on-deck circle in the top of the first inning and gave Kasey a brief smile, then did the same to his parents and sister. He felt as if he was playing his first Little League game, wanting to show them how good he was, to make them proud. He wanted them to know that no player would give more on the ball field than him.

Dustin Shipley, the national collegiate pitcher of the year from the University of Texas, was on the mound for Salem. Major League teams drooled over him, and Tampa Bay had selected him first in the season's draft. He threw left-handed, was tall and rangy, and his fastball roared with movement. His slider dropped under hitters' bats like it had fallen off a cliff.

Cape took a fastball for strike one. Then Dustin threw an off-speed pitch, a changeup, hoping to keep Cape's timing off balance. Cape, who had already begun his stride, froze for a brief second, allowing the ball time to get to the plate. He laced the pitch to third, but the third baseman caught Cape's hit on the second bounce and threw him out at first.

By end of the fifth inning, Salem led 2–1. Dustin had only given up three hits. Cape stepped on-deck, waiting on Caleb to finish his at-bat. Two petite, college-age girls moved to the front row. They tried to control their excitement as one, a cute blonde with a low-cut black tank top, took a picture of Cape taking a practice swing.

"Hey, Cape, we'll trade our phone numbers for an autograph," one of them said. She took another picture. She giggled and her friend tapped her forearm as though she couldn't believe the trade option her friend had offered.

Kasey pretended not to let their antics bother her, but the tint in her face soon matched her auburn hair. Cape paid no attention, watching Caleb look at a two-strike count at the plate. Pauline reached over and touched her husband on the hand, nodding toward the young girls drooling over their son.

"Pay them no mind," Pauline said to Kasey. "They're just crazy kids who'd turn their tails and run if Cape so much as smiled at them."

"It's disrespectful," Kasey said, her arms folded.

When Cape batted, he flew out to deep left field and the girls clapped and yelled as he jogged back to the dugout. Kasey had the inclination to toss her pretzel at them.

The top of the ninth, and the game was tied at two. Dustin strained his throwing arm, so reliever Sammy Tejada took the mound. An animated pitcher from Santo Domingo, Sammy was a crowd favorite in Salem. He would stand behind the mound between pitches, pounding the ball into his glove, staring off to center field, before charging to the mound and throwing the pitch. Sammy struck out the first two men he faced, and needed to retire Cape, the next batter, with hopes the offense would win it in the bottom of the ninth.

He stared at Cape and took a deep breath. Cape returned the stern look. The blazing fastball came high and inside, right at Cape's chin, and Cape barely got out of the way before landing on his backside. His teammates leapt from the dugout.

"What the hell are you doing?" Sam yelled at the pitcher.

"That's bullshit," Caleb said.

Sammy smirked at them.

Again Cape stepped into the box, and cut another stern look at Sammy, who began snorting like a bull. No one stared him down. He was the intimidator. Again he fired inside, and again Cape ended up on his backside. The umpire stepped to the front of the plate, pointing his finger at Sammy.

"You throw at him again and you're out of the game," the umpire said.

"This ain't kindergarten, ump," Salem's coach yelled from the dugout. "Let them play ball."

"That's enough out of you," the umpire said to him.

The Red Sox players clustered on the steps of their dugout. "Hey Jeffers, get back in the box," one of them said. "We don't have all day."

Both teams jawed back and forth and the umpire warned both dugouts to keep their mouths shut.

Cape stepped back into the box, took a practice swing, and then another. He'd gone hitless in front of his family, and that was not acceptable. He remembered his dad telling him that the best players triumphed when the game was on the line.

Sammy removed his cap and wiped his brow. He wanted to throw the ball a thousand miles per hour, but the pitch sailed high and the count grew to three balls and no strikes. The catcher called time and headed to the mound to calm his pitcher.

Sammy cursed in Spanish and the catcher looked like he didn't know what he was saying.

Cape sensed a fastball was coming because he knew Sammy didn't want to walk the batter who had scoffed at his intimidating antics. More than anything, he wanted to strike Cape out. As Cape guessed, Sammy's pitch came hard, and over the middle of the plate. He turned on the ball with an effortless, but powerful, swing. The ball ripped through the sky and smashed against the top of the scoreboard in left field. Sammy slammed his glove to the ground, pointing and cursing at Cape as he rounded the bases.

The Red Sox failed to score in the ninth, giving Myrtle Beach the victory. The autograph seekers began to assemble down the third base line past the dugout. A reporter from the *Roanoke Times* came onto the field and interviewed Cape. Dozens waited, and he smiled and thanked each person who sought his signature.

The last ones were the girls who had offered their phone numbers earlier. The blonde handed Cape her game program and a pen. Kasey watched from the bottom of the stands, trying to be interested in Alicia's chatter about her Harry Potter book.

Cape signed the program and the girls laughed and flirted and touched him on the arm.

Kasey, who now ignored Alicia completely, watched as the blonde stood next to Cape, slid her arms around his waist, and placed her head against his chest. Cape lightly set his hand on her shoulder. Her friend took a picture, and he pulled away and told them he needed to speak to his family. The girls hugged Cape and walked off.

He approached his waiting family and smiled.

"Good game, Cape." Alicia reached across the fence for a hug.

"Nice job, son." His dad put his arm around Cape's shoulder.

"What an exciting game," added his mom.

Kasey stood silently and didn't reach for him.

Cape immediately noticed she was upset, so he tried to talk about the game. "A lot of those guys will be promoted to Boston. And Dustin Shipley is really good."

"He couldn't handle you, though," Alicia said proudly.

"I went hitless against him, little sis." He smiled at Kasey. "How'd you like the game?"

Kasey stared at the outfield fence, her jaws tense and tight. *How could he have the nerve to ask that?*

"Well, I'll meet you guys back at the hotel," Cape said after a moment of awkward silence. "I should be showered and ready to go in about a half hour." He waved and headed for the locker room.

***

They ate late dinner at the Grand Dragon Chinese restaurant, and everybody noticed Kasey's quiet, angry demeanor.

Randy tried to ease the tension by talking about a Chinese restaurant in Santee. He told the story of the woman who ran the restaurant, and how she had gutted an old RV to serve as her dining area. He soon realized he was speaking to a disinterested audience. Kasey did not so much as glance at Cape, and Alicia kept looking between Kasey and her brother, trying to figure out why they were so quiet.

Randy concocted a story about how the woman was caught using cat meat instead of chicken just to see if they were paying attention. They weren't.

"So, Randy," Pauline said to keep conversation going, "Carl wants to come to Myrtle Beach and watch Cape play. Talk with him and see if we can't work something out, okay?"

"Sure," Randy said. "That's a good idea."

Kasey picked at her food. Jealousy consumed her, the worry about true devotion that often runs strong in young hearts. Her dismissive behavior made Cape wonder if she questioned his faithfulness.

After dinner, Kasey went to her room with Alicia, and Cape went to his. His teammate was already asleep. He lay in bed and stared at the ceiling. He wanted to bang on Kasey's door and tell her he'd done nothing wrong.

Kasey curled up in bed. She hadn't shown such a jealous streak since she caught Cal kissing Reagan Maass on the bleachers in the eleventh grade. How often did Cape chum up to girls on the road? What did he do when she wasn't around? *Ballplayers!*

Maybe she wasn't designed to sit idly at home while he went from town to town, worshipped and adored by most every girl at the ballpark. She imagined that it would only get worse the more successful Cape became. When he made it to Atlanta, or New York, or wherever, the groupies would grow in number, wouldn't they? In her mind, they weren't going to be happy with just getting autographs and photographs. She couldn't help but think that thousands of women surely would be coming for her man.

***

The following morning Randy loaded the car while Pauline checked out. Kasey and Alicia stood beside the car, with Kasey holding onto her pillow. She had not spoken to Cape since the afternoon before in the lobby. Cape was in no mood to play games, so he walked outside the hotel, and quietly helped Randy place the luggage in the back of the SUV.

Alicia noticed that Kasey and Cape still weren't speaking, and it bothered her. Kasey was going to be her new sister, and Cape, well, she loved with all her heart.

"Well, son, I guess this is it till next time," Randy said. "It was great seeing you. Keep playing hard and good things will happen."

"Glad you guys could come up. It means a lot."

Pauline hugged her son and tried to contain her tears. "Take care, sweetie. We love you."

"Yes, ma'am."

Randy helped Pauline get in the front seat, and then walked around the front of the vehicle and got in so Cape and Kasey could have a chance to talk.

Alicia hugged Cape without speaking. He rubbed her head.

"Bye, sis. See you soon."

Alicia slid in the car and shut the door.

Kasey stood, holding her pillow tightly, and looked anywhere but Cape's eyes. She began to cry. "Maybe I'm not cut out for this."

Cape took her in his arms, the pillow separating them. "Baby, don't you realize how much I love you? That you're the girl I want to spend the rest of my life with?"

Kasey sighed, but didn't stop crying. "Yes, I know you love me. But it's not easy having to share you."

He pulled her head under his chin. "You're not. I'm all yours. I'm simply here to play baseball. If those who watch me play get worked up over a picture and an autograph, well, there's not much I can do about it. I sure appreciate that they want my autograph or my picture. To me, that's a compliment to the way I play the game." He touched her hand. "But you're what I get worked up over. Well, that and game-winning home runs." He smiled. "In fact, game-winning home runs probably top the list."

Kasey pulled his ear and smiled. "Now, kiss me and get your shapely fanny in the car before they leave you."

"That's not a bad thing. I'd have to stay here with you."

Her tender smile warmed him and he hugged her again. "I wish you could," he said. He gently kissed her and wiped her tears with his finger.

He waved as they drove away.

Chapter Ten

Baseball is a game of failure, especially when it comes to hitting. When a professional player bats .300, it's considered a very good season; it means he got a base hit three out of every ten times he batted. Conversely, it also means the player failed to get a hit seventy percent of the time he stepped to the plate, through the course of an entire year.

When September arrived, Cape was mired in a nine-game hitting slump, the first time he'd ever struggled with hitting a baseball. It had been four games since he'd gotten on base, and with only one hit in eleven games, his batting average dropped from .343 to .309. He became tense when he batted. Right-handed, left-handed, it didn't matter. For the first time in his life, he felt unsteady at the plate.

The Pelicans had a two-game lead over Kinston and faced them in a night game, the first of a four-game series in Myrtle Beach. The crowd was anxious to beat Kinston, the league champs of the previous season. With fifteen games remaining, any win for the Pelicans would add to the slim lead they held in the division standings.

As was customary for late summer, the evening was hot and muggy. The soft ocean breezes subsided, and the humidity made for an uncomfortable setting.

The Kinston team failed to score in the first inning and everyone hoped that was a sign it would a good night for the Pelicans. The leadoff batter walked, giving Myrtle Beach the early lead. Cape grounded out to second base, and the crowd moaned in displeasure. He'd been the fan favorite all season, but they grew tired of his slump.

In the top of the second, Kinston had a runner on first and only one out. The batter hit a sharp grounder to Cape, and the crowd sensed a double play. Cape crouched and lowered his glove to the dirt. The ball bounced higher than he'd anticipated and hit the palm of his glove before ricocheting off his shoulder, landing in the dirt behind him. Boos came roaring from the crowd.

"Make the damn play, pretty boy!" he heard.

"You suck, Jeffers!" came from another. "You should mail in your paycheck."

Cape picked up the ball and threw it to his pitcher. He looked at his glove, rubbing his hand along the palm as if trying to figure out why he couldn't squeeze the ball when it hit the leather. After his error, Kinston scored two runs thanks to a double off the wall in right center.

After the inning, as Cape jogged to the dugout, a fan yelled, "Did you forget how to play the game?"

He had never experienced the home crowd turning on him. On the road, he could deal with it, as it was just their way of voicing displeasure that he led the way in beating their team. But at home, it wasn't supposed to be that way.

Cape struck out in the fourth, and more boos and insults rained down. He sat alone at the end of the dugout. He closed his eyes, visualizing the way he gripped the bat and the way he brought his hands through to the ball when he swung. His teammates tried to encourage him, and though he appreciated their efforts, he felt isolated. His young body had hit the wall, and his mind didn't know how to deal with it. The game had always come so easy for him, but now it seemed foreign and unfamiliar.

Cape came up to bat in the ninth. There were two outs, a base runner on second, and Kinston led by three runs. He tried to block out the vicious comments from the stands. If he could get on base, hot-hitting first baseman Orlando Curtis would bat next. Orlando had been really mashing the ball, and with his power he could tie up the game with one swing.

Cape fouled off the first pitch. He swung at an outside pitch, missing badly for strike two. The pitcher sensed Cape was confused and unsure of himself, and he threw a slow breaking ball that dipped in front of the plate. Cape took a sharp swing at it, missing for strike three.

A beer bottle landed at his feet as he walked to the dugout, head hung low.

"You're a bum," came from the stands.

"A damn disgrace," someone else yelled.

The game ended, and Kinston climbed to within one game of Myrtle Beach for first place. Cape wasn't exactly in the mood for autographs, but he didn't want to disappoint the youngsters who had waited all game for one. But when he left the dugout, no one waited for him. No baseballs, no posters, no caps to sign. No huge grin on an excited child. Cape showered quickly and left without speaking to his teammates. He felt alone, and Santee seemed a million miles away. He wanted to run to the shelter of his apartment.

He sat on the balcony of his apartment and looked out in the distance. The dim lights on the docks hugging the Waccamaw River carved a pale slice from the darkness. He'd left his sliding glass door slightly ajar, and heard loud knocking at the front door. He opened it to see Kasey standing on his welcome mat, a devilish grin on her face. He reached out and squeezed her like he wanted to expunge the air from her lungs.

"Thank God you're here," he said. She wanted to kiss him but he wouldn't let go.

"Are you okay?" She tried to loosen his grip.

"It's been a nightmare."

He finally released her, took her suitcase, and led her inside to the couch. She could see the worn look in his eyes.

"What's going on?" She rubbed her hand along his forearm.

"I'm in the worst slump of my life. I can't hit. I've got no confidence at the plate. I look like I've never played before."

"Slumps are temporary. You can't let it get to you."

"It's more than that. I never thought I'd say this, but it isn't fun anymore. I hate going to the ballpark. It used to be the only place where I felt invincible. Now I feel as though I don't belong there."

Kasey touched his face. "You told me everyone goes through slumps. It's a part of the game, right?"

"I meant that about everybody else, not me. That was, until now."

"Cape, you're playing game after game over half the country, riding buses, staying in hotels. It's going to take a toll."

"Yes, but what if I've lost my ability to hit? I'm nothing if I can't swing a bat."

"You'll get it back. I know you will. What have you got, three weeks left in the season?"

"Something like that."

"Well, you push on through the season, get away from it for a few months, and then start fresh."

"It's not just the slump." He sat on the edge of the couch, elbows on his knees, face in his hands. "The crowd's turned on me. That's never happened before."

"Enough about baseball. Take me to dinner and I'll show you a good time."

Cape finally realized that Kasey had showed up at his door for a surprise visit. He hugged her, kissed her, and took hold of her hands as he looked into her eyes. "I'm so glad you're here."

"I wanted to surprise you."

"As Clark Griswold once said, 'If I woke up tomorrow with my head sewn to the carpet, I wouldn't be any more surprised than I am now.'"

"Tell you what, Clark, buy me a quesadilla to show me your appreciation. I'm starving."

Cape took Kasey to a small Mexican restaurant near the North Carolina state line. He wanted to get away from anyone who might recognize him. He didn't want to be reminded of his rough time on the baseball field.

A Mariachi band played as Kasey updated him on the progress of the wedding plans. Cape watched Kasey's eyes light up as she talked about how she'd found the most beautiful gown, and that the bridesmaid dresses were perfect. She shared that Billy was making sure the groomsmen had been fitted for their tuxedos.

She chattered about the menu for the wedding dinner.

Cape slid his foot out of his Rainbow sandal and rubbed it against her calf to see if he could slow her down. But in her excitement she continued on, so he moved his foot above her knee and rubbed her inner thigh. Her eyes grew wide and she looked around.

"What are you doing?" she asked playfully, her face beginning to blush.

"Just making sure you shaved your legs today. Now, what were you saying about the wedding cake?"

"I can't remember, thanks to you. You took my mind completely off the wedding. I bet you did that on purpose, didn't you?"

"No way I'd do that. I could talk about tulips and snapdragons all day."

She threw a chip at him. "You are going to get it, buster."

"God, I hope so." He knew that day was only seven weeks away.

"Soon enough."

"How about a sneak preview?"

"Cape," she said, placing her elbows on the table. "You're bad."

"I know. Why don't you take me home and spank me?"

Kasey grinned and tried to fake a look of disgust. "Do you know how much I've missed you?"

"I think I've got a good idea. I can't believe how much you consume my thoughts, and I never figured I'd be this way. For me, it was baseball, baseball, and then in between, baseball. And then you had to come along and change all that. Thanks a lot."

"You're welcome. Somebody needed to readjust your priorities, so it may as well be me."

"Just wish you could stay with me and keep my priorities in order now."

"Well, starting next season, you'll have me around all the time, at least for the home games."

"Well, thank God for that!"

***

Kasey took a hot bath to relax after her three-hour drive, and Cape played soft music on the stereo. She emerged from the bedroom smelling sweetly of perfume, wearing a lace tank top and plaid, embroidered flannel shorts. She sat next to Cape on the couch and began to kiss him. A fire burned inside him, and he pressed his hands against her back, pulling her closer. Her lips were soft and supple, her tongue wet and warm. She smiled, stood, and pulled him by the hand, guiding him off the couch. She placed her head against his heart, and they began to slow dance to "Come Away With Me" by Norah Jones. He gently rubbed her soft, long hair.

"I love you," he whispered.

"I love you more."

He gave a shake of his head as they continued the dance. The song ended. She stared into his eyes, and she kissed him. Just a touch of her lips to his. She kissed his face, and his neck, her eyes never leaving his. She angled her face so her lips waited on his, and then he kissed her, softly. He felt her heart beating gently, and it soothed him.

"You don't know how glad I am that you came here tonight," Cape said. "You must have sensed that I needed you."

"Baby, I'll always be here for you."

"Man, am I glad I knocked you into the beer rack that day."

"Who would've ever thought that being a klutz would pay off for you the way it did?"

***

Kasey's surprise visit reenergized him. He got his swing back, finishing with a .322 batting average. Time for the off-season, the wedding, and the beginning of a new life.

Chapter Eleven

The sky was china blue – a ceiling so high and so expansive it appeared there was no separation between heaven and earth, no solar system, no darkness, no stars, no planets. A light northerly breeze had chased away any remnants of summer's humid days. Cape couldn't help but think it would be a great time to toss a baseball with his dad, who stood beside him in the foyer of the St. James Baptist Church. Inside the sanctuary, a crowd that could best be described as overflowing waited for the wedding to begin.

Randy's hand rested on Cape's shoulder as they looked out the window. Cape slid his finger inside the collar, trying to loosen the confining shirt and bowtie.

"Man, this tux makes me feel like I'm inside a boa constrictor."

"Yeah, but you look great," his dad said with a smile.

"Let me ask you something?"

"What is it?"

"Were you nervous when you married Mom?"

"Absolutely. Anybody that tells you they weren't nervous at their own wedding is a damn liar." Randy raised his hand to his mouth and prayed that Reverend Austin wasn't in hearing distance. "But you take a deep breath, keep your knees bent so you don't pass out, and then push on through it. Remember that the wedding is supposed to be fun for everybody but you, so grin and bear it. Your fun will take place later on tonight."

Cape blushed beet-red before realizing his father was simply trying to take his mind off the fact that he would soon be standing in front of two-hundred and fifty people and publically proclaiming his undying love for Kasey. He aimed to repeat his vows without fumbling, as well as not look like a dork passing the time during the soloist's performance.

"It's hard to believe I'm getting married."

"Tell me about it. It seems like you made the pee-wee team just last week. You were only seven. Your uniform swallowed you, and your mother had to cut and re-sew the cap so it would fit. You slept with your bat and glove the night before the first game. And you even managed to sleep with your cap on, though I don't know how you did. I came in your room to wake you and you looked like you hadn't moved all night."

"I remember that night. I was just so excited about getting to play."

"Since you were playing against nine and ten year olds that first year, it took you a couple of games to adjust to the pitching speed. Your first hit was a single off Jack Sprague's boy, Mitchell. I still remember the smile on your face."

Cape's nervousness eased, though he felt a hint of sadness. Gone were the days of chasing Dad's pop flies in the backyard, Mom watching from the picnic table under the maple tree. Gone were Friday night trips after high school games to O'Reilly's Restaurant, a local eatery with wall-to-wall televisions for patrons to watch while eating or sipping on adult beverages. Baseball was still quite an important part of their lives, but it was different now. Games played hundreds, sometimes a thousand miles away from home made it more isolated and independent. It had been an adjustment for Cape to play without his family in the stands.

Cape fought back tears when he saw Kasey walk down the aisle on the arm of her father. Her white satin dress was off her shoulders, and clung tightly to her waist before fanning out in a swirl of beads and lace around her legs and feet. Her hair was pulled tightly in a bun, thereby showcasing her blue eyes and sparkling smile. He took her hand and the ceremony began. They had written their own vows, and the minister, Reverend Austin, informed those in attendance of that before he led them through the ceremony.

***

The reception took place at the Mandolin House, a white, stately two-story mansion with massive columns and a mahogany wrap-around porch. A black wrought-iron balcony was above the ornate front door. Out back, a live band played on a patio deck. Carving stations were manned by gentlemen in tuxedos. Devout Baptists, there would be no alcohol, much to the dismay of Cape's teammates. Jose and Sam talked Lauren and Grace onto the dance floor. Attendees gave speeches and toasts, and the cake was cut and eaten. The party carried on for three hours and then Cape and Kasey exited between two lines of guests down the steps, across the lawn, and into a black stretch limo.

***

Cape and Kasey honeymooned at Daufuskie Island, just off the southern tip of Hilton Head. Kasey had known several people who vacationed there, and after looking at photos and the website of the resort, they both agreed it would be a great place for a honeymoon. Cape had placed $10,000 of his signing bonus into a separate savings account to pay for the trip, and Randy slipped him $500 that he'd saved in a rainy day account. They would make Daufuskie their playground for six days.

The island, which meant "sharp feather" in the Muscogee language, was only accessible by boat, so they took the ferry from Hilton Head for a thirty-minute ride on Calibogue Sound. The island was steeped in history, the site of many battles and skirmishes between the Indian Nation and the British in the 1700s. It was once home to the Gullah people, and author Pat Conroy taught school there in the '70s. The beautiful sea island and its native inhabitants inspired Conroy to create the novel *The Water is Wide*.

They stood along the edge of the boat, Cape's arm surrounding Kasey's waist as they looked off across the emerald water. They docked at a long wooden pier that led to a small, wooden restaurant with a screened porch called "The Paradise." The aroma of boiled shrimp and fried crab cakes greeted them when they stepped off the boat. Two men in khaki pants and white golf shirts came for their luggage that they'd take by pickup truck to the resort. They pointed to a golf cart beside a gray barn adorned with a faded Coca-Cola sign and presented Cape with a map to the resort.

"I strongly encourage you to sample the soft shell crab at The Paradise," said one of the men. "It will add years to your life."

"We'll keep that in mind," Cape said.

"Take your time with the cart," the other said. "Check out the old church on Pine Cone Road. It was built in the 1800s."

Cape and Kasey passed on The Paradise, though the smell of shrimp made it hard to skip. But they were anxious to check in and decided they'd eat at the small restaurant later during their trip. Cape drove the cart with one hand and held Kasey's with the other. They rode along a country gravel road covered in shadows made by giant pines and twisted oaks draped in Spanish moss. The air was sweet and Kasey breathed it deep in her lungs like it might be her last time. Three bellhops greeted them when they drove up to the stately resort. Painted yellow, with intricate, white columns on either side of the front entrance, the inn looked like something from *Gone with the Wind*.

Their dinner took place in a quiet private room at Castleberry's, a restaurant that had been converted from a storage warehouse built in the late 1800s. With small rooms carved into little hideaways and hardwood floors surrounded by walls of deep green adorned with rare paintings, each table draped in white linen and adorned with candle light, Castleberry's offered an ambiance as enticing as its crab cakes and lobster tails. The beautiful couple caught the eye of everyone in the restaurant.

Logs glowed brightly, flames flickering, shifting and bending in shades of red and blue in the tiny fireplace to the side of their table. Cape couldn't stop staring at his bride. She wore a red dress with spaghetti straps, and a black silk shawl that her grandmother had given her as a wedding gift. He wore a Navy-blue sports coat, a white button-down dress shirt, and khaki pants. They ordered filet mignon. The waiter suggested a bottle of wine, and Cape asked him to make the choice. He tried to look calm, though he was worried the man would ask to see his I.D.

The waiter uncorked a bottle of Bordeaux and poured a small amount in Cape's glass. Cape pretended to act like a wine connoisseur, examining the wine in the glass before twirling it slightly. He took a sip and then looked in deep thought as though studying the flavor in his mouth.

"It's fine," he said with a nod. The waiter added more to his glass and then poured wine in Kasey's glass.

"You're now a wine expert, I see," she said as soon as they were alone again.

"I had no idea what I was doing. I was just trying not to look like a fool."

"Well, you were pretty convincing. Had a little James Bond air about you."

He raised his glass, and Kasey did as well. He leaned forward and touched his glass to hers. He watched the candlelight dance in her eyes, and she was the most beautiful girl he had ever seen. "I'm not real good at this, but I'm going to do it anyway." He took a breath and then collected his thoughts, looking intently into her eyes as though trying to study her heart. "To us." He paused. "To the greatest life possible. To loving you with all my heart, and making the most of every day with you."

Kasey looked at Cape as though he were a new creation sent from heaven at that very moment. A gift from God unseen by human eyes until then. "To the sweetest, most incredible man in the world. To watching our love grow stronger every day."

After dinner, the owner of the restaurant stopped by to offer his congratulations, and sent amaretto cheesecake to their table with his compliments.

***

The newlyweds returned to their darkened room. Moonlight slipped through the window's thick wooden blinds, painting perfect shards of pale white across the hardwood floor and casting them in silhouette. Cape took Kasey's hand and led her to the canopy bed adorned in white, sheer draperies. He took her face in his hands and kissed her. She trembled. Slowly, she slid her hands down his muscled back. Their kisses were delicate, though their hearts pounded. A whippoorwill called in the distance, and autumn ferns outside their window rustled softly in the sea breeze.

"I've saved myself for you, Cape," she whispered in his ear. "For you only."

She touched his face with her fingers, looked into his eyes, and kissed him. He put his hands to the back of her neck, and she tightened her hold. Like coals flamed by a breeze, their hunger grew, and their kisses became more forceful. He laid her on the bed as though she were a porcelain doll.

"I can't get close enough to you," he said. He touched his cheek to hers, as if verifying that she was not just a vision. Tears rose as he peered through her eyes into her soul. "I promise to love you with everything that's inside me."

"Is there anything more than love?" she asked. "If so, that's what I feel, even though I can't describe it in words."

He pulled her close, his hands pressing against her lower back, and he kissed her as though he might never get the chance again. He removed his coat and shoes, though his eyes never left hers in the darkened room. She lowered the straps from her shoulder. And then, to the beat of pounding hearts, they joined both body and spirit.

***

Kasey woke to sunshine spilling across the bed and the aroma of shrimp, grits, and fresh coffee. Cape had slipped out and had the kitchen specially prepare the food. Cape served her in bed from a silver tray.

"Good morning, Mrs. Jeffers. Did you sleep well?"

"Yes, I did, Mr. Jeffers. How about you?"

"Like Rip Van Winkle." He kissed her forehead. "Ready to start the rest of your life with me?"

"Can I eat breakfast first?" He nibbled on her ear lobe. "Ow," she said. "Geez, you're so impatient."

"Yes, I am. I don't want to wait another minute."

"If it makes you feel better, I'll set this beautiful tray on the floor and let this wonderful food turn cold and moldy, just so I can be held in your arms."

"Now you're talkin'. Since your attitude is finally coming around, I guess I'll let you eat before you start the rest of your life with me."

After breakfast, in the soft morning light, skin to skin, between the soft, white sheets, they made love again.

That afternoon they rented jet skis and rode in the Calibogue Sound, idling through pods of dolphins that would rise up mere feet away from them. Kasey fishtailed her jet ski, spraying Cape with the warm water. That evening they rode the ferry to Sea Pines, eating dinner as the sun set behind a veil of pale red. Then they watched yachts come and go in the harbor and listened to a man strum an acoustic guitar.

The rest of the week was spent walking the shoreline, lying on blankets under the tall pine trees with lunch prepared by the resort's restaurant, and making love in the quiet of their room. Kasey tried to keep up with the schoolwork she was missing in class, reading a little in the early morning hours by the window while Cape slept.

Their lives were off to a magical start, and Kasey had a hard time believing it was real. Two young lovers, still shy of their twenty-first birthdays, blessed beyond anything they could have dreamed. A lifetime of love and happiness surely awaited.

***

They moved into Kasey's apartment, where they would live, until they found out where Cape would be assigned after spring training.

For their first meal, Kasey prepared sea bass and garlic mashed potatoes from a recipe book she'd received as a wedding gift. Cape set the table with candles and a bottle of wine Billy had given them. After dinner, they shared a piece of key lime pie. Kasey fed Cape a piece, purposely placing whip cream along his upper lip, which he began to lick.

"That's my job," she said, leaning across the table.

She ran her tongue across his lips, removing the whipped topping. He opened his mouth and their tongues met. Cape stood and slid the plates and glasses of wine to one side, clearing a spot on the cherry wood. He pulled Kasey to her feet and lifted her on the table. He began to kiss her neck and her face, and she leaned back on her elbows, craning her neck. The sweet smell of perfume, the soft burn in her eyes, and the slender curves of her body made Cape's kisses grow stronger and more forceful. She squeezed her legs around his and began to sweat. She gave herself to him, and in turn, took him to a level of passion that left him breathless.

***

Dawn had chased the darkness from the bedroom, though the sun was still thirty minutes from making its appearance. Kasey woke when she felt Cape brush his fingers across her forehead. "Morning."

She smiled sleepily. "Hey. What are you doing up?"

"Watching you sleep."

She rubbed his face. "Everything okay?"

"Just trying to figure out how I was lucky enough to land you." He kissed her cheek.

She slid over and placed her head on his chest. "If anyone's lucky, it's me. It scary to think how much I love you."

Cape wanted the touch of his hand, the look in his eyes, to illustrate what he felt in his heart, as his words could not. He wanted her to know that she was a painter in the truest sense. She had softened the canvas of his heart with indescribable pastels, colors that had no names, creating a scene in his life he had never imagined.

***

Their first Christmas as husband and wife was as much about creating the Christmas setting as it was spending the holidays together. They picked out a Virginia Spruce from what seemed like hundreds of potential candidates. Cape found several that to him seemed worthy, but Kasey had some rare symmetrical detection ability that eliminated all of them. The tree had to be perfect, and when they finally got one home, Cape found out why.

He never knew a Christmas tree could hold so many ornaments. Glass snowflakes, crystal hummingbirds, clay figurines of Muppet Santas, and hand-stitched elves and reindeer hung from every branch.

Kasey painstakingly decorated the apartment with nativity scenes, a singing Santa on a tricycle, and candles that smelled like pumpkin pie. The mantle was decorated in garland and lights of green and blue. A twin pair of stockings hung from the mantle as well, personalized with their names.

They spent the night with her family on Christmas Eve. Her sisters made the festivities lively, hiding a lot of presents in strategic places with step-by-step clues on how to find each one.

On Christmas morning, Cape woke early to find a present lying on his pillow in the guest room. Kasey sat beside him, holding a tray with coffee and one of her mother's homemade cinnamon rolls. She wore bright red pajamas, and she reminded Cape of a child who always woke up first on Christmas.

"Merry Christmas," she said softly, her eyes radiant from the sun's first appearance through the bedroom window.

"Merry Christmas. Something smells good." He sat up and held the present. His hair pointed skyward, making him look more like the Grinch than an elf. "What do I do first, eat the cinnamon roll or open the present?"

"The present, goofball."

Inside the small box was a leather necklace with a black pearl cross. "Kasey, this is awesome." He placed it over his head and rubbed the cross where it touched his chest.

"I thought you'd wear it when you play." She handed a cup of coffee to Cape. "It's supposed to keep you safe."

He kissed her. "I'll never take it off."

"Good. Let me touch it from time to time so I'll be safe too."

"Oh, I'll keep you safe. Always."

***

Cape's family Christmas took place at his mother's stately childhood home, decorated in red and gold. It was Pauline's first Christmas there since she was fourteen. She had decorated the house in a Charleston style with the money Cape had set aside for her. Mahogany furniture adorned the den and dining room, as well as paintings of The Battery and the pastel homes of Rainbow Row.

Cape and Kasey made it in time for breakfast. The family exchanged gifts in the den. Pauline gave Kasey an ornament of a tiny fireplace and mantle that said "First Christmas". Like Kasey had done for their own mantle, Pauline had hung a stocking for Kasey, with her name embroidered on it, that was located next to Cape's.

"Now, Kasey," Pauline said, "I just want you to know that we certainly have room for more stockings in case your family grows."

"Easy, Mom," Cape said. "Don't start putting pressure on us to produce you a grandbaby. We just got married, remember?"

Pauline shrugged and said with a laugh, "What are you talking about? I'm just saying…"

Kasey playfully popped Cape on his wrist. "Don't give your mom a hard time. I'm sure I'll be doing the same after our children get married."

***

Later that night, back at their apartment, Cape and Kasey exchanged gifts and sat by the fireplace. With Bing singing in the background, Cape gave Kasey a diamond pendant and her favorite perfume. Kasey gave Cape a black leather jacket. They snuggled in front of the fire, and she fed him fudge her sister had made.

"Just think, we'll be in New York for Christmas next year," Kasey said.

"New York? Is that where you want to spend Christmas?"

"No, I mean we'll be living in New York since you'll be playing for the Yankees." Cape shook his head as if reminding her that he didn't play for the Yankees—yet.

"Don't say anything," she said, waving her finger in front of his face. "Humor me. Just let me see if I can describe the scene as good as you." She sat up, her voice deepening. "Yankee Stadium, bottom of the ninth. Two outs, and fan favorite Cape Jeffers steps to the plate; he's looking so fine in those tight pinstripe pants." Kasey moved her hands in front of her as if she created the scene in mid-air. "The pitcher throws a 200-mile-per-hour fastball, and Jeffers takes a massive swing with a bat that's as big as a tree trunk. Oh my God, the ball explodes off his bat, and it's roaring skyward. Back, back, back the centerfielder goes, and the ball leaves the stadium like a missile. On it goes, out of the city and into the Atlantic Ocean. There's pandemonium in the stands. The streets swirl in mass hysteria. Mothers swear to name their children after the great Cape Jeffers. Women will throw themselves at his feet. Grown men cry and swear on their mother's graves that a better ballplayer there could not be. Cape Jeffers has just become the most beloved Yankee player of all time."

Cape laughed and shook his head. "That's a little different from my version, but I like it. One little problem, sweet cheeks. I play for the Braves."

"They'll trade for you."

"Not with Derek Stringer at shortstop. He's the best in the league."

"Whatever. I don't know who this Stringer guy is, but I do know this: you *will* play for the Yankees. So, be patient." She reached over and kissed him, playfully, tugging on his bottom lip with her teeth.

"Don't hold your breath." He took a quick sip of hot cider.

"Do you like your presents?" she asked, rubbing his hair. She traced his profile with her fingers. He was the most handsome man she had ever seen, and she still couldn't believe he was hers.

"Man, I am loaded up. I like the necklace the best, by far." He rubbed the cross. "How about you?"

"Best Christmas ever." She kissed his cheek.

Cape scratched his chin and looked confused. "Wait a minute. I am such a slacker."

"What are you talking about?"

"I completely forgot, but you still have one more present. Can't believe I forgot to give it to you. The apple cider must have gone straight to my head."

Kasey smiled and playfully grabbed Cape by the shirt. "Holding out on me, huh, Jeffers?"

He stood, took Kasey by the hand and helped her to her feet, then led her to the spare bedroom. There in the corner, wrapped in a big red bow, stood a tall easel. Kasey stood speechless, her eyes moving back and forth between the easel and Cape.

"Oh, my God. A Giant Dulce. I've wanted a Dulce easel since I was in middle school. But they're so expensive, I never dared ask for one."

"Well, now you don't have to worry about asking. Maybe you'll finally paint a baseball picture just for me. Merry Christmas."

Kasey ran her fingers over the easel. Never had she received anything that meant more. She touched Cape on the face and stared into his eyes. She kissed him softly. "God created the perfect man for me." She looked at the easel and shook her head. "Thank you, Cape."

"Just seeing the expression on your face made my Christmas."

"Now it's your turn, bub." She took him by the hand and led him to the den.

Cape watched as she crawled under the tree and grabbed a box hidden on the bottom row of limbs. With all the decorations, the present was easy to hide. Santa Claus himself could have been sitting in there and Cape wouldn't have noticed.

"Here you go." She scooted back beside him and handed him the gift.

"You're just as devious as I am."

"Yes, I am. Now stop stalling and open it."

He tore at the red and white paper, uncovering a small shoebox. Cape knew if it contained shoes, they'd be too small for his feet. He wanted to ask for a hint, but simply removed the top to find the inside was filled with colored tissue paper. He spotted a tiny baseball glove in the paper, and wondered for a moment if it was something for his desk or the bookshelf. He placed two fingers inside the finger grip and turned it so the web faced him.

"What's this for?"

"Well, since you're a baseball player through and through, I figured your child would have no choice but to be one as well."

Cape's eyes widened and he sat straight up. "What are you saying?"

"I'm saying you better get prepared for a new throwing partner."

Cape hugged her. He kissed her. He rubbed her hair. He hugged her again, rocking from side to side like a weighted pendulum. He lifted her shirt, and gently rubbed her stomach. He began to cry. Kasey followed suit.

Life was good for Cape and Kasey Jeffers.

Chapter Twelve

Kasey battled microbiology and morning sickness her final semester. Cape worked out every day, adding muscle to his already ripped frame. He spent his afternoons at the University of South Carolina indoor baseball facility. The head coach, Rick Timmons, had developed a friendship with Cape when he'd recruited him in high school. Cape likely would have played for Rick if he hadn't gotten the multi-million dollar signing bonus to play for the Braves.

Before Cape left for spring training, he bought some plastic baseballs and a plastic bat. Boy or girl, he wanted his child to be able to hit for power. They picked out baby furniture, including a rocker in the shape of a baseball glove, and then stored everything in the spare bedroom. They weren't quite sure whether Cape would be assigned again to Myrtle Beach, or be promoted to the Double A team in Macon, Georgia. By the time Cape headed for Orlando, Kasey had compiled a list of possible names for the baby.

***

Cape indeed was promoted to Macon. It seemed that his progression to the major leagues was going better than he'd originally planned. He had heard rumors that Atlanta wasn't happy with their shortstop, and wanted to move him quickly up the organization. He thought about Kasey's prediction that next Christmas would be spent in New York. Perhaps Atlanta instead?

His season began well. He hit seven home runs in the first month, and was third on the team in batting with a .326 average. He played for far more than himself. He had a wife, a child on the way, and he wanted to give them the best life possible. If he could just make it to the majors and remain on the active roster for at least two-thirds of the year, he would be guaranteed to receive at least the league minimum salary of $260,000.

The top players secured contracts that topped twenty million dollars per season. Such was the reward of being a successful big leaguer.

Kasey missed Cape terribly, but had plenty to keep her mind occupied. She ate healthy, exercised, and took the prenatal vitamins her doctor recommended. She prepared for finals and started packing. Her parents helped with boxing up items from the kitchen and closets. Cape had purchased only the basics for the three-bedroom apartment he leased in Macon, which included a bed that would be moved to the guest room after Kasey and the moving van arrived.

She planned to move the day after graduation. She was glad that her graduation gown was loose enough to accommodate her growing belly. Cape would attend and watch her get her diploma, though he'd be due back at the ball field for an evening game. Kasey's busy schedule cut down on her chance to paint, but she knew she had to choose her priorities.

Kasey's mother had to say her goodbyes at the apartment, since she had a school function to attend at Jordan's school. Doug followed her and the moving van to Macon.

After the movers unloaded the furniture and a lot of boxes, Doug and Kasey placed her clothes in the spare bedroom. They attended Cape's game that night, the first time that her dad got to watch Cape play. Though Kasey thought he seemed proud, he didn't really care much for baseball. His interests revolved around the fresh air of the outdoors: fishing, hunting, and growing timber on their 300-acre tract of land.

The following morning, the apartment took on a somber tone as Doug packed to return home. Kasey walked to the car with him. He had already gone through the separation with his two older daughters, but they lived within forty-five minutes of home. Kasey now lived four hours away, not extremely far, but that wasn't the issue. She was his favorite. He tried to treat all of his girls with the same amount of fatherly love, but something about Kasey made her different from her sisters. He felt that she was more like him than the others.

"Well, I guess that's about it," he said, shutting the trunk of his Lexus. He struggled to look his daughter in the eyes. "Keep in touch. Just let us know if you need anything. I don't care how far the drive is, I'll be here if you need me."

Kasey began to cry and she hugged him. "I love you, Daddy."

"I love you, too, sweet girl." He looked skyward to keep from crying. "It's hard knowing you aren't just forty-five minutes away anymore."

"You and Mom come up and stay with us this summer."

"You can count on it. When you get close to your due date, Mom will be here to take care of you."

He released his hold and opened the car door then got in. He looked at her as he started the engine, and she sighed. She placed her hand on his window and he traced it with his.

On the drive home, he didn't play music or listen to talk shows. He drifted to when Kasey was a child. He thought of the day she took her first steps, and when she spoke her first word. She had awakened before sunrise one morning, crying for him. He could never resist her pleas, and he placed her in bed between him and June.

With his back to her, trying to fall asleep, she touched his back and spoke her first words. "Hey, da-da." His wife would swear that Kasey only mumbled gibberish that day, but he knew without a doubt that her first words were saying hello to her daddy.

***

By the All-Star break, Cape led the league in home runs and runs-batted-in, and had the fewest number of strikeouts on the team. His batting average climbed to .394, and he was so comfortable at the plate that he felt he could get a base hit every time he stepped on-deck. At shortstop, he was a human vacuum, sucking in the ball and throwing batters out from deep in the hole behind third or up the middle behind second base.

Home attendance bloomed as Macon held a six-game lead, much of that thanks to Cape.

Kasey began to paint again. It had been almost a year since she'd picked up a brush, and she felt inspired. As the days passed, the image came to life with the most beautiful of colors. When Cape was home, she draped the painting with an old blanket and hid it in a closet. On some nights when Cape was gone, she'd paint until two or three in the morning. Cape wondered why it seemed she looked forward to his road trips.

***

Roberts, the coach for Macon, called Cape into his office after a game against Durham. "Have a seat, Cape."

"You look a little nervous, skipper," Cape said with a smile. "Something weighing on your mind?"

"Yep. It's a pisser of a day."

"How's that?"

"Well, I just got word that you're to clear out your locker tonight after the game."

"What? What are you talking about?"

"I'm saying you're done playing for us."

"We got a month left in the season. You're trading me? After the way I've busted my tail? This just isn't right." Cape stood and pounded his fist on Doc's desk.

"I know. I know." Doc leaned back in his chair and worked his teeth over with a toothpick. "But it just doesn't make any sense to keep your locker when you're being moved up to Greenville."

Cape lowered his eyes and frowned. "Don't jerk me around, Doc."

"I ain't jerkin'. Your country ass is due to be in Greenville tomorrow. From what I'm told, you're penciled into the starting lineup."

Cape was speechless. He stepped away from the desk and looked out the office window into the parking lot, letting his mind absorb the good news.

***

Kasey put on a fresh nightgown, sweating just minutes after taking a shower. She had battled dizziness earlier that day, and Cape had told her not to come to his game but to rest instead.

"Hey, baby," she said when Cape walked in the bathroom, arching her back to ease the weight of her stomach. "How'd the game go?"

"We lost 8–2."

"Ouch. I miss one game and you fall apart. What's a matter with you prima donnas?" He watched as she poured baby powder down her gown.

"I'm sweating like a pig. I didn't know that being pregnant meant I'd feel like I live on Venus. I may as well start sleeping in a meat locker."

"I just got moved up to Triple A."

"I bet I showered eight times today. I've got the air conditioner on sixty…" It took a moment for his words to sink in. She looked at Cape's huge grin. "What did you just say?"

"I'm heading to Greenville in the morning. Going to finish up the season there."

***

Keeping with his tradition, Cape arrived at the ballpark early. He walked across the field like he'd done in Columbia his first day of Rookie League. Greenville was the last step before Atlanta and the Major Leagues. At age twenty-one, he had almost made it to the majors, and the Braves' organization felt their huge investment was about to pay off.

Cape lived in an extended stay hotel in Greenville. The city was in the midst of a renaissance, and he was impressed with the restaurants and shops that had been constructed downtown. It had a metropolitan look about it. Of course, compared to Atlanta, it was small time. But for someone who grew up in tiny Santee, it was big-city living.

He went two-for-three in his first game, and by the end of the week, was batting .333, facing much tougher pitchers than he'd faced in Double A. He hit well from both sides of the plate. His defensive play at shortstop was impressive. The General Manager in Atlanta took notice. His teammates recognized he was a great player, and that he'd soon be promoted to Atlanta.

***

Kasey's mom, June, came to Macon to tend to her. Her dizzy spells became more frequent, and her doctor recommended she stay off her feet as much as possible. She gained twenty-one pounds, all in her stomach. If one stood behind her, they couldn't tell she was pregnant. But her days of exercising were done until after the baby was born.

Kasey and Cape debated whether or not they wanted to know the gender of their child. Either way, they settled on a name. If it were a girl, her name would be Julia Marie, and they would call her Jules. A boy, Brayden Christopher, called Bray. Though Cape wanted to wait until the delivery to find out, Kasey didn't. She knew, but kept it to herself. She assumed he wanted a boy to follow in his footsteps. But could anybody follow in those massive footsteps?

Kasey had been reading a magazine article on newborns when the phone rang. She looked at the clock on the end table, and when she saw it was 9:00 a.m., she knew it was Cape calling. He phoned her every day at that time to see how the pregnancy was going.

"Hello," she answered just in case it wasn't Cape. Just once, she wanted to shout, "What's up?!" into the phone, but knew if she did, it would surely be someone other than Cape on the line.

"Hey, baby. How are you feeling?"

"Hey, sweetie. I miss you."

"I miss you too. I'm checking in to see how you're doing. Are you getting enough rest? Are you eating good?"

"As a matter of fact, I just finished my morning Bloody Mary. At lunch I'll have a couple of scotches on the rocks, and tonight I'll catch Happy Hour downtown and take advantage of the drink specials."

"If I was there, I'd kick your tail," he said with a laugh.

"Well, there's enough of it to kick around, that's for sure. I feel like a whale."

"Well, you look so pretty to me. You could carry twin rhinos and still look good."

"Right."

"Seriously, how are you doing? Are you staying in bed like the doctor told you?"

"He didn't say I had to stay in bed. He just said to stay off my feet as much as possible."

"Well, I believe that sounds pretty much like bed confinement to me."

"You need to spend more time focusing on hitting a baseball than worrying about how many times I elevate my feet each day." She looked at her swollen feet propped on two soft throw pillows on the couch. "Baby, I'm doing everything I'm supposed to. Wish you could commute to Greenville from here so I'd have you home with me every day."

"I do too. But it won't be much longer. Even though I feel guilty not being there and taking care of you."

"You can't help that. Besides, Mom is here with me now. So you just worry about baseball and we'll take care of the rest."

"Okay. I love you, Kasey Jeffers."

"And I love you, Cape Jeffers."

***

It was mid-September, and the baby's due date was approaching. Cape struggled to focus on baseball, because he wanted to be with his wife. With her basically inactive, there wasn't a whole lot that he could do, especially with her mother there, but he still felt guilty.

The Greenville Braves were in the locker room, getting ready to take on the Louisville Redbirds. The locker room had televisions mounted all along the walls, and some of the players watched the Cubs take on the Phillies in an afternoon game at Wrigley Field. They were changing into their pants and practice jerseys when ESPN pulled away from the game and back to the studio.

"We just got confirmation from New York that shortstop Derek Stringer has suffered an ACL tear today during warm ups," the broadcaster said. "Stringer is done for the season, the postseason, and from what we've been told, it could potentially be a career-ending injury."

"Holy shit," said catcher Benji Falwell. "That's unbelievable. The Yankees will just fall apart without Stringer. ACL. Ain't that a bitch?"

Cape and the guys followed the story closely. They hated to see someone like Derek go down. Not only was he a great ballplayer, he was known to be a great guy who participated in charities and fundraising.

Everyone talked about Derek's injury on the field, in the stands, and in the television booth. Cape tried to push the injury from his mind and focus on the game. But he couldn't help but wonder about possibilities.

Two days after Derek's ACL tear, Cape made a phone call.

"Pete, this is Cape."

"What's up, my man? I'm glad to see you're still lighting up the scoreboard. Shouldn't be long now, and we'll be ready to hit the negotiation table."

"That's what I wanted to talk to you about."

"I'm listening."

"You heard about Stringer's injury, right?"

"Who hasn't?"

"Have you heard his status? Is it a season ending, or career ending, kind of thing? I mean I don't want his career to be over, but if it is, I sure would love to take his place."

"My brother-in-law works in the Yankees office. Let me see what I can find out."

"Pete, you know it's been my dream since I was a kid. Maybe this chain of events is just part of the plan, you know?"

"It's a plan we both could live with." Pete thought of his cut of an eighty million to ninety million dollar, long-term contract with the Yankees.

Cape's phone beeped. "My mom's calling. Let me take this. See what you can find and call me back, okay?"

"Cape." The word came across as terse, but Cape was too excited at the possibility of playing for New York to notice.

"Mom, I just got off the phone with my agent. There's a possibility I might end up wearing a Yankees uniform after all."

"Cape, I just spoke with June. Kasey has gone into labor and she's having complications." In an instant, his childhood dream carried no meaning.

Chapter Thirteen

Cape rapidly entered the front doors of Macon's Northside Hospital, gave a quick glance to the directory, then ran up the three flights of stairs to the maternity ward. There, Cape found June pacing the floor of the waiting area, her arms folded. She'd been crying, her eyes red and puffy.

"Thank God you're here." She hugged him tightly.

"Where's Kasey?"

"She's in surgery. She developed complications soon after she went into labor. I was staying with her in the delivery room when she started bleeding. They had to perform an emergency C-section. They made me leave." Cape saw fear in her eyes. "I'm scared to death, Cape. Please don't let anything happen to my girl."

"I won't."

He ran down the hall to the nurses' station where a young woman wearing a pink and blue top worked at a computer.

"Excuse me," Cape said. "My wife's in surgery. Kasey Jeffers. I need to see her."

The nurse excused herself. She returned in a few minutes, although it seemed like forever. "She's still in surgery. The doctor will be out soon."

"How's she doing?"

"The doctor will be able to tell you when he comes out."

Cape rubbed his forehead, and took a deep breath. His worries about Kasey almost made him forget that she wasn't the only Jeffers patient in the hospital, and a sick feeling of guilt came over him. "Oh, what about our baby?"

"Your baby is doing well. Now, she's a preemie, so we're treating her extra carefully. But she should be fine."

"Did you say *she*?"

The nurse smiled. "Yes, you're the father of a four-pound, two-ounce, baby girl. She'll have to spend some time in an incubator, but that's nothing out of the ordinary."

"But she's okay?"

"Yes. Her lungs need time to develop, and she'll have to learn to feed from a bottle."

"Can I see her?"

"Certainly. Follow me."

The nurse led Cape to the nursery, and made him scrub his hands thoroughly. Four white incubators were positioned side by side, three empty. When he saw his daughter, so small, so frail, wearing a pink beanie, a tiny diaper, and a tube attached to her hand, his eyes began to water. He slowly slipped his hand through an opening of the incubator and placed it on her soft stomach. He felt her heart beat. She trembled as she slept. He placed his finger inside her hand and she took hold. In an instant he knew his heart was no longer his.

"Can I hold her?" he asked the nurse.

"Yes, but just for a moment. She's fragile right now, and we just need to take precautions. I need to go to the nurses' station, but I'll be right back."

He held the baby firmly, almost afraid that he might drop her. She yawned and kicked her legs.

"Hey, Jules," he said. "Hey, sweetie." He traced her tiny face with his finger, feeling the warmth of her soft skin. Tears filled his eyes, and he kissed her forehead. "I'm going to love you in ways that only God knows is possible. You're safe now, and I'm going to protect you. And wait till your mother gets hold of you. She's going to love you like crazy. But between you and me, I'm going to love you just a tad more. Let's just keep that between us."

He watched her sleep, willing her to wake, and she opened her eyes briefly, her tiny arms stretching, her body shaking. Her eyes remained open just long enough for Cape to see the purest form of innocence. June watched from the window, a woman torn between the wonder of new life, and the slow agony of waiting to know the fate of her own child.

The nurse stepped back into the room. "The doctor wants to see you."

Cape patted Jules' stomach gently and handed her to the nurse. "Going to check on Mama. Be back in a bit."

The doctor took Cape and June into an alcove behind the nurses' station. Cape could tell by the serious look on his face that something was wrong.

"Mr. Jeffers, your wife developed complications shortly after she went into labor and began hemorrhaging during the delivery and lost a lot of blood. This caused her blood pressure to drop dramatically. We had no choice but to perform an emergency C-section."

"But she's okay, right?" Cape asked as June took his hand.

The doctor scratched his chin and took a deep breath. "I'm afraid not. We've given her several pints of blood, but she's just not responding. Her blood pressure continues to drop and we've been unable to stop the bleeding."

"I appreciate the update, but shouldn't you go back in there and stop the bleeding?"

"I'm afraid we're past that point now."

"What do you mean you're past that point?" Cape started trembling with rage.

"Her body isn't able to handle the trauma. We've tried all we can, but there's nothing more we can do."

"So what are you saying? She's dying?"

He took a deep breath, and his eyes told the agony he felt in delivering such tragic news. "I'm so sorry." June fell to her knees and began to wail, and a nurse knelt and placed her hand on June's shoulder.

"You can't just give up like that. If you can't save her, find another doctor who can!"

"We've done everything we can."

"My wife's dying and you are just gonna throw in the towel? You're a damn quitter."

"I understand your anger," the doctor said. "We've given her medication to ease her pain as much as possible, but there's nothing more that can be done. I'm truly sorry."

"I've got to see her." The doctor nodded, and led him to her room, then closed the door so Cape could have time with his wife.

Kasey was asleep. She looked peaceful enough, though her face was pale. Cape leaned over and kissed her. He slid the hair away from her eyes. She hated when her hair covered her eyes. He kissed her forehead, and could hardly pull his lips away from her skin. His first thought was to carry her away. He couldn't give up. He just couldn't.

She opened her eyes and tried to focus. "'Bout time you got here," she said, wincing in pain.

"Hey, sweet thing." He took her hand. "You were supposed to make it two more weeks before giving birth. You're just too impatient, aren't you?"

She smiled, but her eyes looked tired and dark. "Well, Jules had something to say about that." Her voice was strained. "Who was I to stop her?"

"You did great."

"How is she? Have you seen her?"

"I saw her just a few minutes ago. She's doing fantastic. She's the spitting image of you."

"Poor baby."

"Are you kidding? She'll thank her lucky stars the day she realizes she looks like her mother."

Kasey coughed deeply, then grabbed her hips.

A nurse entered and checked the readings on a machine beside her bed. She looked at Cape as though trying to convey her condolences, and then quietly left the room.

"I wish I could have held her for more than a few seconds." She looked around. "Why am I in here? I should be with Jules."

"Jules is in an incubator right now. She's got a whole slew of nurses tending to her."

"Incubator?"

"She's on the small side, so they want to keep her in an incubator and make her a little stronger. The doctor says she'll be growing like a weed in no time."

Kasey tried to raise her head but couldn't.

She grabbed Cape's hand. "Ahh. It feels like someone's stabbing me."

A thousand emotions ran through him, a million thoughts surged through his mind. "Rest, baby. You've been through a lot."

"What's wrong, Cape?"

"Nothing. Just hate I wasn't here for the delivery."

"You're a terrible liar. Tell me what's wrong."

"I'm going to get Jules so you can hold her. Your mom's waiting outside too. Rest easy and I'll be back with them both."

Cape's chest began to heave once he walked out of Kasey's room. On the day that should be the happiest of his life, it was the worst. Their future, their plans, gone. She had promised to grow old with him. That was the deal.

Cape felt nauseous and quickly made his way to the bathroom where he vomited in a stall. An elderly man washing his hands went for help, and a male nurse came to Cape's aid. June, who'd been on the phone with her husband, came into the bathroom as well.

"Sir, let me help you," the nurse said, taking Cape by the arm.

He waved them away and sat on his knees. The nurse waited for a moment and then helped him to his feet anyway.

Cape wiped his face and rinsed his mouth.

He looked at June. "I'm going to get Jules. You go see Kasey. Don't let her know what's going on."

June nodded and dabbed her eyes with a tissue. She took a deep breath and went to her daughter's room, trying to summon the strength to see her dying child, to give her comfort while placing her own shattered heart aside.

Within minutes, Cape and a nurse had wheeled the incubator beside Kasey's bed. June held a cup of ginger ale, trying to keep the straw inside Kasey's mouth as she slowly sipped. The nurse placed Jules on Kasey's chest. She asked the nurse to raise her bed, and she smiled when she looked at the baby.

"Hey there, sweet pea." Jules was sleeping but a bit restless. Kasey looked at Cape. "How do we look?"

"The most perfect sight I've ever seen." Cape first kissed Jules on the head and he did the same to Kasey.

"Can you believe we created this? Isn't she beautiful?" Kasey closed her eyes to fight off a sharp pain. "Mama, do you have your camera?"

June nodded and removed it from her purse. "Always."

"Will you take a picture of us?" Kasey grew weaker, and she struggled to keep her eyes open. She forced a smile and June took two pictures.

"Cape?" Kasey whispered.

He leaned over. "What is it, baby?"

"Can we take her to Salem's Crossroads? I want to show her to the whole town."

Cape forced a smile, the hardest thing he'd ever done. "We'll take her anywhere you want to go." He rubbed her hair, kissed her on the cheek. He thought about the first time he'd kissed her, standing outside her door. He remembered watching her close her eyes when their lips first met, so innocently, and then how she'd stared into his eyes like she was trying to peer into his soul. He remembered the soft jasmine of her perfume. He could almost taste the mint chocolate ice cream on her lips that night. He never thought he could love anything more.

"You might better take her on back now," Kasey said. "I'm hurting really bad." Cape carefully gave Jules to the nurse, who returned her to the incubator and rolled it out of the room. "Can you get the doctor? My stomach is killing me." She pulled her knees up under the sheet.

***

It was almost dawn, and Cape quietly sat beside the hospital bed, holding Kasey's hand. June stood on the other side of the bed, rubbing her hair. Doug and the girls had just arrived, and they gathered around the bed. Morgan cradled Jordan as they wept. Kasey's face looked void of color, a washing of her presence from both body and soul. Her chest barely moved, and though her grip was weak, he felt a tender squeeze that let him know she had not left him.

Somewhere, down inside, he felt her trying to comfort him, giving him soft thoughts of sweet moments, tender memories. Thoughts of wanting nothing more than to turn back the hands of time.

She stirred for a moment, and her eyelids fluttered.

He touched her face. "I love you, baby." Her mouth curved slightly, as if her entire being worked to create a smile. Her breathing softened.

Please hang on, sweet girl. Don't leave me. Please don't leave.

***

The funeral took place at the church where Cape and Kasey had married. The crowd spilled into the aisles and along the back wall. Kasey's wedding picture, her high school graduation picture, and a photo of her and Cape on their honeymoon were positioned on metal stands beside the casket. Afterwards, friends and family tried to comfort Cape, but in his numbness, their faces and words never registered in his mind or memory.

Salem's Crossroads was in mourning, though it was nothing new. The town had dealt with the deaths of several young people through the years. Most died in car crashes on the back roads and highways, which at least was a common way for young people to die. But others met their fate from strange situations such as hunting mishaps, illness, and falling off a ladder. Some of the elderly thought the town had been cursed. For Cape and Jules Jeffers, the only truth was that Kasey was gone forever.

The Braves gave Cape time off since the Triple A season was in its final week. He returned to Macon and the hospital the day after the funeral, and stayed beside Jules' incubator for hours at a time, patting her stomach, and letting her hold his pinky. The doctor said Jules was progressing, but slower than expected. They estimated that she would be strong enough, and weigh enough, to go home in two weeks.

He stayed with his newborn, holding her when he was allowed, wondering what the future held. His mom and dad came to Macon for the two weeks, leaving Alicia with a friend so she could go to school. They visited the hospital each day, bringing him food and drink that he rarely consumed. They got a hotel room a block from the hospital, and tried to convince Cape to stay there and rest. But he just couldn't leave his baby.

Jules didn't appear to be progressing as fast as the doctor predicted. Her lungs developed slowly, preventing her from gaining much weight. Once she became strong enough to go home, then what? He had never cared for a child. He couldn't do this alone. What about baseball? Jules would be a little hard to stuff in his bat bag and take on the road.

The nurse who was working the night shift finally convinced him to go home and rest. He had only spoken a handful of words since Kasey's funeral. He felt too numb to comprehend what had happened. He sat in his car and stared out the window, holding the key in his hand. Where should he go? Home held nothing but memories. Kasey's clothes, her makeup, her pink hairbrush, her toothbrush, all reminders that she was gone.

He watched people walk to their cars, the parking lot thinning out as families left their friends and loved ones behind in hospital rooms. He saw a man holding hands with a woman, and saw them kiss. Cape wondered if they understood the importance of the moment, that the kiss could turn out to be their last. The future held no guarantees, and it had been stripped away from him with no regard to heaven, hell, or heartache. His own life had always held a sense of adventure, of looking to the future, a road traveled with no detours and no cares.

Cape eventually decided to drive home. His cell rang and he noticed Pete Bennett's number. "Hello," he said, wiping his eyes.

"Cape, this is Pete. How are you, buddy? I'm so sorry about Kasey. I wish I had the words that could make you feel better. I truly am sorry."

"Thanks, Pete. I appreciate it."

"How's the baby?"

"It's a slow process. Doctor says she might go home next week."

"I'm sure she will be fine."

"Listen, there's something I need to talk to you about. Is this a good time?"

"It's as good as any I suppose."

"I found out from my brother-in-law that the prognosis on Stringer's injury is good."

"I'm glad to hear that. He's a great player."

"Anyway, it looks like you just need to stay the course with the Braves in Greenville and hopefully they'll call you up to Atlanta by midseason next year."

Cape pulled into the empty parking lot of a strip mall. He ran his hair through his hands. Baseball was the furthest thing from his mind.

"I can't even think about that right now. I feel like I'm in some nightmare I can't wake up from. We had it all planned out, Pete. All planned out. Kasey, me, and our baby. Now that's down the tube and all I know is, I have a kid to take care of. And I have no clue how to do it."

"I'll help you. We'll search for a nanny. You know your parents will help out. Don't worry about baseball until February when spring training rolls around."

"There's no way Mom can do it. Parkinson's makes her hands tremble so much that she can't hold a plate of food, much less a child. I don't know. I just don't know what to do."

"I know, Cape. I know. You've been through a hell of a lot. I'll be in touch. You just focus on being a daddy."

***

Cape decided they'd move back to Santee after Jules got released from the hospital. His parents started packing items such as dishes and silverware. When he came home at night, he felt guilty for not helping, though they reassured him his focus should be on his child.

Pauline had played the role of consoler, a mother pouring her heart out for her child. Still, talk was limited. She and Randy feared Cape would break down if they tried to talk to him about Kasey.

Billy came to help with the move. He and Randy quietly packed up boxes, loading them and furniture onto a U-Haul truck Randy rented. They stayed away from Cape and Kasey's bedroom. As if touching Kasey's clothes or personal items, like her hairbrush or toothbrush, would be the same as desecrating her grave.

Those items were concrete in nature, and had nothing to do with keeping alive her spirit or memories of her past. And besides, Randy and Billy didn't know what Cape wanted to do with her things. June and the girls came, and Cape told them to take any of Kasey's clothes they wanted, but only when he wasn't there to see it. He decided to donate whatever Kasey's family didn't take to Goodwill. He would take the easel and paintbrushes back to Santee. Of that he was certain.

The night before Jules was to be released from the hospital, knowing he would be taking her to Santee the next day, Cape let his dad and brother dismantle the bed, loading it on the truck piece by piece. Pauline helped Cape remove Kasey's clothes from the j-shaped walk-in closet. He rubbed a silk blouse she'd worn one night on Daufuskie Island. After the clothing was taken, he noticed something leaning against the closet wall, wrapped in a blanket.

He slowly removed the covering and looked at the painting Kasey planned to surprise him with after Jules was born. He traced his fingers across the blues, violets, yellows. Randy and Billy walked up behind Cape, and their hearts, in some sort of existential way, joined Cape and Pauline's as they saw the image of a man tossing a ball with a small child on the beach. In the background a young woman stood by a lighthouse, watching. The child wore a cap, on backwards, a giant glove on her hand.

Kasey had finally painted him that promised baseball picture.

Randy placed his hand on Cape's shoulder. Cape closed his eyes and touched the painting to his forehead.

***

Cape and Jules went home to Santee on a Sunday morning, a day of clear blue skies and soft, northerly breezes. The humidity that held a stranglehold since early summer was gone, and signs of fall filled the air. The hardwoods behind the house were all cloaked in red and orange, making the long leaf pines appear a deeper shade of green. The day gave no indication that it knew, or cared, that Cape's life had been torn upside down.

Cape spent much of his days in his old bedroom, where he and Jules set up camp. His brother and dad put his things in storage. His mother tried to help with Jules, but was limited. Someone had to hand the baby to her, and then she made her midsection a makeshift crib.

Even when the family tended to her, Cape rarely left his daughter's side. He worried she might be taken from him too, and he dared God to try. In Jules, he saw Kasey, and it gave him comfort. Here was the child they had created, a tangible part of his wife that allowed him to hold onto her.

Cape rocked Jules in his arms each night, holding her close, watching her sleep. He touched her chest to feel her breathe, and when she sighed or moved, he'd kiss her on the cheek and whisper that all was okay.

The days ran together, and Cape had no clue if it was a Tuesday or Friday. Holding Jules in his arms at night made it difficult for him to sleep more than a few hours at a time. He worried that if he slept too soundly, he wouldn't hear if she cried out.

He dreamt a lot about Kasey. One recurring dream haunted him the most: she stood beside his bed, asking to take Jules with her.

Over the months, he lost touch with the outside world, a place that he figured held nothing for him. His dad tried to get him out of the house on occasion, just to see that the world was still moving, but he rarely left. His only purpose now was to care for his daughter. He was very protective of her, the link that kept Kasey's memory alive. He looked severely depressed. He grew a beard, and his hair became thick and shaggy. He lost weight. He looked pale. He didn't care.

***

Cape put Jules down for her morning nap and his cell phone rang. He slipped out of the room and checked the caller I.D. Pete, ready to talk baseball, something Cape was not.

"Cape, how have you been? How's Jules?"

"We're getting by."

"You've been on my mind. Is there anything I can do for you?"

"Unless you want to come change a diaper, no."

"Cape, spring training is just six weeks away. Have you been working out?"

"Haven't touched a bat or ball."

"I know you're the ballplayer here, but if this is to be the springboard year to get you to the majors, don't you think you need to put in the time?"

"I know what it takes. I've been putting it in my whole life."

"I know. I'm sorry. It's just that I'm anxious for you to make it big. Have you got things worked out for a nanny?"

"Not yet. I need to call my investment guy and tap into some funds. Hiring a full time nanny will be costly."

"Jim Cummings will do what's best for you. Give him a call and he'll tell you the way to go about it."

Cape went silent.

"You still there?" Pete asked after a moment.

"Yeah. Still here. Um, Pete, I didn't use your guy. In fact, it took me a second to remember who you were talking about."

"Jim's not your investor?"

Cape could sense tepidness in Pete's question. "No, he's not."

"Who did you go with?"

"Les Jamison, from Columbia. A friend of mine put me in touch with him. He came highly recommended, and since he was local, I thought he'd be best to use."

"Les Jamison!? Cape, please tell me you didn't."

"He's got a load of clients who are pro athletes. Why? What's the problem?"

"The guy is a crook. He ran through his clients' money like there's no tomorrow. He's under investigation for wire fraud, money laundering. His assets have been frozen. The government has put a lock on his yacht, his homes in the Caribbean. He's a snake, and he finally got caught."

"What? That can't be."

"Damn. I should have followed up to make sure you used Jim. Cape, how much money did you give him access to?"

"Over three," Cape said sheepishly.

"Thousand?"

"Million."

"Good God."

"Maybe he hasn't spent mine. Maybe it's still there. How can I found out?"

"From what I hear, there's none to get, Cape. My guess is you'll have to sue him, and you might only get a fraction back, and that could take years."

"Pete, that can't be right."

"I hate to tell you this, man, but I think you've lost it all."

Cape walked outside and stared off into the far distance at nothing. His body suddenly went numb, and he perspired profusely. A cold wind blew through him, though he didn't feel it. Cape felt everything crumbling around him. Twenty-two years old, and already he had been hit across the face by life's sledgehammer. Kasey and baseball had been his world. He'd lost one; was he about to lose the other?

His mother began to cry when Cape explained what Pete had told him. She hugged her son and told him everything was going to be okay.

"Let me call Jimmy Cason," Randy said. "His law firm handles bankruptcy cases. Maybe he can help us look into possibly getting your money back."

"Cape, let us keep Jules, and you go to spring training," she said. "She'll be fine here."

Cape shook his head. "I can't let you do that."

"Yes, you can. We can make this work."

"That's impossible. Your condition won't allow it. And Dad, you can't do it. You've got your job to worry about, and I'm sure you used up all your vacation time. Besides, you've both raised your children. You don't need to raise mine."

"We'll all pitch in, Cape. You can't quit now."

"I think it's time to face the truth, Mom. It's over."

"Honey, there's got to be something that can be done."

"I have to take care of Jules. That's what has to be done. I'll get a job. That's all there is to it."

  "Don't make a rash decision, son," his dad said. "This is something you've worked for since you were a small child."

  "I don't have a choice."

  He heard Jules cry and walked out of the room.

Chapter Fourteen

Cape pulled up in front of Lakeside Plastics. The plant had been in operation since the mid-'70s and had employed more than half the town, with a never-ending rotation of shift workers. Cape, fortunately, got the day shift, only because the manager was one of his biggest fans.

Instead of grabbing an equipment bag and walking to a stadium locker room, Cape took hold of a metal lunch pail and headed to the front door of the plant. No players' entrance, no smell of fresh-cut grass on a sunny afternoon. He stepped inside, his new I.D. badge clamped to his jeans belt loop, and looked across the expansive room of machinery.

Slowly, the folks on the assembly line stopped to watch their hometown hero trudge past them. They looked at each other, as if to verify that the one that they'd placed on a pedestal of the highest degree was about to perform a task so far removed from fame and glory. Without speaking, Cape took his position on the line as Vernon Able walked up. Vernon, who'd been the manager of the morning shift for sixteen years, came to see Cape through his first day, in order to make sure he knew exactly what to do.

Vernon sensed the stares, and knew Cape did the same. Vernon had first watched Cape play in Little League, amazed at the ability of a ten-year-old boy with 'superstar' virtually tattooed across his forehead. After a few minutes of instruction, Vernon looked at the others on the line, who stared like they watched a freak show at the county fair.

"Get your asses back to work!" he yelled.

As his shift came to an end, Cape ran through the safety list to secure his station. Paul Callahan walked by. Before Cape came along, Paul was the town hero. He'd been the All-State shortstop at Santee when Cape was a freshman and signed with Coastal Carolina University. Two months into his first semester, he got kicked off the team for back-talking the coach. He felt like he wasn't getting enough playing time, so he called the coach 'an idiot who only played his favorites'. Paul dropped out of school and came home to work at the plant.

He gave Cape a cross look. "You ain't shit now, are you, Mr. First-Round-Pick?"

Cape stared at Paul as he walked past.

He let the other workers leave first. All that did was to allow time for the second shift to arrive, and the stares to begin again. He finally made his way through the parking lot, past several rows of pick-up trucks and cars belonging to men and women who toiled, year in and year out, at a job they'd work until they were too feeble. The aura was not one of hopelessness, but of indifference.

A place of aching backs, arthritis-laced fingers, and flattened dreams.

***

Randy bought a small modular home and placed it on a small tract of land in a neighborhood on the outskirts of town. Pauline told Cape he could live in her childhood home at Live Oak, but he couldn't commute that far each day. They offered to sell it for him but Cape refused to even discuss the idea. He took the furniture he'd placed in storage, and he and Jules moved into the 1,400 square-foot trailer. He set up a payment plan to repay his father each month.

Pauline enrolled Jules in the infant care program at the Mt. Olive Baptist Church where the Jeffers family had been church members since Cape was four. It opened at 6:30 a.m., allowing Cape to drop her off on the way to work.

Baseball season was underway at the high school, and he purposely avoided driving by the field. Spring training was coming to an end for the professional ballplayers, and they would soon be assigned to their team: Single A, Double A, Triple A, or for the ones deemed the best, the Major League squad. Cape's teammates in Greenville were stunned that their shortstop didn't return, and more incredibly, that he gave up the game he seemed born to play.

It was well past midnight, and Jules had cried for over three hours, her small body shaking in Cape's arms. His crumpled t-shirt was soaked with her tears, and he was so frazzled his knees shook. He couldn't soothe her or stop her from crying, and he'd tried everything his mother had shown him. He couldn't distinguish if she simply had a stomachache, or whether or not she required medical attention. Her face was flushed, but he had no clue if she had a fever, or whether it was the result of crying for so long. He kept repeating, "It's okay," intended to calm himself as much as his daughter. She felt so tiny in his arms. He only wanted to make her pain go away, pleading with God to either end it, or let him carry it for her.

He went as long as he could, but finally called his parents at 3:15 a.m. When Pauline and Randy walked into Cape's house thirty minutes later, Cape sat in the rocker, Jules' body exhausted and limp in his arms. She was asleep, though she seemed restless.

"Cape, you poor boy. Here, let me take her."

Pauline sat on the couch and Randy lifted the baby from Cape's arms and placed her on Pauline's chest. Her hands shook as she cradled the squirming child.

Cape walked outside, feeling defeated.

"Do you think she needs to go to the E.R.?" Randy asked.

It took a moment for Pauline to touch Jules' face, and she slowly wiped the tiny wet ringlets from the child's forehead. "I think she's okay. She's just worn out. Randy, go warm a bottle of water and place a drop of peppermint extract in it. It'll soothe her tummy."

After Randy prepared the bottle, he then helped position it in Jules' mouth and placed Pauline's hands around the slender tube. He then walked outside to where Cape sat on the front steps.

"I don't know if I can handle this anymore, Dad. I can't give her what she needs most of all, and that's her mother. When she gets sick, she fights me, and I can tell she doesn't want me anywhere near her."

"Son, sometimes babies get to feeling so bad that it doesn't matter if they have five mothers. They just feel miserable. And it doesn't mean she doesn't want you."

"But I can't calm her. It's the most frustrating thing I've ever done." He rubbed his hands through his hair.

"You put us through some tough nights when you were young, and that was with both your mother and me playing tag team. Sometimes neither one of us could calm you down and it was just because you felt so bad. The same happened with Billy and Alicia too. That's the way it goes sometimes. And when a child gets that way, the only thing you can do is push on until she feels better."

"I don't know. I'm beginning to think I wasn't cut out for this. Maybe she needs something, or somebody else."

"You're just tired, son. Get some rest and you'll see things more clearly in the morning."

"What rest? I have to be at work in less than four hours. Going to be hard to get much done when I can barely stay awake."

Randy put his hand on Cape's shoulder. "Let us take her home."

"That's okay, Dad. You and mom don't need to worry about it. You've done your time staying up nights. You're retired from that now."

"Nonsense. We'll take care of her. You make it through the work day and then come home and collapse."

"This is harder than I ever imagined."

"It's all part of being a parent. Jules is an angel, and your love for her is unlike anything you will ever experience."

"But being a parent is supposed to mean having a partner to help."

"I know. But God's got a different path for you, and you just have to trust Him."

"I have no clue what that path is to be, or why He's taking me down it."

"Me either, son." Randy gently rubbed his son's shoulders.

****

Cape walked into the cafeteria. His feet ached, and his back hurt. Twice he'd almost dozed off while working on the assembly line. His shifts had become virtually indistinguishable days of monotonous work. His baseball career just a faded memory. He removed his lunch pail from his locker. A ham and cheese sandwich, with an apple and banana to top it off. He took a corner spot at the end of a long metal table, alone.

Jevan Altekruse, Cape's former high school team-mate, saw the ragged look in Cape's eyes. "You look like crap," Jevan said. Cape slid the chair across from him out with his foot and Jevan sat. "Rough night?"

"That's an understatement if I ever heard one. Jules has kept me up three straight nights, and I can barely hold my eyes open. Mom took her to the doctor yesterday. She's got some inner ear infection that seems to kick into overdrive when she lies down."

"Son, I ain't lookin' forward to all that. Whenever we have a baby, Elaine better be ready to work the night shift at home. That is, unless she wants to trade places with me and work at this hell hole."

"You better be good to that wife of yours. She's the only one who can put up with your crap."

Paul and Earl Scoggins took their seats at the same table, a short distance from Cape and Jevan. Earl had a mean disposition and was not well liked at the plant.

"I think we should start a slow pitch softball team," Paul said to Earl, obviously loud enough for Cape to hear. "That way we can get washed up has-beens a chance to relive their glory years. Especially ones stupid enough to think that they were good enough to play in the major leagues."

"Sounds like a slow pitch losers' team," added Earl.

Cape glanced at Paul, then bit into his sandwich and looked straight ahead.

"Really, I think we could find enough guys," Paul continued. "Course, we'd have some that would come up with some lame-ass excuse, you know, like he can't play because he's got no woman to babysit his child."

"Why don't you just go in the corner and screw yourself, Callahan?" Jevan said.

"Piss off, Altekruse. This don't concern you."

Cape grabbed his food and dumped it in the garbage.

"Over-hyped punk," Paul said as Cape headed for the cafeteria door. "Coach Steck just talked you up 'cause you were always up his ass. They say you're the best that's ever played for Santee. They're full of it. Look at you now, Mr. All-American. On the assembly line, just like the rest of us. Heading nowhere."

***

Randy and Pauline had finally convinced Cape to go to the company Christmas party that was being held at the Holiday Inn Conference Center. Cape consented, but said he would pick up Jules by nine. Randy insisted Jules stay the night, and Cape finally agreed. It would be the first time Cape had been anywhere, outside of work, without his daughter.

Cape walked in, and he'd never felt more alone. He also felt out of place when he noticed that the others wore Christmas sweaters and seasonal attire. He wore dark jeans, a black turtleneck sweater, and a leather bomber jacket. He caught the attention of the two girls who worked the front desk of the center, but he didn't know it.

The center was decorated in green and white lights, and a large Christmas tree stood in the corner near a bar where two men in tuxedos served beer, wine, and hard liquor. The plant had had a good year and splurged more for the Christmas party than in years past. Despite the festive setting, Cape wanted to turn and walk out the door. What was the purpose of being there? Just to please everyone who wanted him to enjoy life with the grownups? He got enough of the grownups at work.

Watching other couples dance and laugh, sharing time with ones who had *not* been taken from them, made it hard for him not to be jealous. Why shouldn't he be? He had a right. Maybe his punishment for feeling that way was to just stand on the sideline, left to rely on the faint memories of morning kisses and late-night talks of the future. He thought of how incredible Christmas was last year with Kasey. Decorating the tree, hiding presents from each other, the tender look of love in her eyes when he woke her on Christmas morning. And the news that a baby was on the way.

Before he could leave, Jevan's wife, Elaine, took him by the arm.

"Come on, Cape, darlin'," she said. "Let's have some fun."

She led him to a table where Jevan chatted with a coworker and his wife. Jevan pointed to an empty chair beside him and Cape took a seat.

A disc jockey played music beside a small dance floor, but either no one in the crowd wanted to be the first ones to dance, or they hadn't had enough alcohol to give them the confidence.

Cape pretended to listen to the others at his table, but his mind chased ghosts of a previous Christmas. He felt insignificant.

Elaine's sister, Whitney, arrived, and then Elaine strategically placed her beside Cape. She was home for Christmas break from Francis Marion University, a cute brunette who'd graduated with Cape from Santee High. She tried bringing up old high school days, but it was soon obvious that she was wasting her time.

Cape volunteered to get her a glass of wine so he could escape the forced conversation at the table. Jevan decided to walk with him.

"Come on, pard," Jevan said. "You got to loosen up a little. You haven't had any fun in a long time. Have a beer."

"Fun. I don't know what that word means. I shouldn't have come."

He made it to the bar and asked for a glass of red wine. The bartender handed him the drink, and two guys next to Cape bumped into him and spilled the wine on his jacket.

"You should try and be a little more careful, you dumbass," Paul said. Cape grabbed a handful of napkins and wiped his sleeve, but didn't say anything. "I guess you'll come up with a good excuse as to why you spilled your drink. You've gotten good at that."

"Back off, Callahan," Jevan said. "You and your pal take it on back to your table."

"Why don't you let your girlfriend here handle her own battles?"

"It's alright, Jevan," Cape said. The bartender handed him another glass of wine and they turned to walk away.

"Stop runnin' away from it, Jeffers. You're just a failure and you can't admit it. You're the king of crutches, using your dead wife as a safety net to quit something that you weren't good enough to play in the first place."

Cape spun around and drove his fist into Paul's jaw. The man crashed on top of a nearby table; glasses and plastic plates of hors d'oeuvres flying to the floor. The two couples sitting at the table jumped from their chairs, and one of the ladies screamed. Jevan stood in front of Paul's friend so Cape could deal with Paul one-on-one.

A thunderous rage overtook Cape. He grabbed Paul by his lapel and helped him to his feet. He slugged him again, this time in his midsection, bending him at the waist. Cape took him by the hair, then drove his knee into Paul's nose, and he tumbled into a table beside the bar that held tonic water and mixers. Cape knelt and hit Paul in the jaw. He followed that with a left jab above the eye. The bartenders grabbed Cape, pulling him away from Paul's curled body. The rage in Cape's eyes was pointed and measurable, and he looked angrily at one of the bartenders, who still held on to his arm.

The bartender let loose. Cape straightened his jacket and calmly took a glass of wine back to the table. He placed it in front of Elaine.

"Merry Christmas," he said, and walked out the door.

**

After two hours of searching, Jevan found Cape's car on the side of Old Manning Road. The night air was heavy and cold. Thick oaks and pines clung tightly to the darkness, and frost covered the wild grass beside the highway. When Jevan got out of his car, the sound of the shutting door echoed deep into the lonely countryside. He walked toward the yellow streetlight that stood above the entrance to the Poplar Creek Bridge. The wind caused the light to sway, making the dim path shift as he approached the bridge. He found Cape sitting on a fisherman's bench, holding a pint of whiskey.

"Ain't been out on this bridge since graduation night," Jevan said, taking a seat beside his lifelong friend. "That's the night I got lucky with Rachel Sawyer."

"Bull," Cape said between sips.

"Well, that's the story I've been telling for almost three years, so I ain't changing it now."

"What's Rachel's side of the story?"

"There's no need to concern her about it. Let's just say there's a strong possibility she gave it up for me that night."

"Speaking of giving it up," Cape spoke, before taking a drink, "I'm ready to give it up."

"Give what up?"

"Everything."

Jevan watched Cape take another swig. "You've never been much of a drinking man."

"Well, maybe I should be. It's a great escape hatch, I'll tell you that." He took another swallow.

"Presto. I'm married to Kasey. I play for the Yankees. I've got the best damn life in the world." Another drink. "At least I do tonight. Jim Beam's a hell of a guy, you know?"

"Why don't you let me take Jim for a while? I think you've spent enough time with him." He took the bottle from Cape and took a sip.

"How'd you find me?" Cape's eyes were cloudy.

"I checked the ball field, your house, Conway's convenience store. All the places we used to hang out. This was the last place I knew to look, but I thought even you wouldn't be crazy enough to come out here in this cold."

"We had some fun times on this bridge."

"Sure did, Cape."

"Fun times are over."

"It seems that way for you now. But I got a sneaky suspicion the fun times will return some day."

"Nope. All done. Nothing but working at the plant and playing both mommy and daddy."

"Hey, don't let Paul get to you. He's just jealous because he was the town golden boy till you came along. He can't stand that everybody knows you're the best that's ever been around here. Hell, Cape, you might have been the best anywhere."

"Well, Paul don't play no more, and I don't play no more. Guess that makes us even."

"Yeah, but for completely different reasons."

"Why did life have to screw me over, Jevan?"

"I got no clue, bro." He scratched his head. "Got no clue. But look what you've got. You've got a beautiful baby. You're a great father."

"What makes you say that?"

"I've seen you with her. Man, I hope I can be half the father you are."

"Well, maybe they'll have an All-Dad team for me to play for. I could win MVP for changing a dirty diaper, or cleaning puke off my shoulder. Wouldn't that really be something? All-American cradle pusher."

The friends sat in silence, passing the bottle in the dark cold chill of December.

***

Jevan drove Cape home, then helped him into the house. They staggered to the bedroom. Cape fell across the bed. "The room's spinning."

Jevan retrieved a bucket from under the kitchen sink and placed it beside Cape's head. "You want me to stay with you?"

Cape shook his head and groaned.

***

Cape woke at 4:30 a.m., his head tight and heavy as though it was about to explode. He stumbled down the hall to the kitchen. He shakily filled a glass with water from the sink and choked down two aspirin. He steadied himself by holding onto the kitchen counter.

He snapped the cross necklace from his neck that Kasey had given him their first—and last—Christmas. It was supposed to keep him safe. He twirled it in his hand. Why hadn't she worn it, then? *She'd still be alive!* He stepped outside into the back yard. The stars were bright above, and the air still and deathly quiet. He threw the necklace into the trees. "Damn you. Damn all of it."

Chapter Fifteen

Cape's life became as mechanical as the assembly line work he performed at the plant. Seasons changed and he barely knew it. He hated his job, and though home was a much better place to be, he knew it was always a couple of dirty dishes shy of being labeled a pigpen. Cooking became an real adventure, and any day where food didn't end up burnt, and actually got consumed, was labeled a success. Days were hard and tiresome, and sleep elusive at night.

Through it all he tried his best to make Jules happy. Now a toddler, she looked more like her mother with each passing day. Her eyes the same china-blue, though her hair was dark brown. Her smile seemed to be the only thing that could soften his hardened heart, but it also brought back the reality that Kasey was gone forever.

Cape's rock-hard body softened, and he developed a thick midsection. He dreaded bedtime, since his daughter could keep his mind off the thoughts of Kasey that kept him awake when he closed his eyes. He started drinking himself to sleep every night after he put Jules down for the night. He never drank while she was awake, and worked hard to be a good father. He tried to make sure her life was the best it could possibly be. To ease his pain, each night after she was asleep, Cape found himself with a beer, a notebook and pen. He placed the troubles in his heart on paper.

Late one Friday night, hours after Jules fell asleep, Cape's restless mind stirred. Since he didn't have to work the next morning, he decided to forget about trying to sleep. He got the last beer in a six-pack and removed his notepad and pen from the end table beside the couch. Clouded thoughts, so many things he wanted to say, but none he would ever want others to read. He took a long sip, his beard moist from the cold beer.

He began to write.

Walls close in, a night of suffocation
A crumbling world, a road of devastation.
And then she calls, her voice so sweet
But I cannot reach her, can't move my feet.
Scattered dreams, no rhyme or reason
When she appears, an angelic vision.
I search for answers from the Holy One
But He's just a vapor, a smoking gun.
Nighttime, I'm begging, bring her to me
Ease my burden, her face let me see.
Bring us together, together once more
On a distant land, or a faraway shore.
Damn the morning, damn the light
Lead me back to the dead of night.

Chapter Sixteen

Two more summers came and went. Cape used to set his calendar around the start of baseball season and the coming of spring; that was when the year began. But those days were gone. He had become an average Joe. His to-do list consisted of the menial kind, no longer setting lofty goals of batting .400, or leading the league in home runs. The roar of the crowd? A distant memory, replaced by the steady hum of machinery at the plant. The ringing in his ears came from the assembly line, not cheers in the stadium.

Randy and Pauline unsuccessfully tried to awaken Cape from what they determined was a chronic state of depression. They did everything they could to bring him out of his continual funk. They made appointments for counseling that he never kept. They begged him to let Jules attend family birthdays and special occasions. He always declined, becoming quite good at finding excuses. He even bowed out on a birthday celebration they held for him, saying he was "under the weather". On the occasions Jules attended, he spent the time in bed. Sleep was an equalizer for the pain.

***

Jules sat on a small stool and colored in the den at her father's feet. Randy bought her a child-sized easel, and she was busy at work, drawing a boat with a blue crayon. Like her mother and father, she loved the color blue. Cape tried to concentrate on a self-help book his mother had given him called *Picking Up the Pieces*. It offered ways to become whole again, but he thought the book was useless. He didn't want to become whole, and besides, it was impossible—half of him had died in the hospital three years prior. The book suggested he journal to help ease his grief. He figured his poetry qualified, so he put the book down and watched his daughter draw. He saw Kasey's gentle touch in Jules' hands, as her small fingers moving slowly to stay within the lines.

"You like it?" Jules asked. Her shoulder-length hair curved inside the collar of her yellow pajama top. She brushed her bangs from her forehead with the back of her hand. "Daddy?"

"I'm sorry." He picked up his notepad and placed it on his lap. "What do we have here?"

"I drawed you a sailboat."

Cape looked closely at the drawing, reminding him of the day he first saw Kasey's paintings. "It's just beautiful. You're the best preschool artist in all the land. You need to autograph it for me."

She scribbled a few letters, a "J" the only one that was decipherable. "Here you go." She handed it to him and he hugged her, pulling her close as though he could absorb all the wondrous love contained within her.

"Okay, ankle biter, it's time for bed. You brush your teeth and I'll get a book. You thinking Winnie the Pooh tonight?"

Jules shook her head. "Little Mermaid."

"What? We read that one last night, and the night before. Let's change it up."

"I like that one."

"I do too, but not every night." He picked her up and carried her over his shoulder like a sack of lawn mulch. "How about I tell you a story?"

After she brushed her teeth, and made a potty stop, she hopped into bed. Cape lay beside her, and together they looked toward the ceiling. She lay in his arm, her head on his chest.

"Did you ever hear the story about the Ugly Duckling?"

"No, sir," she said softly.

"Well, this was the ugliest bird you've ever seen. He was so hideous that he even scared himself when he saw his reflection in the water."

"What's id-e-us?"

"Hideous," he said with a laugh. "It means really, really ugly."

"Oh." She stretched her arm across his chest.

"Well, this duck was the nicest duck you'd ever want to meet, but people made fun of him because his bill looked like an oyster shell. Uncle Billy showed you one of those, right?"

"Yes, sir. Looks like a bumpy rock."

"That's right. Well, this duck's name was Gilly, and he didn't have any friends. His mother had to tie a pork chop around his neck just to get the dog to play with him." Jules giggled. "Well, one day Gilly is hanging out next to the pond, and he sees this beautiful duck named Melanie Mallard land on the water. She was the prettiest bird in the county. Her feathers had all the colors of the rainbow."

Jules rose up on one elbow. "Really?"

"Absolutely." Cape smiled and she lay her head back down on his chest. "Well, when Melanie sits on the pond, a fisherman in a nearby boat casts his line, hooking Melanie in the wing. She tries hard to fly away, and the fisherman panics and starts reeling in his line. Melanie cries out in terrible pain and the fisherman starts to think how nice Melanie will look mounted on his den wall."

"Why didn't he let her go? That was mean."

"Tell me about it. If I'd have been there I would have thrown rocks at his boat."

Jules laughed, holding on to her father's words as if they were magical. He took her hand. Her daddy was her hero, and with him, she knew nothing could harm her.

"Well, old Gilly sees what's going on, and without any concern for his own safety, heads across the water. He takes off like he's been shot out of a cannon. He takes that ugly bill of his and rams it into the side of the boat, almost knocking the man clean out of it. The fisherman soon recovers, though, and begins to reel again. Gilly takes off, high in the sky to gain speed, and then dives right back down at the old man, nailing him in the back with his bill. The man yells out, 'I'm hit!' and he drops the pole in the water."

Jules giggled at the pained expression Cape used to describe the fisherman's face.

"Melanie is still flapping like a hen running from a fox, and the pole starts to sink. Her wing is hurting so bad she can't see straight. It was pure agony. Well, Gilly takes to the sky again like Wonder Duck, and he zooms in on the line, cutting it in mid-air. Melanie is now free, though she still has the hook in her wing."

"Did Gilly fix her?"

"No, he couldn't. It's a bummer when you don't have thumbs."

"What'd he do?"

"He carried her on his wings to Farmer Brown's house."

"Whose house?"

"Farmer Brown. He married Old McDonald's daughter back in '73, but she turned out to be an E-I-E-I-Ho."

Jules scrunched her nose in confusion.

"Never mind," Cape said, grinning. "Anyways, Farmer Brown removed the hook, Melanie told the entire duck community that Gilly saved her life, and he went on to become the most beloved duck in the poultry world."

"That's a silly story."

"Well, I'm a silly man." He kissed her on the forehead. "I've got something to show you. Wait here."

In a few minutes Cape returned. He handed her the picture of Jules in Kasey's arms on the day she died. "I've been holding on to this, but I think you're old enough to see it. Your grandma June took it."

Jules held the picture. "Is that Mommy?"

"Yep. You and Mommy."

Jules traced her mother's face with her finger. "She was really sick, huh?"

"Very. But she was so happy when she got to hold you. I'm going to find a good frame, and you can put the picture on your night stand."

"Can I sleep with it tonight? I'll put it under my pillow."

"You sure can. Speaking of that, it's time for bed." He kissed her on the forehead and stood.

"Can I make the pancakes in the morning?" she asked.

"Yep. I will be your assistant. We make a great pancake team."

Jules loved to see her father smile, which wasn't something she saw very often. She hugged him. "I love you, Daddy."

"I love you more."

"I love you *big* as the house!"

"I love you *big* as the sky!"

Cape went back to the living room and started drinking. He was working on his third cold beer when he remembered the stack of mail sitting on the kitchen counter. He rummaged through it, separating bills from the junk mail. In the pile was a complimentary copy of *Sports Illustrated*'s baseball issue. The cover photo featured Rocco Crezdon, Cape's teammate with the

Swamp Hogs, with a caption that read "Atlanta's Rising Star".

Cape opened the magazine, though he'd promised himself that he would never look at anything related to baseball ever again. But Rocco was the only teammate Cape had truly become friends with in his minor league days. The article talked about how Rocco had worked his way up through the minor leagues, eventually becoming one of the top young players on the Braves Major League team. It explained how he'd started a non-profit to give underprivileged Miami youngsters a place to play baseball. Cape smiled at a photograph of Rocco standing among a couple dozen children on a baseball diamond.

Two beers later, Cape finished the article, and though he was happy for Rocco, he couldn't help but wonder what they would be writing about him had Kasey not died. He thumbed through the rest of the magazine, and he saw familiar names on the Major League rosters listed in the issue. He looked at his pooch stomach, and ran his fingers through his scraggly beard. What had he become?

He fell into a restless sleep on the couch. Faces appeared in a dream, short, choppy apparitions, as though his semi-conscious state had spliced bits and pieces of memories from his past and thrown them at him. He woke briefly and the faces faded. He looked about the dimly lit room, the beer clouding reality. When he returned to his uneasy slumber, he found himself walking down a strange, long hallway. Small dark rooms, like alcoves, were located on both sides of the corridor.

Curious figures stood in front of lit candles resting on pearl-white mantles, and they watched Cape as he passed. He turned into one of the rooms, drawn by the sense of familiarity. Although the room was a fold of shadows, with a coldness about it, Cape felt warm and at ease. He walked around a high-back chair, and there she stood, busy at work at an easel. The colors she'd chosen were reds and blues, like the soft flames of a long-burning fire.

"'Bout time you got here," she said, brushing her hair from her eye with the back of a pale hand. She wore a bold, blue dress, long and full as though she had stepped out of a Colonial ballroom. "Baby, can you bring Jules to me?"

Cape immediately began to cry, though no tears fell. He struggled to breathe, and yet he smelled the soft apricot aroma of her hair. "Oh, my God. Sweet girl, is it really you?"

She stroked her brush onto the canvas, which transformed into an open window that somehow held the colors from the room's candles in a prism of light like some neon spider web.

"Bring Jules to me," she said softly. "Hurry, please. My stomach is hurting, and I'm not sure how much longer I can paint. I want Jules to help me finish this."

Cape placed his hand on her back, a collection of fragile bones along her slender spine. Her face glowed radiantly, as though her mind held separate residence from her body.

"Hurry up, Cape. Bring Jules to me. I want her to finish this painting." She bent and winced. "My stomach hurts so bad, Cape. Hurry, baby."

Cape ran from the room, down the hall, frantically trying to find the door to Jules' bedroom. In an instant he was home, but the hallway held no doors. He banged on the wall where Jules' door should have been, and he pleaded for her to find a way out so she could see her mother. He searched left and right for the door, and the hallway seemed to lengthen in front of him. He cried out his daughter's name. They had to hurry if they were going to see Kasey.

He woke up sobbing.

***

Jules awoke around 5:30 a.m. She walked to the kitchen, her hair tussled like strands of cotton candy. She didn't notice Cape asleep on the sofa. She knew the alarm in his bedroom would go off in thirty minutes, so she grabbed the box of pancake mix from the pantry, and tried to hurry so she could surprise her dad. She slid a kitchen chair to the stove, placed a skillet on the front right eye, and turned the temperature on high. She climbed on the chair and tried to pour a dash of cooking oil in the pan, but lost her grip on the plastic jug, pouring the contents all over the stovetop and underneath the burner. Within a few minutes the grease began to smoke and pop, and a startled Jules fell off the chair.

"Daddy," she cried out. Flames began to rise, and they quickly caught hold of the cabinet above the stove. "Daddy!" Cape couldn't hear her cries, nor did he smell the smoke.

She ran down the hall to her father's room, and panicked when she saw an empty bed. As the fire began to spread across the cabinets, Jules ran outside. She screamed for Cape and began to cry. John Swanson, walking to his mailbox to fetch the morning paper, saw Jules and ran across the street to her driveway.

"What's wrong? Where's your father?"

"I don't know." Tears rolled down her cheeks. "I wanted to make pancakes. Daddy's gonna be mad."

"Don't worry. He'll be fine. What'd you do, spill the mix?"

She shook her head. "Fire in the kitchen."

John's wife saw him talking with the obviously distraught little girl through the living room window and walked outside. John carried Jules to her. "Abby, take Jules inside. Call 911. We need a fire truck." He grabbed a fire extinguisher from the carport and took off across the street.

By the time he made it inside, fire reached the kitchen ceiling. He pointed the nozzle and sprayed white foam across the counter and cabinets. Within minutes, the fire was extinguished, but smoke remained thick and heavy throughout the house. He took off in search of Cape amid the dark, smothering cloud. He found him asleep on the couch and shouted Cape's name. Cape moaned and turned his head. John shook him several times before he woke, and led him to the front steps, both men gagging and coughing.

The fire truck's siren roared as it came up the highway. Abby and Jules came running down the drive, and when Cape saw his daughter, he took off for her. He lifted her, squeezing her in his arms.

"I'm sorry, Daddy."

"No, angel, I'm the one who should be sorry. It's my fault. It's all my fault."

"I just wanted to make you pancakes." She began to cry.

"Hush, sweetie. It's okay." He pressed her cheek to his. "I'm sorry I didn't protect you." He kissed her on the forehead, and tears formed in the corners of his eyes. He imagined the fear she must have felt, thinking he wasn't there to help her, and it made him nauseous. "But I promise with all my heart and soul that I will never, ever let that happen again."

Chapter Seventeen

Cape pulled the 4-Runner into Santee Elementary parking lot. He held Jules' hand, and his stomach tightened with every step they took.

She wore pink shorts and a blue, short-sleeve, button-down blouse. The pink ribbon in her hair matched her shorts. She wiped her brown hair from her face and her blue eyes sparkled when she looked at her dad.

Cape didn't realize her first day would be so tough. Tough on him, that was. They had endured a lot together, and he wasn't quite ready to send her into the setting with so many kids; older kids. Church pre-school had insulated her somewhat, and he felt she was much too innocent. He thought about how mean children could be. What if they picked on her? It was hard enough that she had no mother. He thought she should be exempt from the unnecessary pain or sadness caused by classmates, or by anyone else for that matter.

At the doorway, he checked the straps of her book bag, and asked, "Want me to walk you to your room?"

"No, sir. I can do it." He stooped and she hugged him. "I love you, Daddy." Her words melted his heart.

"I love you too, Jules. Remember how big?"

"Big as the sky," she said sweetly, and he kissed her on the forehead.

"That's right. Have a great day, angel."

It pained Cape to watch his baby walk through the school doors. He knew the passage into those halls meant their lives were changing. He thought about those nights after she came home from the hospital, rocking her to sleep and feeling her heartbeat, hearing her breathe. He recalled the sound of tiny bare feet running across the floor when he got home from work and her jumping into his arms. He knew the days of Disney-character pajamas and silly nursery rhymes would lead to prom dresses, cars, and, worst of all, boys.

Cape took off early from work in order to pick Jules up after school. She waited underneath an awning with the other car riders, and waved and stepped to the curb when she saw his car. Her first day of kindergarten was complete.

"Hey, Half-pint," Cape said. She climbed onto the booster in the back seat. "How was your first day?"

"It was great. We got to eat lunch in the cafuh-neria with the big kids." Cape smiled at her pronunciation struggle. "My teacher, Miss Caswell, put my name on my desk. She's the best teacher in the whole world."

"Sure sounds like she is. What would you say we celebrate your first day with a scoop of ice cream?"

"That's a great idea," she said.

They sat at their usual spot, outside the store under a blue umbrella, two scoops of chocolate each. They could be found there most every Sunday afternoon.

Jules devoured her ice cream, the tip of her nose smeared in chocolate. She chattered on about her friend, Andrea, who apparently thought a kick to the shin would convince their classmate, Robert, to give her his cherry Snack Pack at lunch. She dropped her napkin, and when Cape bent to pick it up, his back tightened. The ten-hour shifts and standing on the line at Lakeside Plastics, were taking their toll.

***

Without a college degree, Cape had little choice but to continue working at Lakeside, one of the largest employers in the area. A small community surrounded by two rivers, lakes Marion and Moultrie, and enough swampland to keep the gators happy, Santee relied a great deal on tourism. Anglers came from all over to fish for striped bass, crappie, and catfish. The town was dotted with hotels, restaurants, and convenience stores with self-service gas pumps, bait, and all manner of fishing tackle. Cape had been offered a position with Golden Links golf course, but he didn't want a job that had to do with sports.

His dad sold insurance in a small office downtown, but the parent company wouldn't allow Randy to hire his son, especially since Cape didn't have a business degree.

And so Cape clocked in at the plant each weekday morning, resigned to the fact that life was a regimented routine of button pushing and lever grabbing. Time had calmed the waters at work, so to speak, but many of Cape's coworkers were still disheartened that a legend like him worked the same dead-end job they did. Paul had learned the hard way not to taunt Cape, but he still cut him hard looks when he got the chance. Regardless, the fellow employees had been certain he was destined for great things, and were amazed that he'd walked away from the paycheck, fame, and glory. Being a good father was admirable, but with the money Cape would have made, he could have provided an incredible life for Jules, and for himself, that most only dream about. Many had concluded he'd tossed his career aside unnecessarily. In their eyes, Cape was that rare breed of ballplayer who came around once in a lifetime. Someone they could brag about to relatives and people outside of Santee. He was both celebrity and hero, and they'd wanted to live their uneventful lives through him.

Cape had changed the day of that fire. He quit drinking, and began to take care of himself. He could have lost Jules, and he would never jeopardize her safety again. He started attending family functions, and the Cape of old returned in bits and flashes. A smile here, a laugh there. Especially when he played with his daughter. His parents saw the changes, and it gave them hope that he could once again enjoy life.

Cape was frugal with his money, and set aside a small amount each paycheck for Jules' college fund. Les Jamison had been sentenced to twenty years in prison for siphoning all of Cape's, and the other clients', money. Cape was told that retrieving any of his money from the sale of Les' assets could take several years in the court system, and even then, there was no guarantee that he'd see any of it. Cape refused to harbor any bitterness about it, choosing instead to focus on being the best father he could be.

Life was simple, but good, for Cape and Jules. They settled into a daily routine. He picked her up from an after-care program at school each day, and on the way home she filled him in about what she'd learned, and she always seemed to have a funny story to tell about Andrea. They did homework first thing, and then she helped him cook dinner. Keeping her room clean was something she took pride in, and her toys and dolls sat neatly tucked away when she wasn't playing with them.

Cape's bedtime stories turned into full adventure tales, and she loved how he conjured up stories just for her. He made up magical islands where paintbrushes came alive and colored the sky above them based on the whims inside Jules' mind. He told her about a farm where pigs spoke Spanish and grew giant tacos. He loved to hear her laugh, and see her expressions that somehow seemed to confirm her suspicions that her daddy was the zaniest man alive.

After Jules fell asleep each night, Cape rubbed her hair and promised to always take good care of her. Tender moments that made life good again. He just ached that she had no mother. And she clung closer to Cape than most daughters might. But, mother or not, she was crazy about her father. In her eyes, he was the protector; not only her father, but her best friend.

To Cape, the world revolved around Jules. She represented all that was good. Gentle, innocent. They were inseparable.

* * *

As time went on, Jules asked more and more about her mother. She had a curiosity about her whenever she watched friends interact with their mothers. She noticed mothers brushing their daughter's hair, holding their child's hand, hugging them. She wondered what that was like.

Cape loved to tell Jules about Kasey, how tenderhearted she was, how talented she was, and most of all, how much Jules looked like her. Jules loved to look at her mother's paintings. Two hung on her bedroom wall, scenes of a young girl walking in fields of bright flowers.

She also liked to look at the photographs of her mother, smiling and rubbing her tiny fingers across the pictures as if trying to feel her mother's presence.

Cape set Kasey's Dulce easel in Jules' bedroom, where she used Kasey's brushes to paint on endless rolls of art paper. The one article of clothing Cape had saved of Kasey's was her Piggly Wiggly t-shirt, and Jules wore it when she painted. It looked like a giant color wheel nightgown on Jules' tiny body.

Cape spent so much of his efforts on Jules that he had no interest in a social life. A large part of his heart went to the grave with Kasey, with the rest set aside for his daughter. Sometimes at night he would sit on his back porch, after Jules was fast asleep, and his mind chased the memories of when his life revolved around baseball and Kasey's warm smile.

A few of the unmarried women in the area tried unsuccessfully to date Cape. He'd gone through hell, but his piercing blue eyes could still mesmerize most any woman. Katie Flemming, a girl Cape had dated a few times in high school, stopped by his house to visit from time to time. She adored Cape, and though she settled for being a friend, she wanted much more. Her advances were wasted time.

It was simply a world for two, no room for more.

***

Jules lay on Cape's bed, holding George, her long-legged stuffed monkey, wearing one of Cape's shirts as a nightgown. She rolled over and looked at the framed painting on the wall above his bed. Cape placed his watch on the chest of drawers.

"Daddy, is that one of Mommy's paintings?"

Cape walked beside the bed, his eyes soft and pensive. He reached up, removed the artwork, and sat beside her. "I found this the day before you came home from the hospital. It was in my closet, wrapped with a blanket."

"Why was it in the closet?"

"I think she wanted it to be a surprise, and she was planning to give it to me after you were born. Only she never..." He paused.

"Is that supposed to be me and you throwing the baseball?"

"Yes, Jules, it sure is. Your mother said she only painted pictures that meant something special to her. So, that should tell you that you meant the world to her."

"I wish I could have known her."

"Me too, angel. Me too."

Chapter Eighteen

The aroma of burning coals filled the yard. Billy put a platter of ground beef patties and hotdogs beside the grill. Cape sat at the picnic table, the afternoon sun warm against his back.

Beside him, Jules and her three-year-old cousin, Tripp, worked on a picture from Tripp's *Transformers* coloring book. Billy's wife, Christina, walked onto the patio with a pitcher of ice tea and a bowl of nacho chips.

Cape and Jules had made the drive to their home on Sullivan's Island, on the northeast side of Charleston Harbor, for a weekend getaway.

Billy and Christina had married six months after Kasey passed away. Their wedding was a five-star affair at Saint John's Lutheran Church in Charleston's historic district, and dignitaries from throughout the area attended. The reception was held at Middleton Place Plantation on the Ashley River. Christina's father was a retired general, and a high-ranking member on the Board of Regents at The Citadel.

Billy was in medical sales, and Christina received enough from her daddy's monthly distribution to where she could stay home and be a full-time mother.

Cape and Jules had last seen his brother's family at Christmas, and it was only the second time they had come to Sullivan's Island to visit. As the kids finished coloring, Cape helped Christina with plates and utensils.

"So, Cape, how are you handling Jules being in school?" She handed him a platter of sliced tomatoes and Vidalia onions.

"I tell you, it sure was hard watching her walk through the schoolhouse door that first day. She looked so small with her tiny book bag. I was tempted to find a spot outside her classroom and watch through the window."

"Daddy's girl."

An awkward moment as both of them pondered her statement. Could Jules be anything else?

"Well, it's late April, so she will be out for the summer in just a couple of months," Cape said to cut the silence.

"I've got mixed emotions with Tripp. I still have two years to prepare for it, and I think it will do him good to be around other children. Around here it's just mostly retired people, so he just doesn't have many kids to play with. But I can imagine how emotional it will be when it's his first day of school."

"I think of Jules going off to college and I break out in cold sweats."

"That's a long ways off, Cape."

"It's closer than you think."

After dinner, Christina let Tripp and Jules hand out bowls of banana pudding. The sun hung low in the western sky, and long shadows began to stretch across the yard, making the white blooms of the Bradford Pears and azaleas appear bolder and more vibrant. Cape stepped into the kitchen to help Christina put away the remainder of the uneaten food, while Billy and the kids stayed outside.

"Does Jules ask about Kasey?" asked Christina.

"She does. Especially lately. She loves to look at photos of Kasey. She likes her paintings, particularly the one of Jules and I playing catch. She makes me retell the story of how I proposed about once a week. She thinks the Christmas lights idea is the best part of the story."

"Does she ask you about your baseball days?"

"She doesn't know."

"Doesn't know? You proposed at home plate. How could she not know?"

"I told her my friend was the landscaper of a baseball stadium and that it was his idea to have it there."

"You don't want her to know you played?"

Cape sat down on one of the barstools and drank some tea. "Those days are in the past."

Christina had a puzzled look as she set the tightly wrapped large bowl of leftover banana pudding inside the refrigerator. Had Cape tied baseball with Kasey's death, as if the sport itself had cursed them and caused her to die?

Before she could even respond, they both heard a familiar thump. Cape stood and walked to the window. His brother tossed a white plastic ball to Tripp, who held in his tiny hands a red plastic bat that, above the handle, was as wide as a milk jug. Billy had spent time teaching Tripp a batting stance, and how to crouch, knees bent, pounding the bat on the ground before the ball was thrown to him. As if on cue, Tripp bent his skinny knees, popped the bat on the grass twice, and then hit a line drive to the back fence. He tossed his bat like a baton twirler and began rounding imaginary bases. Jules chased the ball and fetched it from behind the row of azaleas bordering the wooden privacy fence. She threw it to Billy, a hard toss, and it caught him off guard. Tripp slid on the grass to what he assumed was home plate.

"Wow, Jules, what a strong arm," Billy said in amazement. Cape watched but said nothing.

Tripp hit several more pitches, and Jules ran to the ball each time, tossing them to Billy with the speed and accuracy of not only someone twice her age, but also like a boy. Billy asked if she wanted to bat, and she took off wildly to pick the bat up off the ground. On the first pitch, she hit a hard pop fly that carried over the back fence and into the neighbor's yard. Billy ran to retrieve it, but not before high-fiving her as she circled a path similar to the one Tripp had run. When Billy returned, he tossed her another one. She sent the pitch off Billy's shoulder, the ball flying high above his head as he staggered. Cape walked outside.

"Holy crap, Cape, did you see her crush that ball?" his brother asked.

"Watch this, Daddy." She pounded the bat on the ground and then crouched, waving the head of the bat above her.

"Jules, put down the bat," Cape said.

"Watch, Daddy. I'm going to clobber the ball." Billy tossed the pitch and she stung it over the fence again.

"Remind you of anybody?" Billy asked, smiling at Cape.

Cape walked over and picked up the bat as Jules rounded the bases. He handed it to his brother.

"Here, take this. She doesn't need it."

"She's a natural. Watch her hit again."

"I said take it. She doesn't need any part of this."

"Part of what?"

Jules ran to Cape and hugged his leg. "Did you see me, Daddy? Watch me and I'll knock it over the fence again."

She reached for the bat and Billy handed it to her, but Cape took it from her immediately and handed it back.

"She's done. Take the bat."

Billy looked confused.

"But, Daddy?"

"Don't 'but Daddy' me. Go say goodbye to Aunt Christina. It's time to go."

Chapter Nineteen

Jules pulled the permission slip out of her red-and-yellow book bag, an excited look on her face. She was discovering that first grade held more perks than kindergarten; in this case, her first field trip, a Valentine's Day excursion to Potter's Nursery. Virginia and Frank Potter had owned and operated the nursery for twenty-six years, and it was a yearly fixture on the Santee Elementary field trip tour. They specialized in roses, and the children all received not only a quick lesson in how flowers grew, but a half-dozen roses to take home to their mothers. Red, pink, white, yellow, and hybrids, Potter's grew them all. The nursery was almost two acres, and people came from all over the state to purchase flowers and shrubbery.

"Miss Hunt says it's very important you sign this, Daddy. If you don't, I have to sit in the gym all day while the rest of the kids go on the field trip. Oh, and I need three dollars. Did you know we get to stop at The Chicken Hut for lunch?"

"Then I better sign it right this second, don't you think?"

"We get to ride the activities bus. Thad is scared to ride the bus 'cause he gets carsick."

Cape smiled. "It might be a good idea not to sit next to him."

Jules giggled. "Daddy, you're so silly."

The day of the field trip was soft and warm, a preview of days to come. The sun slipped in and out of a thin veil of high, soft clouds. The temperatures climbed into the seventies, and some of the children wore shorts. The Potters waited in the parking lot as the bus drove up. Frank was a short, slender man with curly, silver hair. Virginia was petite, with long, braided brown hair that came halfway down her back.

The children walked in pairs, Jules matched up with her best friend, Kaitlin. The children took turns sprinkling water on the hanging baskets in the covered part of the shop. Carson asked why roses had sharp thorns. Andrea asked Carson why his teeth looked like sharp thorns. Parker knocked over a birdbath in the back of the shop, but it only had a few scratches. When the tour was over, each child was allowed to pick out roses for their mother, in whatever color they chose.

Jules stood behind Parker.

"What are you doing in line?" he asked. "Your mama's dead."

Miss Hunt took Parker by the arm and led him to the parking lot. "Parker, why would you say such a mean thing?" He shrugged. "Can you imagine how hard it must be to not have a mother? You just think about that for a minute. You owe her an apology."

Jules brushed aside Parker's comment and stepped up to the large pottery basket filled with flowers.

Virginia looked at her husband oddly. She knew about Jules' situation, so the thought that she would want flowers caught her off guard.

"There are a lot of pretty colors to choose from," she said. "Take your time and pick the ones you like the best."

"I'll take the yellow flowers," Jules said politely after just a moment. "Daddy said those were Mommy's favorite."

Virginia nodded to Frank, who lifted six beautiful yellow roses from the bunch. He placed the stems in a plastic tube and put water in it.

"Thank you, Miss Potter."

Virginia sighed and looked as though she wanted to wrap her arms around Jules. "You are very welcome, sweet child."

On the bus ride back to school, Jules carefully held the flowers as though they might break if she blinked too hard.

***

Pauline's Parkinson's remained relatively stable, thanks to her medication, and she sometimes picked Jules up after school so they could spend time together. When she got to Santee Elementary, she was confused to see her granddaughter carrying flowers, although she knew about the Valentine's tradition. She wondered if the roses were for Cape, or possibly for her.

"Those are beautiful, Jules." The youngster climbed into the booster seat in the back of the car. "Did you enjoy the field trip?"

"Yes, ma'am. We got to water flowers that grew in big baskets."

"That sounds like fun. Are you going to put those flowers on your kitchen table?"

Jules shook her head. "I want to put them some place special. Can you buy me a pretty vase?"

"A vase? I sure can."

Pauline helped Jules picked out a round green vase at Pampered Plants. Pauline bought a bottle of water at the convenience store next door and poured the water into the vase.

Though her hands moved slowly and deliberately, she was able to help Jules arrange the roses.

***

Randy answered the phone in his office with a cheery hello.

"Hey," his wife said. "Can you leave work a little early?"

"I don't see why not. Is everything okay?"

"Jules needs us to take her somewhere."

Pauline left a message on Cape's cell phone to let him know they wouldn't be at the house when he got off work.

They drove for an hour, and Jules barely spoke. Randy had placed the vase beside her in the back seat, secured in a box by crumpled sheets of newspaper.

When they pulled up into the cemetery, Jules sat forward on her booster seat. She noticed a tombstone with two child-size angels on top. Randy drove on, and when he saw Kasey's gravesite on a nearby slope, he glanced at Pauline. He pulled off the road onto a small strip of grass bordering Kasey's gravesite. Jules stepped out of the car, and Randy removed the flowers and vase from the box. Jules looked about the cemetery, a child standing among markers of finality. He gave the vase to Jules and Pauline guided her along, the vase looking large in her small hands.

They stood at Kasey's grave, a granite marker and vase holder on a six-foot slab. A small easel and a paintbrush were engraved beneath the dates. Randy placed his hands on his wife's shoulder. She fought back tears. A gentle breeze slipped through the trees above them. A bird called out somewhere in the distance, its cries stopping as quickly as it started. The world became silent around them, as if to pay respects to this child who knelt at her mother's final resting place.

Randy removed the vase and its arrangement of plastic flowers. Jules gently placed her green vase in the holder and wiped the hair from her eyes. "This is for you, Mommy. Happy Valentine's Day." She dropped to both knees, and rubbed her fingers across her mother's name, tracing each letter on the smooth granite stone.

Pauline held her hands to her mouth, and then pressed them slowly together as if she were praying. The thought of her youngest granddaughter, denied a lifetime of knowing her mother, was overwhelming, though she kept a stoic front for Jules' sake. She stepped closer and ran her fingers through Jules' hair.

"Do you think she would have liked me?" Jules asked, her blue eyes awash in unguarded curiosity.

"Sweet child, she would have adored you. I'll bet she's smiling in heaven, watching over you as you grow. She was a special lady. And you are every bit as special."

"I wonder if she misses me."

"I know she does. But she wants you to be happy, and not sad that she isn't here."

"I wish I could go to heaven so I could see her."

Pauline took Jules in her arms. "Baby, you'll see her one day. But right now, you need to make the most of your time here, loving your father, your family."

Jules nodded. "Just wish I could talk to her."

"When you say your prayers, ask God and He will pass on anything you want to say to her. She'll get the message."

They walked silently back to the car.

***

The last weekend of March, Pauline and Randy took Jules with them to a Friday night fish fry held by their church. She spent the night with them and Saturday morning. Cape used the time to meet with his income tax preparer. After lunch, his parents pulled up in the driveway.

He could tell Jules was excited when she came running into the garage where he was working to repair a broken slat for the bench that sat on the back patio.

"Daddy, Papa just signed me up. I get to play tee ball."

Cape stopped hammering. "What?"

"I'm going to play baseball. I'll get a uniform and everything. Can we go get a glove? I need cleats too."

"Working on the bench, I see," Randy said as he and Pauline walked into the garage.

"You signed Jules up for tee ball?" Cape asked.

"She was talking about it last night," said Randy. "Some of her friends are playing. We rode by the park and saw that today was the last day of registration, so we went ahead and signed her up." He saw a frown rise on Cape's forehead. "Something wrong? I thought you'd be excited for her."

"You shouldn't have done that without asking me first."

"You don't want her to play?"

"No."

"Why not? You loved it, and we couldn't wait to go to the ball field and watch you play. Thought you'd want to do the same with Jules."

"I don't want her playing baseball."

"I don't understand," his mother said. "Baseball has always been a big part of our family. Jules asked if we could sign her up, and like your father said, today was the last day of registration."

"Let her pick another hobby. She doesn't need to try and follow in my footsteps."

"But it was her idea."

"Can't I play, Daddy? Kaitlin and Carson are playing. I get a uniform and everything."

"No," Cape snapped. "You can't play. And that's final."

Jules ran to her room in tears.

***

One Saturday morning in late May, Cape and Jules set off to run errands, which always required a trip to get ice cream. He enjoyed her company and she didn't care what they did as long as she was with him. She sang a song she'd learned in her Sunday school class. Cape smiled, and shook his head in amazement at the facial expressions she wore. He watched in the rear-view mirror as she moved her hands about like butterflies.

After they got the hardware store and post office checked off the to-do list, he decided ice cream would be best eaten before a trip to the grocery store.

***

As they sat at their usual spot, Jules looked across the street to a small county park. A Little League ballgame was underway and she watched closely and listened to the sounds of the crowd in the bleachers. Cape watched her expressions, though he didn't look at the field. There was nothing there for him anymore. He saw the yearning in her eyes, but knew she wouldn't bring up the subject since he, in no uncertain terms, had told her that baseball was off limits. Her ice cream melted over her hands as she watched the game. Cape looked into those sad eyes. He breathed deeply.

"So, you think you'd like to play baseball, huh?"

Jules nodded, but her answer came with timidity. "Yes, sir. But I won't 'cause it makes you mad."

"It doesn't make me mad." He rubbed his eyebrow as he carefully chose his words. "I was just hoping you'd find an interest in something else like dance or ballet."

"I don't like any of those silly things. I like baseball. It was fun playing at Uncle Billy's."

"You weren't too bad at it either, were you?"

"It was easy. I like hitting hard."

Me too, he thought.

"Well, maybe we can sign you up next spring." She knew maybe meant yes.

"Really?" She squealed and dropped her cone.

Cape took hold of it with his napkin and smiled. "It gets you so excited that you can't hang on to your ice cream?"

"I'm sorry."

"It's okay now, Jules." He heard the clapping and yelling from the ball field. "Are you positive you want to play?"

"Yes, sir."

"Well, if your grades are good next year, you can."

Jules hugged Cape and his neck was sticky with melted ice cream. He didn't mind a bit.

Chapter Twenty

Jules sat on the straight-back chair beside the kitchen table and Cape tied the black laces of her cleats. Her glove on her hand, her bat balanced across her lap, she struggled to remain still. After Cape tied her shoes, he held her tiny feet in his hands and recalled when he'd put on his first pair of cleats twenty-one years prior.

They pulled into the dirt parking lot, and Jules jumped out and ran to the field for her first practice.

"Thank you, Daddy," she said over her shoulder. Her smile and wide-eyed look of excitement told him how thankful she was that he allowed her to play.

Cape stood in front of his car as vivid waves of memories carried him down the path to something much more than just a game of baseball. The place where he learned that great things could happen when he held a bat in his hands. Where his uniform represented the player, not the other way around.

It wasn't just a game. It was security, with mom and dad watching from the bleachers; it was the knowledge that success and failure were equally noble, as long as they were attempted with grand purpose; it was chasing a dream and imitating, in some small way, his childhood heroes.

For a brief moment, Cape felt himself running on that field, holding his glove like it was worth more than any gift ever given. He could almost feel the smoothness of a new baseball inside his small hand, almost see across the field from under the bill of his baseball cap. He was convinced the world looked different when viewed from underneath a ball cap, less harsh, the sun's rays brighter, the grass softer.

Cape walked to the field, his eyes on his daughter. A man wearing a blue cap spoke to her inside the gate, then walked to the dugout and emerged with a cap that he placed on her head. She looked at her dad and grinned.

She was officially a player for Long's Drug Store Cardinals.

She soon paired up with her school friend Kaitlin, and they warmed up down the left field line, standing twenty feet apart and tossing a ball to each other. Though Jules struggled to catch the ball, she threw it so hard that her coaches stepped from the dugout to take a closer look.

One nudged the other and smiled. "Check out the arm on that girl. She throws a bullet."

Cape was nervous for his little girl. He brushed his hand along the wall of the dugout and walked down the third base line. He thought back to his first season. He had played for the Havelock Tire Indians. His jersey had been baggy, his pants the same. He was younger than the next closest player by two years, but he'd played with more heart than the rest of the team combined. His coaches had commented more than once to his parents how they wished for an entire team with his attitude and effort.

He worked his way down the left field line and stood underneath the electronic scoreboard behind the outfield fence, looking up at the spot where his first home run had dented the "o" in *Coke*. He was eight years old, and the youngest to ever hit a home run out of Santee Memorial Field.

Jules waved to him from centerfield. Cape knew since she was a girl, she would have to earn respect from not only the coaches, but the other boys. The coach hit her a slow roller, and she ran to the ball, picked it up, and heaved a rocket to the second baseman. The player winced as the ball popped into his glove. He shook his glove hand after throwing the ball to the catcher.

It seemed that Jules might climb the respect ladder faster than Cape thought.

Cape had stood near the backstop during batting practice. He could hear some of the parents whispering about his playing days, and the sad circumstances that led to him giving up the game.

"Hey Cape." Luke Mayer, who had played for Santee with him, walked up and extended his hand.

"Luke. How've you been? You got a kid on the team?"

Luke pointed to third base. "Jason. He just turned seven. This is his second year. You have a daughter, right?"

"Centerfield." He pointed. "Jules. She's also seven."

"If she hits anything like her old man, we should be in for a good season."

"It's her first time playing, so I wouldn't get your hopes up too high."

"Even though they call this a tee ball league, it's really a coach's pitch league. If a kid can't hit it after five pitches, they'll set the tee up. It's pretty laid back, though some of the parents get into it."

"Well, baseball is big in this town."

"Thanks to guys like you."

It was Jules' turn to bat, and she removed her bat from the blue equipment bag her grandfather had bought her. She held the purple TPX in her hands and stepped into the batter's box. The coach, Arnie Stephens, scooted up onto the grass in front of the mound and lobbed a ball across the plate. Jules hit it straight back at him, and it ricocheted off Arnie's kneecap.

"Oh, my God," Luke said as he watched assistant coach Wilson Mathers run to Arnie's aide. "She mashed it."

Cape shrugged. "Lucky swing."

Wilson stepped in for Arnie, who went into the dugout to nurse his bruised leg. As Wilson delivered the pitch, Jules hit a line drive at Jason's head. He fell on his backside and looked sheepishly toward left field to see where the ball went.

"Think you've got a star in the making, Cape," Luke said, pointing at Jules. Cape tried to hide a smile. "Do you work with her a lot?"

"None. There's no baseball instruction going on at our house. We don't watch it, and we don't play it. She took a few swings once at my brother's house, but that's it. To be honest, it took me a while to finally let her play. I assumed it was more about getting cleats and a uniform than actually playing."

"It's in the blood, Cape. It's in the blood." Cape wondered if Luke might be right.

***

The first game took place on a Saturday morning. Jules had asked everyone she knew, right down to the mailman, to come. Of course her grandparents attended. She also invited Kasey's parents, but they were unable to attend. Billy and Christina made the long drive from Charleston and brought Tripp. It was like old times.

"It feels good to be back at this ballpark," Randy said to Pauline.

"Doesn't it? We've spent a lot of time on these bleachers."

"I thought our days of watching ballgames were over. Sure glad I was wrong." It wasn't Cape on the field, but it was his blood.

Cape wasn't sure what to think. Mixed feelings. He stood by himself down the first base line, watching from a distance. Baseball had brought the best of life to him, but it was not a part of his world anymore.

Sometimes he gave the briefest thought to what life would have been like if Kasey had not died. He had imagined leading the Yankees to the pennant, with fans applauding his monster home runs, and children waiting eagerly for his autograph after games. But, it was just too painful to think about what he had given up, and he never let those thoughts cloud his belief that giving up the game for his child was absolutely the correct one.

Jules batted cleanup, which meant fourth in the batting order, just like her dad. Since defense was the hardest thing for young players to learn, runs were scored easily, prompting the league to install limits of five per inning. When Jules came to bat, the bases were loaded. She adjusted her helmet and stepped into the box, the head of her purple bat moving in small circles as she held it, her hands in front of her right shoulder.

Arnie tossed a pitch, trying his best to throw one that she wouldn't hit off his shin. She launched it above his head into centerfield. She took off running, all knees and elbows, to first base, and the centerfielder cowered as the line drive landed in front of him. He moved to the side and swiped his glove at the ball, a move that a matador would make to a bull.

Jules headed toward second, and it was easy to see she had home run on her mind. The crowd seated in the bleachers cheered loudly, and Cape turned to watch them, amazed at the excitement his daughter stirred. Cape looked again at Jules, coming up quickly on her teammate Jeffery, who had been on first base, as they both headed toward third. For a split second, Jules slowed down since Jeffery impeded her gallop, and she got no more than two or three steps behind him. Her patience quickly wore thin, so she ran around and past him, but not before elbowing him out of the way. Wilson was coaching third base, and stood dumbfounded as Jules rounded third and headed for home.

Jules crossed home plate, and the crowd didn't know whether to laugh or applaud, so they did both.

Pauline yelled her approval. Billy and Randy looked at each other as if to verify that what they'd seen had actually happened, and then Randy looked at Cape with his hands held up, palms to the sky, a 'never saw that before' gesture. Jeffery stood on third base, arms crossed, as Coach Wilson tried to convince him to run to the plate.

It made for interesting conversation at O'Reilly's after the game.

***

Cape and Jules ate spaghetti at the kitchen table. It was her favorite meal and the easiest thing Cape knew how to fix. He looked into those sweet eyes, that window to her mother's spirit, and he smiled.

"Daddy, Coach Wilson says you're the best baseball player, like in the whole world." She spun her fork in her noodles.

"He's just trying to be nice. He probably says that about the other players' dads too."

"Nope. He said it in front of the whole team. He said you played for the Atlanta Braves."

"He did, huh?"

"Did you?"

"Actually, I only made it up to Triple A."

"What's that mean?"

"In pro baseball, each team has several levels. Kind of like school. You start at the first level, and if you do well enough, you move on to the next one. The highest level is the Major League, and I was one level below that. That team was called the Greenville Braves."

"So you weren't good enough to play for the Major League team?"

Cape paused, unsure how to answer. "Yeah, I was good enough."

"Then why didn't you play for that Braves team in Atlanta?"

"Keep eating, missy. You're running your mouth and your food's getting cold."

"You just didn't want to play for that team?"

"No, I wanted to play for them."

"So why didn't you?"

Cape shrugged his shoulders.

"Did you get hurt?"

"In a way."

"Are you still hurt?"

"Sort of."

"If you get better, would you want to play again?"

"I said goodbye to baseball years ago."

"Why don't you play again? That way we can watch each other play."

"Eat your food, motor mouth."

"Want to?"

"Quit yapping and eat."

Jules moved to the pitcher's position halfway through the season. Each game she'd stand beside the mound, beside the opposing team's coach, fielding balls that came her way. She was feared by the first basemen, an ever-changing rotation of kids whose shins, knees, and stomachs got bruised by her rocket throws. During one game, she was so frustrated that the first baseman couldn't catch her throws, she started chasing down the base runners and tagging them with the ball. Cape winced on one play when Jules came across a base runner too fast to catch, and she promptly pegged him in the back with the ball. After that game, Cape had taken her aside and explained that 'beaning' a base runner might be okay in backyard ball, but not on the baseball diamond.

The league hosted an All-Star game on Memorial Day, and issued special uniforms. Each of the six teams put their four best players on the roster, and then divided them into two teams of twelve. Jules was chosen to play the pitcher's position for her team, and was glad to have Brandon Wilson from Dyson's Heating and Air Orioles as her first baseman. Brandon was athletic enough to catch Jules' hard throws. After the game, a large cookout and fireworks show would take place.

Jules stood on the third base line, in her blue and white pinstripes. Cape had told her she represented all of her Cardinal teammates. The field was soaked in sunshine on that cloudless day. A light breeze carried the aroma of popcorn and chili dogs across the ballpark, and in the air the American flag waved on the pole as if queued up for the National Anthem.

Cape watched Jules hold her cap against her heart while the song played. After it ended, she turned and smiled at him. He could see she loved the game, and it reminded him of how he once felt. He missed the passion he'd had for baseball, but there was nothing he could do about it.

Or was there?

Chapter Twenty-One

Cape had never picked up his glove to throw with Jules. He had not hit her the first pop fly or ground ball. He wanted no part of the game. She could sense it, and she didn't press him to play with her. But one summer afternoon that all changed.

Cape sat on a split hickory rocking chair on the back patio. Jules played with their neighbor's puppy, a spunky Black Lab, and Cape wondered if a dog would make a good Christmas gift. After the neighbors took the puppy home, Jules walked to the garage and returned with her glove and a baseball. She began throwing the ball into the air, catching it as it fell from the sky. Being a young child, she could only toss it twenty feet or so. At times it would catch limbs of the maple or pine trees on the way down. Cape watched as she pounded the glove with her fist, waiting patiently for the ball.

After several minutes, she looked at her dad and smiled. Her heart was at odds; she loved her daddy, but felt guilty for wanting him to throw the baseball. Her eyes turned pensive, a girl in love with a game that had hurt her father in some way.

It began to sprinkle, and the hazy, gray sky seemed no higher than the treetops. Cape was ready to call Jules to the porch, but didn't for some reason. Her green cotton shirt turned darker in spots from the raindrops, but she didn't care. She only wanted to catch the ball. One of her throws bounced through several tree limbs, Jules following it intently with her eyes. She didn't see the wheelbarrow Cape had used earlier for raking leaves and pine straw. He called out a warning, but she flipped over the handle—but not before catching the ball. He ran to her. Jules stood and dusted the soil off her kneecaps, a small trail of blood coming from her shin.

"You okay?" he asked.

"Yes, sir."

"Are you sure?"

"I'm sure. You know, it feels kinda good to get hurt when I'm playing."

She was her father's child. Since Cape was old enough to catch, he had loved to come up bloody when diving for balls. It was his badge of honor, his way of showing sacrifice for the sport.

Jules moved back to where she'd first stood, and tossed the ball again. The rain fell even harder. She didn't notice that Cape went to the garage. When he emerged with his glove, Jules' eyes got big, as did her smile.

It felt good to slip the glove on his hand. Without speaking, he held it out and she threw him the ball. He caught it and felt its wet, musty rawhide. There he stood, sharing his first throw with his child, and memories clouded his mind of the first time he threw with his dad, a self-defining moment that many fathers share with their children, where the simple act of throwing a baseball becomes a symbolic passing of the torch.

With each throw, it seemed to pull them closer together, a spiritual metamorphosis. A father and his daughter, joined together by a five-ounce ball. But in that moment, the torch was not being passed. Instead, the torch rekindled dormant coals within Cape.

After they finished playing, she quickly ran into her father's arms.

"Thank you, Daddy."

"I'm sorry it took me so long. I should have done this with you a long time ago."

"Daddy, I heard Papa tell Grandma how much he misses watching you play. Grandma said raising me was more important. Papa wondered if you felt bad giving up baseball."

"That's not something you should worry about."

"You quit because of me, didn't you? I was the reason you had to stop." She leaned onto his shoulders and began to cry. "I'm sorry I made you quit."

Cape pulled away and looked into her eyes. "Jules, there's no need for you to apologize. That was my choice, and besides, I'd do it all over again. You are the most important thing in my life."

"But if it wasn't for me, you'd still be playing."

"I don't care about that. All I care about is you. You know that, don't you?"

The tears continued as Cape held his quivering daughter in his arms. The rain fell harder, and he wondered if Kasey was crying too.

Jules put on her pajamas that night, took hold of George, her stuffed monkey, and walked into the den. "Ready for bed. Tell me a story?"

"Sure thing."

He carried her on his shoulders and dropped her to the bed. He told her a story about a princess who was saved from a raging river by an elf with green ears and a bad case of hiccups. After he finished, he pulled the cover to Jules' chin and rubbed her hair.

"How much do I love you?"

"Big as the sky," she smiled.

"You got that right."

"Daddy, will you do something for me?"

"Anything. I'll lasso the moon with a giant rope. I'll capture a rainbow and hang it above your bed."

"Cool it, Dad."

"What, you don't believe me?" He tickled her rib cage.

After a quick laugh, she pulled his hand away, and with all the seriousness a seven year old could muster, said, "I want you to play baseball again."

"There are no baseball leagues in Santee. The only thing they have is slow pitch softball."

"No, not softball. Real baseball. The kind you watch on TV."

"That's not possible."

"Sure it is. Would you do it for me?"

"It's not that easy, even if I wanted to."

"Mr. Wilson said you were awesome. Coach Paul said the same thing. If you're that good, you should play again."

"Those days are gone."

"Why? If you can grab a rainbow, you can play baseball. We'll get matching uniforms and I'll wear mine whenever you play. It will be like we're on the same team."

"Now you're talking crazy."

"Well, when I say my prayers tonight I'm going to ask God to let you play again. He can make anything come true."

"Well, I think He's going to let this request slide."

"Not if I pray it. Grandma says that if you pray and believe, it will happen. So turn off the lights so I can start praying." Jules slipped off the bed and to her knees. "Night, Daddy."

"Now, Jules."

"I said, *night*, Daddy." She intertwined her fingers and closed her eyes. Cape turned off the light and left her alone to pray.

He walked into the garage and opened the narrow door that hid the water heater. Above the heater, Cape's equipment bag sat on a shelf. He removed it and slid a thirty-four inch wooden bat from the pouch on the underside. He rubbed his hand along the smooth handle, and something stirred inside him.

Cape walked out into the yard, the rain gone, the night air calm and still. He gripped the bat and rested the barrel on his shoulder. He took a deep breath, and then smoothly took a swing. He rolled the wood handle in his fingers, enjoying the feel of the cool wood. He assumed his left-handed batting stance, knees slightly bent. He eyed an imaginary pitcher at the edge of the yard, a ghost in the dark. As the pitch approached, in slow motion, Cape began to step toward the ball, his hands leading the bat over the plate, his hips opening as the bat crushed the rawhide. Off across the knee-high cornfield the ball went, 200 yards, disappearing into the darkness of the tall pines.

Cape touched the bat against his forehead and closed his eyes. The bat was a part of him, as much as his arms or legs. He touched it lightly against his cheek. The dream had been locked away, vaulted so that he would not give it thought. His way of hiding the pain, mainly because it was his choice to quit: no one else's.

Inside, a beautiful child prayed her heart out, and she was worth more than the pursuit of any dream. She was his life, and she extended the life of Kasey. Though Jules hadn't asked to be brought into the world, she showed Cape the truest meaning of unselfish love.

Sometimes he felt guilty for thinking his child was a trade for his wife. As if God had a barter system for souls, a ledger of human accounting that had to remain in balance.

He provided a stable home for his daughter. Would that change if he pursued the game again? What about the road trips, and spring training? Could he stand to be apart from her? But he could dip into her college fund and hire a nanny. With Jules now seven, and more independent, maybe his parents could help. The possibilities started to blossom.

***

Pete Bennett shut the trunk of his Cadillac, his golf clubs stowed away. He had just finished eighteen holes with Clay Person, his latest signee from Marietta, Georgia. Clay had received a $3 million signing bonus to play for the Seattle Mariners, and Clay's father wanted to celebrate on the golf course.

Pete's cell rang as soon as he pulled out of the parking lot.

"Hey, Pete, this is Cape."

"Cape, my main man, how's it going?" Pete said, enthusiastically.

"Not bad. Yourself?"

"Just trying to keep afloat."

"I'm sure that life's a struggle for you. Who's the million-dollar kid this year? Have you signed him to a big fat contract yet?"

"Clay Person. Pitcher. Just finished his junior year at UGA. I played a round of golf with him, his dad, and uncle at Stone Mountain Golf Club this morning. Not a bad way to spend a day. What are you up to now? Still enjoying the simple life?"

"Don't know how much longer it's going to be simple."

"What do you mean?"

"I want to get back in the game."

Pete stopped the Caddy in the parking lot of a convenience store and cut the engine off, as though he wanted complete silence in order to hear Cape explain his statement. "You mean game, as in baseball?"

His mind sprung into action. Seven months till spring training. Seven years out of the game, but the smoothest swing since Ted Williams, widely considered the purest hitter ever to play in the major leagues.

"Are you serious?"

"Absolutely."

"What caused you to have a change of heart? I thought you'd closed the door on baseball forever."

"Jules. I want to do it for her."

The waters wear the stones.
- Job 14:19

Be still and know that I am God.
- Psalm 46:10

Your persistence is your measure of faith in yourself.
- unknown

Chapter Twenty-Two

Coach Amos Steck was tired. He had shoveled dirt for four hours, tossing it from his pickup onto the spot where his new driveway would be, spreading, flattening and smoothing it as though icing a sheet cake. The sun beat down on the back of his neck, and the humidity soaked him to the bone. He thought by starting at 7:00 a.m. he could avoid the heat, but on an August day in South Carolina, he should have known better. When Cape pulled in behind his truck, the coach removed a red and white handkerchief from his back pocket and wiped his forehead.

"You're just in time," Coach Steck said, putting his boot on the side of his pickup. "My back's wiped out, and the wife's lemonade is calling. So, take this shovel and I'll be back in a couple of hours."

Cape smiled as Coach squatted in the bed. They shook hands.

"Hey, Coach. How you been?"

"Can't complain. Good to see you."

"Yes, sir, you too."

"What brings you out to the swampland on a steamy morning like this?"

"I need your help."

"Name it."

"I want you to help get me ready."

"Ready for what?"

"To play ball."

Cape saw the confused look on his former coach's face. "You mean baseball?"

"Yes, sir. I want to give it another chance. Not just for me, but for Jules. Actually, it's her idea. She prayed to God to let it work out. And who am I to get in the way of prayer?"

The coach stepped down from the truck and wiped his face again. He looked off in the distance as if trying to process information he didn't comprehend. He squinted one eye and looked at Cape. "Going to take a lot of work, son. You up for it?"

"Yes, sir. I'm ready to go."

"I mean a *lot* of work. A *lot* of time and effort. The body has been away from the game for what, six or seven years? More importantly, the mind has been away for that long. Baseball is unforgiving."

"I know I can do it, Coach. But not unless I have your help."

"Cape, I want to tell you something." He sat on the tailgate and took a deep breath. "Son, when you played for me, I was tough on you. I was your coach, and I was just doing my job. I expected a lot more from you, because I knew you were so damn talented. And I know the fussin' and cussin' outweighed the praise and any adoration. But you no longer play for me, so I can say this without reservation."

Cape gave him a peculiar look. "Say what without reservation?"

"This ain't easy, so bear with me." He studied the ground and gathered his thoughts. "Cape, I've been around baseball most all of my life. I've coached more players than I can count. Good ballplayers. And I can say without hesitation that you were the most gifted ballplayer I've ever had the pleasure to coach, to watch." Cape shrugged his shoulders. "It's true. You were scary good. But more than that, it's the way you played. Like you and the game were one and the same. And when you quit it was such a letdown. For me; for the whole town. I just knew you were just gonna be one of the greatest pro ballplayers of all time, and then, just like that, you were done. To see you get another chance, well, all I can say is it would be an honor to help you get another shot."

"Well, then, let's give it all we got. And it would be an honor to have you coach me again."

***

Cape and Jules walked through the front door of his parents' home. Randy sat in his recliner in the den watching television, and Pauline read a book on the couch. Jules hopped on her grandfather's lap, kissed him on the cheek, and grinned. "Wait till you hear."

Cape took the remote from the end table beside the recliner and turned off the TV.

"What's going on?" Randy asked.

"Is everything okay?" Pauline followed, uncurling her legs and sitting up.

"Daddy's got big news. *Big* news."

"What is it?" Pauline asked. Her hands trembled as she closed her book.

Cape sat on the edge of the coffee table in front of the television. "Mom, Dad, I know how much baseball has meant to our family. And I know how hard it was on all us when I quit. Not just me. All of us." He smiled at Jules. "But, thanks to that little ankle biter on Dad's lap, I've decided to play again."

Pauline looked at Randy, and then back at Cape. "What? How? Where?"

"Pete is going to shop around and find a team who will take me on. Might be the Independent League. I have five months to get ready, and Coach Steck has agreed to work with me."

Pauline pulled her shaky hands to her lips as though she were praying. "Cape, are you sure?"

"Yes ma'am, I'm sure."

Pauline stood and so did Cape, and they hugged. Jules nodded at her grandfather, still sitting on his lap. "See, I told you it was big. *Big!*"

***

Coach Steck had three weeks before school began at Santee High. Each morning he met Cape at the ball field for two hours before Cape went to work. Coach had Cape start from scratch, beginning with the batting tee. From there he tossed batting practice to him in the cage, and then moved on to the mound where he threw from regulation distance. He gave Cape pointers and tips, just as he'd done in high school.

Baseball was coming to life again inside them both. Coach had grown weary of the way the game had changed in recent years, with the players seemingly more interested in what the game could do for them, instead of what they could do for the game. Varied scholarships and notoriety on recruiting websites. Expectations of mothers and fathers catering to their every need with regard to equipment, baseball gear, and looking the part of a star ballplayer. Young men who lacked respect for the game. There weren't any other Cape Jeffers on the horizon, no one who had that fire in their eyes, nor the love of the game in their hearts. At least not the love Cape held.

Cape thought Coach Steck was the ideal coach. He treated superstars and benchwarmers the same. Being the premier player on the team, and most certainly the best player to ever come out of talent-rich Santee, it would have been accepted for Coach to treat Cape differently. But if anything, he'd worked Cape harder than the rest.

At first, Cape's swing felt odd. His mechanics were pretty sound, but his timing was off, and he had trouble knowing when to begin his stride to the pitch. What he experienced was normal for any player who had been away from the game for even a short while. Timing troubles aside, Cape loved the sound of the ball when he stroked it with his bat. And so he hit, over, over and over. Blisters developed on his hands and fingers the first day, and when he took off his batting glove after he finished hitting, he squirted the wounds with his water bottle.

At the end of the second day, the blisters bled. And yet the pitches continued. On the third day he belted one far over the centerfield fence. His timing was slowly returning and soon Coach was sliding behind the pitcher's screen, an L-shaped fence that provided protection should the ball come back his way, to prevent serious injury from Cape's line shots.

Cape swung right-handed first, as always, and then switched to the other side of the plate. They began to notice that more and more of the baseballs Cape hit were beyond the outfield fence than inside it.

After an hour of batting practice each day, Coach picked up his old fungo bat and hit ball after ground ball. Cape fielded them, tossing the balls softly behind him in the outfield grass. Cape wanted to protect his arm, and he wasn't ready to uncork any throws to first base just yet. On the second week, Coach Steck asked his first baseman to catch Cape's throws to first. By the third week, Cape looked very smooth, and his confidence level grew. Coach swore the first baseman to secrecy about Cape's comeback attempt.

At night, after Jules went to bed, Cape worked out in his garage with some used weights he bought. He got a treadmill and ran after he finished lifting weights. He felt as if life was giving him another chance, and he planned to take advantage of the opportunity.

On the final day of their workout sessions, Coach was impressed, but not surprised, with the way Cape had regained his batting stroke, and his power. After he tossed the last bucket of balls for Cape to hit, the two walked side by side to collect them. Cape held the bucket, his gray t-shirt covered in sweat.

"Coach, it feels great being on the ball field again."

"It's something that never really leaves you. It might become dormant, but all it takes is a few swings for the burn in your gut to return. To be honest, I'd gotten stale myself. No fire, as if I was the only one on the field who understood what the game was all about. You've relit that spark, and now, the very feel and smell of the grass enthuses me again. There's nothing like it. Least not that I've found."

"This might all be a big waste of time, but if I don't give it a shot I'll regret it for the rest of my life. More than that, I don't want to let Jules down."

"Son, you've got the talent to do it. And it looks like you've regained the love for the game as well. I don't see how you can fail. And even if you don't make it, you and your daughter will know you did your best."

"I can't thank you enough for taking time from your summer vacation. I couldn't have done it without you."

"Are you kidding? It was a good excuse to get out of the house. Sally has a honey-do list for me that three men couldn't finish, and since I've been helping you, it's gotten me off the hook. And being that school starts back tomorrow, that list will have to wait even longer." Coach let go a laugh and patted Cape on the back.

"Looks like she'll have your Saturdays all booked then."

"Not unless she can pull me from the swamp. Deer season starts in three days, and she knows better than to stop me from hunting." Coach picked up a ball that Cape had hit fifty feet past the outfield fence. "So, what's the plan of attack?" He tossed the ball to Cape.

"Technically, the Braves hold the rights to me. Pete Bennett, my agent, is talking with them to see if they are interested in placing me back in rookie ball or giving me my outright release. If they release me, I'll shoot for the Independent League."

"What's your preference?"

"As long as I can get a chance, I don't really care."

Chapter Twenty-Three

The Atlanta Braves' organization decided to give Cape his outright release. So much time had passed since Cape last played, and they didn't think it was really worth the wait to get him to the majors, even should that ever happen. They figured it would take at least three years for Cape to work his way through the minor leagues, and he would be thirty-one by then.

So he was free to pursue other options.

What seemed most likely was to sign with a team in the American Independent Baseball League. The league wasn't affiliated with Major League baseball; it consisted of players who'd been away from the game and wanted to make a comeback, or younger players looking for another chance after being released from their minor league club.

They all hoped if they shone in the Independent League, another Major League team might give them an opportunity.

The previous year, the city of Hilton Head had created a team and entered the Independent League in an effort to give retirees something to do besides shop and play golf. Not only was it the only Independent team in South Carolina, it was the only one in the Deep South. Pensacola had a team, but no one in South Carolina would consider Florida a southern state.

And so Pete entered negotiations with Hilton Head. The prospect of having one of the most promising players in the past decade attempting a comeback in baseball would be good for business. The publicity would stir up interest, putting more people in seats of the stadium. The fact that Cape was also a native South Carolinian would make people rally around him with support.

Pete took all that into account and had a contract for Cape to sign in a matter of days.

***

Jules rode on Cape's back as he walked her to bed. He tickled her toes; in return, she bucked and kicked him, trying to tickle him under his chin. He bent and Jules tumbled onto the comforter.

"How about a story?" Cape said as he tucked her in.

"You haven't told me a story in a long time. Did you come up with a new one?"

"Yes," Cape said as he lay on the bed beside her. "I believe this is a new one."

She pulled the covers to her chin. Cape lay on top of the comforter, his hands folded behind his head as he looked at the ceiling. "You ready?"

"Ready," she said.

"Once upon a time there lived a princess. She was the sweetest, most perfect princess in the land."

"What was her name?"

"Let's see...I think it was Jules."

"What a nice name."

"Isn't it? Anyways, Jules' father was the king of the land, and he wanted nothing more than to please his daughter. He was so very proud of her. But she had this one wish, and he would give anything to make that wish come true."

"What was the wish? That he would get her a pet dragon?"

"No, no pet dragon. They outgrow their pen too quickly and they tend to singe the bricks in the castle.

Anyways, at one time, the king had been a great baseball player."

Jules laughed. "They didn't have baseball in the castle days."

"Sure they did. It was called moatball."

"You're so silly."

"Stop interrupting," he said, taking hold of her nose.

"Owww," she said with a cackle. "Okay, I'll stop interrupting."

"So, the king had to quit playing when the queen gave birth to the princess, the most wonderful princess ever. When Jules got older, she found out he was really good at moatball and asked that he play again. And you know what?"

"What?"

"He joined a moatball team in Hilton Head and they moved there and lived happily ever after."

Jules had a peculiar look on her face. "What? Moatball in Hilton Head?"

Cape turned and faced Jules. He took hold of her hand that grasped the blanket. "I'm going to play baseball again. You and me, together. First stop is Hilton Head, and hopefully the last stop is New York City."

"Really?"

"Really."

"That's awesome, Dad. You're going to be the best player ever."

"Don't get carried away, Half-pint. Let me at least play an inning or two before you call me the best player ever."

"I will. But I know you will be."

"One more thing. We have to keep it a secret for just a while, okay?"

"Okay."

Jules slept with a smile on her face that night.

***

Cape had five months before heading to Hilton Head, but there was much to do. He continued to work at the plant, never mentioning his baseball plans. He figured he'd give a month's notice to allow them time to hire a replacement. His parents agreed to keep the news to themselves until he gave them the okay. Pauline enrolled Jules in an after-school art program to keep her occupied, plus Jules wanted to do something she thought her mom would have liked.

Cape met Coach Steck at the high school field three nights a week. He turned up the intensity of his workouts, running long distances, sprinting down dusty country roads. He ran for miles, hearing the roar of the crowd in his head. The rusty weights in the garage were no longer sufficient, and he began working out in the weight room at the YMCA.

One Saturday morning, Cape drove Randy and Jules to the high school field. Cape thought it would be fun for them to throw and hit, and to let Jules experience what Cape had as a boy, the joy of playing ball with his dad. Jules stood beside Randy near home plate, and Cape stood in front of third base. He first threw to Jules, who threw it back to Cape. He threw it to his dad, and Randy took the ball from his glove, examining it as though he was trying to familiarize himself with it.

"It's going to take awhile to get the cobwebs out of this old arm," Randy said. "I haven't picked up a ball in years." Randy tossed one easily and let out a slight moan. "Oww. This is going to hurt worse than I thought."

"That was a good throw, Papa."

Randy smiled. "Thanks, Jules, even though I know you were just being nice."

"She's showing some respect for the decrepit," Cape said.

"Is that what I've been reduced to?"

"Don't listen to him, Papa. I think you're doing really good."

Three generations of Jeffers playing baseball.

After tossing the ball for several minutes, Randy's arm began to loosen. He offered to pitch to Jules, and she took her bat from her bat bag and ran to the box. Randy placed a bucket of balls beside him on the infield grass, forty feet from the plate. Soon the ping of her metal bat rang across the field.

"Nice," Randy said as Jules lined one toward second base. "I think you hit harder than your daddy did when he was your age."

"Really?" She looked at Cape with a proud grin. "Did you hear that, Daddy?" She pounded the end of the bat on the plate, waited on the next pitch, and hit a hard one back at Randy, who barely caught it before it hit his midsection.

"Whoa," he said.

"I think he's right, Jules," Cape said, standing at shortstop. "You're a beast at the plate."

After Randy tossed the last ball in the bucket, which she hit to Cape at short, Randy said, "Cape, you want to take a few swings?"

"Yay, Daddy's gonna hit."

They gathered up the balls, and Cape grabbed a wooden thirty-five inch Louisville Slugger from his bag. Jules ran to center field. "Hit me one, Daddy."

"Going to use the old bat, huh?" Randy asked.

"It might be old, but it still feels good. Still has some pop in it." He stepped in the box to hit right-handed.

Randy threw a meatball to Cape, across the plate, belt high, and he crushed it past Jules, where it bounced at the base of the fence. He hit several more balls across the outfield, Jules giving chase but never quite making it in time to catch one.

"Come on, Daddy. Hit one that I can catch." She ran to the fence in center. "Hit it right here."

"You heard her," Randy said. "Smack it to the fence."

Randy threw the pitch, and Cape turned on the ball, driving a shot that easily cleared the center field fence, hitting the limb of a pine tree that was forty-five feet beyond. After he watched it land, he looked at his bat and noticed a four-inch gash just above where his hands held it.

"Hey, you were supposed to hit it to me," Jules said as she ran through a gate along the right field fence. While she retrieved the ball, Cape and Randy gathered up the balls in the outfield.

"Guess I should toss this into the trash," Cape said as they walked to his vehicle. He rubbed his fingers along the gash. "Man, it was a good one."

"But that's one of your favorite bats," Jules said. "You're gonna throw it away?"

"No need to do that," Randy said. "Take me home. We'll fix it."

In Randy's garage, he removed a small plastic container of carpet nails from a cabinet. He grabbed his hammer from a work belt hanging on a metal hook. "Jules, how about you get that roll of duct tape on the counter." He placed the bat in a vise grip, gripped at the head. Carefully, he took a tiny nail and gently tapped it into the bat where it had split. He hammered two more nails, closing the gash so that the bat looked almost like new, except for a seam that remained.

"Jules, put the tape on the bat right at this seam, and then let's wind it around a few times till we can't feel the nails."

She carefully wound the tape around the repaired bat, circling several times, her grandfather's hands guiding her. He cut the tape, and removed the bat from the vise. He handed it to Cape. "Good as new."

***

Cape sought a nanny, one qualified to home school. Randy pulled money from an account he'd started years ago for emergencies or a special occasion. To him, Cape's comeback attempt couldn't be any more special. The fund roughly equaled two years' salary that Cape would have made working at the plant. Cape had also banked enough to pay for two seasons worth of rent.

Christina's friend worked for the school board in Hilton Head, and she provided him a list of five nannies, all licensed to home school. Cape traveled to Hilton Head in October to interview the potential candidates while his parents took care of Jules. By November, he'd narrowed the list to two, and by December, chose Carnetha Mack, an energetic twenty-six-year-old woman who had grown up in nearby Beaufort. His salary in the Independent league would be enough to cover monthly expenses, and since Carnetha would live with them, he'd only have to pay her to home school Jules. Being a nanny allowed her a free place to stay, and all the food she was inclined to eat.

***

The blustery winds of February rolled along the filled parking lot outside the plant. Cape walked into his supervisor's small, crowded office. Stacks of folders perched on an already full desk. He shut the door so the roar of the assembly line wouldn't drown out what he had to say.

"Got a second, Jerry?"

"Sure, Cape. Take a seat. That is, if you can find one."

Cape removed a briefcase from a chair and sat.

"What's on your mind?"

"I'm turning in my notice."

"Really? You found something better?"

"Better than anything I know."

"What will you be doing?"

"Playing shortstop."

Jerry tried to keep a serious look about him but fought the urge to laugh. "Um, haven't those days passed you by?"

"We're fixing to find out."

***

One of Billy's clients owned a house in Hilton Head's Shipyard Plantation that he rented to vacationers. He gave Cape a great deal on the monthly rent and an open-ended lease. The house was furnished, so much of Cape's furniture was placed in storage. Tucked away on a quiet cul-de-sac, the modest home overlooked saltwater creeks that wove along an expansive marsh. Massive oaks draped in Spanish moss kept the house in soft shadows. A bike route led down picturesque streets bound by creek veins and cord grass.

On a bright, cloudless mid-March day, Cape and Jules moved to Hilton Head. Spring was making an early appearance, the winds calm, the sun warming the car through the windows as they drove. Randy and Pauline followed Cape and the U-Haul in Cape's old 4Runner. Billy drove down from Charleston to help, and to drive his parents home when they were done with the move. After the U-Haul had been emptied and the boxes placed in their proper rooms, Cape took the family to The Drunken Albatross for dinner.

The following day, after lunch at The Have a Nice Day Grill, Randy, Pauline, and Billy had to return home.

Pauline hugged Cape in the parking lot beside Billy's car. "We'll be praying for you. Gonna miss you both, but we're so excited."

"Thanks for everything," Cape said. "And we're going to miss you too."

Randy, who carried Jules on his back, squatted so she could dismount. He gave her a hug.

"If you need anything, just let me know. I expect a daily call too. Got it?"

"Got it," Jules said. She wrapped her arms around his neck.

"I love you."

"I love you too."

While Pauline hugged Jules and said her own goodbyes, Randy gave Cape a bear hug. "I'm real proud of you, Cape. And not just because you're giving baseball another shot. But for the father you've become. For the son you are."

"Thanks, Dad. I learned from the best. I love you. Love you both."

Billy got a hug in as well. "Good luck to you, little brother. Give 'em hell."

***

Cape and Jules tried to settle into their new home. They felt each other's uneasiness. Thrown into a new world, but they had each other.

They hung Kasey's paintings on the walls, and placed Jules' stuffed animals and dolls in their chosen place on the bed, on her dresser, and her glove-shaped chair. Everything had a place and purpose.

As far as Jules was concerned, she had no one but her dad. No friends, no grandparents nearby. She missed Kaitlin. She missed Andrea's daily antics, and being able to tell Cape about them at the dinner table. She wanted her father to be a ballplayer again, but she hadn't known what that entailed when she'd talked him into giving baseball another shot.

Cape had been away from the game so long he felt unsure about his chances. While in Santee, at least he had stability, and his parents nearby. Now, who knew? The only thing Cape and Jules did know was that they would do it together.

Cape and Jules shared a cheese pizza on the back deck. Jules didn't say much, and mostly pushed her slice around on the plate.

"What's wrong, Jules?"

"Why do we have to have somebody live with us?"

It was low tide and the oyster beds along the creek spit water like ballplayers spitting sunflower seeds in the dugout. Jules smelled the oysters, and wondered quietly if something had died, evidenced by the sour look on her face.

"It's the oysters and the mud," Cape explained. "It can get a bit ripe when the creek lowers." He looked into her eyes, trying to carefully choose his words. "We don't *have* to have somebody live with us, but I think it's the only way to make this work."

Cape had brought Jules along with him to meet Carnetha on a final interview. He thought they interacted well, and Carnetha seemed at ease talking about everything from the daily school schedule to what the girls could do to entertain themselves when class was not in session. Since Cape would be on the road a lot, he needed a full-time nanny for Jules. And Carnetha was also highly recommended as a home-school teacher and seemed a perfect fit.

"Carnetha's going to be great," Cape reassured. "She'll not only be your teacher, but I think she'll make a good companion. She'll take good care of you when I'm on the road. You know I'm not going to let just anybody look after you. This lady seems really nice, and smart, and I think she's an important part of making this all work out."

"Wish Grandma could live with us."

"Me too, but she has to take care of Papa. He'd fold like a cheap tent if he didn't have her to take care of him."

"I guess. But does this lady have to live in our house?"

"She can't exactly live in the yard. She's not a Golden Retriever." Cape grabbed Jules' chin and tugged it playfully. Jules laughed.

"What if she cooks stuff I don't like?"

"I'm sure she can fix what you like. It can't be any worse than my cooking."

"No kidding."

"Thanks a lot, smarty pants."

She flashed a mischievous grin.

"We good? I mean, you and me, with Carnetha coming to live with us?"

"Yes, sir. We're good."

***

Jules sat at the kitchen table eating cereal. Cape watched a spring training report on ESPN. He paid close attention to the shortstop rankings for every Major League team. He figured a good season in the Independent League would be enough for Pete to negotiate a contract with a Major League organization.

When the doorbell rang, Cape hesitated to answer it. The fact that he was the tenant, and not a visitor, hadn't fully sunk in. It didn't yet feel like *home*.

Carnetha stood at the door with two worn, canvas suitcases, one on either side of her on the porch. She wore jean shorts and an orange polo shirt. Her wavy hair was shoulder length, dark brown. Her smooth, soft chocolate complexion gave her hazel eyes a greenish tint.

"Hello, Mr. Jeffers," she said with a wide grin. "Welcome to the Lowcountry."

Cape shook her hand and took hold of one of her suitcases.

"Please. Mr. Jeffers is my father's name. Call me Cape."

"That would be disrespectful."

"How so?"

"You're a ballplayer, right? You don't call your coach Ed, or Bob, or Hank. You call him Coach Smith, or Johnson, or whatever. Same goes for me."

"Well, we'll just have to change your way of thinking."

"How about I call you Mr. C?"

"I can live with that." He took her other suitcase.

"Speaking of names, please call me Carnie. Carnie Mack. Has a nice sound to it, don't you think?"

Cape smiled and walked to the kitchen, Carnie close behind. Jules eyed Carnie cautiously while Cape set the suitcases down.

"Hey, girl, how you doin'?" Carnie asked. Almost six feet tall, she towered over Jules as she stood beside her.

Jules shrugged her shoulders.

"Jules, Miss Carnie is speaking to you."

"I'm good," Jules spoke reluctantly.

"What kind of garbage are you putting in your body?"

Jules looked in her bowl to see if something had crawled into it. "Huh?"

"That ain't nothin' but pure sugar. You know what sugar does to your body?"

Jules shook her head, almost afraid to ask.

"It sucks out everything good inside of you. Now let me fix you some real food."

"That's okay," Cape said. "She's not much of a breakfast eater."

"That's going to change. If you're gonna be ready for my class every morning, then you better have a full stomach, child. And I'm talking about food that will make your brain strong, as well as your body. From here on out, breakfast will be grits, eggs, sausage, and liver puddin'."

"Liver pudding?" asked Jules, scrunching her nose. "I don't like the sound of that."

"Child, it's protein overload. Puddin' made of the finest ingredients of a hog: tongue, ear cartilage, and if you're lucky, even the oink." Carnie grinned. "Soul food, little girl."

"I'm not eating that."

"Don't worry. You can mix it up with grits and you'll never know the difference."

"I don't eat grits."

"You will."

"Grits aren't brain food," Jules said. Cape stood, arms folded, observing the conversation.

"You're right," Carnie said, shaking her head, "grits is groceries."

"What does that mean?"

"It's a Lowcountry saying. It means it's food that doesn't necessarily do you much good, but it sticks to your ribs long enough so you don't go hungry. It's the eggs and liver puddin' that will make your brain sharp." She pointed at her own head. "Will make you real sharp."

Carnie's cooking suggestions did little to raise Jules' enthusiasm level.

Cape showed Carnie to her room and there she unpacked. She felt a bit nervous, though she'd done a good job of hiding it. Her experience as a nanny was two and a half years prior, and only for the summer, working for a wealthy couple from Jamaica who owned a home in Hilton Head.

In that situation, she had separate living quarters above a four-car garage. With Cape and Jules, she would be sharing living quarters, sharing it with white people. Now, she saw all people as children of God, but she couldn't help but wonder about cultural differences. She had no doubt in her ability to be a caregiver, or a teacher. But what did Cape and Jules like to do for fun? What kind of music did they listen to? What if she wanted to listen to Alicia Keys, or Jay Z? Would that be allowed? She guessed Cape to be a Barry Manilow or Kenny Chesney kind of guy.

***

Cape reported to the ball field at three o'clock for an informal orientation. The players were given their practice schedule, insights about road trips, per diem amounts for meals, and what was expected of them throughout the season. He felt nervous, something he'd never been before, especially not with baseball, but he'd been away from the game for seven years. He wondered if his teammates knew who he was, knew his story. He didn't want special treatment, and wanted to blend in. A few of the guys appeared to look at Cape as though he was a coach. In their eyes, he most likely looked a little old to be a player.

While Cape attended his meeting, Carnie and Jules rode bikes to the beach. Carnie thought they should get to know each other before school began. Carnie was raised by her grandmother and had shared a home with two brothers and three cousins. She learned the hard way that if she wanted the basics of life such as food, respect, and even love, she had to fight for it. A passive attitude and demeanor didn't go far in her world, and so she grew up strong, aggressive to a certain degree.

"Miss Carnie, how old are you?" They rode side by side along a winding trail covered in shadows made by expansive live oaks and long leaf pines that stood arrow straight.

"Twenty-six."

"Wow, that's old."

"Girl, you don't have any idea what old is. I'm a spring chicken. You know, I been thinking. We need to come up with a nickname for you." Carnie looked out over the coastal creeks, the cord grass blowing in the breeze. "How about Double J?

"Why Double J?"

"Your initials are J.J., so why not? Or, how about D.J.?"

"I like D.J."

"D.J. it is. Well, D.J., you'll find out soon enough that twenty-six is not old. Some days I feel like a child myself. Sometimes I still need someone to show me the way. Someone to tell me all about life before life gets here. You know, like someone who's already seen the movie, and can tell me what happens before I watch it."

"Doesn't your mommy and daddy tell you about all that life stuff?"

"My mama died when I was four. She had sugar diabetes. Not sure where my daddy is. He left soon after I was born." Jules didn't know they shared a common bond, and looked at Carnie peculiarly.

"Tell me something about your mommy. What was she like?"

"I don't remember much. I was little." She looked off into the distance. "I do remember her laugh. Her cookin'. I can still smell those biscuits in the oven, Her hands. I remember her soft hands."

"I wish I had a mommy."

"I do too." She turned her head and caught Jules looking at her. "I do too."

***

The next morning, school began. Carnie set up school in the dining room, and Cape was impressed. That was, until Carnie snapped off the television as Cape watched Sports Center in the den.

"No TV allowed when school's in session," she said. "Now get on up outta here. Git. Read a book. Do a crossword puzzle. Go for a walk. We need silence."

Cape didn't know what to say. He walked into the kitchen and looked around for something to do. Reading had never been a passion of his, and a crossword puzzle was something he was supposed to do when he turned eighty. He drove to the drugstore and purchased every baseball preview magazine they had available. He sat at the kitchen table, poring over the lineups of each Major League roster. He looked at the stats of the previous year's Independent League to become familiar with not only his teammates, but his opponents. He noticed Jose Vargas and Bo Reems, his former teammates in minor league ball, played for the Shreveport-Bosser Captains.

At noon, Carnie and Jules stopped for lunch. A turkey sandwich, an apple, sweet tea, and then time for recess. Jules grabbed her glove.

"Daddy, come throw with me."

Cape looked at Carnie as if to ask permission, and she nodded.

"Go ahead. She needs to exercise her body too. Work hard and you become a leader; be lazy and you never succeed. Proverbs."

"Preach on," Cape said with a smile.

Carnie sat on the back steps and watched Cape and Jules throw. Cape had worked with Jules and it showed—her catching skills had improved. Not only could she catch well, her throws to Cape were dead-on accurate.

School was over at 2:30, and Carnie retreated to her room to read the Bible. She dedicated thirty minutes every day to study the Good Book, and was quick to quote Scripture to whomever she felt needed it.

Jules usually went to her room to paint.

Carnie only had one vice. She loved to watch the Patti Richards Show at four every weekday afternoon. She'd become a fan of Patti in her college days, where she'd watch the show in the Student Center after class. After Carnie studied her Bible, she and Jules watched the show, armed with popcorn or boiled peanuts.

Patti Richards was a former news anchor from New York, and she featured human-interest stories that more times than not had Carnie sniffling and dabbing her eyes with a tissue by show's end. Jules thought watching Carnie's reactions was more entertaining than the show itself.

The rest of the week followed the pattern of the first day. School took place in the dining room, while Cape read baseball magazines in the kitchen and basically tried to keep quiet. Carnie may have been a playful gal on her off hours, but when school was in session, she was serious about doing work. Recess consisted of Cape and Jules throwing in the back yard.

On Friday of that first week, Cape tossed pop flies to Jules, trying to keep them away from the limbs of a massive oak whose arms snaked out in a wide swath across much of the back yard. After a while, Cape could tell Jules wanted him to challenge her, so he threw the ball through the limbs and leafs of the big oak.

Jules patiently waited, watching carefully for the ball's return flight to the ground. She lost sight of it, and wondered if the tree had swallowed it. Cape walked up beside her, looking for the ball as well. He spotted it wedged between the trunk and a limb near the top of the tree, forty feet high, too far up to climb.

"Well, looks like we're going to have to either wait on the next hurricane, or climb up and get that ball," Cape said. "He's not coming down on his own." He put his hands under Jules' armpits and lifted her. "I think I can toss you high enough. Just try not to let the limbs rip your face off on the way down."

Jules cackled. "Daddy, you're a silly man."

Carnie approached from the garage, holding a ball. She looked up at the snagged ball, and moved about until she had a clear view. She assumed a throwing position.

"What are you doing?" Cape asked.

"That ball ain't gonna climb down on its own," she said.

With that, she lowered her right shoulder, pointed her left arm toward the ball, and let go a missile. Her ball headed straight for the one wedged in the tree, and when it collided, it dislodged, both balls falling through the limbs to the ground.

"Nice arm," Cape said.

"Where'd you learn to throw like that?" asked Jules, rubbing her forehead with the side of her glove.

"I played shortstop for the Battery Creek High School softball team for four years. All-State the last two."

"Impressive," Cape said.

"How hard can you throw it?" Jules asked.

"Hard enough to strike your daddy out, that's for sure."

Cape smiled and Carnie laughed.

For Jules to have a teacher/nanny who could play ball was more than she could have asked for. Jules hadn't spent much individual time with any adult women other than Pauline. Grandma June, Kasey's mother, had Jules come visit on occasion. With Carnie, Jules found a strong woman, smart, energetic, and the spunk to handle any man.

Chapter Twenty-Four

The following Monday morning, twenty-two ball players reported to the stadium known as The Home of the Hilton Head Tiger Sharks. Seventeen of them had played for the team the previous season. The league rules required at least five rookies, and Cape was the oldest rookie there. Even though he had quite a strong baseball resume, he would have to prove himself all over again.

He had been taking swings at an amusement park batting cage and, after witnessing Carnie's talent throwing a baseball, began throwing with her on the weekends. With Jules he had to throw rather slowly, but with Carnie, he threw as hard as he cared to. She didn't hold back on her rocket throws to him. She was broad at the shoulder, her arms lean and muscular. She had the body that women at the gym would kill for, though Carnie had never so much as lifted a dumbbell.

The ride to the field was a short ten-minute jaunt. Hilton Head had invested a lot of money in their stadium, and the facility was only two years old. Players had a game room with big-screen televisions and a Play Station. They had leather couches and a stereo system. The locker room was spacious. Each player had a padded stool in front of his locker, made of oak. The stadium had been constructed with burgundy bricks, and a large blue awning covered most of the seating area, providing cover from the brutal sun during day games. The owners had hired a greenskeeper away from Sea Pines Golf Course to keep the field nicely manicured.

Cape eagerly stepped onto the field and stood alone, quietly studying it. He was back in territory he'd sworn he would never set foot on again. He smelled the fresh-cut grass, and felt a sense of rebirth, and a door opened to his past. He recalled being a kid and taking swings from his father; standing in the batter's box in high school with his family watching and cheering; in the on-deck circle smiling at Kasey. He saw himself at the one place he felt worthy of being, the one place he felt like he belonged.

The players sat in the dugout and the head coach, Steve Matlock, walked in. Two assistants walked in front of the dugout.

"Welcome, men," Coach Matlock said. "Are you fellas ready to play some ball?"

"Yes, sir," Cape answered, drawing odd looks from the others, who had simply nodded or looked at the coach.

The coach looked at Cape. "That's what I want to hear." He removed his cap and looked at the bill, rubbing his finger along the edge. "I believe we have a very strong collection of players. A good blend of veterans, rookies, and," looking at Cape, "some that might be considered both. Take a look on the wall behind you. You'll see the schedule for today's practice. I want to see a lot of effort and enthusiasm." He looked at his players, trying to gauge the desire in their eyes. "Okay, let's get cranking."

After the players stretched, they warmed up along the right field foul line. From there the group broke into stations: hitting off the tee, soft toss in the cage, and a drill called pepper, which involved a group of players in a semi-circle, tossing a ball to a batter twenty feet away.

The batter would take half swings at the pitches to improve his ability to make contact with the ball. Batting practice, which Cape looked forward to the most, soon followed.

He and four other players stood outside the roll-a-way cage that surrounded home plate. The other four started talking, leaving Cape to work on his stride and swing. Assistant coach Bump Willis, an ex-major leaguer from the '70s, tossed batting practice from behind the pitcher's screen forty feet from home plate. The rest of the team scattered about the field to grab the balls that had been hit and toss them to a player behind second base, who would place them in a large bucket.

A rookie named Brent batted first, and the sound of balls echoing off the bat soon filled the stadium. Brent hit well, mostly line drives to center and right. After he'd hit close to twenty-five balls, Bump yelled, "Get the hell out of there. Next batter."

Cape stepped into the box to bat right-handed. He adjusted his helmet, breathed deeply, took his two practice swings, and readied himself for Bump's throw. In a smooth stroke that looked effortless, he ripped the first pitch above the pitcher's screen and into centerfield. He hit fifteen or so balls before batting left-handed. He made contact with every pitch, and of the twenty-five hits, four cleared the outfield fence. He felt strong, the bat light in his hands. When Bump yelled for him to get out of the box, Cape placed his bat in his bag in the dugout, grabbed his glove, and jogged out to shallow left field.

Cape was the *man* at the plate, and he commanded attention from everyone on the field. The others could tell that if anyone had a shot being picked by a Major League team, Cape would be the guy. He had the tools and talent that would catch the eyes of scouts, and they knew that diminished their chances. They could see it in the way he handled the bat, the way he carried himself on the field. Just like in Rookie League, he was not just a teammate; he was competition.

After a week of practice and drills, they played an intra-squad game. Cape batted fourth in the lineup for his team, and he faced a pitcher from Ocala, Florida, named Hank Cuthbert. Hank had pitched for three seasons with the Milwaukee Brewers before tendinitis put him on the disabled list. After being sent to Double A for rehab, he never regained his velocity and was released. He worked out on his own for over a year while employed with Home Depot in Gainesville. Like Cape, he was giving the dream another go.

The first pitch to Cape was a fastball that caught him off guard. Batting practice was one thing, but live pitching was another. BP throws came in at fifty miles per hour, tops, and the ninety-mile-per-hour pitch by Hank looked like a bullet. Cape flailed at the second pitch, another fastball, fouling it just enough that it glanced off the catcher's face mask. Cape stepped out of the box, adjusted his helmet, and took a deep breath. When Hank's slider slipped under Cape's bat for strike three, Cape tapped his helmet with his bat and walked to the dugout, feeling completely overmatched. He struck out two more times in the game before grounding out to second on a ball he hit weakly.

The only time he had ever felt lost at the plate had been the stretch in Double A before Kasey showed up unexpectedly at his doorstep. That period was more a problem with hitting the wall mentally than physically. He tried to ignore the whispers. *Looks like Tarzan, plays like Jane.* Maybe he wasn't the guy to leapfrog them after all. Maybe he was just a washed up ballplayer who only *thought* he still had the skills to play the game.

They played three more intra-squad games that week, and Cape failed to get a hit in any of them. He popped out several times, and only once hit the ball out of the infield. He struck out six times. Right-handed or left, it didn't matter. His timing was off, and he couldn't adjust to the mix of fastballs and breaking balls.

Defensively, Cape was strong. He won the starting spot at shortstop, but the coaches thought his hitting was a liability, and penciled him to bat eighth in the lineup on opening day. His first step on his comeback trail was a miserable one. He'd never batted that low in the batting order in his life.

***

Carnie and Jules' grew closer each day. When school wasn't in session, and they weren't watching Patti on TV, they were in the backyard or the ball field at a park three miles away. Carnie threw batting practice to Jules, and gave her tips on hitting.

Cape had done the same thing before, but hearing it from a female made it easier for Jules to understand.

The pair walked the beach one morning, collecting shells, letting the water rush across their bare feet.

"Can we go swimming?" Jules asked.

"You must be crazy," Carnie said with a look of disbelief. "There ain't nothin' but bad stuff in that water. Sharks, jellyfish, stingrays, crabs. Shoot. This is as deep as I go. Besides, we're wearing shorts, not bathing suits." A wave rolled along the sand, the foam just enough to cover her ankles.

"Are you kidding? The ocean is awesome. We can swim and ride the waves. I was hoping you could teach me how to body surf."

"Body surf? D.J., to body surf, your body has to be in the water, and you won't catch mine out there. And besides, that water's dangerous. Waves pull you under, take you out to sea. Then you drown and get eaten by God knows what. Two weeks later they find what's left of you on the shore, the pelicans munching on your bones."

"Ewww. That's gross."

"Exactly. So why do it?"

They walked on.

"Do you miss your mother?" Jules asked. No one had ever asked Carnie that question.

Carnie looked out over the ocean as if she sought some philosophical answer, but it seemed rather foolish to her to long for someone who was never to return. "Sure do," and after a pause, "but spending time thinking about it is like blowing air into a balloon with a hole in it. Since you brought it up, I do sometimes wonder how my life would have turned out if Mama hadn't died. I know I'd have lived in my own house, with just Mama and my brothers. That right there would have been a good thing. I wonder what she would have taught me growing up. My Meemaw told me she was in the church choir and sang like the angels. Maybe I would have spent more time in the choir loft than on a hot, dusty ball field."

"But you liked playing softball, right?"

"Girl, what you talkin' 'bout? I loved it. But you never know which way life woulda gone had Mama been alive to raise me. What about you? You think about your mama?"

She nodded. "Yes. Mostly before I go to sleep. I wonder what it would be like to have her fix my hair, and show me what to wear. You know, girl stuff. Daddy does a lot for me, but he can't be a mother. Carson told me that I was the reason my mama died. Daddy said that's crazy."

"That *is* crazy. This Carson boy should be held down and beaten with a wire brush. If you want me to do it, you just say the word. Don't you pay that boy no mind."

Jules took Carnie by the hand. They walked on in silence, bound by circumstance and cruel fate.

On their way home, Carnie decided to stop in at Mason's Market. The aroma of fresh oregano, parsley, and fresh-baked bread surrounded them as soon as she and Jules walked through the front doors. Carnie wanted to prepare homemade vegetable soup for dinner.

The recipe was a family secret, one she'd learned from her grandmother when she was a teenager. One of her fondest memories was being in the kitchen, listening to her grandmother diligently instruct her on the precise details.

*

Mason's Market was a series of glass counters stocked with fresh fish, beef, and vegetables. The floral department was a colorful display of daisies, lilies, and wildflowers. The market was pricy, and a bit elitist, and it always seemed crowded. Carnie knew to stay on budget, and would limit her purchases to the vegetable section only.

She looked at the produce aisle the way a pianist might examine the keys of a piano before beginning a concerto. She sought out only the finest in celery, carrots, onions, peppers and potatoes. At home a rib roast waited in the fridge, not too lean, so as to have plenty of flavor. She had a slice of fatback in the freezer. The spice rack on the kitchen counter would be her finishing touch, so the vegetables were the only missing pieces of the masterpiece.

Carnie patiently showed Jules how to pick out the best vegetables, pointing out the color and texture that each needed to be considered worthy. Jules watched closely, and Carnie let her touch each vegetable to make sure she understood what to look for. Jules lifted a Vidalia onion, and one rolled off the stand and onto the floor.

Carnie bent down to pick it up and spotted a brown leather Prada wallet.

"Uh, oh, Jules, somebody lost their purse." She stood and glanced carefully at the finely crafted bag. "They are bound to have a fit if they don't find this thing. Come on, let's take it up front."

***

The registers were filled with customers, so Carnie and Jules decided to walk to the manager's office by the front entrance. They rounded a tall display of hanging baskets, Jules talking about how happy the person who lost the wallet would be to get it back. Carnie held it up and nodded.

"There it is!" a woman, donned in an elegant dark skirt and crème-colored silk blouse, shouted from in front of the manager's office. "There's my wallet!"

Those in line, and the cashiers, turned and looked at Carnie, bringing the store to a virtual halt.

A short man in a white shirt and blue tie walked hurriedly toward Carnie, the irate woman close behind.

"Excuse me, miss," he said. "Is that *your* wallet?"

"No, it isn't," Carnie said. "I found it on the floor in the vegetable section. I was bringing it to you guys 'cause I figured you'd know how to get it to the person that lost it."

"That's ridiculous," the woman said. "I didn't drop it. You must have stolen it from me."

Carnie's expression was one of disbelief. "Say what? I didn't steal your wallet."

"I am always so careful with it, so I'd know if I dropped it. Carl, would you please call the police? I want this woman arrested."

"The police are on their way now," a woman said, leaning her head out of the office door.

"She didn't steal it," Jules said. "I knocked an onion on the floor and she reached down to pick it up. When she did, she found your wallet."

"Little girl, please stay out of this," the woman said. "Carl, can't you do something?"

Carl looked uneasily at Carnie. "Ma'am, please give the wallet back to Mrs. Kornegay."

"With pleasure," Carnie said, handing it to her. "Come on, Jules, let's get out of this place."

"Not so fast," Carl said. "I'm sure the police will have some questions."

"You're kidding, right?"

"Look at her," Mrs. Kornegay said with an air of arrogance. "I bet she's been stealing her whole life. And she's made this innocent child an accomplice. It sickens me."

"Lady, I'm getting ready to sicken you if you don't shut that trap of yours. I was trying to be nice, to do what's right, and you make it look as though you caught me doing something wrong."

During the commotion, they didn't notice a petite, elderly woman walking up slowly with the use of a cane. "Carl, you let this young lady go."

"Hello, Mrs. Fields. I'm sorry, but I can't do that until the police get here."

"Nonsense," the lady said. "I saw what happened. You both should be thankful for her good intentions, and you should be embarrassed by the way you've treated her." With soft, brown eyes, she looked at Carnie. "Honey, I think we should take our business elsewhere. What do you say we leave?"

With that, Mrs. Fields, Carnie, and Jules left the store.

"Thank you, ma'am," Carnie said. "I appreciate what you did for me inside."

"Think nothing of it," Mrs. Fields responded. "I have no use for stupidity." She smiled at Carnie. "Have a wonderful day. And the same goes for you, dear child." She touched Jules on the hand, turned, and walked away.

On the ride home, Jules noticed a tear roll down Carnie's cheek and put the brakes on her bike. "Are you okay?" Carnie gave a quick nod. "Why did they think you took that lady's purse?"

Carnie slowed her bike and circled until she was beside Jules. "You don't need to concern yourself with that, D.J."

"But you were only trying to help."

"I know."

"But why would that woman say you've been stealing your whole life? She doesn't even know you."

"Someday you'll understand." She began pedaling again. "And maybe by then, this kind of stupid stuff won't happen anymore."

***

Opening Day for the Tiger Sharks would take place in Shreveport, Louisiana, the first of a twelve-game road trip that would carry Cape throughout the southeast.

The players were due at the stadium at eight in the morning to board the bus. Carnie made breakfast: eggs, grits, sausage, and toast with blackberry preserves. She sensed the sadness in her housemates as they picked at their food. Cape looked at Jules and smiled. Jules looked away, trying not to cry. It would be the first time they'd spent more than a night apart.

"I'm going to call you tonight. I've got my cell phone if you need me, okay?" Jules nodded, shifting her eggs around the plate. "I bet you and Carnie will be so busy, you won't even miss me."

Carnie eyed Jules from the sink, a silent hint that it was time for Jules to go to her bedroom.

She excused herself, walked to her room, and soon returned to the kitchen table. She stood beside Cape and handed him the small blue gift bag that Carnie had helped her prepare.

"What's this?" Cape asked.

"Open it."

Carnie dried her hands with a dishtowel and watched Cape remove two blue plastic wristbands that were inscribed with the words, "Chase Your Dream".

"Jules, this is awesome." He slid one over his left hand and Jules did the same. "I'll never take this off." He hugged her.

"Maybe every time you look at the bracelet, you'll remember this is your dream."

"No, Half-pint, it's our dream."

"Let's say a prayer to that," Carnie said, and for several minutes she prayed fervently for God to keep Cape and Jules safe in His powerful arms, leading them together down the road to not only New York, but also to salvation.

Chapter Twenty-Five

Twelve games into the season, Cape was batting a meager .189. He felt uncomfortable at the plate, swinging at bad pitches, showing little patience. The Tiger Sharks were glad to be finished with the road trip, and Cape was even happier to be home for a two-week home stand. He could spend his days with Jules, minus the class-time hours that Carnie demanded, of course, and at night the girls would be in the stands watching him play.

Jules wore a teal and white Tiger Sharks jersey to her dad's first home game. They were hosting the El Paso Diablos. Her jersey had Cape's number, 7, emblazoned on the back. Carnie wore blue jeans and a white knit top. They sat near the first base dugout in a section designated for players' families and friends. More often than not, the seats were occupied by tanned legs and cleavage—the players' girlfriends, or girls the players might have met the night before. Surrounded by ladies who had come to impress those on, and off, the field, the wide-eyed child and her spunky nanny stuck out like smashed thumbs. Sneakers and flip-flops among pearls and heels.

Two blonde girls in sundresses sat behind Carnie and Jules, and they snickered and rolled their eyes at the pair.

"Must be giving away game tickets in Bluffton today," one whispered.

"Bus tickets sold separately," the other one said with a laugh.

Carnie turned her head, tempted to speak, but took a deep breath instead.

Jules had brought her glove in case a foul ball came her way, but at that moment, she used it to hold a snow cone. The Sharks took infield, and Jules watched her father run from the dugout to shortstop. She had never seen Cape in a uniform, and she jumped up and cheered so wildly her cherry snow cone ended up in her lap. She watched Cape field ground balls while Carnie scrubbed her white shorts with a handful of napkins.

"D.J.," Carnie said, "I sure wish you'd worn red shorts today. Would have at least blended a little better with your snow cone."

"I'm sorry, Carnie."

"It's okay. Next game we'll wrap you up head to toe with paper towels."

Jules smiled. "Good idea."

She looked around the stadium, and thought it was the greatest place in the world. Her father just had to be a superstar to play in such a nice ballpark. The fact that there were only 700 fans in attendance did nothing to change her opinion. Compared to the small crowd at her tee-ball games, the Tiger Shark audience was massive. Though Hilton Head had sunk a lot of money into the 3,000-seat stadium, it was hard to get large crowds to attend. Most were retirees, and a few were vacationers who had most likely gotten tired of removing sand from their shorts.

The game began, the Shark mascot dancing behind the backstop. In a teal and black costume that looked to be a spandex experiment gone horribly wrong, the large-headed shark shook his tail to "I Feel Good". Jules clapped her hands and laughed when the mascot did a split in front of the umpire.

Cape didn't bat until the bottom of the third. The pitcher for the Diablos hadn't allowed a baserunner. Jules knew her father would change that. She watched him as he waited on the on-deck circle, and she saw him rub the wristband she'd given him.

"Did you see him?" asked Jules.

"You know he did that for you," Carnie replied.

Jules stood, rubbed her wristband, and smiled at her father. He nodded, just enough to let her know he saw her.

Cape stepped into the box, feeling uptight. His struggles at the plate were bad enough, but now his daughter watched him, and she was the reason he was back in the game. When he'd played in front of Kasey, or his family, he never worried about them being in the stands. In fact, he couldn't wait to show them what he could do to a baseball. With Jules, he felt an unfamiliar pressure not to disappoint.

Cape watched the first pitch go down the middle of the plate. He swung at the second pitch, grounding out easily to third.

"That's okay, Daddy," Jules yelled as Cape jogged to the dugout. "You'll hit a home run next time."

The girls behind them laughed. "Not swinging like that he won't," one commented.

Carnie became agitated with them, but she bit her bottom lip and recited a Bible verse under her breath.

Cape struck out his second at-bat, and the girls said more derisive comments. Carnie felt heat building in the back of her neck, and rubbed her hand against it while taking a deep breath. She looked down the left field line so that Jules couldn't see or hear her murmuring her thoughts about those smart asses.

In the eighth inning, the Diablos held a 3–2 lead. The Tiger Sharks had two outs and Cape was on-deck. The catcher, Kris Adamle, doubled to right-center. The crowd cheered, and "Start Me Up" by the Stones cranked through the speakers. When Cape stepped up to bat, Jules stood and yelled, "Come on, Daddy, hit one out of the stadium."

Batting left-handed, he ripped the first pitch deep down the right field line, his best swing of the season. The right fielder gave chase, and Cape sprinted to first. But the ball curved just to the right of the foul pole and hooked into the stands. Back at the plate, he worked the count to three balls and two strikes before swinging at an eye-level pitch, missing it completely for out number three.

"Oh, please," said the girl sitting directly behind Carnie. "This guy sucks."

Jules lowered her head, and Carnie knew she'd heard the comments. Carnie stood and turned around. "Girl, you better shut that lip-gloss mouth of yours, 'cause I'm tired of hearing it. You got no idea what it takes to play this game."

"I suppose you do." She flipped her hair off her shoulder and adjusted the strap of her mauve and white pastel dress.

"I *know* I do. I bet you ain't never held a bat in your hand. Why don't you get off your skinny butt and try it?" Carnie pointed her finger at the girl. "And another thing, you best watch what you say because you never know if the player you're raggin' has a family member in hearing distance of your big mouth." The girl took a sip of her drink through a straw and pretended that she wasn't embarrassed. "Yeah, you better keep sippin' before I let you sip on my fist." She sat back down and saw the sad expression on Jules' face. "Don't you pay those girls no mind."

The Sharks lost by one. After the game, Jules and Carnie waited outside the dugout. Cape waved them past the security guard and Jules ran into her father's arms. Cape tried to hide his frustration.

"You played great, Daddy."

Cape kissed her on the cheek.

"What game was she watching?" Kris asked pitcher Travis Earle as they walked by.

"What'd that boy say?" asked Carnie. She pointed her finger at Kris. "Keep your comments to yourself, shorty."

"Easy, killer." Cape took Carnie by her belt loop. "Don't let comments about me get you riled. I'm a big boy. I can handle it."

Cape picked up Jules and held her in his arms. "Thanks for coming, Half-pint."

"You'll hit a home run next game. I just know it."

***

In the locker room, the smell of sweat and musty towels hung heavy in the air. Steam from the showers wafted in, disappearing as it met the air blowing from the air conditioner vents along the ceiling. Cape sat on a stool in front of his locker, a towel around his waist and another around his neck. He'd hoped the hot water would release some of the disappointment, but it really didn't make a difference.

Kris walked up to his locker and rubbed deodorant under his arms. His wet hair hung above his eyes in ringlets.

"So, what's the story with the black girl?" Kris asked. "You two got a little jungle fever thing going on?"

"What?" Cape asked. "What are you talking about?"

"A little brown sugar? Is that it? I bet she's a wildcat."

Cape stood and faced Kris.

"Don't you talk about her like that. Show her some respect."

"Admit it. You're tapping that thing, aren't you?"

"You're an idiot, Adamle."

***

Carnie put Jules to bed before Cape got home. He sat on the porch steps that overlooked the creeks. Bullfrogs sang in the darkness, and the mild night air felt good against his skin. Stars twinkled above the old oak, carving a silhouette of gnarled limbs beneath the sky. Lightning bugs rose from the ground like celestial creatures in search of Heaven's gate, each dim glow of light emitting a calmness to the land. The Lowcountry was showing off her beauty, but it was completely lost on Cape, who couldn't stop thinking about his miserable performance in front of Jules.

Carnie walked out the back door and sat beside him. They looked out at the dark water, both silent in an awkward moment where neither seemed sure whether to speak.

"Low tide," she finally said. "Good time for gigging flounder."

"You've gigged flounder?"

"Growin' up, we didn't have much money, so we ate fish seven days a week and twice on Sundays. There was an endless supply, and it was free. We just had to catch it."

Cape looked into the darkness. "Carnie, I've been thinking. I might have taken on something I can't handle. I'm not that nineteen-year-old kid anymore who could hit anything that came my way without even thinking about it. Now I think too much at the plate instead of letting my instincts take over."

"It's still early in the season, and you've been away from the sport for years. You got a pile of games left to get your groove back. Jules is bustin' over this whole comeback thing. When I tucked her in tonight, she talked about how she can't wait to watch you play for the Yankees."

"It's tough enough trying to play for the Sharks, much less the Yankees. I suck at the plate. I've got no confidence in my swing. I don't know if it's the long layoff, or if something's changed in my stroke. I hit the ball great in BP. But in the game, I got no clue."

"You got to relax. You look all tight and twisted at the plate. Ain't no way you're gonna hit swinging like that. Stop pressing."

"You know, hitting a baseball was what I did best. And against the kind of pitching in this league, I should be ripping the cover off the ball. It's bad enough that I can't hit, but knowing that Jules is watching makes it worse."

"There's your problem."

"What do you mean?"

"You're more worried about letting down Jules than takin' care of business. You can't think like that. You got to go up there like you're Mr. Bad-Ass. When you strut up to the plate, you go up there knowing you own the pitcher."

Cape shrugged his shoulders. "I used to own the pitchers. Every one of them. Now they own me."

"There you go again. If they own you, it's your choice, not theirs. It's got to be about pride. You can't seriously think those pitchers are better than you. Deep inside you, your pride validates who you are. From what I hear, you were as good as anyone who *ever* played the game. So stop your cryin'. This ain't the Little League anymore, and your mama ain't here to blow your nose and wipe your tears. Remember, weeping may endure for a night, but joy cometh in the morning. Psalms."

"This has nothing to do with joy coming in the morning. It's about trying to understand why I can't hit."

"Well, you say it used to be easy. Now, all of a sudden it's not? Put your trust in yourself, and trust in the

Lord. I can do all things through Him who strengthens me. Philippians. You might want to memorize that one."

"With the way things are going, that might not be a bad idea."

"What you think it was like when I played softball, having rich girls from Beaufort and Hilton Head laughing at the glove I used, or the holes in my cleats? I had nothing but pride going for me. And the same best apply to you. You got a girl inside that house who thinks you're a baller. You're the king, baby. You're everything in her eyes."

"That's what's makes this so hard. I know if I don't make it, she's going to be devastated. I think she wants it more than me."

"Then make it more important for you. Hasn't this been something you've wanted your whole life?"

"Yes, but..."

"But nothin'. Here you are with a second chance. So, man up, and take care of your business. How many people you think get to chase their dream? Twice?"

"Are you chasing yours? Is this it, teaching Jules, and cooking and cleaning around the house? I don't see you chasing anything."

"You got no right to tell me about dreams. Spoiled white boy. Everything handed to you. What you take for granted every day is what I chase. A home with stability. My Meemaw raised us the best that she knew how, but nobody gave us nothin'. My older brothers started runnin' with a bad crowd, and we had boys coming in and out our house, on the run from the police, from gang members. We had to fish for our dinner, and wear the same clothes over and over. Did you? No."

"Look, I'm sorry. I had no idea."

"Course you had no idea. Now I get to sleep in a bed without worrying about the police knocking on the door. When I wake up tomorrow morning, food will be in the pantry, in the refrigerator. You talk about a dream. I'm in mine right now."

"Carnie, I'm sorry."

"Dreams mean different things to different people. And you best remember that."

She stood and walked in the house.

***

Cape looked up at the stars, then walked into Jules' bedroom. The light from the hallway carved a path from the darkness and snuck across her face as she slept. He knelt beside her bed. He noticed something thin held between her fingers, and slid it gently from her grip. It was a photo of him and Kasey after a Swamp Hogs game. They were beside the dugout, Kasey sitting behind him as he stood, her arms wrapped around his shoulders, her legs crossing in front of his thighs. Cape looked to his left, his hands holding Kasey's calves.

She wore his hat, backwards, and they looked lost in their own world, two kids in love.

He removed the picture from Jules' fingers and set it on her nightstand. Then, as he pulled the covers up, he noticed she held his glove in her arms, under her chin. He watched her sleep, brushed her hair. It reminded him of the nights he'd watched her sleeping in her crib, listening to her breathe.

When he'd chased his dream with Kasey, it was a magical ride, at least until that fateful day. But on that day he'd been given Jules, a rare gift indeed. And so, there in the dark, Cape vowed softly to his daughter that he would not let her down.

***

At batting practice the next afternoon, Cape had a different air about him. He attacked each pitch with more purpose and more swagger. Before, he'd hit the ball fairly well in batting practice, but now, he knocked pitch after pitch to the outfield wall or over the fence.

After BP was finished, and the batting cage moved from behind home plate, the Sharks went to the dugout to let the Diablos take infield. The players passed the time by talking. Kris recounted the wild time he and Travis had the night before with the girls who'd sat behind Carnie and Jules. Cape walked in, rubbing his face with a towel.

"You planning on getting some hits today?" Kris asked.

Cape saw the others watching him for a response. "I plan on getting hits every day."

"Well, planning and doing are two different things. In BP you put us all to shame, but once the ump yells 'play ball', you go in the tank."

"Well, it's a new day. You just try to keep up."

Cape had trouble curbing his energy, and ran a dozen sprints down the right field line. Twenty minutes later, the Diablos were done taking infield, and it was the Sharks' turn. Cape heard Jules yelling his name as he sprinted to shortstop. "I Won't Back Down" by Tom Petty cranked out over the sound system, and he bobbed like a banty rooster.

"Hey, pretty boy, did you have too many Red Bulls today?" third baseman Manny Fuentes asked.

"Nope. Just loving the fact that we get to play baseball. How many guys get to say that?"

"Well, I'd be a little happier if they'd pay us a few extra bucks for playing. I don't know about you, but I'm tired of bologna and white bread. Steak and lobster, my man. That's what I'm looking for."

"What do you say we hit our way out of this ballpark, this league, and jump to the majors? We do that, steak and lobster won't be far away."

Manny looked at Cape. "You look intense. Are you alright?"

"Never better. Just ready to play some ball."

When Cape came up to bat in the bottom of the second, the game was tied at one. Manny had gotten a leadoff triple, Travis walked, and they had two outs. On the first pitch, Cape, batting left-handed, faked a bunt and Travis stole second. The pitch was a called strike. He worked the count to two balls and two strikes. The pitcher threw a hard fastball, knee-high, and Cape got hold of it and sent it deep to centerfield. He watched the ball as he sprinted to first. The ball hit the top of the backdrop far beyond the centerfield wall, and Cape had hit his first home run in seven years. He trotted quickly, his eyes straight ahead so as not to show up the pitcher, and when he rounded third, Manny and Travis waited behind home plate. They tapped helmets with him after he removed his.

Kris sat in the dugout, arms folded. "It's about time," he called out.

You had better get used it, Cape wanted to shout.

Jules tugged so hard on Carnie's green blouse it appeared she might rip it off completely. She waved at Cape as he headed to the dugout. He pointed at her and smiled. He also gave a quick nod to Carnie, who had challenged his manhood, his self-esteem, and his lack of motivation.

He felt as if God had sent him the perfect person to take care of Jules, as well as to keep him focused. Nothing romantic, but someone to provide encouragement when needed, a butt kicking when needed.

He went three-for-four for the game, knocking in two more runs with a double in the eighth. Each time he stepped to the plate he showed that confidence, that swagger, that had made opposing pitchers fear him.

After the game, Cape took Jules and Carnie to the IHOP to celebrate his resurrection.

Carnie refused to let him get too cocky. "You know, you wouldn't have popped out in the fifth inning if you hadn't dropped your hands when you started your swing."

"Thanks, coach, I'll try and remember that next time," he said with a grin.

"Never rest on your laurels. Stay hungry."

"Speaking of hungry, how many pancakes are you planning on eating?" He looked at her stack of three, plus two of Jules' that she'd snatched.

"Worry about your appetite and I'll worry about mine." She smiled at Jules. "Right, D.J.?"

"Right."

"How come you never talk about your softball days?" Cape asked after taking a sip of iced tea.

"What's to tell?"

"That's what we want to know."

Carnie looked around and shrugged her shoulders as if contemplating whether to divulge a well-kept secret. "Well, let's see. I was All-State my junior and senior years. Had scholarship offers from over twenty colleges but wasn't exactly a bookworm. Schools all backed off because they didn't think I would qualify. So I signed with North Florida J.C. I figured I would get my two-year degree and then the big-time programs would come after me."

"So how'd you do at North Florida?" Cape asked.

"Never played an inning. My Meemaw died in October of my freshman year. I had to come home for the funeral. Never went back."

"Why not?" Jules asked.

"I had to take care of my brothers. I got a job with Marriott and took classes at a local technical school. Got financial aid. Got my degree in Childhood Ed."

"Do you think about what you missed?" Cape asked. "Not playing college ball, I mean."

She shook her head. "Too many other things to worry about. If God meant for me to play, he'd a worked it out. Just like you. God's got a great plan for you. You're going to play for the New York Yankees."

"The New York Yankees," Jules affirmed.

"To the New York Yankees," Cape said.

He tapped his glass against Jules' and Carnie's.

The Cape Train was leaving the station, with its engineer barely tall enough to look down the track.

Chapter Twenty-Six

By the time the Sharks reached the All-Star break, Cape was batting .349. He'd regained his power swing, and was second in the league with sixteen home runs in forty-eight games. His play at shortstop was flawless. Pete Bennett contacted the Braves, the White Sox, and the Devil Rays. He also spoke with Yankee management. They were aware that the Santee Stallion was back in the game, and told him they'd monitor his progress. Cape's teammates knew it was simply a matter of time before a Major League team picked up his contract. And with him regaining his mastery at the plate, there was no way the Sharks could hang on to him.

And they were right.

***

One Wednesday morning in early July, Cape slept late, trying his best to recover from a four-game series with Wichita and the 2,400-mile trip on the team bus.

Carnie and Jules slipped away on their bikes, and Carnie's bike held a crate on the back. She carried bottled water, crackers, and fruit. She also brought weaving tools to make sweetgrass baskets, and a throw blanket to sit on. Jules carried two gloves and a baseball in her book bag.

Whenever they took to the beach, Jules always made Carnie ride to the Leamington Lighthouse, which stood on what once had been known as the Leamington Plantation. It was the only true lighthouse on the island. Jules had developed a fascination because it reminded her of the one Kasey had painted. Jules liked to rub her hand across the base of the tall structure, and she'd pretend it was the one her mother had created with her paintbrush.

After their pilgrimage to the lighthouse, they headed to the beach. The pair rode down a quiet avenue, under a tunnel of giant oaks with twisted, draping limbs. The sun slipped through small openings in the trees, painting the asphalt in random splashes of light. The coastal breeze made Jules' hair dance along her shoulder, and gave her a sense of freedom.

Carnie spread a blanket on the warm sand while Jules removed the crate from Carnie's bike. The beach was busy with bicyclists and joggers. Children built sand castles and splashed in the surf.

Jules and Carnie decided to search the water's edge for shark's teeth.

"Do people ever find whale's teeth on the beach?" Jules asked, trying to rub sand off a tiny black shell that resembled a tooth.

"What do you mean, like Free Willie, the killer whale?"

"Did you know killer whales aren't really whales? They're part of the dolphin family."

"Girl, the only fish I care to know about are the ones I can catch in a creek."

"Wouldn't it be cool to see one swimming out there?" She pointed to the water, squinting as the sun cast a shimmer along the top.

"As long as I'm on land, he can do back flips for all I care."

After tossing the baseball, they spent two hours sitting on the blanket, Carnie teaching Jules how to make baskets, something her grandmother had taught her when she was a young girl.

When the girls' fingers grew tired from making the baskets, Jules was able to coax Carnie to walk into the ocean. Though that meant only knee-deep water, it was an accomplishment. Carnie would squeeze Jules' hand with each wave that raced toward her kneecaps. Jules laughed with every squeal Carnie let fly as the foam waves rushed past them to the shore.

Times like those, they grew closest. In many ways, Carnie became a mother to Jules, and Jules loved it. She decided Carnie was the coolest woman in the world.

***

Cape woke around mid-morning, and with the girls at the beach, he used the quiet time to pay bills and balance his checkbook. After he finished, he walked out on the back porch shirtless, wearing plaid shorts, his face unshaven and his hair tussled.

Cape was a popular figure with the retirees. The men loved to talk baseball, and their wives simply loved to look at him. His broad shoulders and muscular arms enticed his elderly neighbor, Mrs. Farnsworth, to work in her yard most every day, just hoping for a glimpse. He was flawless and ruggedly handsome, and women of all ages were drawn to him, though he was oblivious to it. His focus was on two things, and two things only: Jules, and baseball. Anything else was frivolous and so was not necessary.

Cape waved to Mrs. Farnsworth. The phone rang, and he removed his cell from his pocket. He noticed it was Pete, who rarely called just to pass the time.

"Mr. Baseball! What are you doing?"

"I'm sailing on my yacht, Pete. I've got a crew of bikini-clad girls manning the sails."

"Well, turn the boat around and head back to port. Time to pack your bags, my man."

"Why? Have I been picked up?"

"You bet your country ass."

"By who?"

"The White Sox. They purchased your contract this morning. They want to send you to Class A ball for the rest of the season. If you do well, then they'll want you to report to Birmingham."

"That's Double A."

"You are correct. Cape, you keep your nose to the grindstone and I'll negotiate my tail off so as to get you in Triple A by the end of next season, and with any luck, the big leagues within two years."

The thought of making it to the majors within two years, putting him there by the age of thirty, made Cape pump his fist in the air.

When the girls came in from the beach, hungry and thirsty, Cape waited for them on the front steps.

He smiled at Carnie. "I do believe you're getting a tan."

"Funny, white boy. Maybe you should walk around the yard more often with your shirt off. You look like a manatee."

"Good one. Anyways, I've got some news for you sweet ladies." He pulled Jules on his lap. She held a sweetgrass basket she'd made.

"What is it?" She looked at him with those Kasey-blue eyes.

"As of this moment, I'm no longer a shark. I'm a dash."

"A who?" asked Carnie.

"A dash?" asked Jules.

"You might know them as the Single A affiliate of the Chicago White Sox."

"Wait," Jules asked, no authority on Minor League baseball, "does that mean you're gonna play for another team?"

"It sure does. The White Sox organization bought my contract. If I do well, I could be playing for the actual White Sox within a couple of years."

"That's great, Daddy. Your dream's coming true."

"It's certainly a step in the right direction."

"Does that mean we have to move? What about Carnie? We have to take her with us."

"Well, for the next six weeks I will be living in Winston-Salem, North Carolina. It's not too far from here, so you guys will have to wing it without me for a while. Then, if all goes well, we will probably move to Birmingham in the spring." He looked at Carnie. "You will come with us, won't you? You're family now."

"There's nothing holding me here. You just worry about getting us to Chicago, and Jules and I will take care of the rest. You get me to Chicago, and I'll go on the Patti Richards show. Wonder if she'd let me teach her how to make sweetgrass baskets."

The possibilities.

***

Cape moved into a starting role in Winston-Salem. The Dash were playing the last of a three-game series against Lynchburg. They'd sent their shortstop down to Kannapolis and the lower A affiliate to make room for Cape. That gave Cape six weeks to show the White Sox organization that they were smart to sign him. He had his eyes on Birmingham, two levels away from the Major League.

The hitting groove he'd settled into at Hilton Head continued in Winston-Salem, and the step up in pitching talent did nothing to slow him down. If anything, it made him more determined. After twenty-four games, Cape was batting .404. He batted cleanup, and opposing pitchers walked him a lot for fear that he'd either send one off their chins, or out of the stadium.

The *Charlotte Observer* learned Cape was playing for the Dash, and sent a reporter to interview him. They wrote a two-page, feel-good story about Cape's journey back from tragedy, complete with photos of Cape as a youngster, and of he and Kasey, and of him playing with the Dash. His parents collected every copy they could find. Randy even made the ninety-minute drive to Rock Hill and emptied out the stand at a Travel Mart off the interstate.

***

Carnie and Jules stayed busy: the lighthouse, the beach, baseball, and bikes. On Labor Day, Carnie took Jules to visit her family in nearby Beaufort, where her two aunts and brothers lived. The Holy Tabernacle Church hosted a barbeque, and Carnie's aunt, Cynthia, invited them to come along. Carnie made McClellanville Lump Crabcakes, the spicy aroma of Old Bay Seasoning drifting from the backseat of her car as she drove.

Carnie didn't realize she'd be nervous for Jules, but she was. Carnie knew the sting of prejudice, and she didn't want Jules to experience it. She didn't want other children to experience it either, and she wasn't crazy enough to think that they hadn't, or wouldn't in the future. But Jules was such a delicate flower, a heart too gentle. Jules had become a part of her, and she wanted to protect the little girl as much as possible. Of course Carnie knew it would be foolish to think she could hide Jules away from the cruelties of the world, but she could try and put it off as long as possible.

The day was hot and humid, the sky hazy to the point where it hid the massive white clouds from view.

Carnie wore a black and white patterned dress, the hem just above her kneecaps.

"You look very pretty," Jules said as they walked.

"Thanks, D.J. I'm just trying not to fall in these shoes. Lord knows my feet were made for sandals and sneakers. Dress shoes and me don't go together very well."

Jules wore khaki shorts and a blue knit golf shirt. She'd convinced Carnie to let her wear sneakers instead of sandals. She felt a little uneasy; she hadn't been around other children in some time. The only white child there, Jules received a few peculiar looks, though she had no idea why. Her mind had no predisposition to black or white, even though she'd wondered if the wallet ordeal at the Mason's Market actually had anything to do with the color of Carnie's skin.

Carnie held Jules' hand and walked her to a group of kids playing softball in a field with a chicken-wire backstop. The children were using an old wooden bat and a softball with loose seams. Carnie asked them if Jules could play. A petite girl named Amber, her hair done in cornrows and colorful ribbons, took Jules by the hand.

"Play on our team," Amber said.

Jules looked shyly at Carnie. "Go ahead. Go have fun. I'll be over by the pecan trees helping set up dinner." She nudged Jules with her hand. "Go. It's going to be okay."

Jules and the others played ball while Carnie kept an eye on them. It didn't take long to see that Jules fit right in. They didn't want to stop the game when it was time to eat.

After dinner, Jules walked up to Carnie's aunts.

"Thank you for the food, Miss Cynthia," Jules said, a small dash of barbeque sauce on her chin.

"Baby, it was great havin' you here. You come back anytime and we'll fill your belly and your soul as well."

"Yes, ma'am," Jules said with a giggle.

Chapter Twenty-Seven

The bus pulled into the parking lot of the Myrtle Beach Courtyard Marriott located near Barefoot Landing, a massive collection of shops, restaurants, and nightspots. Traffic was heavy, eight lanes of tourists in search of sand, surf, and shopping. Cape stepped off the bus, the first time he'd been in Myrtle Beach since he'd played for the Pelicans. He filled his lungs with the salty ocean air, squinting his eyes against the sun beating down on the pavement.

His parents planned to attend the game. From what his mom said, half of Santee was coming along too. It would be his first chance to play in front of his parents since he'd hung up his cleats when Jules was born, and he was anxious to prove he could still play.

The team had three hours before they had to head to the Pelicans' stadium. Cape took a shuttle to Barefoot Landing. None of the other players cared to come along, though Cape was kind of glad they didn't. He wanted to retrace the paths he and Kasey had taken along the Boardwalk, making plans for their future. Plans that were never fulfilled.

He walked into The Not So Starving Artist Shop, where he'd bought Kasey a painting of Daufuskie Island. The store was filled with artwork of the ocean, coastal creeks, and lighthouses. Cape found a four-by-six framed painting of a sea turtle for Jules. For Carnie, he found a photograph of two women making sweetgrass baskets on Meeting Street in Charleston.

At Doc's Seafood, he ordered the seafood platter, grilled of course, and a large sweet tea. He looked over a copy of *The Sun News* and read an article about the upcoming game with the Pelicans. The article mentioned that former player Cape Jeffers was returning to the Grand Strand. It felt surreal to see his name in the sports section again. He considered himself a lucky man, but only in that he had a second chance. Luck would not be needed any longer, because it all boiled down to how good a ballplayer he was. In his heart, he knew he was the best.

He had finished his third glass of tea when he glanced out the window toward the pond under the boardwalk. He saw a woman leaning against the wooden rail, watching the turtles surface in the pond. Cape had already paid his tab, so he dropped a five on the table for the waitress and took off out the door.

When he approached, she didn't notice him. He touched her on her arm.

"Angela."

Her eyes grew wide. "Oh my God. Cape, what are you doing here?"

"That was going to be my question for you."

She hugged him tightly, her perfume leaving a delicate scent on his shirt. Her smile was as warm as the night they'd shared nachos in the Winston-Salem hotel nine years ago. She looked even more beautiful than he remembered.

"I'm on my lunch break."

"Break from what? From where?"

She pointed behind the row of shops. "See that high rise? It's the Ocean Park Resort, built last year. I'm the manager."

"You said you wanted to be near the ocean, right?"

"Well, that requires a qualified yes. It's great to be at the beach, but it's not all fun and games. These people are on vacation, not me. While they're off skipping along the beachfront for sand dollars, I'm making sure there are enough clean towels, spare toothbrushes, cleaning ladies, and *USA Today* newspapers. They pay to be pampered, and it's my job to make sure they are. A quite glamorous position indeed. Impressed?"

"Very."

The ocean breeze blew her blonde hair across her face and she brushed it away. Cape had forgotten how her soft emerald eyes sparkled when she smiled. He had trouble staring into them without forgetting his own name.

"You must be playing the Pelicans tonight."

"Yes, ma'am. Seven o'clock. Going to be weird playing for the visiting team."

"I knew you played for the Dash."

"How?"

"Duh. I'm a baseball nut, remember?" She tapped him playfully on the arm, and he moved closer. He again smelled the soft fragrance of her perfume when the breeze turned his way.

"How could I forget? Still wear that Yankees cap?"

"You know it. There's a lot of Yankee fans here. Northern transplants. So I've got company now." Their forearms touched. "How long are you in town?"

"It's a three-game series."

"I've followed your comeback on the Internet just a little. Let me see if I can recall any of your stats." She took a deep breath. "Highest batting average on the team. Averaging a home run every three games. Averaging a run batted in *per* game. But, you're a little low in the number of triples. What's up with that?"

Cape smiled in disbelief. "Good Lord. You're a psycho."

"Psychoville is my hometown." Her laugh was soft and raspy. "Following the success and failure of guys chasing a ball around a field. How pathetic is that?"

"Sounds like you need a hobby."

"Speaking of your comeback, I'm so sorry about your wife."

"Thanks. It's been bumpy to say the least. But I've got a terrific daughter. Her name is Jules, and it was her idea for me to try this crazy comeback. It feels great to be playing again, but it's tough being away from her."

"Is she in town?"

"No, she's with her nanny in Hilton Head. My parents are coming tonight though. Hey, would you like to come?"

"I'm sorry but I can't."

Cape looked out across the water. "It's okay. No big deal."

"No, I'd really like to. It's just that there's a luau tonight at the resort and I have to be there."

"Cooking the pig, are you?"

"Something like that. But I'm off tomorrow. Would you like to eat lunch or something?"

"That'd be great. Should I meet you here with the turtles?"

"How about I pick you up at your hotel? Where are you staying?"

"The Courtyard. A mile down Highway 17."

"Pick you up at noon?"

"I'm eating breakfast with my parents, so noon will be perfect."

"Well, I've got to get back to work." She hugged Cape. "It's great to see you again."

He thought the same.

***

The bus pulled in front of the stadium, where a crowd of nearly 200 waited, led by Cape's parents. When he stepped off the bus, they clapped and cheered. Cape and his teammates had not expected a warm welcome at an opponent's stadium. Pauline and Randy gave Cape a quick hug as he passed. He saw Todd Blakeley, Curtis Wingo, and Jevan Altekruse, guys from his Santee high school team. Coach Steck smiled and Cape nodded his appreciation. Aunts, uncles, neighbors: it was Welcome Home week, the road trip version.

The first pitch was thrown, the game underway. In the top of the first, with two outs and a runner on first, Cape doubled off the wall in right center. From the loud and enthusiastic cheers coming from the stands, it was obvious the folks from Santee were right proud of their hometown hero.

The Dash lost 5–2, but Cape finished two-for-four with two doubles. He also made an amazing, over-the-shoulder catch in shallow left field that not only brought the fans to their feet, but the players. Cape was riding high and loving every pitch, every play.

After the game, Cape went with family and friends to the Calabash Seafood Buffett. Cape's uncle, Pembroke, who was one butterfly shrimp shy of three hundred pounds, did some major damage to the restaurant's food supply. It reminded Cape of his high school days, when family and friends would flock to O'Reilly's in Santee to rehash the game and spend time together. It meant a great deal to him that they came. From the parking lot, he called Jules to describe the reunion scene, and let Randy and Pauline talk with her for a few moments before he hung up.

***

Cape stood at the lobby door ten minutes before noon. Wearing light blue shorts and a white polo shirt, he had a nervous excitement about him, something he hadn't felt since Kasey was alive. Before, he considered the mere thought of another girl to be cheating on her memory. Not only that, the only females he'd really talked to in seven years were either related to him, or named Carnie Mack.

Angela pulled up in a late model red Honda Civic. She wore brief khaki shorts that revealed long, smooth legs obviously splashed by the summer sun. Her purple blouse made her eyes appear a deeper shade of green. She looked stunningly sexy, but in a sweet, adorable kind of way.

"Hop in," she said.

He smiled at her when he got in the car. "What's up? How's your day going?" *What an original question,* he thought. *Real smooth.*

"Good. Still riding my morning high from jogging the beach at sunrise. While you were sleeping like a baby, I was running five miles."

"At sunrise, huh?"

"Yep. Want to run with me tomorrow morning?"

"At that time of the day? That's a big negative."

She shook her head in mock disgust. "Slacker."

"You got that right." He rubbed his hands together. "So, where we going?"

"I thought we'd eat at Sea Captain's House. Then, depending on how much time you have, I want to take you someplace. When do you need to be back?"

"I'm good till about three, three-thirty."

"Well, let's see if we can't stir up some fun."

They sat beside a window. looking out over the Atlantic Ocean. Sea Captain's was the last of the original restaurants on the beach. It had been built as a cottage in 1930, and opened its doors as an eatery in the early '60s. Small and cozy, it looked like a time warp from the days when Myrtle Beach was nothing but quiet dunes and quaint beach houses. Cape couldn't complain about the atmosphere, the view, or especially, the company.

"I don't see nachos on the menu, but maybe the boys in the kitchen can whip you some up," Cape said.

"Oh, I get it. Because of that night at the hotel. So you've labeled me, huh, Jeffers?"

"If I remember correctly, you ate the whole plate, in between sucking down, what, a six-pack of beer?"

"You're full of it. I ate two or three chips, tops. But, you," she hesitated for effect, "you were a disgusting sight. Cheese hanging off your chin. Black beans wedged between your teeth. Scary. And, I didn't even finish two beers, thank you very much."

"Whatever. I'll be happy to ask the waitress to tap a keg for you and bring it to the table."

"If I wasn't a southern belle I'd reach over and kick your shin."

He liked her spunky attitude.

Contrary to her culinary reputation with Cape, Angela ordered nothing resembling nachos. Rather, she chose mussels and she-crab soup. Cape went with seafood pasta, and while twirling the long strands with his fork, he listened as she spoke about life at the beach. She wasn't too enthused about the traffic congestion and the sheer volume of tourists, but it didn't dim her enjoyment of her living at the beach.

"So, now that you're a local, do you consider yourself a surfer girl?" Cape asked.

"Oh, yeah, definitely," she said, her words dipped in heavy sarcasm. "When I surf, I focus on two things: not looking like a complete fool, and trying to do it without getting a wedgie. And I suck in both categories."

"And there you have it, ladies and gentlemen. Surfing commentary by Angela Dennison."

"Think I should write a book about it?"

"With that kind of knowledge, why wouldn't you?"

Angela told him about a deep-sea fishing expedition where she'd tossed her breakfast over the side of the boat a mere twenty minutes after they left the dock. She had become so sick that she spent the entire time hanging onto the edge, white knuckled, emptying her stomach.

"Not a very fun trip, huh?" asked Cape.

"Hardly," she said with a smile. "I begged the boat captain for a refund when we got back to shore."

"What did he say?"

"Lady, there ain't no barf-free guarantees."

Cape laughed. "Ain't no barf-free guarantees," he repeated.

She had a softness about her that Cape liked. Her voice was gentle, but raspy in such a way that made him wonder how it might sound if whispered in his ear, under a full moon. She appeared prim and proper, but was also unafraid to let her laugh carry across the restaurant. She was a head-turner who seemed to have no clue that she was. Cape couldn't help but stare at the way her full lips took on a sultry hue when she flashed her smile. Like a strand of pearls and costume jewelry, she looked the kind of girl who could wear an evening gown in a pickup truck and not look out of place.

Cape talked about the long journey he'd been on since Kasey's death. He talked about his daughter, and the things they liked to do together. Angela seemed touched by how the mention of Jules' name lit up Cape's face. She asked about his comeback, and he could tell she knew her baseball.

"What about you?" he asked. "Did you play ball growing up?"

"I played softball for one season, but stopped when I realized I couldn't do one very important aspect of the game."

"What was that?"

"Hitting. I was terrible."

"Then how do you know so much about the game?"

"Actually, from watching Dylan play in high school. I learned how to calculate batting averages, earned run averages for pitchers, and on-base percentages. All which qualified me for the geek squad."

**

After lunch she drove down Ocean Boulevard to the old part of the beach. They found a spot to park in front of The Gay Dolphin, a landmark gift shop that had opened in 1946.

They walked through a large crowd of teenagers gathered outside a body piercing shop.

"What *exactly* have you got in mind for us?" Cape asked, looking at the skull and crossbones on the sign above the shop.

"Thought we'd get matching navel piercings." She laughed and took him by the hand. "Actually, let's live on the edge a bit. You're not afraid of a little speed, are you?"

"Speed is my middle name."

She pointed toward a spot in the distance. "Good, because The Screamer awaits."

The Screamer was one of the oldest roller coasters on the east coast. It looked almost ancient compared to the newer, flashier coasters that had popped up all over the country, but it was built to go fast. They slipped into their seat, side by side, the safety bar locked at their lap, and Angela asked, "Just a side note: do you get sick riding these things? You did consume a plate of creamy Alfredo sauce, you know."

"You're the barfer, remember?" He tugged at her small purse. "Besides, I'll barf in this if I get sick."

"You do, and you're going to need someone else to play for you tonight."

The coaster pulled out of the loading platform, and began a rickety climb. Cape looked to the east, and miles of beach became visible. As it crept higher and higher, Cape's palms began to sweat. "Is it too late to back out?"

The long assemblage of cars rose to the peak, coming to a halt for a brief second, and the world below looked very small, and very far away. "Well," Angela said with conviction, "it's go time."

The Screamer plunged straight down, pushing the pair against the back of their seats. The roar of the steel cars against the rails was deafening, and Cape wished he could put Angela in a headlock. After what seemed like an hour of terror, the coaster finally pulled back into the loading platform.

"Remind me to kill you later." Cape rubbed his hand upwards on his face and through his hair.

"Next time, how about you wear your big boy pants and leave your bellyaching at home?"

"Hey, you didn't hear a peep out of me."

"That's because the sound of the coaster drowned out your screams."

He wanted to pinch her ear, and then kiss her. For the first time in years, his heart began to feel emotions he hadn't thought possible, not ever again.

To make up for Cape's ride of horrors, Angela offered to take him on the beach, promising she'd hold his hand if the sand shook too much under his feet. He did pinch her ear after that comment, but refrained from kissing her.

Gray skies had chased away the sun, and the ocean breeze gave a rare chill to the air. The clouds sent most of the sunbathers and swimmers indoors, limiting the beach to the occasional beachcomber, jogger, or child playing in the sand. Cape and Angela walked close together and their arms touched.

"I have always loved the ocean." She looked out at the iron-colored water, brushing the hair from her eyes, sandals in her hand. "Our family vacationed here every summer and I wanted to live here. I thought this was the best place in the world. There's something about it, you know?" She stopped walking. "Just look at it. It's the one place where, if you provide the vessel, it will take you anywhere you want to go."

"A vessel, huh? Well, I hope mine comes with satellite TV and ESPN."

"We'll have to remember that when we start the design process."

"We've been coming to Myrtle since we were kids too. First week of August, like clockwork. Had to wait until summer baseball was over."

"I've decided you can't be sad at the beach. It's impossible. Just look around. The waves and the surf. The sun rising every morning over water that stretches further than the eye can see." She looked at the gray skies. "Well, not today, but you get the picture."

She laughed, then continued. "Families everywhere. Little kids running around the shore finding more things to do with sand than I thought humanly possible. Guys trying to look cool so they can meet cute girls. Great sunsets. Moonlit walks at night." She shook her head. "Listen to me. I think I sound a lot like a Chamber of Commerce infomercial."

"That's an impressive selling job. I'm glad you see it that way. But I don't think everyone looks at it the way you do."

"Oh, no? You don't?"

"Once upon a time."

"Are you telling me you're not feeling warm and fuzzy right now? I mean, besides still looking green from the roller coaster ride. Look around. How can you top this?"

"For most people, yeah, I think they'd agree." He shrugged his shoulders. "But for me, well, all it does is remind me of what used to be. Of a time when life couldn't get any better. I was in love, had the girl of my dreams. Baseball was going just the way I wanted it. You know, Kasey and I had some really great times here when I played for the Pelicans. And we honeymooned at Daufuskie Island down the coast. So it's a reminder that those days are gone."

"I'm sorry, Cape. I wasn't thinking."

"Don't apologize. You were talking about something that means a lot to you. I prefer your story to mine when it comes to the past. I'll bet yours was a lot more simple."

She frowned for a second and appeared in deep thought about Cape's statement. "What do you mean?"

Cape shrugged his shoulders again. "Oh, nothing."

"Are you saying I never had pain and anguish growing up?"

"I can't answer that. I'm just saying, for me, the beach is a reminder that the girl I had planned to spend the rest of my life with is gone. I signed up for seventy or eighty years with her, but only got two."

Angela looked embarrassed. "I'm sorry, Cape. I can't imagine."

"I tell you, after she died, there were days when I wanted to stay in bed and never get up. I felt God had set me up for a life of misery. Like He held some grudge, standing on the mound on a baseball field in heaven, throwing a cosmic fastball at my head, smiling as I lay sprawled on the ground." Cape kept his eyes on the long horizon in front of him.

"I'm sure it's been hard, but I just can't believe that God has it in for you. That He intentionally caused you pain and heartache all for the sake of some twisted amusement."

"All I know is He took away the person I was supposed to spend the rest of my life with."

"But He gave you your daughter."

"Maybe He's waiting for the right moment to plunk me again and take Jules away too."

"You think God is going to take everyone you love from you?"

"I don't know what I think. All I know is that He set me up with a little taste of heaven before sending me into a world of hell. I wouldn't wish it even on my worst enemy."

The trip back to the hotel was quiet.

"I really had a good time," Cape said as he opened his car door.

"Me too." A pensive smile followed.

"Can you come to the game tonight?"

"I'm not sure."

"Other plans?"

"That's not it."

He looked into her eyes. "It would mean a lot if you came."

She gave a soft nod. "Good luck tonight."

"And if you don't make it, will I be able to see you before I leave?"

"Let's see about tonight first."

His words, his eyes, had told her everything. The way she saw it, his bitter heart had erected a virtually impenetrable wall. She was extremely attracted to him, his kind heart, his sense of humor, and she thought he was as fine looking a man as she'd ever laid eyes on. But with such bitterness, not to mention the distance baseball would put between them, what kind of a chance would they have?

***

Cape stood in the on-deck circle in the first inning. His parents, and the town of Santee, were in the stands in full force. He glanced around, but didn't see Angela. In the sixth inning, Cape again stood on-deck. He took a practice swing and noticed her standing along the walkway of the third base line. She wore a bright red sundress. With the setting sun catching her face, she cut a striking figure. He had no idea how long she'd been standing there. She smiled at him but he'd already turned his head toward the action at the plate.

Manny singled sharply up the middle, and Cape stepped to the plate. His hometown fan club clapped and shouted his name. The Pelican fans remembered his days there as well, and were familiar with why he'd quit the game. He sent the second pitch out of the park, a towering shot that cleared the scoreboard, and then got a standing ovation. The Santee Stallion, the one an entire town had pinned their hopes and dreams on, had delivered again. When he stepped on home plate, he pointed to the sky, a signal of sorts to Heaven, then smiled at his parents.

From the edge of the dugout he looked up at the portal and smiled at Angela, tipping his cap to her. She nodded and slipped into the shadows. Gone.

He called her cell phone after the game, but only got voicemail. The next day he tried her again, assuming she was at work. He hoped she would return the call, but his phone stayed silent. They played their final game of the series that night, and he looked into the stands, but saw no sign of her. The bus ride home was quiet, a lonely night of sleepy towns and deserted streets.

Chapter Twenty-Eight

A great baseball player zones out everything but the game once he steps on the ball field. The uniform goes on, the cleats are laced, and the only thing that matters is what takes place on the diamond. Cape knew that as well as anybody, so he put his thoughts of Angela out of his mind when it was time to play.

His hitting streak continued through both July and August, and he played with a controlled fire. Batting .417 into September, he was determined to raise his average even higher. He wanted to be the ultimate player, the greatest of all time.

Sports Illustrated ran a feature on his comeback. He had daily requests from the media for interviews.

The Cape Jeffers Fan Club website was launched, where updates were posted daily on his rise to the majors. He'd given the General Manager his permission to let the organization create the site, but only after much prodding and after he'd been told the benefits of having a site where Jules would always be able to keep up to date with her father's accomplishments. It quickly became a huge success, with thousands of fans joining in. The female contingent was large, with many of them looking for the pictures that the team photographer uploaded each week. He didn't know it, primarily because his focus was on his being the best ballplayer possible, but he was becoming a heartthrob and hero combined in one. He developed a cult following though he had no clue.

During bus rides, and in his hotel bed on the road, Cape found himself thinking of Angela. He easily blocked her from his mind at game time, but when he was alone, he thought about her often. One night, he used a computer in the lobby of his hotel to search for the phone number at the resort where she worked. He called the front desk, and left a message asking her to return his call.

He didn't understand why she'd turned so cold so fast. Why did she come to the game, simply to watch, wave, and disappear? He thought she'd had as good a time as he did the afternoon they'd spent together. He could see it in her eyes while they ate. He could tell by her playfulness on the roller coaster. He had tried to be open and honest when they walked on the beach. Did she not want him to share his feelings about how hard life had been for him? He replayed the day over and over, with no idea how his comments had affected her.

All he remembered was how funny and adorable she was, and how she seemed completely at ease around him. Was it all an act?

***

Cape placed his luggage in the baggage storage compartment of the bus and noticed the coach pointing at him. He stepped out of the line of players boarding the bus bound for Kinston.

"Cape, we just got a telephone call. They want you in Birmingham in the morning, so crank up 'Sweet Home Alabama' and pack your gear. You're scheduled to start tomorrow night against Chattanooga."

"Yes, sir."

One step closer.

After the bus pulled away, he phoned Jules and told her the news. She screamed and told Carnie. He could hear Carnie yelling, "Come on, Chicago. Come on, Patti Richards."

Carnie kept Jules busy. She wanted Jules to make friends and develop social skills with children her own age, especially since her school days were spent at home. She signed Jules up for the Brownies, which gave her a chance to hang out with other girls and do arts and crafts, singing and dancing, and basically, anything that children typically do. Jules' desire to paint continued to grow.

Carnie made sure she had plenty of art supplies, especially acrylics. Jules didn't know how much she was like her mother.

Though Jules developed a few friendships, she wanted to spend all her time with Carnie. To Jules, Carnie was smart, pretty, athletic, and could do no wrong. She was the only person Jules knew who had lost her mother, and that reason alone made her cling to Carnie's side.

Kasey's love for painting may have passed through the bloodlines to Jules, but it was Carnie who provided a strong influence on Jules' likes and dislikes. Jules loved to make sweetgrass baskets, and became quite good at it. She found herself trying to emulate Carnie when she sang, danced, or even laughed. Jules loved her father immensely, but a man is not privy to the many things in the mind of a girl, which made Carnie's role a prominent one.

Jules didn't realize that sometimes the color of a girl's skin determines a preconceived notion on how she should behave, the way she should dress, the way she should speak, the way she should carry herself. Wasn't that the American way, or at least, the Southern way? How long could Jules be sheltered from that perception?

***

Season's end rapidly approached, and Cape had fifteen games left to show how well he could hit against Double A pitching. He'd had no problem with it when he'd played for Macon almost a decade earlier, and his confidence was even greater now. He had come into

Birmingham, the heart of SEC football and NASCAR, to make upper management take notice.

He hoped Birmingham would be where he, Jules, and Carnie would live next spring. With a good year, he could then make the jump to Triple A, and from there, on to Chicago to play for the White Sox.

***

Cape ended the season with a outstanding .401 batting average, belting five home runs in fifteen games, and headed back to Hilton Head. He had five months to spend with Jules and Carnie. It would allow his body to rest, and give him time to clear his mind of all things baseball. He knew that in his short stint in Birmingham, his performance surely had convinced management to send him back there in the spring.

On the ride home, Cape decided to call Angela. Again he had no luck, but the girl at the front desk had promised to give Angela his message.

***

Cape had been home three days, and Jules and Carnie had a surprise for him. He'd been helping plan Jules' eighth birthday party, set for Saturday afternoon. But those plans were of no concern to the girls that Wednesday night. They made Cape wait outside in the passenger side of Carnie's faded Corolla, only telling him they were taking him for a ride. When Jules walked out in a baseball uniform, glove in hand, Cape smiled.

"Can you guess where we're going?" She opened the car door and got in the back. Carnie got in the driver's seat.

"Scuba diving?"

"No, Daddy. Look what I'm holding in my hand. A glove. Baseball. Hello?"

"Oh," Cape said, stringing out the word long and slowly as though he'd just been told the meaning of life. "Baseball. I don't know why the glove didn't tip me off."

Cape and Jules weren't the only ones strapping up the cleats. Carnie had joined the ladies' softball team at St. John's Baptist Church.

Jules' team was in a fall baseball league for nine and ten year olds. At first, they'd told her she had to play in the coach's pitch league, since she was just shy of her eighth birthday, and because she was a girl. But Carnie pleaded with league officials to let her attend tryouts.

After her first three swings sent balls to the fence, and after they learned she was Cape Jeffers' daughter, they allowed her to play.

The baseball field was at the county recreation park. Jules played second base for the Dragons. Carnie took a seat on the bleachers and Cape stood next to her. He never could sit in the stands, and preferred to walk around to burn nervous energy. Though he never felt nervous when he played, it was a different story watching his daughter on the field.

Jules came up to bat in the first inning with two runners on base. She took one practice swing, and then another. She lowered the bill of her helmet. She had learned, and copied, Cape's batting rituals. Jules batted right-handed. Cape had toyed with the idea of teaching her to switch-hit, but she wasn't interested. She swung at the first pitch, hitting a hard liner to left-center. Carnie rose to her feet.

"Go, D.J. Go, girl."

Jules was on her way to second when she realized the center fielder had just picked the ball up at the fence. She rounded the bag and headed for third.

Carnie's decibel level increased with each bag Jules touched.

The ball was thrown wide of third and rolled toward the third base dugout. Jules' coach waved her around the base and she headed for home. The shortstop picked up the ball and threw it to the catcher, who tagged Jules' knee as her foot slid across the plate. The umpire called "Safe!" and Jules hopped to her feet. She removed her helmet, did an awkward pirouette, then took a bow toward the bleachers. The catcher for the other team tried to push her off the plate, and someone from the bleachers yelled, "Show some class, kid. This isn't the circus."

"Hey, Jeffers," someone else yelled. "Why don't you teach your kid to show some respect on the ball field?"

Jules saluted her dad as she jogged to the bench.

"What in the hell?" Cape said quietly to himself. He walked to the dugout, stuck his head inside, and called Jules out. He took her firmly by the arm and led her down the right field fence so no one could hear him but her.

"Just what do you think you're doing?"

"Sir?" She saw the anger in Cape's eyes.

"What was that crap you pulled at the plate?"

"Um, I was… I was just celebrating my home run. You hit home runs for me, and I wanted to hit one for you."

"That's great, but you never, *ever,* show up the other team. That's not how I taught you to play the game, and you should know better. This game is about respect. Don't forget that." He poked his finger into her chest, still holding on to her arm. "Now, if you do that again, I'll yank you off the field so fast you'll come right out of your cleats." He let go of her arm.

She'd never seen him so upset, and when she walked into the dugout, it was all she could do not to cry in front of her teammates. He was the last person she wanted to disappoint.

Carnie walked up to Cape, who stood alone at the fence, arms folded, his face beet red. "Mr. C., don't be so hard on her. All mornin' long she talked about how she wanted to hit a home run for you. She wanted to make you proud, and she got a little carried away, that's all. You remember what it was like when you were a kid, right?"

"It's inexcusable. There's a certain way to act on the field, and that wasn't it. It's called sportsmanship. Or is that something they never taught you in Beaufort?"

Carnie bit her lip, looked toward the field, and shook her head. "What's that suppose to mean?" She took a deep breath, her palms facing outward as if she were trying to stop an oncoming car, and said, "Mr. C., she's *just* a little kid having some fun."

"Fun," he repeated. "Well, then, she needs to learn to have *fun* the right way. The fun comes from playing, not celebrating; certainly not at the expense of showing up the other team."

"She wasn't really trying to show up the other team. Anyway, who put you in charge of deciding how a player's supposed to carry himself on a ball field?"

"It was something decided way before I came along. All I'm saying is there's a certain way a ballplayer is supposed to act when he steps on the field. Maybe you both should pay a little more attention to how the game is meant to be played."

She fought hard to bite her tongue. "So, we need to learn some class? Is that it?"

"I didn't say that."

"You didn't have to."

The ride home was deathly quiet.

Cape and Jules ate dinner that night alone. Carnie took her meal to her room, saying she needed to put Jules' progress portfolio together for the state school board. Jules picked at her food with a fork, and she didn't speak.

She was in trouble, and she knew it. And by Cape's demeanor, Carnie was too.

The next morning, Carnie tended to breakfast without speaking. She placed two bowls of scrambled eggs, full of green peppers and mushrooms, on the table. After loading the dishwasher, she went to her room.

Jules tried to make eye contact with Cape as he glanced over his *Baseball Weekly*. "Daddy, I'm sorry for what I did in the game yesterday."

Cape hated to see Jules hurt, but he was adamant on the subject of showboating. "I know you didn't mean anything by it," he said. "And maybe I overreacted. I just want you to understand a ballplayer's reputation follows him wherever he goes. If he loses it, even once, it's hard to win back."

"Yes, sir. I won't do it again."

Cape slid his chair away from the table and pointed to his knee. Jules went over and sat on his lap. He pulled her to his chest. "It's okay, Jules. I should have talked to you more about that kind of stuff when you first started playing. It's my fault."

"No, it's mine."

"It's over and done with, okay?"

"Okay, Daddy. I love you."

He held her tight. "I love you too. Remember how big?"

"Big as the sky."

"You got that right."

"Can I see if Carnie will eat with us?"

"Sure."

Jules stood in the doorway to her room. "Carnie, aren't you going to eat with us?"

"No, baby, I've got some work to do before we begin class." Carnie kept her eyes on the course planner, worried that if she looked at Jules, she'd see the hurt in Carnie's eyes.

"But we always eat together. Can't you do your work later?"

Carnie shook her head and pretended to look over the planner.

Cape worked in the yard that day for over four hours. He mowed the grass, trimmed shrubbery, and edged along the driveway. He'd removed his shirt soon after he began, and his body shimmered from sweat. He was raking the clippings into a concise pile by the road when next-door neighbor Bernie Perkins walked up. He was a retiree from Akron who'd lived in Hilton Head for almost twenty years.

"Yard looks as smooth as Astroturf," Bernie said. He wore brown and tan plaid shorts, and an untucked aqua half-silk, half-polyester shirt, along with calf-high white socks and white sneakers.

"Well, anything's an improvement. It sure looked ragged when I got started."

"So, how'd your ballclub do this season? I hear you knocked the hell out of the ball."

"I don't know about all that," he said modestly, "but I did alright, I guess. I know I can play better. There's always room for improvement. Regardless, it feels good to be back home. The hardest part is being away from Jules."

"Well, Edie and I try to look out for her when we can. Sometimes she'll come over and have some of Edie's chocolate chip cookies. She likes our dog, Winston."

"I appreciate that. I know I've sheltered her somewhat since she's had to grow up without her mother, and outside of Carnie, she doesn't interact much. So any attention from the neighbors is welcome."

"I've noticed she and the gal sit on the porch from time to time and make those baskets. It's kind of an odd hobby to teach a little white girl, don't you think?"

"What do you mean?"

"Well, it seems more suited for the ladies down in Charleston that you see by the roadside. You know, the ones singing those spiritual slave songs."

"You got something against those *ladies* that sing and sell sweetgrass baskets?"

"No, not at all. But, it just seems an odd choice for the nanny to teach Jules."

"It's a hobby, not a career choice."

"Well, I guess it's none of my business."

"No sir, it's not."

Bernie glanced down the road. "Here comes Edie. I better get back to work in my own yard."

***

The next afternoon, Carnie and Jules returned from errands to make last-minute birthday preparations. Carnie had invited fifteen girls, most of them Brownies, as well as some kids from church. She invited Jules' grandparents, Doug and June, neighbors Bernie and Edie, and a five-year-old neighbor named Clint, who liked to play ball with Carnie and Jules in the yard. Of course all of Cape's family would attend.

Carnie ran yellow and blue streamers across the den and Jules blew up balloons, most of them blue. After Carnie had finished, she walked to her room and returned with her CD player.

"This house is too quiet," she said. "Let's listen to some tunes while we turn this place into a par-*tay*." She plugged in the CD player. "Let's see now, what's best for blowing up birthday balloons?" She unzipped the CD case, and began flipping through her large collection. "Oooh, girl, I think this calls for a little Missy Elliot." She placed the CD in the slot and turned it on.

Carnie began placing small toys and silly items in colorful bags and singing the words to the hip-hop sounds of "Lose Control". She took hold of a candle on the table and used it as a microphone. There was such a child-like innocence about her, and Jules smiled as Carnie shook her backside to the beat. When she twirled, Jules laughed.

"Come on, girl," Carnie said, "show me some rhythm." She took Jules by the hand. "'Everybody here, get it outta control'," she sang along. She raised her arms, elbows out, and slid her feet. "Come on, D.J." Carnie stepped to her left, and Jules did the same. She stepped to her right, and Jules followed. Carnie began to twirl, and Jules did too, giggling like the little girl she was.

Cape finished washing off the wooden deck out back, and stepped inside for some water. For a moment, he stopped and watched the pair dance. Carnie noticed and tried to hide her embarrassment.

"Mr. C.," she said, setting the candle on the table, "I didn't hear you come in."

"What kind of influence are you?" he asked with a smile. "You're corrupting my child."

"You're scared," Carnie said. "Admit it."

"Scared of what?"

"That I'll put a little 'sister' in her."

Walking into the kitchen, Cape said, "She knows better."

He didn't see the puzzled look on Carnie's face.

***

On Saturday, Jules helped Carnie put snacks and drinks on the kitchen counter. The party was set to begin at two, and the Santee gang arrived first. Randy pulled into the driveway and Jules took off toward the car. Along with Pauline and Alicia, Jevan Altekruse had come along. Jevan and Cape had not seen each other in over a year, and Cape looked forward to catching up with his old friend.

Soon Jules' friends and the neighbors arrived, and the party was underway. Carnie was the ultimate hostess, setting up games for the children, giving them goodie bags, serving drinks and snacks, as well as leading the singing of "Happy Birthday" and the cutting of the cake.

Pauline and June helped by refilling chip bowls and plastic cups with tea or lemonade.

Randy took pictures and talked with Doug.

Jules opened her presents on the patio under the shade of the oak, surrounded by piles of wrapping paper and the other children. Cape just enjoyed watching Jules have a good time.

By four, most of the guests had left. Jules played ball in the front yard with twins Mary and Maddy Conroy. The sisters played on a slow-pitch softball league at the park, and were intimidated by how well Jules could hit and throw. Each time Jules hit the ball, the sisters would scream with fright. She thought they needed to toughen up.

Randy helped Carnie and Pauline in the kitchen, and Alicia worked on removing streamers and balloons from the living room. Jevan helped Cape clean up the deck. Cape gathered paper plates and cups from the picnic table.

"Looks like things are going really well for you." Jevan opened the trash bag so Cape could toss in a stack of cups.

"We're doing okay, Jevan. We're doing okay."

"So, you expect to return to Birmingham next spring?"

"That's what the skipper told me when the season ended."

"Are you taking Jules with you?"

"Oh, yeah. We're going as a team."

"What about the girl? Carlie?"

"Carnie," Cape clarified. "What about her?"

"Are you taking her too?"

"Sure. Why wouldn't I?"

Jevan hesitated. "Hmm," he said, scratching his chin.

"Something wrong with that?"

"Never mind."

"No, what is it?"

"Maybe it would be best to get someone, you know, a little more your own color."

"What color did you have in mind? Pink? Carolina Blue?"

"I'm not trying to get all Jim Crow on you, but maybe Birmingham ain't the place for a black girl and a white guy and his daughter. I'm just thinking about you guys."

"I appreciate your concern, but I don't give a crap what others think. She's part of our family."

"Well, it's something to think about. You know?"

Cape shook his head and bit his lower lip, and the more he thought about Jevan's comments, the madder he got.

Carnie stepped outside to return a cooler to the storage room behind the garage. She noticed a wayward balloon at the side fence and went to retrieve it. She picked up the purple balloon and heard Cape's voice.

"Yeah, it's probably best not to take along the *black* girl," she heard Cape say. "She just might end up teaching Jules some ancient tribal dance while eating fried chicken and watermelon." Carnie didn't detect the sarcasm—or anger—in Cape's voice. "Next thing you know, they'll be throwing spears at the neighbor's dog."

She looked to the sky, tears appearing, her heart absolutely crushed. She turned, lowered her head, and walked back inside.

"Easy, Cape," Jevan said. "I didn't know you'd be so sensitive. I stepped over the line. I'm sorry."

"Carnie is an amazing girl, Jevan. We couldn't have asked for a more perfect person. For Jules. For our family. She's the best. She keeps our priorities straight, and I wouldn't be in the position I'm in if not for her. We love her."

"I'm really sorry. I was way out of line."

Cape's family soon headed back to Santee. Carnie told Jules she had a headache and went to bed early. As the sun set, Carnie lay on her side, crying. She'd never felt so hurt. She loved Cape and Jules with all her heart. She'd envisioned herself staying with Jules until the girl went off to college, and even then, staying with Cape to make sure he was well taken care of. She'd thought she was as important to them as they were to her.

***

Jules woke up and walked to the kitchen. Her dark hair was tussled and she wore a pair of orange-colored cotton pajamas. She figured Carnie would already be working on breakfast, and wanted to thank her for the fun party. The kitchen was empty, so she walked to Carnie's room. The bed was made, and a hand-written note sat on the comforter.

Jules cried when Cape read it aloud.

Chapter Twenty-Nine

Cape drove up in front of Sea Oats Elementary School. Jules looked at the children walking inside. Cape placed his hand on her shoulder.

"It's going to be okay, Jules. This will be a good experience. You're going to make all sorts of new friends."

"I don't want new friends. I want to go home."

"You can't go home yet. I haven't had any luck finding someone to home school you, so this is our only choice."

"Why can't we bring Carnie back?"

"Look, I'm just trying to do what's best for you."

"Her note said you hurt her feelings. What did you say to her?"

"I didn't say anything *to* her. I was just making sarcastic comments to Jevan because of what he'd said about…" He saw the confusion in Jules' eyes. "Listen, it was a total misunderstanding."

"Then tell her you're sorry. Get her to come back."

"I've called her cell phone a hundred times, but she won't answer. I've left messages, but she hasn't called me back. I have no idea where she might have gone. I guess she went back to Beaufort, but I don't know."

"You didn't try hard enough. She's part of our family, Daddy."

"I *have* tried. And I know she's part of our family. I miss her too. But she's gone, and we've got to move on."

Jules began to cry. "Please don't make me go to this school. I want Carnie. I want it the way it used to be."

"Come on, now. Don't cry. You don't want to start your first day with puffy eyes, do you?" He gently rubbed his hand through her hair and looked out across the parking lot. "It's going to be okay. I promise it will if you just give it a chance. And you liked going to school in Santee, remember?" Jules lowered her head and gave a half-hearted nod. "You want me to walk you to your class?"

"No, sir. I can do it."

***

The blistering guitar sounds of Metallica roared over the gym's speakers, drowning out the ringing of Cape's cell phone. He'd placed it on the floor beside the shoulder press machine, and just happened to glance down and see the display light up. He grabbed it and stepped into the locker room. Taking a deep breath so he could speak without panting, he looked at the unfamiliar number on the caller I.D. and pressed the 'talk' button.

"This is Cape."

"Good morning, Mr. Jeffers, this is Wendy Baker, the principal of Sea Oats Elementary."

Cape's first thought was that Jules was sick or hurt. "Is Jules okay?"

"Yes, she's fine. She's in class right now. Listen, I wanted to see if you could come to the school and discuss her progress. We're just not getting much out of her in the classroom. She seems unmotivated. Listless."

"But she's an excellent student, and smart as a whip."

"Yes, she is quite bright. But we're having trouble getting her to participate in class. She rarely turns in homework. She tends to sit and stare out the window."

"Homework? I make sure she does her homework every night."

"Well, she tells her teachers that she didn't do it."

"What time do you need me there?"

"How about three this afternoon?"

"I'll see you then."

When Cape walked into the principal's office, she and four teachers waited in chairs arranged in front of Wendy's desk.

Ken Copeland, her art teacher, spoke first.

"Jules is a talented student, but she has hardly any interaction with her fellow students, or with me," Ken said. He pointed with a pencil to three drawings laid across Wendy's desk. "I'm impressed with her artistic skills as well as her expressive ability when it comes to drawing and painting. But she looks depressed. I've not seen her smile once."

"Art is the only class where Jules is performing well," Wendy added.

"I just don't think she cares about her schoolwork," said Allison Crompton, Jules' math and science teacher. "She's more than capable, but I think she's just slacking off."

"I don't understand," Cape said. "She doesn't slack off at home. She does her homework assignments. I go over it with her to make sure it's always completed."

"Well, if she's doing it, as you say," Allison said, "she certainly isn't turning it in."

"Well," he said sarcastically, "I *say* she does it every night."

"I think maybe we should have her meet with the guidance counselor on a weekly basis," Wendy said. She sat behind her desk, fingers intertwined and folded on her desk. "Would it help if Jules' mother gave us her thoughts?"

"Her mother passed away the day she was born."

Wendy looked at the floor for a moment, taking a breath, and tried to hide her embarrassment. "I'm so sorry. I apologize for that oversight."

She glanced at Jules' records, and cringed. "Maybe that has something to do with why Jules is struggling."

"That's not why," Cape said. "Well, that's not completely true. I'm sure growing up without a mother plays a part in Jules' life to some degree. But, in this case, she's having withdrawal issues from Carnie."

"Who?"

"Her nanny."

"Well, if we can't get this resolved soon," Wendy said, "she may be looking at repeating the third grade."

***

Early November. The red and gold of autumn were a fading memory, and most of the trees were barren and gray. Jules had become reclusive, spending most of her afternoons in her room painting. Crumpled sheets of drawings filled the trashcan beside her dresser. She didn't want to play with other children, and stopped going to her Brownie troop meetings.

She showed no emotion during her baseball games, though she seemed to take her frustrations out at the plate, constantly ripping liners to the outfield fence. She wanted to quit, but Cape wouldn't let her. He told her if she didn't want to play the next season, that was her choice. But she needed to finish what she'd started.

The school guidance counselor met with Jules twice a week, but she still performed woefully in all courses except art. Cape tried talking with Jules, even threatening to take away certain privileges, like painting, if she didn't show more effort with her schoolwork. They were butting heads, and getting nowhere.

Cape sat beside Jules' bed one morning.

"Time to get ready for school," he said, tickling her toes. She flinched and pulled her feet under the covers toward her chest. Cape tried to rub her hair but she pulled the sheet over her head. "Jules, wake up."

"I'm sick."

"What's wrong?"

"My stomach hurts." Cape had sometimes used that same excuse to get out of going to school when he was a boy, because it was the hardest ailment to prove. He suspected her stomach was fine.

"Well, I bet after you take a good hot bath, and get a little food in your stomach, you'll be good as new." He waited but she didn't move. "Come on. Up. Now."

"I told you I'm sick."

"Get up, Jules. You gotta go to school. The way you're struggling, you certainly don't need to miss class time."

"I want to stay home."

"You can't."

"This is all your fault."

"My fault?"

"She was my best friend. She was the only person I could talk to about stuff you don't know anything about. She knew what it felt like to grow up without a mother. She made me see that it wasn't my fault that Mommy died. And she taught me so many things. She played with me. She was my teacher. But you ran her off."

"I didn't run her off. Like I told you before, it was a misunderstanding."

"Whatever."

"Listen, I'm not going to put up with your smart mouth."

"What difference does it make now? Everything's ruined."

Cape forced Jules to get up, get dressed, and go to school, but she didn't speak a word along the way. She opened the door, got out, then turned and looked at him. Crying, she said, "I hate you." She slammed the door and walked to class.

Those three words felt like a dagger struck straight into his heart.

Jules was right. He had no one to blame except himself. He somehow had to find a way to make Carnie understand, but how could he? She wouldn't answer her phone. He didn't know where or how to find her. The one thing he knew was that he had screwed things up, and he had to find a way to make it right again.

***

That afternoon, Cape watched the children and cars line up at the school pick-up zone. The line slowly began to move, a buzz of controlled activity, and when Cape pulled up, a teacher opened the back seat door on the passenger side. Cape expected Jules to hop in, but the teacher dipped her head inside the car.

"Who are you here to pick up?"

"Jules Jeffers."

The woman called out Jules' name, and some of the children started looking around. The line of vehicles behind him grew. "Doesn't look like she's here. Maybe she's in the office. Park in the lot and come inside."

Cape walked into the office and a teacher's aide paged Ken Copeland's room to see if she was still there. He said she'd left with all the other students when the bell rang. The T.A. walked with Cape down the halls, by the cafeteria, and then back to the loading zone just as the last two children in the line climbed into the back seat of a passenger van.

The principal sent the maintenance man to check the school grounds, and also made an announcement over the P.A. for anyone to call the office if Jules was with them. Cape began to worry. This wasn't like Jules at all. After twenty long minutes they determined that Jules was nowhere on the school grounds.

Cape drove home, thinking maybe she'd caught a ride with someone from school. After all, she was mad at him. But the house was empty. He called Wendy to see if she had shown up in the office, but the answer was no. He stood in his bedroom, tapping his phone against his chin as if trying to conjure up the magic phone number to dial

He noticed a broken picture frame sticking out from behind his dresser. He carefully lifted it and realized it was the frame that held the painting Kasey had made of Cape throwing a ball to Jules. The painting was gone.

He called the Hilton Head Police, and they took down her vital statistics and issued an Amber Alert. They wanted a recent photo. A million scenarios ran through his mind, and he tried to sort through them to decide where to go, what to do, who to ask for help. His stomach knotted up, and his hands were sweaty.

He asked Bernie to wait at the house, and if Jules appeared, to call him. He drove back to her school and looked along the sidewalks. He drove by the ballpark. He thought how difficult it was going to be to tell his mother that her grandchild had been kidnapped, or worse. What if someone took her to get a ransom? He thought of who he'd call to raise money to get her back. What if some madman took her, one with an underground bunker? Maybe it was a satanic cult.

His mind became like a television where someone kept changing the channels in rapid-fire succession, each one worse than the last.

He passed Sims Park, a small playground with picnic tables and a bike rack. He spotted a payphone and pulled off the street. He found a quarter in his ashtray and exited the car. *Maybe she'll answer if I don't call from my cell phone.* He pushed the quarter in the slot and punched the numbers on the dial pad as fast as he could.

"Hello," the voice on the other end said softly.

"Thank God," Cape's voice shook and the words tumbled out. "Carnie, Jules is missing. I went to pick her up from school and she wasn't there. We had a fight this morning. She told me she hated me. That I ran you off."

"Just you stay calm, Mr. C.," Carnie said, in an authoritative tone. "Where all have you looked?"

"Everywhere. Home. The school, inside and out. I drove the streets between the school and home and back again. Bernie is waiting at our doorstep in case she shows up while I'm out looking for her. I've called the police, and they're looking for her too. She's nowhere to be found." He rubbed his hand along his temple. "I can't make it if something happens to Jules."

"Don't even talk like that. We're gonna find her. But you gotta stay focused." She took a deep breath. "Does she have any friends from school she might have gone home with?" As she waited on Cape's reply, she made a three-point turn and headed for Hilton Head, a forty-five minute drive from Beaufort. As she sped down Highway 170, her mind raced like the engine in her Corolla.

"I don't think she has any friends at school," he said. "Or at least none that she talked about."

Carnie had never wanted to be able to transport herself magically from one place to another, but she did right then. The straight, lonely highway allowed her to speed, and she tried to remain calm. Scary thoughts clouded her mind, and she vowed silently to hunt down anyone if they had done Jules harm.

"Can you think of anywhere she might be that I haven't checked?"

"Did you check the beach?" Carnie asked. "How about the ball field?"

"She wasn't at the ball field. Haven't tried the beach."

"Get in your car and then call me back. Go to the beach."

Think, Carnie, think. Where is she? Still fifteen agonizing minutes from Hilton Head, she talked with Cape on the phone as he drove to the beach. She battled fear and anger, but willed herself to remain calm for Cape's sake. And for Jules.

Cape arrived at the beach parking lot and sprinted from his car, phone to ear. He looked north and south along the shoreline, and thought every child he spotted was Jules. Carnie told him to head south, since Jules loved to walk toward the Sound.

"I don't see her," he said with fading hope as he ran. "I just don't know where else to check, Carnie. I'm running out of options. Help me, please, help me find my girl."

She could hear the anguish in his voice. She let out a yell and popped her forehead. "The lighthouse! Check the lighthouse. I'd bet a ham to a sow's ear that's where she is."

He sprinted along the shifting sand and it made him feel he was running in slow motion. When he made it to the car, he said, "You know, I think she took Kasey's painting this morning. I found the empty frame in the room behind my dresser."

"The one with the lighthouse?"

"That's the one."

"Jackpot."

Cape spun his car around and worked his way along the winding road to the lighthouse. Carnie crossed the bridge and onto the island. The sun was setting fast, and shadows began to slip out from the dense trees and cordgrass, overtaking the creeks and flat roads that cut along the island.

Cape parked next to an old brick house that was located fifty yards from the six-legged lighthouse tower, daylight all but gone from the sky. He ran toward the base. Carnie drove in, her headlights carving his shadow onto the side of the tall structure. She left the car running and sprinted toward Cape, the ground a pale yellow in front of her from the lights. The shrill, noisy sounds of crickets filled the air.

Cape called Jules' name at the top of his voice. Carnie, without hesitation, passed him on the way around the tower. His heart raced as he followed her. A single streetlight cut shapes from the shadows.

"Jules!" Cape yelled again. Carnie stepped closer to the giant structure. She saw a tiny silhouette against the tower.

"Mr. C.," she said, pointing to the figure.

Cape ran to it, and there was Jules, crying, her head against her knees, her mother's painting rolled up in her hand.

"Jules Jeffers," he said, swooping her off the ground and squeezing her in his arms. He wanted to both smile and scream. She wrapped her arms tightly around his neck.

"Daddy."

"Do you understand how much you scared me? What were you thinking?" Though his words were harsh, his voice was kind and his heart overjoyed to have her safely in his arms.

"I'm sorry about what I said this morning. I didn't mean it."

"I know you didn't."

She wiped her tears with the back of her hand and saw Carnie, who also had tears streaming down her face. She yelled Carnie's name, and Cape set her down. She ran into Carnie's arms so hard it knocked her on her back in soft pine straw the nearby trees had dropped.

"Oh, child, what kind of nonsense are you pullin' here?" Carnie asked, cradling Jules' head to her shoulder.

"Please come back home, Carnie. Please come back. I need you."

"I need you too," said Carnie.

Cape knelt beside them. "Carnie, you need to know that what you heard me say was a stupid, sarcastic response to Jevan's comments. I have never had anything but respect for you. I love you. *We* love you, and you do belong with us. You're part of our family."

Jules kissed Carnie's cheek, the salty taste of tears on her lips. "Please don't leave us, again. Never, ever."

Carnie shook her head. "Never, ever."

As Cape helped them both to their feet, he brushed the straw off Carnie's shoulders. "Come on ladies. Let's go home."

Chapter Thirty

Carnie spent Thanksgiving morning cooking. Macaroni and cheese, stuffing, pole beans, corn on the cob, and sweet potato pie. Jules drew turkey heads and feathers on slits of brown paper, and glued them to thick, round pinecones. The prickly gobblers were arranged in a circle, facing each other as though they were waiting on someone to lead them to the nearest pine tree.

Cape cooked the turkey in the smoker on the back deck for hours. All through the house and across the yard, the aroma of home cooking caused hunger pains to stir.

Pauline, Randy, and Alicia arrived just past noon. Billy had stayed in Charleston to share Thanksgiving with Christina's family.

At the dinner table, they held hands and gave thanks. Carnie said the blessing, and then she went into a sermonette as she expressed gratitude for her "adopted" family.

As Cape sat at the table, warm in the company of his family, he thought of Angela. He wondered how her Thanksgiving was going; if she was with family. Was she with a boyfriend? Was she thinking of him at all? He truly felt blessed to be with his own family, but part of him thought the dinner table would be a little warmer, a little brighter, if Angela were with him.

***

It was a week before Christmas, and Angela had just finished talking with the shuttle service director. They provided a shuttle to and from Barefoot Landing, located next door. She'd gotten complaints that the shuttle was slow in picking up guests waiting for rides back to the resort. Angela couldn't understand why, other than the elderly, they couldn't just walk the short distance, but her job was to keep the guests happy, and the shuttle driver promised to make the rounds quicker.

She looked through the mail, and in the usual bills and junk was a red envelope addressed to her. When she opened it, she found a Christmas card with a picture of a manger scene.

Inside, it wished Christmas blessings. Below the message a hand-written note said:

Angela,
I hope you are doing well. Maybe Santa will be extra good to you this year. You have been on my mind lately, and I've been thinking about the day we spent together at the beach. If you find the time, please give me a call. I would love to hear from you. Even more, I'd like to see your pretty smile. It's no big deal, but I wonder why you haven't returned my calls. Was it something I said? I thought you had a good time that day, and I'm sure you could tell I really did. Would be nice if we could do it again some time.
Merry Christmas,
Cape

Angela held the photo that Cape had included. Cape, Jules, and Carnie sat on the limbs of a large oak. She smiled and touched Cape's face. His blue eyes shone brilliantly, and his wide smile practically jumped off the picture at her. She placed the card in her desk drawer.

After she finished the day's work, she walked into her office to grab her purse. She reached in the drawer and looked at the photo Cape sent, picked up the phone and began to dial. She heard the faint tap of knuckles and her office door opened.

"Mind if I come in?" a voice asked.

"Cole," Angela said, surprised. "What are you doing here?" She placed the phone back on the receiver.

"I thought I'd surprise you." He held a bouquet of roses behind his back, and when he pulled his arm around to show her the flowers, surely he saw the stunned look on her face.

"This is very unexpected."

"Hopefully that's a good thing. I came to take you to dinner. Are you free?"

"Oh, no. Not a good idea. Dinner will only make you think we are getting back together. We're supposed to be making a clean break, remember?"

Perhaps the fact that they had dated off and on for two years gave him the right, so he asked, "What's one dinner going to hurt? It's not like you have plans, right? Come on. It will keep us from being bored."

"Cole…"

"A nice meal at the club. A glass of wine. What harm is there in that?"

She sighed. "Let me get my purse."

* * *

They entered the dining room of the Dunes Club, the premiere club of Myrtle Beach. The hostess, who wore a black skirt and crisp white blouse, smiled and then removed two menus from underneath the cherry bureau.

"Good evening, Mr. Devereaux," she said. "Miss Dennison, it's good to see you again."

"Thank you, Brittany," Angela said, with the sense of being reeled back in like a blue marlin destined to hang on Cole's wall. "Nice to see you too."

Cole and Angela followed Brittany to a table that looked out at the 18th green. Brittany handed them the menus, and informed them that Annalise would be their server. Cole placed his hand on Angela's.

"I've been putting a lot of thought in to what we discussed last week," he said. "And I'm determined not to give up. We make a really great team and I am sure we belong together."

I didn't realize I was on a "team", she thought. *Are we competing against other teams?* She sighed and shook her head as if she didn't have the energy or desire to deal with Cole's determination. "Cole, it's just not working. This relationship is going nowhere."

"How can you say that? We're perfect for each other. For the last year we've been *the* elite couple of this town. We've attended every high society event; we run in the finest social circles. This city has already carved us out as the next great couple."

"I don't want to rub elbows with the social elite of this town."

"I can give you anything you want. Dad will be turning over the business to me in the next couple of years, and I'll be able to give you the life of luxury you deserve."

"I don't want luxury, Cole. I want someone I'm head over heels in love with. I'm sorry if that hurts you, but I have to be truthful." Cole didn't appear to give the remark another thought. "Somebody who will be happy with me dressed in sweat pants and my hair pulled in a bun. You just want me as a decoration on your arm."

"That's not true. I love you. And I know I can make you happy."

"There's so much more to it than that."

"What do you mean? Is it that baseball player you told me about? Is he the one you want? What can he give you? A long-distance relationship comprised of phone calls and emails? He lives on the road. And doesn't he have a rug rat or two? You want to become a full-time baby sitter? What kind of life is that? You deserve so much more." He rubbed his hand against her cheek.

The mayor, Andrew Campbell, and his wife walked up to the table.

"Well, hello there, Cole," the mayor said. He shook Cole's hand. "You remember Sheila."

Cole stood. "Yes, sir. Mrs. Campbell, it's good to see you again. I believe you remember Angela." Angela nodded.

"How could we forget?" Sheila said. "You two make the prettiest couple in Horry County."

"That's because of Angela," Cole said. "I got the best one in the sea when I snagged her."

Angela bristled, though Cole seemed oblivious.

"She's a trophy all right," the mayor said, "but I'll put my Sheila up against anybody."

"And so you should, sir," Cole said. "She is so absolutely beautiful." Sheila appeared to blush, though she was used to compliments.

"Well, we know you've got more exciting things to do than talking with an old couple like us," Andrew said. "We'll let you get back to your dinner."

"Nonsense," Cole said. "Let's schedule dinner for the four of us soon."

"Great idea, son," Andrew said. He took Angela by the hand. "Angela, always great seeing you."

"Thank you, sir," she said.

"A trophy?" Angela said when they sat. "You called me a trophy?"

Cole took Angela by the hand. "I meant it in a good way. Don't you see how everyone in this town loves us? Just give me another chance. I can make you happy, Angela. I can provide you with all the stability you need. You will want for nothing."

"It's not stability that I'm after. I can take care of myself. What I *need* is someone whose interest is my heart, not my comfort."

"I can be that guy."

She shook her head. "Let's just eat our dinner."

Cole drove Angela back to her car at the resort. She stood next to her Honda and watched him drive away, his red Lamborghini roaring out of the parking lot. She felt so confused. On the way home she thought of Cape. Was he worth the trouble? Could she take the place of Kasey's legacy? She recalled his comments of how he'd lost his soul mate when she died. Didn't people have only one soul mate in their lifetime? Could Cape have two? And what about the distance between them? Surely she'd only get to see him a few times a year in the offseason. What kind of relationship would that be? She had a career too, and couldn't just up and leave whenever Cape was in town, or home during his offseason. At least with Cole, he would always be there, and he did love her. But was comfort and luxury enough to offset her lack of love for him?

Chapter Thirty-One

Spring training for the White Sox took place in Glendale, Arizona, the furthest distance Cape had ever been from Jules. It was for only short six weeks, he kept reminding Jules, and himself, and then they'd be together in Birmingham. At least that was his hope. The way he'd finished last season, he knew he wouldn't get sent back down to Single A ball in Winston-Salem.

After spring training, Cape indeed got assigned to Birmingham to play for the Barons. He flew to Hilton Head where Carnie and Jules had already packed up their clothes and personal belongings. Jules rode with Carnie, her Corolla following Cape's new, black 4Runner on the seven-hour trip.

Cape rented a three-bedroom furnished apartment in Hoover, a suburb of Birmingham. It had the basics as far as beds, couches, and a kitchen table, but it just wasn't anywhere near as nice as the well-furnished house they had rented in Hilton Head. Cape guessed they would need the apartment for five and a half months, then would move back to Hilton Head with the hope that Cape would be assigned to the Triple A team in Rock Hill.

Cape started off well, hitting .354 through the month of April. The fans loved him, and the autograph seekers flocked to him after every game. He made a point to show his appreciation to everyone who wanted to have his signature.

Jules made only a few friends, but it wasn't a big deal. She had Carnie to share her days and nights with. They attended all the home games, and like Cape, loved being at the ballpark. Although Jules graduated the third grade ahead of schedule, other than a two-week break, Carnie kept her on a tight regimen. Cape was known to declare a field trip every now and again to the ball field to "study" the history of baseball.

Carnie took Jules to the public library once a week. Jules had a fascination for baseball stories, mostly non-fiction. Her favorite book was *The Rookie*, about Jim Morris and his comeback to the Major Leagues in his mid-30s after retiring due to an arm injury. Jules knew her dad's story was similar, though the reason for his detour from baseball was completely different.

She was also familiar with Josh Hamilton, one of the top home run hitters in Major League baseball, and his comeback from drug addiction, but since she didn't know what drug addiction was all about, she preferred the Jim Morris story.

Because of Cape, she became interested in comebacks and second chances. One day on the way home from the library, she noticed a different building, the Greater Alabama Children's Home, a collection of faded brick dormitory wings.

"What is that place?" she asked.

"It's an orphanage," Carnie replied.

"They don't have mommies or daddies?"

"Either that, or their parents just couldn't raise them."

"I think not having a mommy is bad enough. Bet it's really bad to not have both."

"I would think it would be a hard thing to deal with."

"Maybe we can play with them or something."

"Huh?"

"Maybe we can help them out."

Carnie learned that the orphanage had a ball field, but it was sorely lacking in equipment. Maybe she and Jules *could* help.

At the breakfast table, Jules picked over her eggs. "Daddy, you think it's been hard on me not having a mommy, right?"

Cape was caught off guard, worried initially that maybe Jules had picked one out for him. "Yes, I know it's been hard." He could see her brain working through the gleam in her eyes. "Where are you going with this?"

"Don't you think it's even harder for kids who don't have a mommy *or* a daddy?"

"You mean orphans?"

"Yes, sir."

"I can't imagine what it's like."

"Well, Carnie and me found some orphans. They have a baseball field but they need baseball equipment. Will you help them?"

"You and Carnie found an orphanage? How did you find them?"

"Phone calls, Mr. C." Carnie poured orange juice into his glass. "It's amazing what you can accomplish with a phone and a phone book," she said, grinning.

"Anyways, Daddy, they have a ball field to play on, but they need bats and balls and gloves. So, we thought maybe you could help."

It touched Cape to see Jules' tender, caring heart.

At Cape's request, the Barons donated thirty gloves and ten dozen baseballs. The team's sales rep from Louisville Slugger provided ten metal bats.

The headmaster of the orphanage put two teams together, and invited Jules, Carnie and Cape to their first game. Since the Barons were in town, and had a night game, Cape attended. He let Jules hand the headmaster tickets to the game for Sunday afternoon, a block of forty in an area that would be roped off, with pizza and drinks for everyone. The tiny headmaster, five-foot-four at the most, looked overwhelmed with gratitude.

Cape brought Baron caps and autographed balls for all of the children. Jules was proud of her father for taking time to help, and she smiled when all the children surrounded him before the game.

Carnie gathered a few girls who seemed afraid to play, taking them past the outfield grass to play catch.

The children pleaded with Cape to hit a few baseballs, and he obliged. The largest bat they had was a thirty-one inch composite, four inches shorter than his normal bat length.

Cape yelled for Carnie to pitch to him. The kids watched from behind the backstop, a wise decision since Cape didn't want any broken noses or busted chins. The children seemed as impressed with Carnie's lively arm as they were with Cape's ability to hit. She threw some easy pitches, and Cape hit several liners deep in the outfield after adjusting to the shortness of the bat. He looked at Carnie and smiled.

"Scared?"

"You must be crazy, Mr. C. I can handle anything you hit. I'm holding back so I don't embarrass you in front of all these children."

Cape laughed. "Don't hold back on my account. Let's see what you got."

Carnie delivered a fastball, belt high, and Cape ripped it into the sky. Across the long field it went, rising like a missile. The crowd went silent as they watched the ball disappear into pecan trees surrounding the driveway entrance almost four hundred feet away.

Cape smiled at Carnie.

"Not bad for a soft country boy from back-water Santee," she said with a grin.

"Not bad for a country girl from muddy-creek Beaufort."

Cape, Jules, and Carnie enjoyed watching the first three innings of the game before heading home so Cape could get ready for his game.

***

In late May, the Barons made a long road trip to Raleigh for a four-game series with the Carolina Mud Cats. They took the opener 3–2, and Cape went one-for-three with a walk. He was batting .376, and the Mud Cats felt lucky to only give up one hit to him.

The next morning, he rented a car online from the computer in the hotel lobby. Fortunately he chose the agency with the motto, "We'll pick you up." At 8:00 a.m., Cape dropped off the young man who had brought him the rental, a black Cadillac DTS. Soon Cape was heading east to I-95 for a four-hour ride to the coast.

He was nervous, and twice almost pulled off at an exit to turn around.

He arrived at the Marriott Ocean Resort a few minutes past noon. He worried that Angela had gone to lunch, or worse, it was her day off. But since she hadn't returned phone calls, or answered his card, he decided seeing her face to face was his only chance of finding out why she had cut off contact. He had a one-hour window before he had to book it back to Raleigh to catch the bus to the stadium.

He walked to the front desk, where a college-aged girl asked, "How may I help you?"

"Is Angela Dennison here today?"

"I'm sorry, but you just missed her. She went to lunch."

"Do you know where she went?"

"Even if I did, I'm not at liberty to say."

He nodded his thanks and headed to Barefoot Landing, looking for any sign of her on the busy sidewalks outside the shops and restaurants. When he came to the boardwalk, he prayed he would be lucky enough to find her watching the turtles. He jogged across the long walkway, around tourists and mothers pushing children in strollers.

He saw her leaning against the rail, looking out at the water, and his heart began to beat faster. She looked beautiful in a white sleeveless dress, her skin tanned. He walked slowly up to her, nervously rubbing his fingers against his palms.

"Hi, Angela."

She turned. *No way.* "Cape. Oh my God." She hugged him awkwardly. "What are you doing here? In Myrtle Beach, I mean? Aren't you playing the Mud Cats tonight?"

He was surprised that she still kept up with his schedule, but it made him wonder if maybe, just maybe, she held feelings for him.

"Yes, we play the Mud Cats. But I had to come here, to find you. Why haven't you returned my calls, or my letters? I can't stop thinking about you. About us." Angela looked across the pond, and Cape could tell she was deep in thought. "I just don't understand. I thought we had a great time together. I was thinking it was the start of something. Was I imagining it?"

"No, you weren't imagining it. But, Cape, it's very complicated."

"Is there someone else?" Angela sighed, and Cape took her hand. "I've come a long way. The least you can do is level with me."

"The day we spent together was one of the best days of my life. I had a wonderful time. But when we walked on the beach, I could hear the bitterness in your voice. It was easy to see you are still very much in love with Kasey, and it was apparent, to me anyways, that no one could take her place. I don't think I can compete with a ghost."

"You wouldn't be competing with a ghost."

"That's easy to say."

"Look, I know Kasey will always be a part of me, and for the longest time I thought I'd never want anyone else. But all that changed on the day that you and I spent together. You awakened something inside me."

"Well, even if you take Kasey's memory out of the mix, there's the distance factor. You're so far away. We'd never get to see each other."

"That's not true. The offseason is five months long. We could use that time to see each other. And you have vacation time, right? You could come during the season. I think there are ways to overcome the distance issue if we try."

He pulled her close and softly touched his lips to hers. She stepped back, and tried not to look into his eyes. She knew she had no chance if she looked into his dark blues. He placed his hand gently on her chin and guided her face to his, and her heart jumped when she looked at him. They kissed, surrounded by the busy crowd on the boardwalk. Angela began to cry and Cape took her in his arms.

"Cape, I really would like to make it work, but…"

"Then come to my game tonight."

"What?" She pulled away and looked at him as if he were joking.

"Come to my game."

"That's crazy. Besides, I have to work. I don't get off until five."

"Then come after that. The game will go on till at least ten. You'll get there mid-game and we'll eat dinner afterward. Do you work tomorrow?"

"Yes. I work from noon until nine."

"Stay the night with me."

"Cape, I can't do that."

"Yes, you can. Please. Please." He touched her hand. "I'll see you tonight." He kissed her cheek and then hurried back to the car.

***

Angela stood outside the will-call window. She was nervous, but in an excited way. She made her way to her seat, the crowd cheering after a Mud Cats triple. She wore a white and yellow sundress, and Cape noticed her from where he stood at shortstop. By the number of heads that turned, it was obvious the other men noticed her as well. Her shoulder-length hair was highlighted with soft blonde streaks, and her sleek shoulders were tanned and firm. She commanded attention from the crowd without even trying.

She found her seat, and then she found Cape. He looked great in his uniform, the white jersey and pants, black pinstripes, and black hat. She soon noticed he was wearing 7, and she wondered laughingly if he'd paid the equipment manager to ensure he received that number. She watched him for a few minutes before glancing at the scoreboard. She may have been mesmerized by the man, but the baseball junkie in her turned her interest to the numbers on the board. It was the bottom of the fifth, the game tied at two. The Barons had gotten five hits, and she wondered if Cape had any of them.

The people around her seemed like locals. She saw no one wearing Baron gear, typical for an away game, hundreds of miles from Birmingham. There were a few rowdies in the crowd, and two guys in front of her who seemed to enjoy throwing insults at Baron players as they ran off the field at the end of each inning.

Cape flashed a quick smile at her on his way to the dugout. Her seat was eight rows from the field, close enough for him to see the uncertainty in her eyes.

She couldn't stop wondering why she had come. She felt guilty for telling Cole that she wasn't feeling up to going to the Grand Strand Oyster Festival with him. He had offered they skip it entirely, and just relax at his place. But she'd convinced him to go without her.

So she sat there, watching a baseball game four hours from home, wondering how she could be so stupid. But when she saw Cape climb to the on-deck circle, her heart fluttered. He was confident, athletic, and Lord, he looked better than any man had a right to. She watched him warm up and thought that maybe he was Mickey Mantle reincarnated. Still the All-American kid, no matter that he was approaching thirty.

Cape singled to right and the fans around Angela voiced their displeasure. The next two batters failed to reach base, and with two outs, the Barons' first baseman doubled down the right field line. Cape rounded second. When he headed for third, the third base coach waved him toward home. The ball reached the catcher just as Cape began his slide. A cloud of dust kicked up as the catcher dropped and tagged Cape on the shin.

"He got him!" the umpire yelled, peering on one knee beside the plate.

Cape dusted himself off and the two men in front of Angela stood as he jogged to the dugout.

"Nice job, Jeffers. Who taught you how to slide?"

"Get another hobby, Seven. You suck."

Angela shook her head, tempted to kick them.

Yeah, like you could have scored on the play, she thought. *I'm sure you were an All-American in your day. Have another chilidog.*

Cape flew out to shortstop his final at-bat, ending up with only one base hit for the game. He was very much disappointed, and Angela felt bad for him. She didn't care that he only got one hit; she knew even talented players like Cape couldn't have multiple-hit performances every night. But she figured Cape would be hard on himself for not putting on a better show for her.

After the game, Cape motioned her to the bottom of the steps and asked her to meet him at Gate Three in fifteen minutes. She made her way there, telling herself she would head home after dinner.

Cape took her to Damon's Steakhouse. He wore seersucker shorts with black stripes and a black polo shirt. He talked her into sharing a calamari appetizer, and she ordered a glass of Chardonnay. Their conversation seemed forced at first.

"You look great tonight," he said. She blushed. "It was hard to concentrate with you wearing that dress."

"The great Cape Jeffers, distracted? No way."

"Why do you think I only got one lousy hit?"

"Then maybe it was my dress that distracted you. I bought it two months ago and have been waiting for a good reason to wear it."

"Does that mean you think I'm a good enough reason?"

A setup question, right off the bat. She hesitated. "Maybe." Her eyes sparkled from the flame of the glass-encased candle on their table.

He took her hand. "Thanks for driving up here. You don't know how much it means to me."

"I'm glad I came. Other than the one at-bat when you played for the Pelicans, this is the first time since high school that I've been able to watch you play."

"Well, I didn't do much to impress you."

"It wasn't your hitting that concerned me."

"Oh yeah? What was it?"

"The play at the plate. You should have begun your slide sooner. You don't want a broken ankle, do you?"

He shook his head and smiled. "No, no, I don't. Thanks for the tip, coach."

"Happy to help," she said with a nod and a smile.

Dinner arrived and they talked about Jules, and of course, baseball. Angela wasn't happy with the recent play of the Yankees, and Cape told her to stop whining about it. Angela slowly lowered her guard as the evening progressed. Her intentions of shielding her heart were not going the way she had intended.

After dinner, she drove him to his hotel. There was an uncomfortable moment of silence when she pulled into the lot.

"Well, I guess I should be on my way back home," she said, but he sensed her uncertainty.

"Please don't leave. Come to my room. I have something for you." He took her hand and looked at her as though worried he'd never see her again. "Please."

"I just don't want to make the situation more complicated."

"I understand. Just stay a little while."

She didn't know Cape had requested a two-bedroom suite so she could have her own room. He didn't intend to get her into bed, but to convince her he'd fallen for her. He wanted her to know for certain that he wanted to be in a serious relationship. With her. Heart-to-heart, soul-to-soul.

Inside the suite, Cape had a dozen lilac roses in a crystal vase on the dining room table. In front of the vase sat a package wrapped in blue and gold. He turned on the small silver stereo on the kitchenette countertop, and soft music began to play. He then took her purse and placed it beside the stereo. He guided her eyes to his by touching her chin with his fingers. She sighed, and knew the wall she'd built was crumbling. When he took her in his arms, she forgot about her fears, Kasey's legacy, Cole.

"Dance with me," he said softly, "What if You" by Josh Radin playing on the radio.

The lights low, they moved slowly, in unison, no words spoken. He wrapped his fingers around hers, and looked in her eyes, as if trying to search her heart's thoughts. He kissed her, and she trembled. She had never received a more tender kiss. She placed her head against his chest and closed her eyes.

After two more songs, Cape took her hand and led her to the table.

"I have something for you." He handed her the gift.

"Cape, what did you do?" Her eyes lit up like a child. "You shouldn't have gotten me anything."

"Too late."

She took the slender package and sat on the couch, and Cape sat beside her so that their legs touched. Her skin felt good against his. She tried to open it carefully so as not to destroy the wrapping.

"You don't have to be gentle," he said. "Go ahead and rip it open."

She quickly peeled off the paper. In a burgundy frame was a four-by-five black and white photo of a young boy standing next to a baseball player wearing a Yankees uniform. The boy looked around eight years old.

"Wow, that's Mickey Mantle," she said. "He looks so young." She kissed Cape on the cheek. "Now I've got an actual photo of Mickey. Thank you, Cape."

"That's not just Mickey. Look again."

Mickey's hand rested on the boy's shoulder. The kid wore a Yankees cap high on his head so that his entire face was visible. He wore a wide smile and a look of amazement that he was having his picture made with one of the greatest baseball players of all time.

"Who's the boy? Is he someone you know?"

"Look closely. See if he looks familiar." His eyes did look hauntingly familiar. Where had she seen him?

"You know, he kind of reminds me of Dylan. But this picture must be fifty years old."

"It's exactly fifty years old. You sure you can't figure out who the boy is?"

She pulled the picture closer. "Wait. Is it? It's Daddy."

Cape smiled and gave a brief nod. He took the frame from her and slid off the back, then removing the picture. "Turn it over."

She flipped it over and read, *Yankee Stadium— '58. Mantle and Dennison boy.*

"Oh my God." She covered her mouth with her hand. "How did you get this?"

"My agent's brother-in-law is the Media Relations Director for the Yankees. I told my agent what you'd told me about the picture. He knew they had an archive of old photos. So, he paid his nephew a hundred bucks to go through the stack of unclaimed photos and pull out any he could find of Mickey Mantle posing with a boy. He found three, and they all had writing on the back. He saw the writing on this one and figured it had to be it."

Angela hugged Cape. "Oh, Cape, you don't know what this means to me. Daddy talked all the time about this picture. He told family, neighbors, co-workers. He would have given about anything to track it down. I only wish he were alive to see it."

Cape rubbed her back. "I do too."

She kissed him and he wiped a tear from her cheek. She pressed her face to his, and she felt certain she was skin to skin with the sweetest boy she had ever known. He lit a fire inside her, and stirred her soul so that thoughts of stability and the future evaporated. Gone went the reality of the situation, of a loving relationship that would no doubt cause her pain and loneliness because of the distance between them. At that moment, she cast all her fears aside to chase a crazy love affair that might not extend past the morning light.

She lowered him onto the couch so that his head was on the armrest. She began to kiss his neck, tender kisses. He felt her breath on his skin. Her lips moved up his chin, along the cheek, and then she found the corners of his mouth. She kissed along the edges, working her way to encase his lips with hers. As she kissed him, the passion and forcefulness grew.

She rubbed his chest, following the curve of his pectorals before tracing the muscles in his shoulders. She kissed him again and helped him remove his shirt. She kissed his chest, and his neck. Her perfume smelled so sweet, and he felt a faint trace of perspiration on her lower back. She felt the soft pulsing of his heart, and he smiled when he touched the curves of her contoured waist.

***

Angela awakened and the clock on the bedside table read 4:56. She looked at Cape, breathing steadily, heavy in sleep. She tiptoed to the bathroom and closed the door. Finding the light switch, she looked at the mirror, combing her hair with her hand, and noticed Cape's gray t-shirt hung loosely off her shoulders. She spotted a photo on the counter of Cape holding Jules in his arms, both of them laughing as if they were in on a secret that the whole world wanted to know, but were not privy to. Angela looked at the beautiful father and daughter, thinking about what they'd been through. She wondered how Jules would react if she became a part of their lives. She heard her cell phone vibrate on the bathroom counter and noticed she'd missed a text message. It read: *Hope you feel better. Sleep well. Looking forward to our dinner on the yacht Saturday night. I love you so much.*

When Cape woke, the sun had slipped through the creases of the curtain. He looked at the bedside clock.

6:42. He wanted to make sure Angela was up in time to make it back to work by noon. He walked into the living room. She sat on the floor in front of the couch, her legs pulled to her chest, her arms around her knees.

"Angela?" Cape sat beside her and put his arm around her shoulder. "What's wrong?"

She shook her head for a moment, capturing her thoughts carefully before she spoke. "I haven't been up front with you. I planned on coming here last night to watch the game, eat dinner, and then tell you there was no way to make this work." She took a deep breath. "But then you blew me away with an incredible, unbelievable night, and all I want is to stay here with you. But I can't." Again a deep breath. "Cape, I'm involved with someone else. He is loyal, and he loves me. But what is it that do I do in return? I come up here and I spend the night with another man."

Countless questions ran through Cape's mind, but the one that seemed most important was the only one he thought needed an answer. "Do you *love* him?"

"He's a great guy. He provides stability, and he's there for me." She rubbed tears on the sleeve of the tee-shirt. "But with you, I feel alive, like part of me that's been trying to burst out has been set free. God, you stir my soul like I never knew possible."

"Then call it off with this other guy."

"I can't be one of those long-distance relationship kind of people. I would want to see you every day. Be with you every day. In a few minutes I have to leave, and it's tearing me up. Besides, I owe it to Cole."

"Do you love him?" he asked again.

She stared at the wall for a long moment, and then nodded.

"But are you *in* love with him?"

"He's always there for me. He's so good to me."

"You didn't answer my question."

"I'd like to think that I am."

"That proves you aren't. And it's crazy to settle for someone you're not in love with."

"But, Cape, you'll be so far away."

"I told you, we'll make the most of the offseason. We'll schedule times during the season. We'll absolutely take advantage of every opportunity."

"And what, you're going to leave Jules behind and come to Myrtle Beach? I can't quit my job for five months a year and move to wherever it is you will be. It's just an impossible situation."

Angela dressed and gathered her things, and Cape walked her to her car. He didn't want her to leave. He figured if she did it was over. But what could he do? Quit baseball and move to Myrtle Beach? Get a job selling tee-shirts so he could be near her?

He hugged her, and again her tears flowed. "Please don't give up on us," he said. "There has to be a way to make this work."

Her phone vibrated and she saw another text from Cole. *Hey, sweetie*, it read.

"This is crazy," she said. "Cape, chase your baseball dream. Give it everything you have. It's what you were meant to do." She kissed his cheek softly, then placed her cheek to his. "It's what you were meant to do," she repeated.

He watched her drive away, and knew he had lost her for good.

Chapter Thirty-Two

Mid-August, the season was winding down. Cape was determined to not let thoughts of Angela interfere with his game, though at times she crept into his mind. She belonged to another, and it was simple as that. All he could do was hope for her happiness.

Cape decided to take Angela's advice, and he treated every game as though it would be the last one he would ever play. As a result, the Cape Train bore down toward the major league. His batting average climbed to an amazing .391. He led the Southern League in home runs and runs-batted-in. His fielding percentage was tops of all shortstops, and his fan club website became even more popular. His weekly blog on his perspective of baseball received thousands of hits.

At the stadium, a banner that said 'The Cape Town Ladies' hung from the rafters in left field. Hundreds of women sat in that section, wearing tee-shirts with Cape's picture on the front. On the back was the Barons' home schedule, with the label "Cape Tracker".

***

Carnie took Jules and Cape to the Broadwater A.M.E. Church one Sunday morning. A neighbor who attended had offered Carnie an open invitation. With his traveling schedule, Cape had not had much chance to find a place of worship. His church in Santee was small and everyone knew everyone else. He was hesitant about walking into a place where all eyes would turn to him, to become the visitor that everyone would want to welcome after the service was over. He didn't mind all eyes on him on the ball field, but the House of the Lord was another matter.

"Let's just go on back home," Cape said as Carnie drove down I-20.

"This will do you good," she responded.

"I know that. But I'd feel more comfortable at a church where I knew somebody."

"You do know somebody."

"Who?"

"Jules and me." She laughed and slapped Cape on the forearm.

"You are one funny girl."

"It's time to experience new things, new people. You need a little cross-culture."

"We'll stick out like sore thumbs. I hate being stared at."

"A little soul singin' and preachin' will be good for you. What, you worried about God turnin' you black? Think He'll strike you with lightning if you yell 'Amen' in an A.M.E. church?"

"No, I'm pretty certain I'm ust going to stay this color. So, you're telling me this is the kind of church where people stand and shout?"

"Shouting will do you good. It'll stir the devil out of your soul and bring Jesus on in. Halleluiah! Praise the Lord!" Carnie clapped her hands. "Give me an amen, D.J."

"Amen!" Jules shouted.

"You're starting to scare me," Cape said.

Jules laughed from the backseat.

Cape made Carnie sit on the back row. Of course, heads turned to look at the visitors. They were greeted with warm smiles.

"See, I knew they'd like you. They think you're Opie Taylor."

"Shut up," he whispered as he returned a smile to a sweet-looking elderly woman in a white hat.

Cape had placed his phone on vibrate, so when it shook in his pant pocket, he tried to muffle the sound by smothering it with his hand. A couple of minutes passed and it twitched, and he knew someone had left a voicemail. He looked toward the pulpit where a teenage girl began to sing, slipped the phone out of his pocket, and glanced at it quickly. It showed a missed call from his parents' home.

The diminutive preacher, wearing a black suit, white dress shirt, and gold tie, wiped his bald head with a gold handkerchief as he spoke. He warned that a day of reckoning was coming, and pleaded for the congregation not to get blinded by the bright lights of the world.

"Stay on the narrow path," he yelled as a chorus of Amens echoed across the room.

Afterwards, many stopped by to express gratitude to the visitors for coming to their sanctuary. Cape was almost embarrassed by the fuss, the handshakes and pats on the shoulder, but something about the genuineness in their smiles made him feel good. Outside, he removed his phone and listened to the voicemail. His mother's voice sounded strained.

"Hey, Mom," Cape said as he walked to the car beside Jules and Carnie. "Sorry I missed your call. Carnie brought us to church. What's up?"

There was brief silence, the kind where he could tell something was wrong. He heard sobs. "Mom? What is it?" The crying continued for a few moments before he heard her take a deep breath.

"I've got some sad news." Cape stopped walking. "It's your father."

"Something happened to Dad?"

"He was on the way over to eat breakfast with Tate Oliver before church. He was hit by a pickup truck after it ran a stop sign."

"Is he okay?" Cape's palms grew sweaty. Mom's sobs were agonizing. *Please be okay, Dad. A little banged up, maybe a broken bone, but all will be fine.*

"He didn't ..." An eerie moment of silence.

"Didn't what?"

"He didn't...survive."

Cape turned white and fell to his knees. He heard his mother crying and then his phone fell to the pavement.

***

Vehicles filled the driveway and yard. Cape found a space to park, and he, Carnie, and Jules stepped quickly from the car and into the house. Pauline fell into Cape's arms when he walked into the kitchen. Many stood around them, laying their hands on the shaken mother and child. Christina walked up and hugged Jules, smiling through her tears.

"Hey, sweetie," Christina said. Jules was afraid, and she held tightly to Carnie's hand.

Sadness hovered about the quiet house, a solemn blanket. Every picture and piece of furniture reminded them of Randy's presence. Randy always loved working with wood, and he had redesigned the kitchen cabinets, redone the hardwood floors, and created several pieces of furniture. All over the house hung photographs of the family, Randy's smile visible in most every one.

***

After the funeral, Cape drove to the ballpark alone. It was home to ever so many childhood memories created with his father. He walked on the lonely field, softly touching his foot to third base as he followed the foul line down left field. In the outfield, he found a baseball against the fence. He picked it up, studying it as though its age could be determined by the gray, scuffed rawhide. He ran his fingers along the worn seams, and he suddenly felt five years old again.

June 1985

Cape flipped a baseball into his new glove just to feel the soft leather squeeze the rawhide. He sat in the passenger seat of his father's Ford pickup, and couldn't wait to get to the ball field. He decided to give the plastic glove he had gotten when he was two to his baby sister Alicia. That she would later use it to store hair bows didn't matter.

He wore a white uniform with navy pinstripes, and a navy-blue fitted Yankees baseball cap. His jersey was number 7, just like Mickey Mantle. The truck came to a halt near the backstop, and Cape quickly opened the door and jumped from his seat. The sun, brilliant in its decline toward the tree line behind right field, cast the outfield grass in soft hunter-green, the red clay infield a pale burnt-orange.

Randy placed a bucket of balls in front of the third base dugout before setting Cape's aluminum bat against the cyclone fence bordering the backstop. Cape jogged to third base and touched the bag with his cleat. The young ballplayer was ready to play, standing in front of third base, straddling the faded foul line. Randy walked to home plate, and when he threw the ball to Cape, he threw a lifeline between father and son.

A particular magic takes place when a father and son play catch on a baseball field. In that moment, they enter a world of perfect meaning. The mere act of tossing the baseball becomes an invisible but palpable bond that bridges a generation. Not only does it weave father and son together, it transports them to the days when our country was young at heart. It provides a snapshot of when the game embodied the spirit of a great nation. It carries them back to a time when baseball eased the pain of the Great Depression and two World Wars. It provides tangible evidence that something good comes out of playing a game for the pure love of it: unselfish effort, team camaraderie, a desire to achieve greatness, as well as the realization that a perfect afternoon is found under a soft blue sky and a warm breeze, the loud sound of rawhide meeting leather creating a most perfect tune.

Randy saw the look of concentration in his son's eyes. Every one of Cape's throws went arrow straight to his glove. "Looking good, son. Always focus your eyes on your target. Let your arm be your guide, and let your mind enjoy the moment. Mechanics may be the key to accuracy, but love of the game is the key to being great at it."

He tossed the ball back to Cape, the ball nestling softly in the pocket of his glove as though it were crystal that could break easily. Randy watched Cape line his shoulders, hips, and feet each time as he stepped and threw the ball. For several minutes they played catch, and to some it might look uninteresting and ordinary, but to Cape, it connected him to the ghosts of baseball past.

Cape's arm was loose and he was ready for infield practice. He looked at his father, and nodded as he ran to shortstop.

"And now, playing shortstop for the New York Yankees, number seven, Cape Jeffers," Randy said in his best public address announcer voice.

Chills rose on Cape's arms and he tried to stop his smile by biting his bottom lip. His dad walked to the plate with a bat in his right hand, a glove on his left, and a baseball in the glove. He tossed the ball from the glove into the air and hit it one handed. Cape attacked the ball, stepping forward, intently watching the ball enter the pocket.

"Mickey Mantle never looked better," his dad said, even though Mantle had been an outfielder, not a shortstop.

Cape didn't care. His dad's words made him bounce on the balls of his feet and pound his glove for each ground ball coming his way. Randy hit nearly fifty. Cape, running to his left, then his right, caught every one.

He'd squeeze each tightly, as though it had legs and might try to escape his glove, before throwing it back to his father.

When they were done, Randy carried the bucket of balls to the mound. Cape grabbed his bat and stepped to the plate. A gentle breeze brushed against his face as he took a practice swing, and then another. Cape hit the first pitch right-handed, a line drive that went over his father's head on its way to center field. He hit fifty more, and after he helped his dad retrieve the balls and place them into the bucket, he stepped to the plate and batted left-handed.

"Smooth swings, big man," said Randy, who had played for the Stallions in his high school days. "Drive it hard. Line drives. That's where the base hits are." After Cape hit fifty more, scattering balls all across the outfield, Randy removed the last ball from the bucket. He pointed the ball at Cape. "Are you ready?"

"Yes, sir." Cape ran to the front of the concrete dugout. "Say it real loud so everyone can hear it."

Showtime.

"Okay. Here we are, ladies and gentlemen. It's a do-or-die situation. The bottom of the ninth, and the New York Yankees are trailing by one to the dreaded Red Sox. The tying run is at first base, and the mighty Cape Jeffers walks to the plate."

Cape stepped stoically to the plate with his bat to mimic his father's words.

"The crowd is absolutely beside themselves. It can't get any more dramatic than this, folks. Two outs, and the pennant on the line. If there was any one player Yankee fans would want in this situation, it would have to be Jeffers. The crowd is on their feet now, and the roar has become deafening. Jeffers steps into the box, takes a practice swing, and then another." Cape followed along. "The pitcher looks nervous, and I would be too if I was going up against the greatest Yankee since Mantle. The pitcher winds and delivers." Randy pitched the ball. It crossed the plate, and Cape turned his hips and swung as hard as he could. He mashed a liner toward centerfield and raced out of the box toward first base. "Jeffers gets hold of it, sending a bullet to deep center. It's been hit a ton, folks, and the centerfielder is backtracking. Back, back, back, and by God, this ball is ouuuuutta here!" Cape slowed into a home run trot halfway to second base. "The Yankees win the pennant! The Yankees win the pennant! It's pandemonium."

Cape pumped his fist.

"My God, it's the most amazing scene I've ever had the pleasure to witness. I will never forget this day for as long I live." Randy jogged to the plate and then stood behind it. After Cape rounded third and headed for home, his small legs churned faster. He stepped on the plate and leapt into his father's arms.

"Cape Jeffers has broken the hearts of the Red Sox and secured his place in Yankee history," his dad said, lifting him onto his shoulders.

***

Cape looked across the field, and for the first time, it felt empty, lifeless, as if the baseball gods had deserted it. He walked slowly toward home plate, clinging to the memory of his dad standing there. He remembered the jubilation he'd felt when he jumped into his father's arms, sharing his game-winning moment with his biggest fan, his baseball partner, his teacher. Cape dropped to one knee and cried.

Chapter Thirty-Three

The White Sox gave Cape a week to grieve, and then told him to report to Charlotte to play for the Knights, their Triple A team. He packed the car early one morning while Jules and Carnie slept. He asked them to stay behind for a few weeks to comfort Pauline.

The day was overcast, the air sticky and deathly still, though the temperature hovered in the low 70s. Cape looked into the distance, the thick and endless walls of motionless pines and hardwoods, a dull gloominess that mirrored the atmosphere inside his childhood home.

Pauline walked outside wearing a white robe. Cape hugged her silently. He didn't want to leave. She dabbed her eyes with a tissue.

"You keep your focus on the game, sweet boy, not me. Now you're carrying your father's memory on the ball field, and he'd be upset if you let this get the best of you."

"It doesn't seem right to go off. Not now."

"I'll be okay, Cape. I've got Jules and Carnie to keep me company, and after they leave, you know Ms. Imogene will take good care of me. Go make your daddy proud. They've assigned you to Charlotte, son, just one step below the majors. You're so close to making it to the big leagues. Now, show those boys how to play the game."

Cape managed a slight smile and nodded. "Yes, ma'am."

Fortunately, the season would be over in six weeks and he could return.

***

He arrived at the Knights stadium in Rock Hill, just below the North Carolina state line. When he saw his name on the locker, it didn't have the same effect as when he got promoted to Greenville nine years ago. He hardly noticed or cared that his jersey number was 24. At least he would play in his home state.

But that provided little consolation because he'd be apart from his grieving mother and daughter.

The first time he had played Triple A, Kasey was taken from him. And now the White Sox brought him one step from the big leagues, only to have his father pass away. Too many casualties for one ballplayer. Cape just wondered if the pursuit of his childhood dream would require any more sacrificial lambs. Maybe it was God's sign to quit for good. He'd walked away once before, so he could do it again. He never imagined playing baseball without his dad. But then, he hadn't planned on losing Kasey either. He just hoped they both had box seats in heaven.

He had twenty-six games before the season was over, and had mixed emotions. His dream of playing in the major leagues finally looked within reach. But losing his father drained him. He felt lifeless, and had trouble sleeping at night. He had little energy during the day, and managed just five hits in his first ten games. He struck out eleven times, something that would normally take him half a season. He had no spark, no desire. He felt like he was cheating the Sox out of a paycheck. Even in his home state, he felt alone.

The Knights prepared to play the first of a four-game series with Gwinnett. The players were in the locker room, changing into their batting practice gear. They wanted to stay indoors and avoid the heat and humidity as long as they could.

The team manager sent word for Cape to see him in his office. Cape walked in and was told to shut the door behind him. He sat and felt the uneasiness in the air.

"Everything okay, Skip?"

"I just got a call from Chicago. They know you've been through a rough stretch here lately. That's why they've been patient. But they're starting to wonder if the jump to Triple A is what's making you struggle. Your window of opportunity is closing quickly. If you aren't able to turn things around in these last fifteen games, they plan on reassigning you back to Birmingham for the next season."

"I understand, Skip. But I'll be the first to say it's been frustrating."

"You've got to find a way to light that fire again. I know circumstances have made it hard on you, but you've got to leave all that outside the white lines. I think you're a hell of a ballplayer, and I would like nothing better than to see you in Chicago next season. But that's up to you. You and I know you've got the talent. Just find a way to get that hunger back."

"Yes, sir."

Cape tried his best, but he struck out his first at-bat. The home crowd booed and tossed a few verbal jabs his way. He batted again in the fifth, and tried to lay down a bunt to advance a runner from first to second. Instead of bunting it on the grass, he popped the ball into the air. The catcher caught it, and then threw to first base before the runner could return to the base for a double play.

In the bottom of the eighth, he sat at the end of the dugout and decided if he got sent back to Birmingham in the spring, he would hang up his cleats for good. He didn't have another year or two to chase his dream. No team would want a rookie in his thirties. It wouldn't be a wise investment, knowing that his shelf life as a Major League player would be just a few seasons.

The next two games, he floundered at the plate again. He came to the conclusion that his baseball career would end in the dugout of the Charlotte Knights. At least he'd made it to Triple A, something only a small group of men could say. And he'd made it twice. He'd given all he had. He could go back to Santee with his head held high, and he and Jules would be just fine.

Before the final game with Gwinnett on Sunday afternoon, a sparse crowd slowly assembled under the staggering Carolina heat and humidity. Cape showed no enthusiasm during batting practice, and didn't bother to take swings left-handed. What was the point? *May as well give some of the other players more time in the cage; guys who stand a chance of moving up to Chicago.*

When Cape finished batting practice, he walked toward the dugout, and noticed a pretty teenager smiling at him. He turned and looked behind him; he thought she must be looking at someone else. She waved, and when he waved back, she stepped closer to the railing. Her eyes looked familiar, but he couldn't place her. Behind her stood a couple he assumed were her parents, and he *knew* he'd seen them before.

"Hi, Cape," the girl said. "Do you remember me?"

Cape studied her face, and again, there was something about her eyes.

"I autographed your baseball cap for you when I was a little girl," she said.

"Becca?" he asked.

"You remember my name?"

"I sure do. And I could never forget those eyes. My God, you've grown. How old are you now?"

"Seventeen."

"Good Lord. Wow, it's great to see you. I still have my money on you to win Miss America."

She blushed and looked at her feet. "I've still got the ball you autographed when I met you in Columbia."

"Do you know I still have my hat that you had autographed?"

"No way."

"Sure do. I keep it with a display of hats from the minor league teams I've played for. Whenever I see it, I think about you. Course I think of that little five year old, and not this grownup beauty queen you've turned in to. Do you guys still live in Columbia?"

"Yes. We've followed your career, and saw on your website that you'd been moved up to Charlotte. We always said we would come watch you if you were close by. I'm very sorry about your wife." Cape nodded. "My mom and I sent you a card when it happened. Did you get it?"

"A card? No, I don't think I did."

"We didn't have your address so we sent it to the Braves main office."

"Well, I appreciate that very much. I'm sorry it wasn't delivered to me."

"I think it's awesome that you were able to raise your daughter on your own, at such a young age. And now, to see you making this comeback is amazing." Her face held a sincere look of caring, of innocence.

Cape looked at her parents. "You've done a great job with this young lady. She's something, isn't she?"

"We think so," her mother said.

"I could see it in her eyes that first time I met her."

Becca blushed, and then reached into a green linen bag.

"I've been wanting to give this to you for a long time," she said, handing him a large manila envelope.

Cape opened it and removed a crayon drawing. Blue, green, and orange. It was a picture of a baseball player, with the name "Cape" written across the jersey. Above the player, in the sky, was what appeared to be an angel. Under the picture was a caption: *She watches from heaven.*

Cape bit his lip, his heart was really touched by the thoughtfulness.

"I drew this when I found out about your wife. I was only seven years old at the time, so it's not drawn very well."

"It's absolutely perfect. Looks like I'll need your autograph one more time." He handed the picture back and her mother removed a pen from her purse. Becca smiled, and it lit Cape's soul. She had taken the time and effort to track him down, ten years later, just to give him something she'd made as a child. He knew Kasey *was* watching from heaven, and so was Dad. He knew they were. And it wasn't just heaven following his successes and failures on the ball field. It was Jules and Carnie; Mom and his brother and sister; the town of Santee. He couldn't let them down.

He took the drawing to his locker so it wouldn't get messed up.

Cape got three hits with two doubles, driving in four runs. In the eighth inning he wowed the crowd by making an over-the-shoulder catch in shallow left field while turning a somersault.

He batted .409 the last fourteen games, and the management was pleased. He had regained his focus; Becca's visit reminded him that he played for so much more than himself. He began thinking of Jules every time he took the field, knowing his daughter had brought his dream back to life. He thought of Kasey every time he scored, remembering how she cheered him on. And when he stepped into the batter's box, memories played through his head of his father pitching to him when he was a boy.

***

Cape, Jules, and Carnie moved to Santee to be close to Pauline during the offseason. Cape took his old room, Jules took Alicia's room—she was in graduate school in Chapel Hill—and Carnie got the guest bedroom. Carnie turned the den, located on the bottom floor of the tri-level house, into a classroom. Mornings would find Jules and Carnie there, with Jules working on fifth grade material.

Cape helped his mother around the house, tending to yard work and things that Randy had always taken care of. Carnie had volunteered to take over the kitchen duties, but Pauline didn't want to hurt Ms. Imogene's feelings. Pauline and Jules spent a lot of time together, and they grew even closer. Carnie found herself with spare time, and she began attending the Jericho A.M.E. Church, which, not by coincidence, had a softball team that played in the Marion County Recreational league.

***

Randy had loved Christmas, and each year he'd turned the front yard into a winter wonderland. Although everyone felt melancholy because of his absence, they planned to celebrate in his memory. Pauline, Jules, and Carnie got all the Christmas decorations out of the attic and made the inside of the home festive.

Cape tried to duplicate his father's handiwork in the outdoors, but admitted his efforts were amateurish at best. Placing the mechanical reindeer on the lawn wasn't so tough, but assembling Santa's workshop was more than he could handle.

On Christmas morning, the family gathered around the tree and opened presents. Billy and Christina were there, and the lively voices of Tripp, his little sister, Allie, and Jules took away some of the sadness. Alicia brought her boyfriend, Cliff, a neurosurgeon at Duke.

The smell of coffee and hot chocolate filled the den, and soon the floor was littered with wrapping paper and ripped boxes. Carnie felt the warmth of family, though she couldn't help but wonder what Christmas might have been like if her mother hadn't died.

Pauline, Carnie, and Christina then prepared a huge breakfast. The enticing aroma of Pauline's fluffy biscuits battled with the aroma of bacon frying in the pan. The rays of the brilliant December sun filtered through the windows. Frost held to the windowpanes.

Cape heard a tap on the kitchen door.

"Merry Christmas, Cape," the old man said.

"Merry Christmas, Mr. Jacobsen. Please come in." Ira Jacobsen had worked with Randy for nineteen years.

"Thanks for the offer, but I really can't stay. I just wanted to drop this off. It came to the office yesterday morning. Your father wanted to surprise you with it for Christmas." He handed a box to Cape. "Give my best to your family."

Cape walked into the kitchen and cut the brown tape with a pair of scissors he found in a kitchen drawer. He opened one end and slid out a picture frame. He set the eight-by-twelve burgundy frame on the counter.

It held a canvas painting, which Cape recognized from a photo that Carnie had taken the previous summer on Sullivan's Island. Randy stood on the beach, Jules on one shoulder, Tripp on the other.

Beside him stood a smiling Pauline, Cape's arm surrounding her. Billy and Christina were positioned on Randy's other side, Billy was holding Allie, and Alicia sat on her knees in front of them all.

Cape rubbed his forefinger gently across Randy's face, his smile captured forever in the image.

Carnie said it was a true sign from God that Randy was with them on that cold Christmas morning.

Chapter Thirty-Four

Cape maintained a rigorous workout schedule in the offseason with Coach Steck. He pushed himself to limits he'd never reached before, and told Coach not to ease up on him. Each afternoon, the loud crack of the bat echoed across the baseball field at Santee High as Coach threw hundreds of pitches to his favorite player.

Coach saw the fire in Cape, evident in every ground ball he fielded, and in every ball he crushed at the plate. Baseball was a simple game, but to be great, one had to understand its intricacies. It was so much more than hitting and throwing, wins and losses. Rather, it was about searching within one's own self to discover that the effort, pain, sweat, and sacrifice was where greatness could be found.

Cape was one of the rare breeds who understood that.

In late February, Cape left Jules and Carnie in Santee and headed back to Arizona for spring training.

After breakfast on the first morning, the team met with the coaches. The first few days were typically eight hours of hitting stations, fielding, base running, and other fundamentals. One of the coaches read the list of guys that management wanted to train with the Major League team of the White Sox. He called Cape's name and two others, Bobby Wanstadt and Marcus Wilson. Bobby was a catcher and first round pick from LSU. Marcus, on the other hand, had signed a free agent contract out of high school, spending six years in the minors.

"Well, boys, here's what we've been waiting for our whole life," Cape said as they jogged slowly across the spacious training complex on their way to Camelback Ranch Stadium, the spring training ballpark shared by the White Sox and the L.A. Dodgers.

"I don't know about you fellas, but I feel breakfast coming back up," Marcus said.

"Relax, man," said Bobby as they ran. "You better take advantage of the opportunity 'cause you won't get a second chance."

"It's what we've been busting our tails for," said Cape. "Baseball is baseball, no matter if we're with the guys in Rookie League, or these boys in the big leagues. Don't try to do anything differently. Just battle, one pitch at a time."

"One pitch at a time," Bobby repeated.

When the three walked onto the field, Jose Perez, a muscular right fielder, was on the grass, stretching. He had led the league in runs-batted-in the previous year, and was also second in the league in home runs, belting forty-three out of the park. "Welcome ladies," he said as some of the other players laughed. "Hope you get to hang out with us for a while. The last guys they sent over didn't make it past lunch time." The three nodded mutely.

The Major League squad had already been at spring training for two weeks, and they looked relaxed and confident. It was an entirely different atmosphere than the madness of the minor leagues where players worked like rented mules to keep their major league dreams alive. These players had reached the top, so their goal was on fine-tuning their proficient skills for the long season ahead.

Cape, Bobby, and Marcus tried to act nonchalant.

"Hey Jeffers, I hear you got some pop in that bat of yours," Jose said as the players warmed up along the left field line.

"If the wind's with me," Cape said with a smile. He looked around the field. It felt surreal to see players he'd watched on television warming up around him, some he'd watched since his high school days. "I'd sure be happy with your numbers, dude. You were a machine last season."

"Got to keep the fans happy, you know?" Jose said.

"That's what they say."

Cape practiced with the infielders, and Darian Wheeler, the shortstop, didn't say much. He knew Cape was there to challenge him for his position. Strong as he was defensively, he'd batted only .221 for the previous season. He was in the final year of his contract, and he sensed the front office didn't much care for last year's performance.

Cape worked out with the team all week, and felt good with the way he fielded. At the plate he was in total control and relaxed, hitting the ball with what seemed an effortless motion. The other players took notice, but more importantly, so did the coaches. Jose commented out loud to anyone who cared to listen that he'd not seen a player who could hit with power from both sides of the plate like Cape.

In the first game, which kicked off a thirty-game exhibition season known as the Cactus League, Cape sat the bench. Darian started at shortstop, only because he was the returning starter, not because he outplayed Cape in practice. Darian looked intense in the way he carried himself on the field, and he obviously intended to retain his position.

Cape wasn't used to sitting on the bench, and watching the game from the dugout made him restless. He observed the guys as they took the field, how they acted in the dugout, the camaraderie they shared. These men were at the top of the ladder, the best of the best, a team, with goals of winning championships. The walls they'd built around themselves in the minors were gone. There was no competition between them, no more steps to climb, no more worry of being stepped on.

There were egos, and each player knew that his individual stats not only brought more fame, but also higher dollar amounts in contract negotiations. But the only competition was with players who didn't perform well, causing management to see if guys like Cape could challenge them into retaining their spot.

Darian went hitless in the first game, and afterwards, kicked over a cooler in the dugout.

The next day was a double header against the Dodgers, and Cape started the second game. He fought a smile when the manager let him know he was playing.

In his first at-bat, he faced right-hander Kerry Tate, a split-fingered fastball specialist. Batting left-handed, Cape adjusted his helmet, took his two practice swings, and took a deep breath. *It's just baseball*, he thought. *No need to do anything any different than I've done my whole life.* He loved the challenge, the one-on-one duel of pitcher versus batter.

He took a fastball for strike one, trying to get a feel for the speed of the pitch. The second pitch was a split finger fastball, a bit too low for a swing, for strike two. A split finger came his way again, knee-high. He made a nice stroke, and hit it hard up the middle. He was sure he had a single, but the opposing second baseman made a diving backhand for the ball, popped to his feet, and threw Cape out by a split second. He didn't get a base hit, but he did impress the coaches with his smooth swing.

For the next five weeks, Cape batted .324 and took over the starting shortstop position. Darian was in the same hitting funk from the previous year, and the pressure Cape put on him seemed to make it worse; he pressed more and more at the plate.

As the exhibition season ended, Cape got called into the manager's office, where he was informed he was heading to Chicago, and that Darian was being sent to Charlotte. Cape had three days until the season opener, and couldn't wait. After a decade of delays and re-routes, the Cape Train was finally boring full speed ahead.

***

Carnie and Pauline sat in rocking chairs in the atrium of the Columbia Airport. Jules bounced from foot to foot, her eyes glued on the corridor where her father would soon walk. When she finally saw her dad coming towards her, holding a bear in a White Sox uniform, she took off running toward him. He squatted and braced himself for the impact. She wrapped her arms around his neck and he squeezed her back.

"I missed you, Daddy," she said, refusing to ease her grip.

"I missed you too, Jules. I tried to get the pilot to fly the plane faster so I could make it home to see you as soon as possible." He realized she was growing up, now getting tall. Soon she would be eleven years old. "I know you're kinda big for a teddy bear, but I thought this one would look good on your dresser in Chicago."

"Chicago? You got moved up to the White Sox?"

"You bet your sweet smile I did."

Jules turned and ran toward Carnie and Pauline. "Daddy's in the majors. Daddy's in the majors." Most everyone in the busy airport turned to watch.

Pauline began to sob and soon was wrapped in Cape's arms. "Oh, Cape, your father would be so proud."

Carnie put her arms around the pair as best she could, and Jules nudged her way between their legs. Two men walked by and Carnie smiled.

"We're moving to Chicago," she said to one of them. She then raised her clenched fists as high as she could. "Hello, Chicago. Hello, Patti Richards."

Cape decided to fly to Chicago, and have Carnie and Jules drive up at the end of April. He spent the weekend searching for a three-bedroom furnished apartment. He knew it wasn't worth it to hire a moving van, and he wanted to see whether or not he would actually become a permanent fixture with the White Sox. If he had a bad start, he might be sent down to Rock Hill again. He also wanted to adjust to life in the big leagues, and Jules to finish the school year at his mother's house. He knew it would be good for his mother too.

On Opening Night, Cape drove his Buick rental car to the stadium and a guard directed him through a tunnel to a reserved parking spot underneath, just outside the locker room. It was a nice change from parking in back lots, away from fans and errant foul balls. The vast locker room was the nicest he'd ever seen, with carpeted floors, leather couches, and large screen televisions in every corner. Each locker contained large oak cabinet compartments.

He was early, as usual, and when he found the locker with his name on it, he got chills. He smiled when he saw his jersey hanging in the locker. No. 17, with the name Jeffers above it. He decided as long as it contained a seven, he was happy. From a manila folder, he removed a photo of his father carrying Jules on his back, and placed it on a shelf. He also removed the drawing Becca had given him and set it beside the photo.

Cape walked onto the field for batting practice, and stood along the first base dugout. He studied the giant structure, the triple deck, the skyboxes, and the massive video screen scoreboard behind center field. He looked across the manicured diamond, and the sounds of bats thumping balls echoed across the empty stadium. Twenty-five years in the making, Cape finally stepped on a Major League field in a team uniform. He would be playing with the best in the world, but since he wanted to be the best of the best, he still had much work to do.

He stepped into the batter's box, the stadium active around him. His teammates were scattered about the outfield, waiting for the line drives and fly balls that Cape would hit. Fans were filling the seats, and vendors walked the aisles. The flags along the top of the scoreboard popped in the breeze. The late afternoon sun was showing the outfield grass in gold, and it felt exactly like the scene Cape had imagined as a child.

He fouled off the first three pitches.

"Easy there, Jeffers," Jose said from behind the cage. "Just see the ball, and don't try to over swing."

Cape lined the next pitch to right field. By the end of BP he had knocked five balls over the fence. He stepped out of the cage and Jose tapped him on his helmet with his bat.

"You'll remember this day for the rest of your life, rookie. You've made it to the show. A billion kids have dreamed about making it, but they never will."

Cape nodded. He was ready now.

He jogged to shortstop, and between fielding balls from Brandon Griner at first base, he looked at the 40,000 fans who'd come to watch a baseball game.

Cape had only been to two Major League games. The first was to Yankee Stadium when he was nine, and at the time he couldn't believe so many people could fit in one place. Both times, he'd imagined what it might feel like to actually be between the white lines, and now he was finding out.

***

Half of Santee met at O'Reilly's. Pauline, Carnie, and Jules arrived an hour before game time to get a large table with a great view of the biggest television. Friends came. Coach Steck, donned in a White Sox cap, was ready to root for the hometown hero. It had been a long journey, not just for Cape, but for the entire town. Never had such hope been placed on a local boy, and they all wanted something to cheer about, something to make them feel good again. With the blow Cape was dealt in Kasey's death, and then Randy's, some had wondered if the town was cursed.

The game began and the visiting team, the Kansas City Royals, came to bat. Crowd noise rose as the first pitch was delivered, and the season was underway. A grounder was hit to second, where it was fielded and thrown to first for the out. The next two batters struck out, so Cape's first opportunity to field a ball would have to wait.

Cape batted fifth in the lineup, and he took his bat from the rack and began rubbing it as he sat on the bench. He was anxious to hit, but a three-up, three-down inning prevented it.

In the top of the second, with one out, Cape got his first chance to make a defensive play. A ball was hit toward second base, a high bouncer that Cape had to charge quickly. With the batter sprinting to first, Cape fielded the ball with his bare hand, zipping a bullet to Brandon and beating the batter to first by mere inches for the out.

In the bottom of the second, Cape stood on-deck, swinging his bat in windmill fashion like he always did. The first batter popped out to left to start the inning, and Cape stepped to the plate. Cape adjusted his helmet and took his two swings. *Focus on the pitcher*, he thought. *Do what you do best.* He'd waited for what seemed like two lifetimes for this moment. He called time and stepped out of the box. He looked across the stadium at the crowd. He looked into the twilight of the western sky, clouds soared high and endless, much like the day of his championship game in high school.

"Play ball, batter," the umpire said.

Cape smiled and stepped into the box.

"Can't blame for you soaking it in," said the catcher, a seven-year veteran.

Cape worked the count to two balls and two strikes, and felt surprisingly calm for his first at-bat in the majors. He tried to guess what the pitcher would offer, and when a fastball headed for the outside corner of the plate, Cape made just enough contact to slip the baseball between the first and second baseman and into right field. He ran down the first base line faster than he'd ever run before. He stood on first and thought of the time long ago when he'd gotten his first hit in Little League. He'd yelled, "Hey, Dad, now I have a batting average." How he wished he could yell that to his dad right then and there.

The White Sox won 3–1. Cape went one-for-three with a walk. It wasn't exactly a storybook performance, but it was solid and he'd felt confident each time he walked to the plate.

After the game he stayed for autographs, and was overwhelmed by the size of the waiting crowd. He called his mother's cell phone as soon as he got to the locker room.

"Hey, Mom, did you watch the game?"

"Of course," she said loudly over the background noise of people talking. "We wouldn't have missed it for anything. Half the town is here at O'Reilly's. We're so proud of you." She felt a tug on her sleeve. "Hang on, someone wants to talk to you."

"Hey, Daddy. I saw you wearing the bracelet."

"I always do. Are you wearing yours?"

"Yes, sir. You were great tonight. I miss you."

"I miss you too. But I'll see you in just a few weeks."

"What's it like playing in a major league stadium on television?"

"Not bad. Not bad at all." He smiled and rubbed his hand through his hair.

"Grandma wants to talk to you one more time. Carnie says to tell you hi and that you played great, but she says she really needs to work with you on your power hitting."

"Okay. I'll let her help me when you guys get up here. I love you, Jules."

"I love you too, Daddy." She handed the phone to Pauline.

"Coach Steck said to tell you he knew you'd make it to the big leagues, but he just didn't realize it would take this long."

Cape laughed. "Tell him he's a very big part of the reason I'm here."

"I sure do wish your father was here to see it. He'd be beaming."

"I know, Mom." Cape's eyes welled, and he looked skyward. "But somehow, something tells me he was watching."

The Cape Train was picking up steam, and about to pull into the station.

Chapter Thirty-Five

By the second week of June, the Sox were a game and a half out of first place behind the Detroit Tigers. Management was quite happy with everything except the pitching situation. One of the starters, Joshua Carlisle, was on the thirty-day disabled list due to tendinitis. George Whiteside, a relief pitcher, was having shoulder problems.

Cape was second on the team in hitting, batting .351, and tied with Jose Perez in home runs with fourteen in fifty-one games. *Baseball Weekly* wrote an article about him titled "A Seasoned Rookie". The early ballots for the All-Star game were coming in. Cape was second in the league in votes received. Not bad for a player ten years removed from the first time he'd stepped on the field in Rookie League.

Cape made the league minimum salary, close to $300,000. He bought a refurbished two-story brick home in a tree-lined neighborhood near the Oak Street Beach bordering Lake Michigan.

It had a sunken den where Carnie and Jules could hold class, and a narrow back yard just big enough for them to play catch.

Jules and Carnie became regulars at the home games, and began to make friends with the families of the other players.

By the time most players made it to the majors, they had settled down, replacing the line of girlfriends with wives and children. The sons and daughters of the White Sox players took to Carnie's childlike personality.

The players' wives were entertained by her passion for the game, and how quickly she'd stare down anyone who chose to make rude comments about their husbands, or when the situation called for it, to stand up and verbally defend the team. She became the unofficial White Sox security guard/number one fan.

* * *

The White Sox were scheduled to play the cross-town rival Chicago Cubs at Wrigley Field on Wednesday afternoon for a 1:00 p.m. start. Wrigley was synonymous with old-time baseball and had a rich history, a place where many legends of long ago once played. Where players, fans, and the ball field became one. Unfazed by time, Wrigley Field had been the heartbeat of the row-house neighborhoods of the north side since the '20s.

Cape couldn't hide his excitement. Behind Maui Jim sunglasses, his Stallion cap pulled low, in jeans and a sweatshirt, he boarded the Redline train for Addison Street. His teammates drove to the stadium, but Cape had always wanted to ride the "L" to Wrigley. Even though he was surrounded by Cub fans dressed in blue and white, he made it to the stadium without detection.

The streets bordering the stadium were noisy, just how Cape had anticipated. The smell of Bratwurst grilling in onions tempted Cape to grab his wallet and have a taste. A four-piece band played in front of Harry Caray's statue, the beloved Cubs' announcer who was famous for leading the fans each game in singing "Take Me Out to the Ballpark" during the seventh-inning stretch.

Like tourists at Disney World, people snapped photos of everything in Cub land.

Minutes before game time, dressed in his White Sox uniform, Cape looked across the stadium, into the upper decks, and imagined fans from sixty and seventy years ago, watching their heroes play the greatest game in the world. When he stood outside the dugout, he felt the ghosts of Rogers Hornsby and Ernie Banks, two of the greatest Cubs players of all time, beside him.

He imagined life in those golden days, the men in the stands dressed in white shirts, ties, and fedoras. Based on the sold-out stadium that day, it was obvious that time had not diminished their love for the Cubbies. These were the most loyal fans in all of baseball.

In Cape's second at-bat, he drilled the second pitch deep in the gap in left field. He watched the ball carom off the famed ivy-covered wall, and when he stood on second base, he looked across the outfield bleachers to the balconies of row homes where people gathered to watch the game. Cape loved playing baseball, but he was almost tempted to walk into the stands and watch the rest of it from the outfield bleachers. He considered himself a lucky man to play in that perfect atmosphere. He wished every stadium had the purity of Wrigley Field.

The Sox beat the Cubs 3–1, and Cape felt bad for the Cub fans and the dejected looks on their faces as they made their way out the exits. He kept one of the baseballs used in the game, a memento that was to remind him of his experience that day at Wrigley. He held the ball, watching the sun dip behind the upper deck, the shadows swallowing the field, turning the grass into a deep shade of emerald. A cool breeze touched his face, and on that crystal clear day, he knew he'd felt the true heartbeat of baseball. As he gripped the baseball, he realized that baseball actually gripped him.

***

After several weeks of trying, Carnie was finally able to get a ticket to the Patti Richards Show.

Unfortunately, the audience members had to be eighteen or older, so Jules went to Brandon Griner's house to play with his daughter.

After the show, the director sent his assistant to invite Carnie to meet Patti. Carnie said a silent thank you to God and tried to keep from fainting.

The assistant led her down a hall and into a room where Patti sipped on bottled water and looked at a recent ratings chart. Patti extended her hand.

"Carnie, could you please tell me more about Cape Jeffers?"

"Yes, ma'am."

"Please don't call me ma'am," Patti said matter-of-factly. "It makes me feel old."

"Yes, ma'am. I mean, I'm sorry, ma'am." Carnie took a deep breath, her palms facing Patti. Carefully she said, "I'm a little nervous. Yes, Miss Richards."

Carnie explained the chain of events, in full detail, of Cape's long journey to the Major Leagues, thinking Patti probably had more important things to do than listen to her ramble.

Patti listened intently for a few minutes and asked a couple of questions, knowing she would soon be whisked away to a meeting for the next day's show.

"We would like to get Cape on the show. You think he would do that?"

"If I have to knock him out with his bat, and heave him 'cross my shoulder, I guarantee you he'll be on your show."

***

White Sox owner Charles Bennington sat in his luxurious office and looked out over the outfield of White Sox stadium. In front of him sat Jim Baxter, the general manager, and head coach Flip Peterson.

"Guys, we have a big offer on the table from the Yankees," Charles said. He looked through his reading glasses at a contract on his desk. "With Carlisle on the disabled list, and now Whiteside out with rotator cuff problems, our pitching is in a hell of a mess. The Yankees have offered up Yancey and Goodwin, their ace from Triple A who's literally shut down the whole league this season."

"What's the catch?" asked Flip. "Those guys would help us tremendously."

"They want Jeffers."

"Bullshit," said Flip. "He's too good to let go."

"He's a talented ballplayer," said Jim. "But if we don't get help with pitching, we've got no chance to win the pennant."

"You want to go with Wheeler at short?" asked Flip. "He couldn't hit his way out of a wet napkin."

"We'll work around him," said Charles. "We've got plenty of offense. But we've got to get pitching help immediately, or we may as well hang up the season and go home. The trading deadline is less than a week away, so we don't have much time to make a decision."

***

Angela stood beside the indoor pool and removed the 'No Swimming' sign. The repairman had packed up his gear and the pump was back in proper working order. She was surprised how many people preferred the indoor pool on a beautiful Carolina summer day when the resort had a spectacular outdoor pool, not to mention the beach.

She placed the sign in a closet and went to check the water cooler in the exercise room. The room was empty, not uncommon for that time of day. Most people were at the beach, by the pool, or touring around Myrtle Beach.

She glanced at the television bracketed on the wall in front of the treadmills, and quickly grabbed the remote to turn up the volume. Confused, she squinted her eyes toward what looked like Cape talking to Patti Richards.

"Cape, can you take us back to that day when your mother called and told you Kasey had gone into labor?" Patti, in a crème-colored pantsuit, crossed her legs on her sofa chair. Cape sat next to Patti on a long, brown couch. He wore blue jeans, a black v-neck shirt, and a tan blazer.

"I was playing in Greenville with the Braves. We'd beaten Chattanooga 4–3. I had just pulled into the parking lot of my apartment building after the game." Angela stood motionless. *No way* Cape was on Patti Richards' show. "I had just spoken to Pete Bennett, my agent, and I'd asked him to contact the Yankees. Their starting shortstop, Derek Stringer, had suffered a serious knee injury. They thought it might be career-ending, and I knew the Yankees would be looking for a replacement."

"I understand it's been your lifelong dream to play for the Yankees."

"Yes, it has. My dad and I went to the ball field almost every summer day when I was a kid. He'd hit me grounders, pitch me batting practice. I would pretend I was playing for the Yankees, and Dad would pretend he was the Yankees' broadcaster.

"We would end each practice with me hitting the winning homerun against the Red Sox to win the pennant, and him announcing the home run. I know it sounds corny, but to me, it was great."

"It sounds like you and your father were very close."

"We were. Unfortunately, he passed away last year."

"I'm sorry to hear that." The crowd murmured, an audio outpouring of compassion.

"Thanks."

"So take us back to that day, when you got word that Kasey was having complications during labor."

"I felt terrible that I wasn't there when she went into labor. It was a two-hour drive, though it seemed like it took a week to get there. When I got to the hospital, they told me Kasey was hemorrhaging and there was nothing they could do." Cape looked toward his feet. "She died the next morning."

"I can't imagine the emotional rollercoaster you were on. You have the miracle of birth, your only child. Your hopes for playing for the Yankees are looking like a possibility. But then, you lose your wife."

Cape tried to contain his emotions. "Jules, our baby, was premature and in the hospital for almost a month. I didn't want to leave her side. I was afraid I might lose her too."

"But your plans were to return to baseball for the following season, correct?"

"Yes. I was going to hire a nanny for Jules. That way she'd be taken care of while I was on the road. Mom offered, but she has Parkinson's, and there was just no way I could let her."

"But you learned some disturbing news before you were to report to spring practice," Patti said, guiding Cape perfectly so he could detail the events.

"I found out my investor had squandered away my signing bonus. I was broke."

"And so you had no choice but to quit."

"I didn't see any other option. I wanted what was best for my baby, and that option was me being there for her."

"But the dream of playing Major League baseball didn't completely die, did it?"

"For a while it sure seemed that way. I went back home, got a job, and spent my days raising Jules. I'll be honest with you. I took a lot of grief from the people of the town. I can't blame them, I guess. Maybe some of them had hooked their dreams to my wagon, and when I quit, their dream died too. I had no experience raising a child, and many nights I wondered if I was in over my head. But, when Jules was six years old, she found out I once played pro baseball, and soon realized I quit for her. She told me she wanted me to pursue my dream again. So, here I am."

"For those of you who don't know," Patti said, checking her notes, "Cape plays for the White Sox and currently leads the team in hitting, and also in home runs with thirty-seven." The crowd applauded and Cape tried not to blush. "I don't know much about baseball but that sure sounds like a lot of home runs." Patti held her hands out, palms up. "What do you think, audience?" They clapped enthusiastically. She smiled and looked at Cape, her demeanor becoming more serious. "Tell us what the last ten years have been like."

"Where to begin? It's had its share of ups and down. Many nights I'd rock Jules to sleep, her on my chest, both of us literally exhausted. I'll admit I hit rock bottom. I was depressed, and figured life had screwed me over. Jules meant everything to me, and she's the reason I got through it. And the little rascal is the one who got this crazy comeback started. We also have the best nanny-slash-teacher in the world, Carnie Mack. She loves you, by the way, and could hardly control herself when she found out we were moving to Chicago."

"Well, she's why you are on the show today."

"She's the best."

"If you would, tell us how hard it was to lose your wife at such a young age."

"You are just not prepared for something like that, especially when you're twenty-two years old. You take it for granted that you have your whole life together ahead of you. Kasey was special, and Jules is so much like her." Angela turned up the volume. "But, I know she's never coming back, and I've had to move on. I can't let my love for her prevent me from having a future with someone else."

"So, are you saying there is a 'someone else'?"

"I don't know if I feel comfortable talking about it on television."

"Well, you're a gorgeous guy."

The audience began to clap, their way of agreeing with Patti. She smiled at the audience's reaction.

"You're athletic, and financially, I'd imagine, you're in great shape. So I'm sure you're highly sought after."

"I don't know about all that. There was one girl who was special. But it didn't work out. With me there comes a lot of emotional baggage."

Angela wiped the tears from her cheeks as two women entered the fitness room. She placed the remote on the water cooler and walked out the door.

"Well, Cape, before we let you go," Patti said, "we have someone here who is anxious to see you."

Pete Bennett came on stage. Cape stood and hugged him. Pete was short and stocky, with neatly trimmed brown hair. He wore a navy-blue pinstripe Armani suit. "Cape, it's great to see you."

"It's good to see you too, Pete." Cape smiled.

"Pete has something he wants to tell you," Patti said with a devious grin. "By the way, audience, Pete is Cape's agent." Pete sat on the couch beside Cape and placed some papers on the table in front of them. Cape gave Pete a strange look. "Go ahead, Pete," Patti said.

"Cape, I want you to know that everything that you have endured, and how you had to overcome all the adversity in your life, is inspiring. I know it sounds sappy, but you truly make me want to be a better person. You are an amazing guy, and I've been fortunate to have you not only for a client, but a friend." Pete unfolded the papers. "And that's why it gives me a huge amount of pleasure to present this contract to you."

Cape leaned forward in his seat. "A contract for what?"

"Not what, Cape, but who."

"I'm not following you."

"Pack your bags, my man, because you're heading to New York."

Cape looked at Patti, who smiled and nodded like someone already in on a secret.

"A six-year deal, Cape. Ninety mil. You are going to be a New York Yankee."

Cape rubbed his hand through his hair. He looked at the ceiling and bit his lip in hopes of halting his tears. He was unsuccessful.

The audience stood and clapped, some yelling in excitement, and Jules and Carnie ran onto the stage. When Jules leapt into her father's arms, Patti began to cry. The audience followed suit.

Chapter Thirty-Six

As soon as he arrived in New York City, Cape took a cab straight to Yankee Stadium. He walked through a portal down the left field line and dropped his bags at his feet. A lifetime of dreaming, along with years of persistence and dedication, had led him to this moment. His mind couldn't process the distance he'd traveled, and the seemingly long odds he'd overcome.

He thought about restless nights when Jules was a baby, tending to her all alone, baseball nowhere in his thoughts. He remembered lying in his bed at night as a child, imagining what it would feel like to play for the greatest baseball organization in history. He thought of past days in the back yard, and the Little League field, passionately playing the game with a dream to someday stand at home plate in Yankee Stadium.

Though the stadium was empty and silent, he felt the presence of his heroes. Mantle, Ruth, Gehrig, as well as DiMaggio. The Bronx Bombers, the Yankee Clipper. He thought of Gehrig's speech at home plate when he had announced his retirement, his career cut short due to the crippling ALS disease, proclaiming that he considered himself the luckiest man alive. He looked at the outfield, and imagined Mantle and DiMaggio chasing down fly balls in the alleys. He pictured Ruth smiling from right field, waving to the girls in the stands while he waited his turn to hit another towering home run.

Cape moved into a small three-bedroom apartment that afternoon, though he had little time to unpack. In two hours he was due back at the stadium to begin a week-long, west coast road trip. His debut in Yankee Stadium would have to wait.

Carnie and Jules had stayed behind in Chicago. Cape put the house on the market, and though he wanted them with him in New York, he didn't want them to be confined to the apartment, especially with all the time he would spend on the road. As a result, the girls temporarily settled for watching Cape play on television. Carnie let Jules stay up late to watch the games, and they both found themselves taking catnaps during their class breaks.

On the plane to his first game as a Yankee, Cape sat beside Charlie Wiseman, the third baseman. Charlie had been with the Yankees for six seasons, was a fan favorite and a solid ballplayer. Cape had always followed his career, and was glad to be paired with him for the flight.

"So, just how does it feel to be a thirty-year-old rookie?" Charlie asked after taking a sip of ginger ale.

"Like I'm old. In more ways than one."

"You can't tell it by the season you've had. Hard to do what you have done your first year in the majors. Especially when you're *old*."

Cape was surprised to receive compliments from an established major leaguer. He had never accepted compliments easily, and it made him uncomfortable to have praise heaped on him. He simply considered himself a ballplayer who loved the game. It wasn't about the money or even the fame. He would play for basic living expenses if he had to. He knew how to hit, to field, to throw. He knew extemporaneous things clouded the game, and he'd gone through a truckload of them to make it to the big leagues.

"I've done alright, I guess," Cape said. "You know how it is when you're in the zone, and the ball looks the size of a grapefruit when you're at the plate."

"I know all about the zone, but you're putting up huge power numbers from *both* sides of the plate. That's pretty damn impressive."

"If you're trying to make me feel welcome, you're doing a great job." Cape took a glass of diet soda from the flight attendant. He looked at Charlie. "You're having a good year yourself."

"Doing alright, but I would love to have your numbers."

"Take 'em. They're yours."

Charlie smiled, and it was obvious he liked what he saw in his new teammate. The way Charlie and the rest of the team viewed it, Cape very well could be the one addition they needed to win the pennant. They were three games behind Boston and one game behind Baltimore, and they knew, with the right boost, they could still take the title.

***

The Yankees entered the visitor's locker room, and Cape quietly moved along the row of lockers until he found his. He touched the sleeve of his gray jersey, and smiled when he saw the number assigned to him, 77. Mantle's number, twice. Since they were traveling, the team wore the solid gray pants and jerseys, so Cape would have to wait till his first home game to wear the famous pinstripes. That didn't matter to him because at long last he was a Yankee. A New York Yankee.

Adrenaline took over when Cape fielded the first ball hit to him in infield practice; he threw a laser to first baseman Victor Morales. Charlie smiled and pointed at Cape with his glove. "Ease up, rook. You're going to knock Morales' glove off his hand." Cape grinned.

Family and friends watched from O'Reilly's, and the manager cordoned off a section with a sign that read

"Cape's Corner". Cape wished the family could be there in person to see his first game.

* * *

The west coast trip went well. The Yankees swept Oakland in a three-game series, and took two of three from Seattle. Cape continued his hot streak, hitting .346 for the trip with two home runs, one a three-run blast that rallied the Yankees from a two-run deficit in the eighth against Oakland.

Cape walked into the locker room as the Yankees prepared for a six-game home stand against Minnesota and Detroit. When he saw the pinstripe uniform hanging in his locker, he brushed his hand across the interlocking "NY" embroidered on the chest of the jersey. Since he was a boy, the Yankee pinstripe uniform had fascinated him, and the one he'd worn as a child still hung in a closet in his parents' home. To him, it represented every baseball dream and wish he'd ever had. It reminded him of the photographs his father used to show him, and pictures on baseball cards. Mickey Mantle taking a home run swing. Babe Ruth leaning against his bat on the on-deck circle while Lou Gehrig stood at the plate, just biding his time before he knocked the rawhide off the baseball.

He looked around the locker room, and he was alone. He removed the jersey from the hanger and slipped it over his blue, button-down dress shirt. He quickly walked to the mirror in the bathroom, buttoning the jersey along the way. He had been told so many times just how handsome, how good-looking he was. If asked, he'd deny it. But in that moment, staring at himself reflected in the mirror inside Yankee stadium, he knew he looked quite impressive. And he didn't feel bad thinking it.

Back in Santee, O'Reilly's became the place to be, showing Yankee games every time they played. The manager hired extra help to accommodate the crowd.

By the end of August, the race for the pennant involved three teams. The Yankees were a half game out of first place, and Baltimore had drawn even with Boston atop the standings in the AL East. The Yankees headed to Boston and Fenway Park intent on leapfrogging them in the standings.

The crowd was rowdy on that Friday night opener. Beer flowed and tensions were high. Boston and New York's general dislike for each other would have made for great reality television. Babe Ruth's trade from the Red Sox to the Yankees back in 1919 had started the rivalry, and it showed no signs of easing.

The Red Sox took game one 4–0, the result of a brilliant pitching performance and a three-run homer in the sixth inning. Cape went hitless, thanks to a diving catch the Red Sox's second baseman made in the fourth inning.

Game two went much like the first—Boston shut out New York 2–0, putting the Yankees two-and-a-half games out of first place. They needed to win the Sunday matchup to keep from falling too much further behind in the standings. With the score tied at three in the eighth inning, New York took the lead on Cape's sacrifice fly to center, allowing Charlie to score from third. In the bottom of the ninth, with the Yankees holding onto the slim, one-run lead, the Sox leadoff batter walked. The crowd screamed, directing their venom toward the relief pitcher for the Yankees, Aaron Prescott. A sacrifice bunt moved the batter over to second. Aaron struck out the next batter, and was one out shy of inching one game closer in the standings and avoiding the sweep.

Trey Williams, the first baseman and RBI leader for the Sox, stepped up to bat. He'd been a major thorn in the Yankees' side all season. Aaron got ahead of Trey in the count, working a one ball, two strike count. After fouling off two pitches, Trey launched the next pitch over the Green Monster and out of the stadium. The sweep was complete, the noise from the Red Sox fans deafening. The Yankees headed home, dejected.

By mid-September, Cape was batting .407. He had hit forty-eight home runs, and led the league in runs-batted-in with one-hundred and twenty-two. The Yankees were just two games out of first. They took two out of three from Baltimore, which moved them into second place.

Baltimore then proceeded to lose all three games at Toronto, making it a two-team race between Boston and New York for the pennant.

***

Cape sat in his apartment, eating his usual pre-game meal, the minutes passing slowly before he could leave for the ballpark. He ran through the contacts on his cell. Angela's number was the first one on the list. He still thought about her from time to time, wondering if she did the same about him. He understood her stance, yet he still felt he could truly love her the way she deserved to be loved. After he finished lunch, he took a deep breath and dialed her number. When her voicemail kicked in, his heart jumped. He was almost glad he didn't get in touch with her in person.

He left a brief message and an invitation.

***

October in New York City, a chill in the air as the town ended its summer siesta. Crystal clear skies hugged the skyline, and at night, people walked the city streets in jackets and sweaters. The Red Sox had come to town to finish off the Yankees, holding a two-game lead with only three games left in the season. All the Sox needed was one win to clinch the pennant, and they looked forward to taking the Yankees down in the Yankees' own backyard.

Cape flew his family to New York for the series. He had not seen his daughter in two months, and he missed her terribly. He had to go to the ballpark, so he left a key with the doorman.

Jules and Carnie's plane arrived thirty minutes before Pauline and Billy's family, and after exchanging hellos and hugs, they all rode a shuttle to the downtown hotel. After Pauline and Billy checked into their rooms, Carnie and Jules went to Cape's apartment to drop off their bags. Alicia flew in from Durham and met them at Cape's. Two hours before game time, they climbed in a limo that Cape had arranged so they could all ride to the stadium together.

After the driver had dropped them off, the family hurried to their seats in order to watch Cape take batting and infield practice. The players' family seats were just behind the backstop, and Cape saw Jules when they walked through the portal. Her hair had grown, and it was in a ponytail tucked under a Yankees cap. She waved at him, and he motioned for her to come to the dugout. He hugged her over the railing.

"Hey, Half-pint," he said, holding her tightly. "Girl, have I missed you. I've been counting down the days." He smiled at his family. His mother placed her shaky hands to her face, and her eyes sent her love to him.

"I've missed you too, Daddy." Jules pulled back and looked at him. "Wow. You were made to wear that uniform. You look awesome."

"Did you think this day would ever come?"

"Yes, sir. I surely did. Remember the night I prayed for it?"

"I'm just glad you're here. I wouldn't be standing on this field if not for you."

"I guess it's been worth the wait, huh?"

"You know it." Cape looked at players who were taking batting practice. "Guess I better get back to work. I'll see you after the game. Tell the others I love them."

"I will." Jules turned to walk to her seat.

"Hey, Jules." She stopped and looked at Cape. "But not as much as I love you."

She smiled. "I know."

"Cocky, aren't you?" Jules nodded and turned again. "Hey, Jules?"

Jules shook her head and stopped. "What now, Daddy?" she asked with a laugh.

Cape held up his arm and rubbed his bracelet. "You wearing yours?"

"Always," she yelled and raised her arm. They smiled at each other and she ran up the steps. He watched her go, his little girl not so little anymore.

The Red Sox jumped on the scoreboard in the first inning, scoring a run off back-to-back doubles. The few Red Sox fans who had found tickets were loud and very rowdy. They had come to party at the Yankees' expense.

In the bottom of the first, Jose doubled down the left field line with two outs. Cape stepped to the plate. Batting right-handed, he calmly watched the pitcher, Dustin Shipley, who he'd faced years ago at Salem. Dustin had averaged fifteen wins a game for seven straight seasons. Cape sought his eyes, as much to give him an "I'm back" look as to figure out what pitch was coming. He worked the count to two balls and no strikes, and felt a fastball was next. The Red Sox coach sensed that too, and instructed the catcher to signal a breaking ball. When Dustin threw a curve ball, Cape ripped it to left center, and Jose scored to tie the game.

In the eighth, the Yankees on top 3–1, the Red Sox loaded the bases with one out. Trey Williams stood at the plate. He crushed a line drive that hit past the mound on its way to center field. Cape moved to his left. It went past second base, two bounces away from the outfield grass. Cape, his arm fully extended, cradled the ball as his body fell to the ground. Just before his knees and elbows made contact with the dirt, he flipped the ball from his glove to Chris Howell, the second baseman. Chris barehanded the toss, pivoted and turned as his foot moved off second base. He tossed a side arm bullet to first, beating Trey by a split second to end the inning without any runs being scored.

The Yankees held on, putting them within one game of Boston. If they could win on Saturday, Sunday's game would determine who would take the pennant.

Security escorted Cape's family to wait outside the locker room. He showered quickly and stopped for two interviews before making his way to them.

His mother was first in line to hug him, and she kissed him on the cheek.

"Cape, I'm so of proud of you. To see you in Yankee Stadium, dressed in pinstripes, I can't even begin to describe the feeling."

"Thanks, Mom. I'm glad you're here. You are a big part of all this."

"This is more exciting than anything I've ever seen."

"Well, we're not done yet. Two more wins to go." He kissed her on the forehead before Jules nudged her way between them. He lifted her into his arms. "How did I look out there?"

"Awesome, Dad. Awesome."

He felt her shoes rubbing against his kneecaps. "My God, you are getting tall. I don't think you're my Half-pint anymore."

Cape hugged Billy, Christina, and then their two children. Three-year-old Allie, with brown hair and browner eyes, kissed Cape on the chin. "Hey, Uncle Cape."

"Hello, babycakes."

He hugged Carnie and told her how much he missed her turbo-charged spunk. "I alerted the town that you were coming. They said you were a little too laid back for this city."

"Funny white boy. See what drinkin' swamp water as a kid has done to your brain?"

Cape took everyone to eat at the Knickerbocker Bar & Grill in Greenwich Village. He bought them all steak dinners, and throughout the meal other patrons stopped and congratulated Cape on the big win. It was as if New York had become Cape Town.

The Yankees blasted the Red Sox on Saturday 8–2, setting up the final showdown. The entire city had a feeling of excitement, and the Yankee fans in the bars and restaurants were cloaked in team attire. What better way to win the pennant than by sweeping those hated Red Sox?

***

Cape set aside tickets for his family, writing their names on the envelope for the will-call office. He added one extra name, one more ticket, just as he had for the two previous games. A ticket that had gone unused.

When he handed his ticket form to the equipment manager, he was tempted to remove the extra ticket, but decided it didn't make any difference. She wouldn't come.

Around two in the morning, Cape woke to find Jules crying beside his bed. He turned on the lamp. She wore a light blue gown, and her eyes were red.

"What's wrong, Jules?" He placed his feet on the floor and took her in his arms, placing her on his lap. He marveled at how much she'd grown.

"I heard Uncle Billy and Aunt Christina talking tonight with the people who sat beside them at the game."

"Talking about what?"

"Uncle Billy said he never thought you'd play again, after the way your life was ruined when I was born."

Cape looked carefully into her eyes, and like so many times before, saw Kasey staring back at him. "He didn't mean it like that. They knew I had always dreamed of playing for the Yankees, and when I decided to quit to raise you, they thought the dream was dead."

"If it wasn't for me, you'd still have Mom. You'd have played baseball, instead of working at the stupid plant. Instead of having to be Mommy and Daddy to me." She sniffled.

"Baby, what happened to your mother was not your fault. Nothing is your fault. I really would have been content to spend my life raising you, just the two of us. If you hadn't asked me to play again, that would have been okay by me. I had you, and that's all I needed." He wiped her tears with his thumb. "Remember that time we were playing at the ball park with my old wooden bat, and it splintered?" Jules nodded. "Papa hammered carpet tacks in it and taped it, and we still use it when we play ball at the park. Well, that's pretty much what happened the day you were born. The dream splintered a little, but it wasn't shattered. And now it's been put back together because of you."

"That's not really true," she said, grinning like a sly fox.

"What do you mean?"

"It won't be put back together until tomorrow night."

"How do you figure that?"

"I can't explain it, but I can see it in my mind."

Cape smiled and rubbed her soft hair. "See what in your mind?"

"You'll see tomorrow night."

"What are you talking about?"

"Patience." She hugged him tightly. "Go to bed, Daddy. Big day tomorrow." She walked to the door, turned, and smiled at her father. "I love you."

His heart melted at that moment, and he smiled at his daughter, the one who gave him purpose, who gave his life meaning. "I love you, too, Jules. More than you'll ever know."

Cherish your vision and your dreams, as they are the children of your soul, the blueprints of your achievements.
- Napoleon Hill

And also that every man should eat and drink, and enjoy the good of his labour, that is the gift of God.
- Ecclesiastes 3:13

Chapter Thirty-Seven

A large group of Yankee fans had gathered outside the players' entrance of the stadium. Normally when Cape arrived, no one was there but the security guards.

"Give 'em hell, Jeffers," an elderly man shouted.

"You da man," a college-age kid yelled. Cape waved to acknowledge the compliment.

Cape prided himself on being first to the locker room, but when he walked in, he realized Charlie had beaten him to it.

"A little anxious?" Cape asked.

"You're damn right," Charlie said. "Lisa kicked me out of the house. I've been pacing the floor of our apartment since 7:30 this morning and she said it was driving her crazy."

"It's just a game, right?" Cape asked as he sat in front of his locker.

"And the Ark was just a friggin' canoe."

"Well, maybe it is more than just your average game."

"Haven't you ever wanted something so bad you could feel it deep down inside you?"

"You've no idea."

"I want to win the pennant, and the American League championship, and then the World Series. But that can't happen if we don't win today."

"Nothing to worry about, dude. There's no doubt in my mind."

What he'd imagined as a child had come true. Cape *was* a New York Yankee, playing against Boston for the pennant. And now it was up to him to finish the dream. For Kasey, for his father. Jules. His family. His hometown.

New York celebrated the game in style. Fighter jets flew over the stadium as an Italian tenor from the New York Opera belted out the Star Spangled Banner. The governor threw the ceremonial first pitch. Celebrity sightings were common. Scalpers sold what remaining tickets they had outside the gates, filling their wallets. Cape's family sat twelve rows from the bottom, bundled up like the Southerners they were.

Billy snapped photos of the players, and the field. He took pictures of the family. Carnie and Jules thought it'd be fun to make goofy faces. He had planned on taking pictures of Cape throughout the game.

The Yankees had eighteen-game winner Jason Norton on the mound. The tall lefty had a fastball that consistently stayed in the ninety-seven mph range. He could make his slider drop like a drunken nun. The Sox decided to go with Matthew Vaughn, a tough righty who had won his last six outings.

The night was crisp, the skies clear, temperatures in the fifties. The perfect matchup, the perfect setting, and after one-hundred and sixty-one games, it all came down to the final one. The deep sea of Navy-clad fans adorned in coats and jackets made the stands look dark and distant. The field, however, was lit up like Times Square.

The first two innings were uneventful; Norton and Vaughn retired the first six batters. In the top of the third, Boston struck. A leadoff walk by the catcher got the Sox players up on their feet. The next batter hit a ground ball that Chris Howell fielded on the grass deep behind first base. He had to settle for the out at first, but the runner moved over to second. The next batter hit a hard grounder to Cape, who looked the runner back to second to keep him from advancing to third, before throwing to first for the out. The next batter, however, doubled to left, driving in the runner on second. The Sox took the lead 1–0.

The score stayed the same until the fifth, when the Sox doubled to start the inning. After a strike out and a walk, Trey Williams knocked a slider down the first base line, allowing both runners to score. The fans fidgeted in their seats. Jules looked at Carnie.

"Don't worry, D.J.," Carnie said. "Wait on the Lord, and He shall strengthen thine heart. The book of Psalms."

"Well, God needs to strengthen us all, and really soon," added Pauline.

A rowdy fan several rows behind them yelled, "Get Norton out of there. He's a bum."

Carnie stood and turned. "Get up outta here with that trash talk. This ain't Sunday afternoon softball. This is the big leagues, fool."

"Shut the hell up," the man replied.

"Boy, I'll shove that pretzel up your nose if you don't watch that language. There's children present."

"Easy, Carnie," Pauline interrupted, touching her sleeve.

Carnie bit her lip and cut the man a mean stare. She pointed her finger at the obnoxious fan. "You just made the list."

In the bottom of the sixth, the Yankees finally got their bats cranked. Charlie singled to right, and then Jose singled up the middle. Cape stepped into the box and stared at the pitcher. *I've got him right where I want him,* he thought. He knew Vaughn didn't want to walk him, as that would load the bases with no outs. The pitcher also knew that a walk was better than a three-run homer, but either way, he didn't want to get behind in the count.

The first pitch was a fastball on the inside corner of the plate, knee high. Cape turned on the pitch and the crack of the bat echoed across the field. The ball headed for the gap in left-center, and both runners scored.

Boston's lead was now a slim 3–2. The energy in the crowd rose.

Cape stood on second base and nodded to his teammates in the dugout. He tugged on his bracelet and smiled at Jules, who stood and tugged on hers.

In the top of the eighth, the Red Sox had a runner on third with two outs. Their right fielder was at bat, and he hit a blooper down the left field line. Charlie gave chase but had no chance to make a play on the ball, and Cape went after it. The soft pop fly headed to a spot just inside the foul line, and Boston looked as if they were about to take a two-run lead. As the ball fell toward the grass, Cape slid on his backside, his left leg bent as if he were sliding into second base. He turned his glove toward third base, and caught the ball just before it hit the ground. The crowd jumped to their feet, screaming and applauding. When they showed the replay of the catch on the video board, Jules stood and shouted, "That's my daddy."

The inning was over.

The Red Sox brought in their closer, a stocky hard-throwing right-hander named Michael Stonebreaker, after the Yankees got a runner on first with two outs. His fastball could reach speeds up to one-hundred mph, and he blew three fastballs by catcher Adam Edwards to end the eighth. The Yankee fans began to grumble. Three outs away from defeat to their archrival. They just couldn't imagine anything more painful.

Yankee relief pitcher Gabe Joyner got the first two batters out in the top of the ninth, but then gave up back-to-back singles, with Trey Williams next up at the plate. Being down one run in the ninth, the Yankees knew if Boston scored again, their chances of winning would be greatly reduced. Gabe was clearly rattled, especially at seeing two relievers warming up in the bullpen. Cape called time out and jogged to the mound.

"How you feelin'?" Cape asked. He took the ball and rubbed it with the palm of his hands.

"How do you think I'm feeling?" Gabe removed his hat and wiped the sweat from his forehead with his sleeve. "Not too damn good."

"Listen. You're going to get us out of this jam so we can win it for you in the ninth. Williams is a fastball hitter so he won't be expecting one. Jam him high and hard. He can't lay off 'em."

"Coach will staple a one-way bus ticket back to Single A on my earlobe if I serve up a fastball. I need to stick with the breaking balls on the outside of the plate. I'll just nibble and see if he'll go for a bad one."

"Gabe, you're one of the reasons we're one win away from the pennant. This guy can't beat you if you give it all you got. It all comes down to who wants it more. Now dig down deep and throw with everything you got."

Cape patted him on the backside and returned to his position.

Gabe toed the mound and took a deep breath. The catcher, Adam signaled for a breaking ball, and Gabe nervously shook his head. Adam again flashed the sign for a breaking ball, and Gabe again shook him off. He gave the sign for a slider, and Gabe slightly jiggled his glove for a 'no'. He called for a changeup, and again, Gabe brushed it off. When Adam laid down the sign for fastball, Gabe nodded. Adam stared at Gabe like he was an idiot. Gabe smiled.

He reared back and threw the fastball with all he could muster, and the pitch jammed Williams high and inside for strike one. The Yankees pitching coach leapt from his seat and threw his hat before going into a tirade of profanity.

Gabe looked at Cape as he walked back to the mound. Cape smiled and nodded. *Not again*, Gabe thought. *Oh yes, again.*

Gabe once again shook off Adam's sign for the breaking ball, and he fired another fastball to the inside of the plate. Williams swung, the ball hitting the bat just above his hands, and the soft pop fly landed safely in Gabe's glove. The inning was over.

So it came down to the final at-bat. The tension was thick, and Boston looked as uptight as the Yankees. The Sox just needed three outs to win the pennant. Jules rubbed her bracelet. Carnie began humming "We Shall Overcome".

Stonebreaker picked up where he left off, striking out the leadoff batter. The crowd became deathly quiet. Carnie hummed louder. When Charlie popped out weakly to second base, the only sounds in the massive stadium came from the small group of Sox fans. Most of the New York fans had their heads buried in their hands.

Cape stepped up on-deck and Jose walked to the plate. With bat in hand, Cape rolled his arm like a windmill, staying loose as the temperature steadily dropped. He turned his head from side to side, calm and relaxed. He looked at the crowd, and he saw the worry in their eyes. He also noticed a figure standing at the top row of steps on the lower deck. A familiar silhouette carved by the concourse lights behind her. When she stepped from under the shadows and smiled, he knew it was her. She had come.

She nodded in his direction, her face shielded under her trademark New York Yankees cap. The crack of the bat rang out, and Cape turned to see Jose beating a path down the first base line. By the time the left fielder threw the ball to the shortstop, Jose stood on first with a single.

The tying run was at first. The winning run coming to the plate, the Santee Stallion, Cape Jeffers. He rubbed his bracelet and adjusted his helmet. He took one practice swing, and then another. The crowd was on their feet, and Cape ignored the noise. He began to hear his father's voice. *Now batting, the greatest player to wear the Yankee pinstripes, Cape Jeffers.* Goose bumps rose on his forearms. Cape looked at Stonebreaker. *He's nervous,* Cape thought. As the pitcher wiped the sweat from his brow, he heard Randy's excited voice again. *Two outs, one runner on, and the pennant on the line. If there was a player Yankee fans would want in this situation, it would be Jeffers.*

The scene was eerily familiar to Cape's final at-bat in his high school championship game. However, the stakes this time were so much bigger. The outcome of this game would affect the disposition of millions of Yankee fans everywhere. It would affect the mood of the largest city in the country. It would stamp a mark on history that would last for all time. The pressure of it all rested on the broad shoulders of Cape Jeffers. But, instead of feeling nervous, Cape felt a calmness. Twenty-six years he'd waited and rehearsed this situation in his mind and body.

The first pitch from Stonebreaker was a scorcher that just missed the outside corner of the plate. Cape stepped out of the box for a second, and looked at the crowd. He had them where he wanted them. They were pleading for greatness, and he was ready to give it to them. He stepped back in the box, took his two practice swings, and the pitcher threw a fastball up and in. Cape didn't swing because he wouldn't have been able to extend his arms enough to send it out of the park.

With a one ball, one strike count, Cape sensed that Stonebreaker would bring the slider. He guessed right, and the slider, close to ninety-five mph, came roaring to the plate at kneecap level. In what seemed to be like slow motion to Cape, he turned his hips and his hands exploded toward the pitch. His eyes squinting, his teeth biting down on his lower lip, tasting the saltiness of his skin. His broad shoulders twisting, his powerful front leg stepping forward. Everything in his body, fluid and smooth, pushed toward the ball. When he made contact, the bat crushed the ball.

The crowd fell silent as the centerfielder sprinted to the wall. Stonebreaker dropped to his knees, unable to watch. Cape charged down the first base line, watching the ball as it flew higher and higher into the New York night. The centerfielder stopped at the warning track and watched the ball sail over the scoreboard and out of the stadium. The crowd began to roar, a deafening, rising wave of sound, and Cape felt the electricity coming from the fans. On his way toward second, Jose rounding third and on his way to the plate, fireworks exploding above centerfield, Randy's voice told the story in Cape's head.

The Yankees win the pennant! The Yankees win the pennant! It's pandemonium. My God, it's the most amazing scene I've ever had the pleasure to witness. I will never forget this day!

Cape rounded third. Tears flowed down Pauline's face. Jules was in Carnie's arms.

"Praise Jesus," Carnie screamed repeatedly.

When Cape stepped on home plate, he felt his dad's arms surround him.

Cape Jeffers has crushed the Red Sox' dreams and has secured a place in the hearts of Yankees fans forever.

Cape's teammates swarmed all over him and he disappeared under the dog pile. The dream was complete, splintered no more. He felt Kasey's presence too, and knew he hadn't performed the task alone. The fireworks continued to boom as Frank Sinatra's voice belted "New York, New York" over the sound system.

Cape had a huge smile on his face when he finally slipped out of the pile. Amid the wild melee of yelling and hugging, he searched for his bat. He found it in the grass behind home plate. He rubbed his fingers down the handle to a five-inch gash near the label. He cradled it in his arms and looked to the sky.

His family made their way through the crowd and to the security guard beside the dugout. Cape grabbed Jules and slid her over the railing. Pauline leaned over and hugged them both, allowing her tears to flow freely.

"You did it, Daddy." Cape barely heard her over the continued celebration from the stands and the loud speakers. "Your dream came true."

"No, Jules," he yelled, "our dream came true."

For minutes he hugged her, knowing she had delayed the dream, but she also brought it back from the ashes. He set her down and the guard helped Pauline through the gate.

When they hugged, Cape's body began to shake. They fell to their knees, Cape's tears washing away ten years of heartache, of the fear of reaching a dead end when it appeared the Cape Train had ran out of track. What he'd accomplished, he had done for his family; he had done it for all the boys whose dreams rose from the baseball field. He did it for Coach Steck, and the players at Santee who'd come before him. Most of all, he did it because of his love for the greatest game in the world.

***

The players' families waited outside the locker room. Excitement continued to pour through the crowd, as if the child had been rediscovered in hearts young and old. Cape, the new darling of New York, was the last to come through the locker room door; it had taken a while to complete the post-game interviews. Cape handled each interview with poise and class, thanking his teammates, his family, and God. Number 77 would become the hot item in sports stores all across America.

Billy and Christina were the first to hug Cape, and Cape lifted Tripp in his arms and placed a Yankees cap on his head. Emotions still ran strong, as if Christmas and New Year's, Easter and the Fourth of July had all come at once. Cape walked with his family to the limo waiting at the entrance.

Cape looked into the jubilant crowd as they called his name and clapped. He waved and smiled, and was about to slide into the limo when he saw Angela, her hands in her coat pocket, her Yankee cap perched on top of her head, smiling. He ran toward her, and she pushed past a guard and ran toward him. She found his arms, and he kissed her. He'd thought he'd never hold her again. After they kissed, he stared into her soft, green eyes and touched her face.

"I didn't think you'd come."

"I wouldn't have missed it for anything. You were unbelievable." The noise of the crowd seemed to fade as the pair looked into each other's eyes.

"What about the guy back home? And the distance situation?"

She placed her hands around the back of his neck and kissed him softly. "He's not in my future. Cape, I'm so sorry for pulling away. Can you forgive me?"

"Shh. There's nothing to forgive." Cape smiled and kissed her again as the crowd cheered. Jules nudged Carnie and they watched through the window.

"I just hope I'm not too late."

"Your timing is perfect." He removed her cap and ran his fingers through her hair. "Absolutely perfect."

Chapter Thirty-Eight

The wind blew, and leaves tumbled across the cold, hard ground. The trees had turned gray and lifeless, and the sun struggled to warm the day. Cape carried a baseball in a glass case and carefully stepped across faded tombstones in the Eternal Springs Graveyard. He made his way to a familiar granite marker, and placed the glass case on top.

"Hey, Dad." Cape cleared his throat. "I've got something for you. It's the ball I hit to beat those crazy Red Sox. The kid who ran it down outside the stadium gave it to me in exchange for an autographed bat. And the guys who work here at Eternal Springs said they'll encase the ball into your tombstone, so it can stay with you. You know, when I hit it, it was just like you described when I was a kid."

Cape looked skyward, gathering his thoughts. "Pop, I sure miss you. I miss seeing you in the stands." He ran his fingers through his hair. "It's just that," Cape rubbed his eyes, "when we won that game, I wanted you there. It was wild, Dad. Amazing. But it wasn't the same without you." In the distance, a hawk screeched as it sailed high above a row of cypress trees. He touched the glass case. "Anyways, this ball belongs here. With you." He knelt and touched the tombstone. "Thanks, Dad. I love you. Can't wait to throw the baseball with you again one day."

Cape had one more stop to make, and he headed upstate.

***

He stood in front of Kasey's grave, a pink and white bouquet of silk flowers in the vase in front of the granite marker. He held a bat in his hands.

"How are you, sweet girl? Well, it's been quite a trip, huh? I sure wish you could have been here with me. You were such a big part of it all. A part of me. So much of who I am is because of you." He brushed a leaf away from her marker. "You should see Jules. She's growing up so fast. She looks just like you. When I want to see you, all I have to do is look into her big blue eyes."

He touched the bat against the tombstone. "This is the bat I used to hit the game-winning home run. It splintered when I hit it, but I mended it with a few carpet tacks and some grip tape." He held the bat out in front of him, rubbing his fingers along the tape. "It's whole again, and I think I finally am too. When you passed, I thought life sucked, and I was angry at God for taking you from me. Sometimes I still feel that way, and I know you'd kick my tail if you could. I know you want me to move on, but it's not easy. I'll never stop loving you, and I thank you for giving me your best, and for giving me Jules. God, how she would have loved you." Cape slumped to his knees. "One day, when we meet face to face again, I'll tell you all about the day we won the pennant." He leaned over and kissed the granite.

***

Cape walked in silence under the barren oak trees that stood above the cemetery, the bat resting on his shoulder. He would later mount it on his wall, in order to commemorate the love they shared. A souvenir of his journey, brought to life the first time he held a bat in his tiny hands, the first time he threw a baseball, the first time he slipped on a glove, the laces loose and touching the back of his wrist. He'd chased a dream that boys everywhere, young and old, pursued, if only in their minds. It began where all things were possible, between dusty lines of chalk, on fields with crumbled fences, with bases dry and brittle, with endless summer skies of blue beyond the center field fence.

It was a journey that not only kept alive the spirit of a father who had taught his son what the game of baseball was truly about, that kept alive the memory of the woman who gave her life for her child, but also one that showed that a man, with the unconditional love of his daughter, could realize that a dream is not so much the accomplishment itself, but the bumps, bruises, laughter, and love shared along the way.

Meet our author
Chuck Walsh

Chuck Walsh is a graduate of the University of South Carolina. He discovered a passion for writing in 2004 and, since then, has written human-interest articles for a dozen publications and co-authored *Faces of Freedom* (featured on Sean Hannity's book list), which recognizes the noble lives of U.S. soldiers who died while fighting in Iraq and Afghanistan. He has the following out or coming out next year: *A Month of Tomorrows* and *A Passage Back* (Vinspire Publishing); *Shadows on Iron Mountain* and *Backwoods Justice* (Champagne Books).
www.chuckwalshwriter.com

Made in the USA
Charleston, SC
19 April 2016